THE CAULBEARER
Young Tierney

LEEJOHN

authorHOUSE®

AuthorHouse™
1663 Liberty Drive
Bloomington, IN 47403
www.authorhouse.com
Phone: 1-800-839-8640

*In the work of fiction, the characters, places and events are either the
product of the authors' imagination, or they are used entirely fictitiously.
Any reference to an actual person living or dead is purely coincidental*

First published by AuthorHouse 10/10/2011

ISBN: 978-1-4567-7765-4 (sc)

Printed in the United States of America

This book is printed on acid-free paper.

R.I.P

Thomas 'T-BAR' Bradley
(1972-2011)
Departed, but never forgotten.

Acknowledgements

First and foremost, I thank my Co-writer and best friend in Berlin Germany, Michael A Martin, for his research, belief, and hard work and bearing with me on all the changes I have personally made over the years, not once did he complain (well, almost).

I thank the writer's workshop, in Oxford. Harry Bingham, Paul.A.Toth, and Mike's daughter, Grace Corbett.

To the best parents a kid could hope for, a big thank you to Ernest and Maureen Fearnehough for everything, especially looking after my twelve year old daughter, Zora.

For their generous assistance in the research of the book, I would like to thank the staff at the Sheffield City library, which provided information over the years regarding Nostradamus, the Knights Templar, and the Crusades, not to mention the background to the book's Sheffield connection.

A big thank you to former Tapton Masonic Hall Freemason, Bill Ayres, my 82 year old, neighbour, for his support and fantastic teachings over the years, not to forget the sherry!

For the technical areas, we have so many people to thank, Dr Stefano Perale for his help with the Vatican secret archives and his insight into *Processus contra Templarios*. Dr Carlo Ginzburg *"The night battles"*. Robert George Crosbie *"The Seven signs, the seven seals, and the seven Veils"*. Denis McGowan for his in-depth knowledge of the complete subject. Kwamè Foster, (Foster Media Corp) for great support and pointing us in the right direction, time and time again. To John Sulph-Johnson and Andrew Rowland, thanks lads. To Kim Fearnehough, Jimmy Daly, Melanie Hill and Lorrie Porter.

We would also like to extend a huge thank you to each and everyone who contributed to our project, should we have forgotten anyone, this includes the people who wish to remain anonymous, you know who you are.

Christopher left the upstairs bedroom and walked out onto the landing. He was stunned. He had just become a father for the first time. Rose had given birth to a premature baby boy. The smell of a newborn child was still in the air, accompanied by loud crying.

Christopher looked over to his boss, Tommy Collins, and said, 'I'm a father Tommy, a father.'

Tommy hugged Christopher and shook his hand. The bedroom door was slightly ajar. He saw the midwife holding what appeared to be a piece of skin up in the air. It looked wet and shiny, something not unlike chamois.

'Be careful with that, will you please,' Tommy said. 'Wrap it up in brown paper right now.' The authority in Tommy's voice was indicative of an order.

Christopher was confused. *Why*, he thought, *what do you know about that?*

Tommy was distant, as if he was in a dream; he was thinking back to when Rose was born; he had also been present then. He pictured the day he'd first seen a baby born with a membrane completely covering its face. The membrane covering was extremely rare; it was identified as a 'caul' by the few who know about it. Rose was also born this way, just the same as the child that she had just borne. Tommy was aware of the caulbearer links within the Tierney clan, and being a lifelong friend of the family, he had been sworn to secrecy.

Tommy looked at Christopher with a more than perplexed expression. It was blatantly obvious to Christopher that Tommy knew something he wasn't talking about. Whatever was on Tommy's mind was shrouded in mystery, and it was beginning to scare the hell out of Christopher.

THE CAULBEARER

LEEJOHN

"Science without religion is lame,
religion without science is blind."
Albert Einstein

Facts

The birth caul or veil is a full face mask that may be sometimes found covering the face of a child at birth. More accurately described, the caul is a separate membrane, or skin covering, found on the face of some newborn children, extending from the hairline downwards to below the chin, with loops of skin attached behind the ears. These caul births should not be confused with ones in which the amniotic sack (amnion) or placental remains cover of partially cover a newborns face, although this misunderstanding appears to be widespread.

The correct name for those who are born with a caul is 'Caulbearer'. Such people are often referred to as being born behind the veil, as the caul is also referred to as the veil in many cultures. A true caul cannot be washed off or simply rubbed away, as some references to the phenomenon claim, with midwives allegedly wiping the baby clean. A caul must be correctly removed by a physician or experienced nurse-midwife.

In all cases, the caul must be perforated around the nose and mouth to allow the child to breath. The proper way to do this is to first cut a small hole for each of the nostrils and the mouth. Then, the practitioner must release the loop on the left ear and peel or roll back the caul across the newborn's face, from left to right. Finally, he or she must release the loop from the right ear.

Such births are rare and hold special significance for the child born in such a manner. There are many stories and myths about the caul, many of them erroneous. It should be noted that caulbearers may be male or female and may come from any social class, racial group, or religious group. There are no geographical boundaries to the phenomenon. However, it has been observed that caul births do have tendencies to run in family bloodlines. Sometimes, but quite rarely, more than one member of an immediate family, usually a parent and child, may be born with a caul.

There are many stories, both old and new, about caulbearers, many of which are unproven references to famous people who were or are, allegedly, caulbearers. It is sometimes said that, in ancient times, certain caulbearers could predict future caulbearer births. However, there is no actual proof of this, though legends and folk stories indicate that only some caulbearers know the secret of how these predictions are made. This is a highly unusual phenomenon, and members of the Brotherhood of Nazarenes, a caulbearer-only group, have calculated that caulbearer births may be as few as one in eighty thousand. However, this does not necessarily mean that there will be one such birth in every eighty thousand births in a particular geographical area. Nor does it guarantee that there will not be more than one in any grouping of eighty thousand births.

The knowledge of the calculation of caulbearer births is secretly passed down from generation to generation in certain families and fraternities, for fear of what has happened to caulbearers in the past, particularly in the Middle Ages, where accusations of heresy and witchcraft were laid upon such people who did not fall into line with the rules of the Roman Catholic Church.

***

For those who are interested in the subject, please go to www.the-caulbearer.com, where you can find some fascinating information. We are also extremely interested to hear stories from those who have reason to think that they were born 'behind the veil,' especially those of you who still have your caul.

PROLOGUE

Paris, France - 1307

Being warrior monks and military defenders of the Catholic Church, the Knights Templar existed purely for the Crusades; or so it was commonly thought. When Jerusalem finally fell, under the never-ending onslaught of Saladin, the Holy Land was lost and support for the Order quickly faded.

King Philip IV of France, deeply in debt to the Order, took advantage of the situation. In 1307, under extreme duress, Pope Clement V was forced to issue an arrest order for the Knights Templar on the charges of heresy. Pressured by the King to act, the Holy See operated more swiftly than could be anticipated.

Overnight, Templar strongholds throughout France were raided simultaneously. The knights were arrested by the King's men, tortured into giving false confessions, and burned at the stake.

Outrage spread throughout the land and as far away as England. Due to the continuous quarrelling, Edward I King of England, who was Philip's brother-in-law, did not condemn the Templars, prompting many of the French-based knights to flee to England.

Philip's daughter, Isabella, married the Prince of Wales, becoming Queen of England, producing an eventual English claimant to the French throne itself, and war – a war that was later to be known as the 'Hundred Years' War.

Back in France, things had taken a decidedly bad turn for King Philip. Villagers rioted, and fires burned. The Templars' Grand Master, Jacques de Molay, called for a crisis meeting and summoned one of his most trusted knights, Vladimir Gaudin, son of the former Grand Master, to the helm of the meeting. It was a grisly atmosphere. Eleven Templar brothers stood in waiting.

'Vladimir, your father's plan to persuade everyone that the Templars had always been the guardian of the sacred bloodline was the work of a genius. He even managed to convince our so-called friends and allies, the Catholic Church, that it was the bloodline of Jesus Christ and Mary Magdalene that we were protecting.

'It seems, however, that tonight our allies wish to see the evidence. Your father passed on the knowledge after the fall of Acre – the knowledge of more than two thousand years of religious turmoil, which has been recorded in the book of *the way*. Within lie the truth and the details about the real guardians of the bloodline, along with the bloodline itself. This book has been in our possession since the beginning of time, and has graced the hands of the Lord.'

De Molay opened the casket and removed the face covering of the leather box inside, being very careful not to touch the contents. As he tilted the box up to be viewed under candlelight, a gold pentacle could be seen on the face of the book, along with numerals and ancient writings. The Templars bowed in awe and immediately knelt on one knee; only Vladimir remained standing.

'No matter what happens to me or to our brothers in this room, it shall remain the responsibility of all brothers to serve and protect this manuscript. Without it, our very existence shall perish. King Philip will attempt to take the rest of our treasures, the daggers, the jewels, and the goblets; he is not to be crossed. We shall sacrifice our gold for our future. I have faith in our church and our holy father the Pope; he shall not fail us in our hour of need.'

A commotion broke out among the knights, only to be subdued by Geoffroi de Charnay, de Molay's right-hand man.

Vladimir looked distraught over the task ahead. De Molay passed Vladimir a small parcel wrapped in a brown paper like material, stood up, and placed his hand upon Vladimir's shoulder.

'Within this package is my caul, Vladimir. It is the only way you can prove your identity and the only way the Brotherhood will accept you. Should you be captured along *the way*, it must be destroyed? The Catholic Church must never be allowed to possess such a powerful symbol. Therefore, I must remind all of you before you depart that our main joint objective is to preserve the existence of the Brotherhood at all costs; this means protecting the manuscript. When I talk of the Brotherhood, I use the term loosely. You all know that we are many singular groups; nevertheless, we all worship the Grand Architect of the Universe, and we are all governed by God's personification here on earth, the Brotherhood of Nazarenes. Your journeys will take you to lands far away, and along these journeys, you will encounter many enemies; however, you all know where to seek shelter.'

De Molay hugged Vladimir, whispering an ancient Brotherhood blessing, as a tear trickled down his cheek. 'You must travel to Salon-de-Provence, Vladimir. Once there, you will be greeted by the monks of the Order and led to a place of safety. They will then ask to see the caul. Being high priest caulbearers, the monks will know it belongs to me. Then, and only then, will you receive your final orders.

'You will choose four Templar brothers to travel with you on your journey to our leaders. The rest will stay by my side and fight for our honour. You must travel swiftly, Vladimir, for our very existence depends on you.'

The meeting was interrupted; the King's men had arrived. The charge was heresy. The plea was not guilty. The result was fatal.

With the sacred manuscript intact, Vladimir and his companions managed to escape. De Molay and de Charnay were arrested, but the remaining knights were true to their oath and were brave till the end. The five Templar brothers were murdered, stabbed in the left side of the neck with ceremonious daggers, and later burnt at the stake. De Molay and de Charnay were imprisoned.

Constantly under pressure from King Philip, the Pope disbanded the Order in 1312. Almost two years later, on March 18, 1314, three cardinals sent by the pope sentenced de Molay and de Charnay to life imprisonment. Realizing that all was lost, de Molay rose up and recanted, proclaiming the Order's innocence. Philip immediately ordered de Molay and de Charnay to be taken to the Isle des Juifs, where they were executed, burnt at the stake. From the flames, de Molay cursed both Philip and Clement V, saying that he would summon them before God's Tribunal before the year was out.

Believing the two to be the last remaining leaders of the Templars, the king, with his debts now cleared, could put his plan into action.

However, a little over a month later, Pope Clement V died on April 20, 1314. Seven months later, King Philip fell from a horse while out riding and died on November 29, 1314.

Unknown to Philip at the time of his death, the caulbearer fraction had taken refuge amongst another secret brotherhood and, thus, under this secret umbrella, lived on.

THE CAULBEARER

LEEJOHN

Chapter I

The bantering crowd of solemn villagers didn't disperse as John Tierney barged his way through on his way to the bedside of his long-suffering friend, Michel de Nostredame. Tierney had been travelling for days after the horrific news of his friend and mentor had reached him.

Jean de Chavigny, Nostradamus' constant companion, knelt at the bedside of his master and whispered, 'John is here. John is here.'

Nostradamus, pupils straining in the light, replied, 'Jean, at sunrise thou will not see me alive. I must see John before I depart. Send him to me; then please leave us alone.'

Nostradamus removed a handkerchief from his mouth. Jean's eyes were glazed with sadness as he slowly moved backwards, noticing blood around his friend's mouth. Jean knew this would be the last time he would see Michel de Nostredame alive.

John burst through the door, conscious of what may confront him. His lungs burned with the need for clean air. The bonfire smoke, coupled with the breakneck running pace few Olympians could maintain, had taken its toll. The sight of his best friend neatly tucked up in bed conjured a spiritual-like atmosphere, a powerful man so easily enslaved to the spell of the deathbed. Death was imminent, as John was well aware of the predictions Nostradamus had made. John was now humbled and, forgetting his own pain, obeyed when beckoned to the bedside of his one-time tutor.

A gust rushed through a window left open by de Chavigny. Was the gust a sign? Nostradamus was a master of senses and controlled the elements to some limited degree, or so John believed. Walking to the bed, John paused and sat beside his friend, Nostradamus, who rested a hand on John's shoulder.

'Hello, my friend,' John said. 'I'm sorry I couldn't come sooner. I tried my best, but my journey was full of hazards, and—'

'Shh. Speak no more, John.'

Nostradamus pulled John closer. His deep black pupils startled John, who saw his image reflected in the glassy pools. Nostradamus spoke with urgency, intensifying his already arrhythmic breathing. 'Listen, John, for I have words and objects of grave importance for you.'

The grip on John's shoulder loosened as Nostradamus' hand slipped away. John could hardly bear the lost vigour in his friend's voice, but Nostradamus, apparently unaware of his own weakness, continued. 'My time here has come to an end, John. I've given de Chavigny my full instructions. I've wanted to tell you something for many years, but the timing would've been all wrong, and my courage wasn't strong. John, I have a son, a secret son. His name is Joseph, and he'll be the most surprised of all when he learns the truth.'

'A secret son, Nostradamus, and you never told me?'

John wondered what to expect next. He remembered a time he guarded Nostradamus' house with passion and loyalty, until King Henri II of France made Michel de Nostredame his personal physician. John looked to the floor in dismay, as if the panels would reveal why it had taken his friend so long to share that which he, of all people, surely ought to have been trusted to know.

'I'm sorry, John. This is a closely guarded secret known by no one, other than the guardian monks. My profession has always caused me to imprison secrets within my soul. In due course, I will reveal many more secrets to you my, friend – you, and you alone. You must guard these secrets with your life, John, for you, as was I, will be in grave danger. I have kept this secret since the day my son's mother died giving birth.

'In any event, John, I want you to take care of my son. Treat him as if he was your own son. You'll find arrangements are in place to assist you, and the details are at the monastery. There you shall find aid with the help of de Chavigny's instructions. Thereafter, you must leave the Languedoc and take my son with you to Ireland.'

'I shall follow your requests, though you've told me so little, my friend.'

'You of all people must understand, John. I, too, was fearful. For hundreds of years, the Catholic Church has sought the secret bloodline. They failed to wipe away its seed. I ordered Jean to destroy many of the transcripts I wrote, in fear they would burn me for being a heretic. However, our common enemies hide themselves amongst us. But the knowledge in the book will make them visible to you, John. I have not accomplished my achievements by chance. Everything that has happened throughout my life happened for a reason, a reason set out for me by *the way* of destiny John, and you're part of that destiny.

'You see, John, I was born behind the veil. I'm a caulbearer, like so many before me. Many belong to the

Brotherhood of Nazarenes, all who have much to say, but fear of suppression and discovery has kept their knowledge hidden – Leonardo da Vinci, Jacques de Molay, and many, many more. John, even Jesus was a brother caulbearer. They were all Nazarenes. De Molay was burned at the stake under the orders of Philip IV after the Processus contra Templarios, whereby he was accused of heresy. They destroyed him because of his power, power achieved through greatness born not of strength but through his birthright, just as they did with Jesus. The Catholic Church developed a white paper called the Witch's Hammer, a new law created purely to justify burning caulbearers as witches. The caulbearers were kings through right of birth, John, and as a king, I shall leave this place.'

Nostradamus gasped for breath. John placed a pillow behind Nostradamus' head then passed him a cup of cold water. 'You must rest, my friend. It is time to sleep.'

'The next time I sleep, John, my eyes shall open no more.'

Nostradamus moved his crumpled bed sheet aside, revealing a leather-bound manuscript. 'Here is the sacred book of the Brotherhood, John. My grandfather, Jean de St. Rémy, passed it on to me. He was a Merovingian and a great man. The book was given to him from within the Brotherhood. Each generation has added knowledge, truth, reason, and logic, all gained over many, many years. I've guarded this book and its secrets for over fifty years, John. No living man has seen this, barring you, and the monks of the Order. This book has graced the hands of King David and the Lord Jesus, our brothers the Nazarenes, and now yours, my friend. You now belong to a small group of elite people who, under severe suppression, have shaped our world into what it is today. This is your destiny, John.

'With this book comes great responsibility. Never forget

the grave danger that follows it. Over the years, bearers of the book have managed to resist the powers that be. It contains the prophecy of the arrival of the high caulbearer and all that comes with such a momentous event.

'From this book, John, you'll soon learn that the Antichrist sits in the city of the seven hills. This means nothing to you now, John; but if you use it wisely, the sacred book will explain all. The Antichrist will come for the soul of the high caulbearer. You'll be one of the protectors, John. I've recorded the knowledge passed on from the great ones to me.

'Teach my son, Joseph, about life and, more importantly, the contents of this book. Later on in his life, he'll have three children, the last of which will be a son; the third child will be the successor who inherits the book. This will shape the future of our planet. The book will be passed on from generation to generation to the third-born son.

'Far in the future, I've predicted the division of Ireland by war. At that point, your future family will move to England, not by choice, but because I have predicted that there the high caulbearer shall be born.

'Remember, John, that these events are only my predictions, and they can only become reality if you fulfil your destiny and follow the prophesy.

Nostradamus began to cough, his chest expanding as he held a cloth to his mouth. John noticed blood on the bedding.

'Be gone now, John. Hurry.'

Nostradamus' expression darkened as the strength and will to live showed little signs of any ensuing miracle. He removed a small creased ancient-looking paper package from within the book.

'This is my caul, John; you must promise me that it stays with me, just as Joseph's caul must stay with him. It's of vital importance. Whatever happens, they must never lay their hands upon it. Ensure that de Chavigny knows it must be buried with me.'

'Have no fear, Michel; your wish is my command. Now get some rest, please. I shall see you in the morning.'

'I've seen my last morning, and now I shall see my last night.'

John stood trembling, feeling hollow and devastated at his inevitable loss. He paced to the opposite side of the bed. Grasping the manuscript, he embraced the book tightly against his chest. He paused and looked at his friend for the last time. A cold shiver ran down his spine, like someone walking over a gravestone.

For a moment, John imagined a curtain swaying. A veiled suspicion of treachery swept over him. Edging towards the window, John's shadow against the back wall blackened out the room. The townsmen; where were they? The bantering crowd had been replaced by a cold, deadly silence. John scanned the outlines of the woodland, his imagination-running wild, playing games, illusions beyond his control.

Rustling branches or leaves – a simple explanation must exist. Yet John sensed a phantasmal presence in the room. He grimaced, noticing the taste of his own bile. Fear had him by the throat and, at any given moment, would paralyse him.

The hinges of the heavy door creaked as John opened the door to leave the room. Breathing heavily, he rushed to the landing and tried to calm himself. Outside the room, John heard Nostradamus muttering a strange chant. He could barely make it out until finally Nostradamus said clearly.

'Oh Lord, my God, is there no mercy for the widow's son?'

Fear was the only emotion John felt. Searching for help, John opened the book near the centre and read a few words:

From the stars, an almighty King will be sent to join us. Born on the eleventh minute, eleventh hour, and the eleventh day of the eighth month, he will be the saviour. The solar eclipse shall begin its cycle. He will show you *the way.*

A creak from the floorboard behind startled John. He closed the book and turned in response. De Chavigny had appeared from nowhere, like a spook beneath a child's bed.

'Hello, John. It's been a long time.'

'Jean, how are you?'

Jean was inquisitive, looking at the book. He seemed in a trance-like state. 'What do you have there, John?'

John could see the jealousy burning in Jean's eyes. 'Michel gave me a book. Within it is a gift – a gift for you, Jean, a small package. It's his caul. He said you'd know what to do with it, as Michel instructed you so clearly. You're the one he's trusted. The responsibility lies with you, Jean. Please don't disappoint. Your task is crucial.'

Knowing de Chavigny as he did, John knew his reverse psychology would goad Jean into doing precisely as John wished.

Jean said, 'Fear not, my humble friend; we've walked this path together for many years. Why do you think it is I whom he has entrusted with his final plans?'

Nostradamus had accomplished his work, and the hours had passed quickly. Already it was early morning. Jean returned to the bedroom.

John smirked, sighed, and finally hurried down the staircase. As he reached the hallway by the front door, the last lantern flame flickered to an end. In the darkness, John fought his thoughts. He felt that this was some kind of a spiritual signal. He looked to the heavens with thoughts only for his dearest friend. John crossed himself; his emotions were at war with his mind. He was uncharacteristically frightened, outnumbered. Encircled by the eerie darkness, he could vaguely see the surroundings. He was now alone.

Chapter II

John closed the house door behind him with the sacred book under his arm. Sunrise had, once again, produced a crowd, now gathered outside, their expressions glistening with sweat, observing one another in the yellow glow cast from the lanterns' firelight. The peasant children lingered, grim as corpses, dressed in rags, their faces smeared with dirt, and the elders muttered like gossiping grannies. A medley of voices- philosophers, scientists, surgeons, teachers, holy men, holier women-floated on the wind.

John walked through the crowd slowly, until he rejoined the rest of the clan. They gathered their belongings and set off towards the monastery where Joseph was hidden, according to de Chavigny's instructions. They travelled through the forest for several hours in rain and wind until the road ended.

The way forward seemed to have been obscured, until John saw what appeared to be a tunnel through the trees deep in the forest. Instantly, he knew this must be the way he'd been instructed to follow. After walking through what seemed a never-ending stretch of woodland, John came to an involuntarily halt. Something startled him, an inner feeling that his mission must be kept a secret. He told the rest of the clan to remain at the forest's edge and await his return. Continuing the journey alone, he fought his way ahead, refusing to stop until he reached a weather-beaten old granite-stoned cliff illuminated by constant flashes of lightning and echoes of monstrous thunderclaps. Looking up, he saw that the craggy mountain revealed a path leading up to its peak. John estimated that peak at a thousand metres or so – or a two-hour journey, in John Tierney time.

He rested for a moment then continued his climb. By the time he reached the monastery, the wind and rain had reached unbearable levels. John faced two wooden doors, high and arched, lending the building a Gothic appearance. Elaborate carvings marked the entrance, which was entwined with vine more poisonous than a viper's bite. Careful not to expose his skin to the ivy, John brushed the vegetation away with his clothed arm.

He peered through the slit between the doors. Against the billowing wind, he could hear only the rustling of leaves chasing each other over the rocks far behind.

'Hello?'

The echo of his voice faded without response. He pushed the door, and a cold wind rushed over him. The iron hinges moaned with the burden of the door's weight as it swung farther open, for it hadn't been completely shut before his arrival. John recalled the morning's events at Nostradamus' house, but perhaps everything could be explained as coincidence.

He stepped inside, once again disoriented by darkness, though at least candles flickered on windowsills, illuminating deep cracks in the walls and arched doorways leading to other rooms. John couldn't see or hear anyone. Then, in the doorway nearest to him, he caught a glimpse of a shadow. A flicker of light had tricked his mind, or was it a ghost?

Moving closer, he spotted a symbol there, on the wall above his head. Securely fixed by a large rusty nail, the symbol was shaped like a shield and coloured by a red Maltese cross against a white background.

John noticed something behind the shield, a bizarre creature. He wanted to witness this being, which had its jaw open and held its breath. John reached out and stroked the weird sculpture. As much as he wanted to believe this must be a person, the creature that stood behind the shield bore seven horns on its head and six wings that fanned in both directions, all grotesquely implanted upon a human-like body. The image reached the depths of John's memory, for it was a sight he wouldn't forget for a long time.

The sudden clatter of the pans in John's bag sent him over the top; he was now on maximum alert, right on the edge. Somebody, or something, had run past him. He again felt paralysed, but he twisted to see what stood behind him.

A hooded man now stood motionless. This sight alone was enough to set John's pulse racing. The figure was a monk wearing a plain brown robe, fastened around the waist by white rope. The monk dropped his hood, and the candles around the room rendered a gleam of yellow on his naked scalp. Until now, John had only previously seen a monk from afar, and the one standing before him was unique, for he was of Mongol origin. He glared boldly, stepping forward.

'Can I help you?'

Feeling foolish, John aimed for an authoritative voice. 'I'm a friend of Nostradamus. He told me to come here.'

The room's palpable atmospheric change eased John's suspicions. The monk nodded, observing John's clothing, thinking back to the time Nostradamus told him of a man who would come looking for Joseph.

You'll see a fair-haired man, robust in stature and curious by nature.

John smiled.

'You're Tierney, John Tierney.'

'That's right. How do you know my name?'

'We are of *the way*, my friend. The how is surely something else!'

With that, the monk turned, robe brushing his ankles as he began to walk. 'Follow me, please.'

They passed through several doorways before stopping in a narrow corridor. The monk pointed to the room in front of them. 'You'll find what you came here for.'

John nodded. 'Very well.'

He noticed the engravings on the walls around him as he followed the monk across the cold flagstones. John remembered illustrations of some of these engravings from the book. Inquisitively observing the room's contents, John almost collided with the monk, who had unexpectedly stopped walking. Hands clasped, the monk looked down at something. John followed the monk's gaze, his senses more attuned than ever.

There, on the chapel floor, a few paces ahead, a boy knelt deep in prayer, unaware of those in his presence. A statue of Jesus Christ hung from the wall. A nearby compass-like circle matched an illustration in Nostradamus' book.

The monk cleared his throat. 'Joseph will be finished shortly.'

For a moment, John's concentration diminished, but then it intensified when he realised who the person he saw before him was. 'Joseph.'

With this delayed introduction, the boy rose to his feet and walked towards them. The monk laid a hand on the boy's shoulder.

'You must know that Joseph is the one to carry the sacred book and pass it on to the next in the bloodline.'

Jealousy possessed John. He felt betrayed in an unusual way, for he'd been led to believe that he was the only one to know of the sacred book's existence and Nostradamus' true purpose. Obviously, he'd been wrong. Joseph spoke softly like a choir boy.

'I've been waiting for you with great faith, Master John.'

Frowning, John guessed the gaunt boy's height at about five feet six inches, a good head and shoulders below himself. This boy, perhaps sixteen years old, lacked parents and had no idea of his purpose, yet he exuded patience and gratitude. He had grown up fast but not nearly fast enough, considering the boy's future responsibilities. Empathy replaced John's jealousy.

The monk stepped forward. 'I think it's time you were on your way. I'll accompany you beyond the monastery walls to the mountain path.'

After collecting Joseph's belongings, the trio set off without further conversation until the end of the flat road. There, the monk embraced Joseph and placed a hand on his head.

'May the Lord be with you, my child.'

He kissed Joseph's forehead and departed. Every now and again, the boy turned back, only to see the figure of the monk diminishing into the mist. On John's journey to the monastery, fighting through the atrocious weather had taken his mind off his task. Amazingly, the weather had changed. Gone were the howling winds, replaced miraculously instead with a calm mellow breeze. Heads down, John and Joseph started their return journey, which was a little more comfortable now.

When John arrived at camp, the family looked up with

surprise. John mentioned nothing about the boy to them. They asked no questions anyway. They all simply packed up and moved out, heading back in the direction of their village, located deep in the heart of the hills and valleys of the Languedoc.

Joseph knew nothing about his father; it was too early. Soon, John would reveal all, including what the book foretold. As the monk had informed John, the boy knew of the book's existence but not its purpose. After internal debate, John decided it best the boy adjust to his new life without intrusion.

The clan walked day and night, pausing only to allow Joseph an hour of prayer at dawn and dusk. One night, John took Joseph aside. 'In the morning, you'll meet the rest of the Tierney clan.'

He explained to Joseph that the Tierneys had relocated to France earlier that century and that the family was known for producing bare-knuckled boxing champions, John being one of the finest among them. The family tended towards fairness but retaliated whenever crossed. They had earned respect, and their company was appreciated.

John's older brother, Eamon, had related stories about their father, who had remarried near the end of his life and played his part in the conception of many children. John found the memories distasteful and the subject of the book too difficult to breach. Instead, he engaged Joseph in conversation. 'When you pray, to whom do you pray?'

'My master instructed me never to answer that question.'

This answer disappointed John.

Joseph mischievously replied, 'Except, of course, I am allowed to tell you, Master John.'

They both laughed. Joseph looked to the stars, leaning

on one hand and twisting strands of grass with the other. 'I pray for the coming of the high caulbearer.'

Joseph ripped a handful of grass from the earth and pitched it skyward. 'What do you know about the high caulbearer, my boy?'

'He'll come from the sky in a time of great war, the last war.'

'Go on; tell me everything.'

Joseph, in a rather more serious mood, stood. 'He'll carry the world on his shoulders, and he'll confront evil and destroy it.'

John, recalling the single candle's flame flickering in the boy's eyes, moved closer. 'What then?'

'Commanded by the Sun Gods, the black hole will open and send the high caulbearer to earth.'

John looked confused.

'The black hole is that place where the Sun goes every morning and night, into and out of the sea.'

Joseph smiled at John. 'My master learned from his master, and so forth. The caulbearers prophesied the high caulbearer would arrive. He shall have six wings and seven horns.'

John blinked and grabbed Joseph's arm. He hesitated momentarily and, remembering the monastery, replied, 'The shield, that figure with six wings. I saw it on the walls of the monastery. It was the same image I saw in your father's book.'

'Yes, you saw it there. That was recorded shortly after the crucifixion of Christ.'

'Recorded by whom, Joseph?'

The boy watched the fire that, unleashed by the breeze, burnt wildly. 'It was written by Jesus' disciples, the caulbearers.'

John struggled to stand while brushing his trousers clean of debris. 'And these so called caulbearers, who are they?'

Joseph gestured for John to follow. They walked at ease, kicking pebbles from the path. 'They were followers, all chosen by Jesus himself, all born behind the veil. Their writings come from stories Jesus shared with them before the last supper.'

John again grabbed Joseph's arm. 'So the high caulbearer will join us in the second coming, but not Jesus?'

Joseph shrugged his arm loose, turned with what seemed to be an angry tone, and said, 'They say Jesus was of two minds before the high priests arrested him. He was fighting another soul from another world. He was fighting the devil. Peter tried to talk to Jesus. Jesus sent him away, for the devil wanted his soul. Instead, he sold his soul to save humankind. That will never happen with the high caulbearer. He won't be so merciful; he has little faith in humanity, for he'll allow us one chance and one chance only.'

They resumed walking. Joseph, oblivious to John's concern, continued, 'The course of the sacrifice will take its path, and his soul will go to the Gods. There are no intersections, no shortcuts, and no other routes, only a wide circle with a destination point. Once the message is revealed, human life will know how to prepare for the releasing of the souls come Judgement Day.'

'Judgement Day?'

Joseph paused with John under the shelter of a tree. '"Yes, Judgement Day – the day the world, as we know it, comes to an end, Master John. The heavens know our destiny lies beneath the stars in another realm.

'My first master was the last of the Knights Templar monks. He told me that, after the Cutting of the Elm in 1188, the Templar split from the Order, and it was then generally believed the order had collapsed. It led to the formation of a

secret group of former Knights Templar, who were known as
the Angelic Angels. The Angels' leader was called Vladimir.
He was to be given the instruments that once belonged to
Jacques de Molay and the Brotherhood of Nazarenes. These
instruments would be passed on, as would the sacred book
that all of Catholicism became obsessed with in their search
for whatever the Holy Grail might have been. The Templar's
division could only be healed by sharing purpose through
travel overseas to different countries, including America,
Scotland, and England. It was believed they took refuge
within the realm of the Freemasons. The only reason they let
this become open knowledge was to protect the whereabouts
of the Grail, which, according to the Order, was said never
to have left France."

'The circle in the book, what is it?'

Joseph looked to the skies, searching for a quick answer.
'The enlightened ones wrote that all the Gods start out
as dream makers, and when they die they turn into star
makers. The star of Bethlehem fell from the sky when Jesus
was born. From the beginning of time, the rules of evolution
dictated the world as we know it – a life for a life. Contrary
to scholarly historical revelations, Christ was thirty-three
when they crucified him.

'This time, it will be different. Before we reach the
destination point, in the year of our Lord two thousand
and twelve, the Sun Gods will call Horus's name. From
the core of the earth, he'll rise, and Rome will tremble with
fear the day after Christ's Sunday crucifixion. It will be a
sign to those who betrayed him, before the high caulbearer
is unveiled to the world. He won't fail the world. He won't
fail us.'

Joseph studied his palms, as if he could somehow find
the answers on them. 'From the lessons my masters taught
me, only the high caulbearer has the tools to decipher the

circle. Among these tools are knowledge, reason, truth, and logic. These tools, along with the sacred book, allow the high caulbearer to decipher the secret of the Roman numerals, which consist of dates, times, and places, and the way to find the information leading to Judgement Day.

John felt belittled as he realised this boy knew the most important aspects of the book and the origins of the religions. Not only had the monks been watching over him, but they had also finely groomed him to pass his knowledge on to the next generation.

Chapter III

The years had passed, and Joseph was now twenty. John's health had declined. The Tierney clan gathered outside the room, leaving John with his sister. He had lost half his body weight in the past six months alone. John could feel the pain inside his body, darkness closing in as he remembered when he'd first met Nostradamus, just outside the capitol of Lyon.

***

John had watched from a distance as Nostradamus was ceremoniously robbed. His screams had been desperate. 'Hey, you, thieves, thieves, come back with my scrolls.'

John remembered how he had been determined to catch the thieves and the look of delight on his newfound friend's face the next morning, as John returned the scrolls.

'It seems, old man, that someone of your stature and wealth needs someone to protect you and your possessions. I could be of great service to you. I am John Tierney, of the Tierney clan.'

***

John closed his eyes, thinking of the boy before muttering his name, 'Joseph.'

Joseph lingered at the entrance, hesitant to see his friend and father figure in such poor condition. He turned to leave, with the family following.

John's sister pulled Joseph to one side. "He wants to see you. Go to him, Joseph. Please go to him."

Joseph entered the room, knelt beside the bed, and placed a hand upon John's heart. 'Can you hear me, John? It's me, Joseph.'

There was a moment of silence before John looked up. 'Joseph, my boy, listen to me carefully. Your children must be of Tierney blood. No outsiders – none will be acceptable. Your father followed the way of the prophecy all his life, Joseph. If you stray from the path of the prophecy, it will no longer remain sacred, and his actions will have been in vain.'

John sighed, and with his words and strength now fading, closed his eyes.

Joseph looked away, with the tears that John had once bled for Nostradamus. 'John, please don't leave me, not now, not here. Don't leave me alone. Please, John, Please.'

But the time had come. John's breathing slowed until he spoke his last words. 'Tierney blood, Joseph, Tierney blood.'

***

The day of the burial arrived quickly. It was the eleventh day of November 1570; the skies were grey and heavy with rain, cracks in the ground visible between scattered blades of grass. On a slanted mound, the Tierney family stood alone, coal-coloured figures melting into a stony background. Hand in hand, they comforted each other as they witnessed the last shovel of earth fall upon the coffin.

Joseph dropped to his knees in desperation, gazing at his beloved father figure. He closed his eyes and searched his memory. He recalled his childhood days, playing with a man in a field.

That man had pointed to a monk. 'Go to him, Joseph.'

These words were the last his father, Nostradamus, had spoken to him.

Joseph opened his eyes, the icy breeze teasing wisps of curled hair into his hazel eyes, but Joseph shed no more tears.

'You'll live again, John Tierney. Live again.'

Oblivious to the sobs and moans around him, Joseph focused on those familiar words that provided a portal to the future, a future only he could see.

***

Joseph was now regarded as a true Tierney. No one asked about the sacred book and its prophecies anymore. He had married Irene Tierney and fathered two children. Her father, Eugene, followed the family tradition of bare-knuckled fighting. After many long discussions about family history and word of a third child on the way, Joseph knew the time had come for the clan to leave the Languedoc and head for Le Havre, the shipping port to which travellers and gypsies brought their goods. From there, they would relocate. They jointly settled upon the roots of their family tree in Galway, Ireland, just as Nostradamus had predicted.

***

The journey, battling against the harsh weather conditions, had been treacherous. Even though the clan came across many obstacles, they'd managed to travel around without problems. Around this time, the law had made it evident that the gypsy way of life was unwanted within certain lands. In England, Henry VIII forbade gypsies from entering the country, and some years later Queen Mary sentenced gypsy travellers to death for travelling this way.

Once settled, the Tierneys took over the previous clan's

power with ease. All was well, and the family prospered for a while. Wealth wasn't easy to find in times of hardship. The bare-knuckle fighting tradition put bread on the table.

Just as the prophecy had predicted, Joseph had passed the book on to his third son, Marcus, now forty-two years old. The son's face resembled the father's, but the former's small frame distinguished him from the rest of the family men. Yet Marcus possessed the sacred book and stood at the head of the bloodline. Fate, as written by the caulbearers and prophesied by Nostradamus, had run its course.

The Tierney clan dug their feet in deep turning a small village on the outskirts of Galway into a festival place, with showmanship of a circus quality. Romany gypsies, Welsh travellers, new age travellers, and even Druids came in on the barges for the summer festivals. Stories of the clan had travelled far and near.

The Tierney family lived within the ruins of an ancient rundown castle overlooking the festival grounds. It was partly rebuilt from natural stone by Marcus and the clan in the early 1620s with the aim of keeping it within the family and passing it down over the centuries.

Knowing his way around the grand circle, Joseph reminded Marcus that the prophecy told of a time when the British would divide Ireland, and until this time came, the sacred book must remain hidden within the walls of the castle. This would ensure that the Tierney clan remained in Galway, and only after the prophecy became evident, would the family move on. Thereafter, they would leave for England.

***

The Tierney's, had become businessmen, and making money was the way of life. The decades rolled by, and the population surrounding the festival lands had expanded rapidly. They owned every liquor and market stall in the village and had become property owners themselves. Every week, the clan collected their rents, and when cash was scarce, cattle exchanged hands. Keeping order in the town was one thing the Tierney's knew how to handle.

A favourite attraction for the fairground visitors at midnight on the last Sunday of every festival season was the telling of a dark story. This was not just a tale, but a dark prophecy that seldom left the thoughts of the gypsies who heard it.

Callum Tierney was born in 1830. A forty-five–year-old man and father of two sons, he had inherited the story from his grandfather and the Tierney genetic line, and now he was the storyteller. On this particular night, the sky was clear, and a full moon was evident. The campfire burned, and the lanterns glowed, and hundreds of traveller families were waiting silently outside the tent of Callum Tierney. Dreamcatchers hung from the clump of trees that surrounded the audience. Tierney clan members blew out the lanterns.

There, in front of the crowd, standing at well over six foot, stood Callum Tierney. His beard hung down to his chest. He puffed upon a long wooden pipe, trying to light it as he rested his foot on a tree stump. He looked around smiling at all the children staring at him as though they were waiting for a bedtime story to fall asleep by. Well, this story was not for the faint-hearted, neither should it be heard by children, but Callum always started in an understanding manner, choosing his words wisely.

'I have a story to tell you all tonight, a story about a boy and a book. This boy is not just any boy,' Callum said, pointing his finger in the air, 'but a boy who will come from another world.'

Callum started to walk, puffing on his pipe. He stopped and knelt among a group of children allowed to stay up past their bedtimes. Callum's eyes observed each and every child, before he carried on talking. 'Before the twentieth century, the Sun God will come from the sky, and he shall present us with a star, the same way he did when Jesus Christ came to our world.' Callum reached into his pocket and took out what appeared to be a leather cloth in the form of a mask. He hid his face in his hands before springing his hands away. The children screamed. One child ran into her mother's open arms, frightened, just as a young child would be. All the while his mother was laughing. Callum had attached the mask to his face.

'And when the high caulbearer is born, we shall not be able to see his face, as he will be born with a membrane covering his face, similar to the skin I have here. This will be the sign of his power, for he will be able to see into the future and he shall tell us about the ending of days.'

Callum slowly removed the mask from his face. He looked at the bewildered faces in the crowd and slowly walked over to an old oak tree, where a dream catcher was hanging down. Callum ran his fingers through the bell chimes. Not a sound could be heard, apart from the sound of the crickets.

'The high caulbearer, a beautiful boy, will be the family's third born child, but he's not to be hurt. The angels and demons around him will make his decisions and protect him from any severe fate thy shall put before him.'

Callum walked back slowly to the tent of the dream catcher. He turned round to say his last words. 'Tell your children the story of the high caulbearer, so that the world will be prepared for his arrival. Our children are our survival, and our survival lives on in our dreams.'

The last flames of the fire flickered, and the crowd slowly dispersed as Callum turned and disappeared into the tent.

Later that night, Callum returned to the castle with the

clan. After putting his two sons to bed, Callum joined his wife, Maria, in bed. A candle flame glowed in the corner; Callum lowered his ear to Maria's stomach. 'I can feel him move.'

Maria was pregnant, just over seven months.

'Well he's the special one according to the prophecy,' Maria said.

Callum turned over onto his back. 'Yes, he will be the third born son, and he'll be the first to see the sacred book since my forefathers buried it within the walls of this castle.

'Maria, I've decided on his name. I hope it suits you, for it follows a long line of Tierney tradition.'

Maria's head turned. She knew her husband had been thinking about this for a long time. She realised how important a task this would be for him. 'Eamon, I'll call him Eamon.'

***

Three centuries had passed since the Tierneys had crossed the channel from France. Maria had passed away shortly after giving birth. Unfortunately, this was the sixth birth of the third born child, who had taken the life of the mother. For many years, the families had worried if this unusual occurrence was completely natural or if it had something to do with the prophecy.

The Tierney clan now consisted of four brothers and two sisters. Leader of the clan and holder of the sacred book, Eamon Tierney II, son of Callum, had become another great fighter, remaining undefeated throughout the gypsy camps. The families felt at home, back where they belonged, back to their roots, and, above all, back where they knew protection was close at hand. They were happy in Ireland, even if the years between 1910 and 1920 presented the family more hardship than previously imagined.

Meanwhile, Eamon had retrieved the sacred book of Nostradamus concealed within the walls of the castle. The prophecy had survived, unlike Callum, who had passed away shortly before the country-dividing politics of Ireland had gathered momentum. Eamon knew, too, that, according to the sacred book, his soon to be born third child should be a son.

Chapter IV

The Government of Ireland Act had just been passed, only two years after the Easter uprising. The country was split in two. Eamon knew it was time to call the clan together for a secret meeting. They must move to England, as Nostradamus had foretold. Eamon tried to wait as long as possible but, ultimately, told the clan it was time to move on.

He soon found things were easier said than done, for part of the family chose to stay in Galway, regardless of his advice and pleas.

The following day, Eamon called another meeting in the barn. His wife, Connie, twenty years younger than he, and his two young sons, Thomas and Roy, stood by his side. The meeting attracted more than thirty people, most of them clan members, but families who had travelled with the clan from the Languedoc those many moons before were also in attendance.

With a clap, Eamon silenced the crowd. 'You all know about the prophecy regarding the Tierney clan. I know you've all been waiting years for me to tell you the truth about it. As I've told you before, it is the fate of your grandchildren to know the truth, just as it has been for generations before us – our fathers, our fathers' fathers, right back to Joseph, son of John Tierney the first.'

One of the other settlers bellowed, 'My forefathers have followed *the way* of the Tierney clan for over three hundred years, which led to my respect for you and your present family to this very day. Nevertheless, I don't believe it right that we should separate our children from their homeland. I say we stay and fight for the Irish. Is anyone with me?'

Applause and shouts of approval answered the question.

Despite the opposition being sent his way, Eamon decided to let his argument stand. He spoke slowly and softly. 'I can understand your concerns and the reasons for your objections, but you must understand that Ireland will never be the same after dividing. Believe me, you don't want to be living here through all of this torment. The only way forward is to protect ourselves. Either you're with us or you're not. Listen to me, please. There will be no second chance. We'll prepare to leave in three days time.'

Those who didn't agree trailed out of the barn. Those left behind stood in a dishevelled silence.

***

The clan was on the move, horses roped to the caravans, leashes in the hands of the cart drivers. Belongings had been stowed in the back of the carts. Weighing on Eamon's mind was his wife's condition. The fifth month of pregnancy was not the ideal time to travel; nevertheless, Eamon had a prophecy to fulfil.

Once again, Eamon rose on his cart and addressed the small crowd that had gathered on the road. 'You'll all be remembered and sadly missed. Now, we set off for our destination. We'll go to Nottingham. Please, one last time, join us. I'm begging you.'

As he expected, no response met his final plea.

Unconvinced by Eamon's reasons for the family's relocation, followers of the clan had decided to remain in Ireland. Relocation was out of the question for them, regardless!

Defying those sentiments, the family of the Collins clan put their trust in Eamon and decided to travel with the Tierneys. They had accompanied the Tierneys on their journeys throughout time, right back to the early days in the Languedoc. It was the gypsy way. They weren't about to quit now.

Days later, the bloodshed had already begun in Northern Ireland. In the meantime, Eamon had commanded each cart to travel to the south of Dublin, where they would take a boat to Liverpool. Eamon knew it wouldn't be so easy for the Irish Republican Army to recruit either of his sons if they bypassed Dublin.

Chapter V

Nottingham, England – 1921

After giving birth to a beautiful baby girl, Connie passed away. The burial ceremony, which the clan held along the way, was extremely sad. The journey had been too much for her. The baby was premature, and Connie lost too much blood.

Eamon was deeply saddened but he concluded that, within the sacred book, the family tree indicated that Connie's death was a distinct possibility, a secret he had kept to himself. Eamon had known before the pregnancy that this day could come. It was the one and only time he'd hoped that the shape of the family tree would start to change.

***

The Tierney clan had settled in a remote gypsy camp on the outskirts of Nottingham, along with the Collins family. Eamon's two sons, Thomas and Roy, now had a baby sister, Kate. She was the youngest and most important family member, according to Eamon. Following Connie's death, Kate's birth was the only thing that kept him going, especially as it confirmed within him the incredible accuracy of the sacred book.

Work was immensely difficult to find, especially when the only skill perfected by the brothers was fighting. At fifty-two, Kieran was the eldest, but he never questioned the fact that Eamon was by far the best fighter, especially with Eamon's ability to show deviance towards his enemies and anyone else. Nobody dared provoke him, a reflection of his sincerity and mastery of his craft. Through the fair operation of their business in town, the brothers had gained respect and built a good reputation for themselves.

One day, a tall, moustached stranger arrived in the village. He was looking for John Tierney. Eamon was the first to notice the stranger. He strolled over. 'You're looking for John Tierney, I hear?'

The man scanned Eamon's expression and shrugged casually. 'I could be. Who are you?'

'I'm his brother. What do you want?'

The man slowly removed his grey cap, folded it, and shoved it into his pocket, cold eyes constantly focused on Eamon.

'My name is George, George Mooney.'

He scratched the side of his moustache and offered a greasy handshake. Eamon resisted, staring at the hand in disgust.

George continued. 'I want to know if your brother will fight for me next week in Sheffield.'

The tone of finality in the stranger's voice convinced Eamon he was serious. In the distance, Eamon saw the outlines of his brothers. He nodded in their direction, so George could see them. 'You'd better ask. That's him over there, on the left.'

George traced the direction of Eamon's nod, and was

succumbed by John's intimidating stature. 'Jesus Christ! That's why they call him Big John, then. He don't bite, do he?'

Eamon smirked. 'John, someone to see ya.'

John trotted over to them, stopping directly in front of George.

George disbelieved that John wasn't at all out of breath, considering he had covered thirty metres' distance in a few seconds.

John softly spoke. 'What can I do for ya?'

George glanced at Eamon, who stood watching John. Half a minute's silence passed before Eamon spoke. 'He wants ya to fight for him in Sheffield next week,' he blurted, breaking into a half grin.

George nodded and turned back to John. He cleared his throat, running his left hand through his surprisingly thick, grey hair. 'That's right, John, next week. Winner takes all, and if you win, maybe I could set you and your brothers up with some work.'

'Who am I fighting and what will I be paid?' John said.

George dug his foot in the dirt. He deliberately pronounced his words with sharp clarity. 'Well, does five pounds sound okay, John?'

Kieran grinned. 'That'll do. Doesn't matter who he's fighting.'

George seemed relieved. 'So, it's a deal then, is it?'

Noticing George's dirt-encrusted nails, John nodded, humming an almost inaudible sound of approval under his breath. George, with his tired aged exterior, smiled at John.

The next morning, John and Eamon rose at dawn for a training session. Though Eamon had never been defeated, due to his age, his self-confidence seemed nearly non-existent, all the better for his hidden willpower. Eamon could better teach John how to focus on strategy, as opposed to audience reactions, which ranged from disturbed to derogatory.

John's thirtieth birthday approached. As John was younger than Eamon, he always remained primed for fights. Eamon, concerned for his own health, had an eight-year-old son, and already John's reign had come, as did the revelation of the prophecy.

Well past midnight, Eamon studied the sky and all its shades and textures with the clouds barely visible, seaweed green and purple against an inky backdrop. Straight above, he spotted a strange area where the clouds had parted, revealing a disquieting sheet of pitch black sparkling with the diamond shine of stars. The night wind brushed his fingers. Several clouds drifted. Suddenly, silver beams slit the darkness, and the moon emerged, full as it had ever been.

Though Eamon had heard John calling to him, his own name rang in his ears, as if it had been uttered from some faraway place and echoed between. Eamon, startled, felt John's icy fingertips grasp his shoulder. Eamon dared not look to the sky, having seen enough. The time had arrived. Eamon returned to the campfire.

John couldn't fathom Eamon's odd behaviour. His pulse quickened. A solid figure blocked the intensity of the raging light. Something was out of place. What year was this?

Metres away, Eamon rose, adjusting his trousers accordingly. He felt as though he were swimming deep into the flames. He picked up a stick and threw it onto the pile, orange sparks like fireflies alighting, only to fade.

'Remember that time in Galway' Eamon said, 'when I made the speech to all our brothers and sisters?'

Eamon knew something perplexed John, yet he displayed no tension.

'Yes,' John finally answered. "I think I had just turned twenty-eight. You spoke of our aunt's sisters and the sacred prophecy of the Tierney clan.'

Eamon involuntarily exhaled, the ghosts of unsaid words almost escaping his parted lips. He clenched his teeth. 'That's right. That's why our family split, because the prophecy had to be kept sacred. If I had told you the truth, all of us might be together now. But the worry of outsiders joining would have been a disaster. That's why' – he leaned close to John – 'that's why, John, I gotta tell you the truth about everything.

'Let me show you our family tree, copied from Nostradamus' sacred book and passed from generation to generation. Besides me, you're the only one who's seen this. I have a feeling that my daughter, Kate, can't be told the truth about her birth. That's why we have to change the shape of destiny, and you must teach Thomas all about the prophecy.'

'Why not Kate?' John asked.

Eamon continued his explanation as if John had never spoken. 'Look closely, John. Here's Joseph, Nostradamus' third born, who passed the book on to his third son, Markus. The pattern continues, always the third child, a son.'

'But what is all this leading to, Eamon?'

'The sacred book professed the high caulbearer would be born, but what that means, only God knows.'

This was too much for John to absorb, especially when the situation denied him a choice. 'Do you believe it, Eamon?'

Even in the shadows, Eamon looked downcast. 'It's in our blood. The caul has existed throughout our bloodline for centuries. It's all we've believed in for hundreds of years. The strange part – the part that's hard to accept – is that nothing was written within the sacred book to indicate that a baby girl would be born when we were all expecting a boy. And, what's more, who would have guessed that she would be born the same way as all those boys many years before. Neither one of us should let our family down and break the prophecy.'

'When will all of this happen?'

'The handwritten notes from Nostradamus stop all of a sudden in 1920, as though he's trying to tell us something.'

'Tell us what?'

Eamon replied, touching the book's ember red cover. 'It says he'll be born before the end of the century. I'll be dead, but before then, you'll teach Thomas all of it. Kate cannot be told. You must promise not to let me down.'

This responsibility made John uneasy. He went to his brother and placed his arm around his shoulders. 'You've never let me down, Eamon. There's no chance I'll let you down, especially now.'

***

The week had passed quickly, and the Tierney family had arrived in Sheffield for John's fight. Because George lived in a large house, it was only logical that he offered the family his hospitality.

'Well,' Eamon said, 'it's a fine house you have here, George. Seems you've done well for ya'self.'

Kieran had underestimated George's abilities.

George said, 'They say the harder you work, the more life pays you, and things have been going well for me lately. Anyway, let's talk about tomorrow's fight, shall we?'

The brothers circled George.

'The man you're up against has won his last eight fights. He's a big man, but not as big as you, John. The fight takes place in town, tomorrow night at eight o'clock. Normal rules – no kicking, and when a man goes down, you wait for him to rise.'

***

By the next evening, George and the boys had arrived in town. John sat beneath a wire in the dingy cloakroom. Above him, a nearly exhausted bulb swung limply.

George reached into a cupboard and removed a cloth. He threw it to John. 'Do you feel fit then, John?'

The light bulb flickered.

John rubbed his forehead with the cloth. 'Reasonable.'

The uncertainty in his reply had George regretting the investment he'd made on the fight, as well as his bet with the bookies. George turned away, hiding his worried expression from John. If he acted as if everything was fine, then perhaps it would be. 'Well, come on, then, get stripped down. The fight starts soon.'

Minutes later, they entered an intimidating full tavern, the onlookers packed wall-to-wall, spitting and shouting. George calculated some 200 faces around him. Not a single one cheered for John, since the Tierney name was unfamiliar to the crowd. They had good reason to place money on John's opponent.

George quickly stepped up and threw John a fresh towel, who gratefully received it. He swiftly wiped the clumps of mucus off his back and angrily tossed it back into the baying crowd.

A bookie shouted, 'Even money.'

John raised his right fist to his mouth then blew on his knuckles while simultaneously cracking them, letting his opponent know the crowd hadn't intimidated him.

George watched John's every move. His ten-pound wager increased his anxiety. How stupid he felt, since John was as much a stranger to George as the big man was to the crowd.

A diminutive man appeared under the spotlight. He stretched out his arms, signalling for the crowd to spread out. Checking the circle around himself and the fighters, he calculated an adequate space. The crowd silenced as the man spoke, his voice deeper than his height had suggested it would be. 'You know the rules.' He raised one of his arms. 'Let the fight begin.'

The colours of the crowd blurred into the background as John and his opponent stalked one another in a slow-motion dance. Finally, both raised their hands.

Straightaway, John felt a cold rush of air as the opponent's fist clumsily met cheekbone. John felt a burning sensation, blood trickling down his face. His opponent pounced, and John received two blows to the left eye socket. He stepped back, trying to blink away the sudden darkness. Hatred pumped through his veins. George's voice pierced the stupor. 'Come on, John.'

Remembering what Eamon had taught him, John tried to push away thought. He focused on the opponent as they gripped one another in a struggle for control.

From where George stood, victory appeared doubtful.

John pushed away his opponent. George clenched his teeth as his fighter outmanoeuvred his opponent and landed a perfect uppercut. John had thrown his first and last punch. The referee knelt, checking the other fighter's pulse. George was stunned, speechless. The tense electric atmosphere had dissipated, and the once deafening screams were no more, replaced instead by silence. George watched the motionless, comatose opponent.

'It's over; the fight's finished,' the referee announced.

John, still gasping, stood. Eamon placed a fresh towel over John's shoulders and patted him on the back. They walked over to a rejuvenated George, whose face lit up.

'Reasonable? Reasonable! Well, you sure as hell know how to put the bloody frighteners on me, John Tierney.'

The crowd dispersed, leaving the bookie standing without a queue waiting to collect their money. He glanced over to where George was standing and winked defiantly. George laughed.

***

Later that evening, everyone gathered at George's place. George, sitting on a stool, raised a half-empty bottle of sherry and, speaking with a slur, said, 'You know, John, me and your entire family shall get on well with each other.' George's cheeks reddened as he drank still more. 'I said I'd give you five pounds. Hell, let's double it, providing you and your family stay here and work for me.' He swayed.

John and Eamon, seated by the fireplace, glanced at one another. Eamon stood. 'I can't see that being a problem at all, George.'

George swung a heavy arm around Eamon and nearly sent the latter tripping over the rug.

John grabbed the bottle of sherry and shook George's hand. 'It's a done deal then."

George shook hands with his new army. It was the same day that the British Legion was formed, 24 May 1921.

***

George and the Tierneys had become infamous throughout Sheffield in a short time, soon controlling every district in town. The number of gang members had soared. George was known as the 'Boss.' The Tierney clan had become an integral part of the Mooney gang. They were tough and, if necessary, brutal, yet displayed a courteous attitude towards those who wished to join them. Gradually, they united all aspects of their operations and soon controlled Sheffield.

Just as things were getting better, unexpectedly, a

massive loss occurred. Eamon Tierney, the gang's thinker, had passed away with cancer at the age of fifty-one.

John was distressed by Eamon's death, much more than anyone could know. Although John had been aware that Eamon knew his time was running out, John reacted so badly that no one could get through to him. John mourned for weeks on end.

Meanwhile, the pressure of a rival gang had overwhelmed George. He knew the problem had to be solved immediately or serious consequences would result. A simple solution seemed improbable.

Eamon's funeral took place on City Road, behind the Manor Estate. The entry process was comparable to that of a football match, attended by friends and enemies alike, all displaying tokens of tribute and respect.

George demanded that business operate as usual. Everything seemed in order, or as much as could be expected, until members of the rival gang arrived. George remembered the gang leaders face from, London Road. Oddly, the fellow's name was Stacey. George combed his hair and willingly stepped outside to attend to the matter.

'What can I do for you gentlemen?'

George's rival was a good six inches taller than George. Stacey was thin with broad shoulders. Dark eyes provided contrast to his greased and pale blond hair. The rival had three men for back up, with a look of mock concern. Stacey's black leather glove squeaked as he rubbed his hands together.

'Well,' Stacey said, stepping closer to George, 'I wanted to sort this out last week. I couldn't find ya. I thought it best to wait till the funeral.'

'What do you want exactly?'

Removing his gloves, Stacey pulled a silver case from his pocket and lifted a cigarette from it. Gripping it between his teeth, he struck a match and lit the cigarette, blowing smoke in George's face. 'Come on, George, cut the bullshit! You know what we want.'

George leaned forward, and whispered in Stacey's ear, 'As I said, *what exactly?*'

Stacey's guards shuffled from side to side. Stacey threw down his cigarette in irritation, snuffing it with a heel. 'We want in. We have workers, and we want our own patch. If you don't agree, I won't be happy.'

George could feel his anger rising.

'We have rules in this firm. What's ours stays ours, but I don't want a war, son. We can sort this out another way. If you win, you get what you want. And if I win, you can all piss off. You're a sick bastard, Stacey, to come to a funeral to tell me this."

Stacey looked satisfied with the reply. 'It looks like it's my best man against yours then, right?'

George nodded stiffly. 'Correct, son.'

Stacey reached for a handshake. 'That's all I wanted.' His hand met George's; then he walked away with his guards, disappearing as quickly as they had arrived.

George knew it was neither time to face opposition nor to reveal weakness. Circumstances had forced an agreement.

George was the leader of the Mooney gang for a good reason. He figured that, if he portrayed the right characteristics and approached the situation with the right attitude – in this case, the right attitude being to act like a hard bastard, which he actually wasn't – he would gain the respect of those wishing to cooperate with him. Either that or he'd scare the shit out of them. After all, George hadn't been known to lose his rag at the drop of a hat. If someone got in his way, a firsthand experience of a personal demonstration would put anyone in his or her place, which was very rare. Still, it would be something to tell the kids about, providing the entertainment got that far.

This time, Stacey got lucky because, where the Mooney gang was concerned, it was all about the dance, and Stacey had selected the song. This meant he had plenty of time to exhibit some fancy footwork, if he had any!

***

The date of the fight had been arranged. George had to contact John, but nobody knew where the hell he was.

Since Eamon's death, the secrets of the prophecy occupied and terrorized John's mind. He had to take care of Thomas. His path lay before him; he just had to stick to it, though fate was already throwing things at him that were obscuring his vision. Still, had he known George's position, he would have turned back long ago to help.

Noon the next day, George sat in the centre of a small circular room of sombre-looking faces. He concealed yearning for John, the only one not present. Since the negotiation with Stacey, George had hoped a gang meeting might return him to his usual clarity. His efforts had failed. Either John didn't know or he didn't care or both.

George sounded weary and looked so, too, with insomnia-induced bags beneath his eyes. 'As you all know, I had a meeting yesterday with a rival boss. He wants our patch. We made a deal that each of our gangs would put up their best man. I must decide who fights him.'

Aside from John, the best fighter in the gang was Harold, despite him not being a member of the Tierney clan. Harold had the gang's respect. He stepped forward.

'I'll fight 'im, Boss.'

George realised that, without Harold, he'd have probably left the gang to resolve the mess without him, a thought he could never have shared without forever losing his crew's trust. 'Okay. We have forty-eight hours. Get yourself ready, Harold, and don't let me down.'

Any other day, George would have held open the door as a gesture of equality to his underlings. This time, he departed first.

The gang seemed convinced that Harold's techniques would serve as an adequate substitute for John's. George however, doubted John's stand-in fighter. He was beginning to feel like an actor playing a Mafia boss and one with bad news accumulating.

Two people upon whom he could rely remained, though he didn't know it. Tommy Collins and Patrick Tierney set out to find John.

Fight day arrived. George had received no information concerning John's whereabouts. The gang rushed into town, this time without a bookie. George waited in the cloakroom, staring at the cockroaches. It was half past seven, half an hour before the fight. The trainer massaged Harold.

Fat lot of good that'll do, George thought, shaking his head miserably. The dripping tap continued to aggravate him. George got up; the door behind him creaked open. He looked over his shoulder and froze.

John stood in the dust-speckled light. 'Everything okay, Boss?'

George stuttered in disbelief. 'J-John, what you doin' here?'

'Thought you might be needin' me, Boss.'

George grasped John's shoulder. 'You don't know how pleased I am to see you, Johnny boy. It's been a hard week for me, John. How ya doin' big man?'

John shrugged. 'You know me, Boss, reasonable.'

Reasonable. Hadn't George heard that word before? In a sudden wave of excitement, he jumped onto his stool, shouting, 'That's why we're called the Mooney Gang.'

To John, George appeared as triumphant as a soldier who'd just found his platoon and a last chance for survival.

Harold stretched his arms and legs. He walked over to John and said, 'Thank God.' His expression suggested that he had predicted his own defeat.

'You're a good man, Harold. I'd happily fight by your side any time, but this is my time, my day, and my fight.'

Harold thanked John and stayed to work his corner. George had never felt so much respect for a man.

As the fight began, both fighters strolled casually into the centre of the room, accompanied by their bosses. They stood with patience and dignity before their watchful enemy.

Many venues had experienced trouble with the police, so George and Stacey had decided to keep it a low-key affair. Thus, the crowd John had expected never appeared, only scattered fans. Rumour had it that a secret police force had been sent from Scotland to keep eye on events. Everybody knew the Gavins Gang had recently run straight into the law.

Now John stood centre-stage, facing his opponent. They shook hands and backed away, neither expecting what was about to occur.

The moment they raised their fists, a stool crashed through the window, sailing in a huge arc across the room. Glass shattered like an explosion of razors. Everyone dived to the floor. The double doors heaved with a force shoving against them. The bar across them wouldn't hold long. Briefly, the chaos ceased, but everyone remained sheltered under tables.

From the streets came a thunderous voice, 'Police. Open up!'

George maintained an indifferent pose as he watched Stacey light a cigarette. It had all been a set-up. People ran like rabbits, trying to escape. The venue owner had climbed halfway up the stairs, stopping only to shout, 'Quickly, up the stairs. We can get through the window and onto the next building.'

Several made it to the other side of the wall before the police breached the barred door. John and George were two who made it out. Those left behind soon found themselves under arrest.

Edging past the window, they leapt for the street. Upon landing, George twisted his ankle. Police whistles screamed. Out of breath, John tended to George's ankle. Palpitations shook his heart, and nausea permeated his guts.

George struggled, out of control. 'Run, John, run. Leave me.'

John took George's hand for the last time, the sadness between them too obvious for words.

Turning in the opposite direction, John sprinted down Campo Lane. With every step, he heard the boots of two police officers on the cobbles. The sound grew louder. He swerved onto St. James Street, head on with another officer. John stopped. His only hope was to face a fight outside the ring.

The officer facing him said, 'Stand still. You're under arrest.'

John thrust a knee into the cop's crotch, grabbed him by the throat, and lifted him into the air. The consequence was like setting off dominoes, with the latter officer landing and cracking his skull on the kerb.

The next day, the incident spread across the front pages, for the police officer died soon after the accident. The police had already broadcast an official statement across the radio waves that announced the impending arrest of John Tierney. A reward of fifty pounds provided decent bribery for information on a suspect's whereabouts, especially the killer of a police officer. If arrested, John could be executed by hanging.

By the next morning, the police had already cordoned off the Tierney's residence. Kieran, Thomas, Roy, and Patrick, carrying young Kate, were taken to the station.

Chapter VI

Twenty-five years had passed like a breeze. The Tierneys' decline continued. Patrick had recently died, killed in the war. John's name was a family ghost; no one knew where he had fled, and no one, except Thomas, spoke of it, for fear of the repercussions. Thomas repeatedly suggested John might have taken a boat trip to Boston.

Meanwhile, John's promise to Eamon seemed broken. If some better future awaited the family, the way to it seemed obscured.

***

For John, the only comfort was knowing Kieran and Thomas would be safe, so that they could watch over Kate.

By then, Thomas was forty-three years old, Kieran had gone back to Ireland, and Kate had two young daughters, Christine and Rose.

The name Tierney no longer invoked respect or fear. It had vanished from history and public interest; it was now just another family name.

Had the prophecy been a mere family legend, passed

from generation to generation, but never questioned despite its unlikelihood? Nostradamus had insisted the prophecy had to be fulfilled. It had been written that the 'High Caulbearer' would be born before the year 2000.

Chapter VII

It was clear that another cold winter was approaching. Nature seemed silver, as winter's first snowflakes fell from a smoky sky. The family gathered around the fireplace. Kate watched the flames consume the white cabinet she had chopped into pieces.

Rose had developed into an attractive young teenager, but fate had pushed her out into the coalfields, as this was the only alternative for staying warm.

At home, a shadowed movement caught Kate's attention. She went to the window. It was only the postman approaching from the path. Checking the clock, Kate wondered why the post had arrived at such an unusual time. In fact, she wasn't even expecting mail at all. A snap of the letterbox announced the arrival of a package, which fell to the floor. She rushed to the hallway and retrieved it. The handwriting proved unrecognisable, the stamp unidentifiable. Feeling the package, she guessed it contained plenty of unpaid bills and a possible eviction notice. Kate ripped open the package. Notes of money drifted towards her feet. A folded letter remained within the package. She read its contents.

Kate, it's been a long time. Much too long, in fact. We need to meet today, by the quarry. Eight o'clock. ~ JT.

She crumpled the letter within her palm. It couldn't be.

Thomas grabbed her shoulder with concern. 'Where's all that money come from? Who's the letter from?'

Kate hurried to the front room and tossed the paper into the fire. Thomas had followed her.

'What is it, Kate?'

She hesitated before touching Thomas's chest. 'Come upstairs. We must talk.'

Thomas followed Kate into the bedroom. Clutching the cash, Kate sat precariously on the edge of the bed. Thomas guessed she would cry, but instead she explained the situation. 'John sent the package. He's here and wants to meet me tonight. We can't tell anyone in case the police get a sniff.'

'What time are we going?'

Kate handed him the money. She knelt and held his hands. 'Thomas, I have to go alone. That's what he asked.'

Though the letter hadn't specified whether Thomas might accompany her, John had to be kept as safe as possible.

Thomas knew his father had shared a secret with his uncle. For sure it was all connected; why else would a condemned old man return to the country that had issued his death warrant? However, Thomas had no clue of the secret's importance.

***

Later that evening, Kate headed for the quarry. The snow had intensified, covering any tracks she might have followed. She tightened the scarf around her neck and remembered common voices and some unknown ones, from stories that Thomas had told her. The voices were echoing in her head.

That's why they call him big John.

Providing you'll stay here and work for me.

This enabled her to recall the radio announcement from years ago. She could remember it clearly, as if it was yesterday.

A man believed to be around six feet four inches tall, with thick dark hair. He spoke with a northern accent. Today, a warrant has been issued for the police to search the Tierney household.

It was all coming back to her now, John's voice and touch, his pain and loss, and all the years that had passed since his disappearance.

At the quarry, she sheltered her eyes to get a better view of the surroundings. Fear encouraged her retreat as a car's horn sounded nearby. A grey car stopped just metres in front of her. The window came down slowly. A face partially hidden by dark glasses appeared, but she couldn't yet guess whether it belonged to a woman or a man.

The words were delivered in a male's foreign accent. 'Are you Kate Tierney?'

How to respond? He had some connection to John. She backed away from the window. 'Yes?'

'Stay there. The next car will pick you up.'

Kate waited with apprehension until a black version of the first car approached from the opposite direction. It stopped farther from her than the previous car had. The door swung open. Kate ran to the car and closed the door. The car idled. Kate tried to get a look at the driver. He had blonde hair, appeared slightly older than Thomas, and wore a dark suit. She aimed for his attention by clearing her throat. 'Where's John?'

The man replied without looking back. 'You'll meet him soon enough.'

Anxiety weakened Kate's courage. 'Where are you taking me?'

The driver didn't reply. Kate gripped the door handle. She had never seen such a luxurious interior. In fact, she had never owned a car, but the silence overcame these impressions.

The driver brought the car to a halt outside a well-lit hotel. Three men, all dressed in black suits, waited at the entrance. Remembering John's business acumen, Kate believed everything had been going according to his plan.

As soon as she exited the car, one of the dark-suited men commanded that she follow him. A few people stood in the hotel foyer, and they all filed into an elevator. The second button turned orange at the push of the man's forefinger. The bell rang, and Kate trailed down the corridor. They stopped outside a door bearing a large golden '11.' The man opened the door and gestured for Kate to follow him inside.

The atmosphere was tense; Kate could hear her own heartbeat as she stepped forward. The light was dim.

'Hello, Kate.'

She turned to see her uncle John on the other side of the room, where he opened the curtains. The guard, who had been waiting behind the door, locked it closed. Now she saw John's face for the first time in years. She immediately noticed how much it had changed during his absence.

John rubbed his palms together. 'It's been so many years, Kate.'

They moved towards each other. 'Too many,' Kate replied. 'Far too many.'

They embraced tightly until John pulled back. Beyond his appearance, something else had changed in him. Kate couldn't guess how guilty John felt for everything, for failing to fulfil all he had promised to her father, Eamon.

'Not one day has passed that I haven't thought about you, Kate – not one day.'

Kate took his hands. 'We all understand, John. You had no choice but to run. You killed a police officer. Now you're back, and for good this time, I hope.' She looked at him pleadingly.

'That all sounds good, Kate; unfortunately, I must go back to the place I've called home for the last few years. Tell me, how's Thomas?'

'He's fine, but he's missed you awfully badly over the years. He wanted to join me. I thought it best I come alone.'

John glanced at his watch. 'Tomorrow night, I'll arrange to pick you up. We'll all have dinner. That's already been organised.'

She suddenly remembered the guard, who had been standing behind them. 'Who do these men work for, John? And what have you been doing all these years?'

John nodded at his guard, who checked his watch.

'You know me Kate, I never did hang about. These men work for me. Kate, you must trust me.' He nodded at his guard once more. The key in the door turned. 'Now, you'd better leave. Remember to meet me at the same place where you were picked up today.' He paused. 'Wait. How are things financially Kate?'

She lowered her eyes, remembering the burning cabinet. 'You know me, I like to gamble. I owe money to the local bookie. It was only a couple of bets, John.'

'Who's the bookie?'

'Smiths Limited, in town.'

John took her by the shoulders and lowered his voice. 'Listen, Kate, I'll sort it out for you, but you have to promise you'll keep your wits about ya over the coming months.'

Kate looked back at the guard when she left. This

time, she noticed herself in the mirrored elevator walls. *Fifteen years; I could've at least brushed me damn hair.* The luminosity of the foyer upset her nerves still more. She exited the elevator and walked towards the sliding doors. She stepped into a chilled breeze and, pulling at her scarf, reached for the car door. From the open window above, John shouted to her. 'Kate, is everything all right with Rose?'

Confused, she nodded.

***

The next evening, the family gathered at a large dining room table. Kate studied their faces. She realised John had been jig sawed from the Tierney puzzle. He looked amused, leaning sideways towards Rose, who chattered into his ear.

Kate excused herself. In the toilet, she splashed cold water on her face, trying to wash away the most unusual feeling of jealousy. *How can I envy my own daughter?* She was tired.

Yawning, she returned to the table. A silver plate shimmered at the centre of the table, and upon it rested a perfect cut of meat. Throughout dinner, Kate couldn't help but think about the bookies. John looked as if he'd forgotten all about it. The uncertainty worried her even more.

John stayed at the house overnight. Everybody awoke early, for he was leaving soon. 'I'll be back,' he told them. He kissed Rose on the cheeks and whispered a personal message. Kate noticed how much longer John had spoke to Rose, rather than he had to her or Christine.

He handed a small gift to Thomas, a poem Eamon had written. Thomas was surprised that John had maintained something so fragile throughout the many years he'd been gone. They embraced.

As John walked the path towards a black Mercedes, the rest of the family gathered at the window, wondering if they'd ever see him again.

***

One person who would see John before he departed for Boston was Tommy Collins. Shortly before John's departure, his Mercedes pulled into a lay-by next to the quarry. Another vehicle was waiting by the roadside. Tommy Collins stepped out of the car. The wind was gale force, and the dust it created was like a desert storm. On the opposite side of the road was the Mercedes.

Tommy stood still, waiting for the dust to settle. As the wind relented slightly, it made the car more visible to the eye. When the image was clear, John had already gotten out of the Mercedes and was standing by the quarry fence. His hand was on his head, trying to keep his hat on. Tommy walked over to John.

'Did you do as I asked?'

Tommy cleared his throat before answering the question. 'Yes, John, you're the new owner of Smiths Limited, and I'm fronting it for you. I also employed the young man you asked me to give a job to.'

John turned to face Tommy. His face bore the look of an old hardened criminal. 'You just make sure he looks after her, do you hear me?'

Tommy heard an order from an old voice going back to his teenage days in Nottingham.

John turned and walked back to the car, walking stick in hand. His minder opened the car door. John removed his leather glove and shook Tommy's hand. 'I'm leaving for Boston, Tommy, so make sure you send me a monthly report on the situation. Old age is catching up with both of us. I have a feeling we're so close.'

Tommy patted John on the back, as John climbed back into the Mercedes. Whatever John had planned, Tommy knew, there was no room for error.

Chapter VIII

Ten days after John's departure, life had apparently regained its normality, until Kate heard car tyres crushing gravel then the slight screeching sound of a car skidding to a halt. As she peered through the small pane of glass to the left of the door, she could see three men exiting an old-fashioned car. They looked neither dangerous nor in the mood for laughs. She reached to the coat stand and pulled down a cardigan.

Kate opened the door slowly. Looking down, she saw two shiny shoes at the bottom of pinstriped suit trousers. It was a long way from the man's shoes to his face. He was a stocky lad who looked to be in his early twenties. The other two stayed behind him. They appeared to be in their late fifties. Kate tried to look relaxed. It didn't work.

'Kate Tierney?'

'Yes, that's me.'

The young man leaned against the door frame, getting closer to Kate he said. 'Your account hasn't been paid. You know that tomorrow you'll be paying interest on the debt that you owe Smiths Limited, right?'

John had forgotten. He'd broken his promise. Why?

The man continued. 'You get three days to pay, or we'll

come back to visit you.' He stepped down to leave. The car sped away, disappearing as swiftly as it had arrived.

What can I do? John can't help me now. He's back in Boston, far away and beyond my call.

***

Late the following afternoon, Kate headed to the local working men's club with her daughters, Christine and Rose. She played bingo there every Sunday. It was close enough for them to walk.

As always, the place was small and shadowy. Cigarette smoke permeated the air. Teenagers surrounded a pool table at the opposite end of the bar, and men sat in a corner playing cards.

Kate, Christine and Rose sat at the first free table. Midweek meant fewer regulars than usual. Rose offered to buy the first round. She went to the bar and ordered the drinks then lit a cigarette.

A man appeared next to her, as if from nowhere. She exhaled smoke through her nose, exhibiting her disdain for his presence. *Another creep*, she thought.

Oblivious, the man happily sipped a pint. *Good work, big man*, he thought.

Actually, Rose noticed, the man was quite attractive. Now she was staring at him. He seemed familiar.

The man put down his glass and gave a pleasant smile. 'Hello, we've met before, haven't we?'

Rose corrected her posture. 'Oh, I'm so sorry, I'm such an idiot! You came 'round to our house the other night. That's my mother in the corner.'

He traced the direction of her glance and nodded in recognition. 'I remember. My name's Christopher Bronks, by the way. Nice to meet you.'

'Hi, Chris, I'm Rose,' she said.

He took her hand. 'Such a beautiful name.'

58

Rose smiled as she stubbed out her cigarette. Some chemical reaction passed between them. Rose laughed and grabbed the drink tray. Kate approached Rose.

'Where the bloody 'ell have you been?'

Placing the drinks on the table, Rose leaned forward. 'Mum,' she said, sitting down. 'You've seen that guy at the bar before. What do you know about him?'

Christine giggled, while Kate squinted and shuffled along the seat. 'Can't say I've seen him before. I don't know who he is, Rose.' She fumbled in her bag. 'I've left my glasses at home.'

Huge help she is. Rose was now certain that she'd seen Mr Bronks's face before, apart from when he came to the house.

***

The next day, the sound of someone banging on the front door interrupted Rose's daydreaming. The debt collectors had arrived early. She gathered the few notes lying on the mantelpiece. She calculated they had half the money to pay Kate's debt.

Two knocks on the door later, she rushed to find only one man waiting, Christopher Bronks. When she saw his face, she blushed, for she wished Christine had answered the door as she had yet to apply makeup.

'Chris. Just a minute, I'll get my mum.'

Christopher had a strange expression on his face, as if he knew something Rose didn't. 'Wait. It's you I came to see.'

Rose turned back and opened the door wider. Christopher took a nervous step towards her. 'I came here to ask you if you'd like to go out tonight.' Like a small child standing by a Christmas tree waiting to open gifts, he seemed wistful and pensive.

Rose heard her mother's voice. 'I don't have a problem with it,' she said, 'providing she's back by eleven.'

Her mother could tell she was genuinely interested in Chris. Kate walked past, ignoring the scene.

Chris shouted after her, 'She will be. I promise.'

Rose couldn't grasp the moment. He hadn't even given her a chance to get out of it. Perhaps a date would help. Maybe he'd allow more time to find the money Mum owed. But she could hardly let him know that was half the reason she'd agree. 'Okay. What time?'

He said nothing after she had agreed to the date. She waved a hand in front of his face. *Five minutes together before the first date, and already he's ignoring me.* She tapped her watch. 'What time?'

He ran his fingers through his hair. 'Eight.'

***

As if by fate, four months later, Rose and Christopher were deeply in love. Kate's debt had remained overlooked. Why hadn't Chris mentioned it?

John knew.

Chapter IX

Sheffield, England – 1971

Between the showers on a Sunday afternoon in April, Rose stood beneath a pure blue sky. She stepped out of the shade and into the sunlight. It was a beautiful spring day. There was a sharp transformation in the air. A dark bubble burst into white-hot beams. The concrete sparkled.

Rose often spent Sundays at the lake. She had met her friends alone, as Chris dealt with overdue payments. Fancy bloody bothering him on a Sunday.

Rose had known Kathleen and Mel since school. They knew her as a great swimmer with countless medals to her credit. Naturally, she always reached the small island first. It provided a fantastic sunbathing spot.

Kathleen and Mel met Rose by the tree, and they decided to leave their bags beside its trunk. They knew it was safe enough to leave their things unattended.

They all walked into the waist-deep water. Kate savoured the water's coolness rippling across her skin; despite the sunshine, the water was still damn cold. They kicked off from the riverbank and made their way to the island. Kate smoothed out a patch of grass and sat down while Kathleen and Mel still paddled along. Once her friends arrived, they spread out across the island's bank. It wasn't long before Mel slept under the warmth of the sun.

Rose turned to Kathleen. 'You know, I'm so happy with Christopher. He does everything for me. He's a proper gentleman.'

Kathleen adjusted her sunglasses. 'I wish I could say the same about my man. In fact, I doubt I'll last much longer. We've been together five years now. He hasn't once told me he loves me.'

I should have kept my mouth shut, Rose thought.

***

Across town, Christopher was driving along Coleford Road with his boss, Tommy Collins, who had insisted a backup vehicle come along just in case.

'Think you can handle Hodgson's gypsies on your own? These boys are the best he's got.'

Christopher sat motionless before turning to face Tommy. 'Had bigger,' Christopher said.

He had a debt to collect, and he screeched to a halt in front of the large black wrought iron gates of Richmond Refractories Ltd. Christopher clenched his fists, got out of the car, and walked inside.

Two men appeared immediately. Both had the appearance of gypsies. Christopher stepped to one side as the wind blew sand and grit into his eyes. The gypsies worked for Hodgson, another small-time local gang boss, one yet to gain the slightest respect. These blokes had no idea of the trouble they faced as they approached Christopher.

'What d'ya wants like?' the gypsy said while wiping his hands on a rag.

Christopher spoke with mock patience. 'Tell your boss

62

that tomorrow's bill paying day or, next time, he'll be seeing me. Is that clear enough, lads?'

Christopher could see Hodgson looking through his open office window. He wasted no time in displaying his anger.

'What's up with you boys? Get him off my property.'

The gypsies looked at one another with a grin. One wasted no time in showing his aggression. Christopher replied with a short burst of rabbit punches. Within seconds, both gypsies were on the floor, one out cold. Christopher wedged his foot on the other's jaw. Hodgson closed the window before appearing in the doorway.

Christopher shouted, 'I'll be back, same time tomorrow if the bill isn't paid.' Christopher looked down at the gypsies 'Do ya hear me, you two scum bags?'

One of the gypsies tried to raise his head to nod but could only groan in acknowledgment. That was enough for Chris. He knelt to wipe the blood from his shoes. Rolling down his sleeves, he dropped the tissue and stepped over the bloodied rival gang members.

Tommy and his colleague had been waiting by the open car door. 'Good job, son. I'm betting he'll pay tomorrow.'

Chris had shown them he needed no assistance. He got in the driver's seat of the car. Suddenly, he realised how dark the sky had turned. He must have been dealing with the gypsies far longer than he had guessed. It was highly unusual for the weather to change so rapidly in such a short space of time. Then he remembered Rose and hurriedly clicked his seat belt into place.

Leaning out of the window, he shouted back to Tommy, 'Do you mind taking the boys' car back? I'm driving to the lake now. Looks like a storm coming. Those clouds over there are as black as the ace of spades.'

Tommy Collins watched Christopher drive off at speed.

He glanced up towards the storm. Blinking twice. He took a deep breath. 'Jesus. Mother of God' Tommy knew this storm was something else!

***

Back at the lake, the wind had become a gust. Leaves and litter drifted past the girls. In a panic, Rose motioned for Mel and Kathleen to follow. 'We'd better head back. You two take the dinghy. I'll swim and meet you over there.' The girls paused, as if waiting for Rose to change her mind. 'It's okay. Just go!' Rose said.

Mel grabbed the paddles as Kathleen pushed the dinghy into the water.

Meanwhile, Rose inspected the water, which tore into itself under the heavy rain. Mel and Kathleen sped away. The wind blew pin-like raindrops into their faces. Rose tried to conquer the overpowering rush of water. Her friends glanced back at the sound of thunder echoing from a mass of clouds. Rose remained twenty yards behind. Lightning shot, gunning the sky.

The girls landed safely ashore. They jumped out of the dinghy and dragged it uphill, across the now muddied bank. But Rose was way behind, held back by an even stronger wind. She tried to shout, choking on water as the waves began to overcome her. Her arms ached. Her legs had become nearly impotent. A cramp in her side intensified. A headache announced its approach. *If only I could lie down.*

Heart pounding in her chest, she watched a terrifying white fork of lightning strike the water beside her. She had one last conscious thought: *Sleep.*

***

Rose lingered in the water, her face lit up from the headlamps of a parked car. The door slammed. A figure emerged, whom the girls soon recognised as Chris. Mel tapped Kathleen on the shoulder.

64

'Where's Rose?'

Kathleen hurried to the bank. Chris followed her.

'Where the hell is Rose?' Chris repeated.

'Oh my God, I can't see her. She was there just a minute ago, right behind us. She must've gone under! I'll call an ambulance.'

Chris ripped off his jacket and tossed his shoes over his shoulder. He yelled, 'No need,' and was gone. He jumped into the water that ran like rapids, yet he was soon fifty feet from the bank. He circled, searching.

Mel grabbed Kathleen's shoulder. 'Where is she?'

'Don't worry. Chris has it under control.'

The clouds blocked the moonlight and darkened the surface of the lake.

'What's he doing?' Kathleen asked.

They trailed down the bank. 'That noise. Didn't you hear that noise?'

Mel shook her head, hoping it was an ambulance.

'It's Chris. I think he's got her.'

Chris, splashing, came into sight, holding an unconscious Rose in his left arm, pushing towards them with his right. The girls ran to them and helped drag Rose by her arms onto the bank.

Chris, exhausted, dragged himself out of the water and ran straight over. He fell on his knees and felt for a pulse, which was not to be found. He heard a whistle as another gust swept around them. He pushed Rose's chest. 'Come on, girl, don't give up on us.'

Chris parted Rose's lips, pinching her nose and holding her mouth open as he breathed forcefully. Nothing.

He tried again.

'Come on.' He hoped the air would trap itself in her throat and cause some reaction, and it did.

She wheezed and choked, her mouth ejecting water.

Chris collapsed onto his back. 'Thank God.'

After vomiting violently, Rose leaned forwards, gazing at those watching her. 'What the hell are you looking at?' She burst out laughing, until more vomit flew in every direction. Finally, she collapsed and fell asleep.

Chris ran to the car and grabbed a blanket. He returned and wrapped Rose in warmth.

The girls, still huddled together, looked stunned, witnessing a near-death experience hardly being part of their original plan.

'I think,' Chris said, 'we'd better go to the hospital.'

The girls squeezed into the back seat with Rose between them. They held her upright, allowing her breathing to even out. Upon their arrival at the hospital, the girls shuffled out of the car. They gathered Rose between them and carried her past the sliding doors. Chris ran to the reception desk.

'I need a doctor. Make it sharp.'

The nurse fumbled about before picking up the phone. 'We need a doctor at reception.'

Chris leaned on the desk, tapping his foot.

'Someone's on the way down,' said the nurse. She smiled sarcastically and began filing her nails.

Chris muttered under his breath. 'Typical, an emergency situation, and she's worried about how she looks. Half of 'em are only in here for free medication. Anyone who actually needs 'em gets to pay.'

All the while, Mel had been out of breath. Kathleen shook her. 'Mel, what's the matter?' She pointed at her stomach.

'Are you hungry?'

Mel shook her head. 'Insulin — I forgot my injection twice.'

Kathleen ran towards the desk just as a doctor burst

through the doors. 'My friend needs insulin. She's missed two doses already.'

The doctor, holding a clipboard, said, 'No problem. Right this way.'

Kathleen led Mel into the small cabinet room next to the desk.

Meanwhile, Chris and Rose were on their way to a ward on the floor above.

Chris sat in a chair, watching the medic. 'Any serious problems, doc?'

The medic, glancing at Chris, said, 'No problems, none at all. She could've developed pneumonia pretty quickly if you hadn't gotten her here so fast. We'll be keeping her overnight before giving the all-clear.'

Chris fidgeted. The medic poured a glass of water for him. 'Relax, sir. You've had enough excitement for one night.'

'I've had enough bloody water!' Chris replied.

The medic left Chris alone in the ward. Chris pondered the contents of the glass. Footsteps resounded down the corridor. Chris's face came closer to the small square of reinforced glass. Mel swung the door open.

'All clear, everything's fine,' Chris said.

***

As Rose regained consciousness, her family came into focus. They watched over her in a room yellow with sunlight. Rose savoured the warmth. She remembered dark, cold, heavy water.

A white doctor's sleeve parted Thomas and Christine. This older man with his posh London accent said, 'It won't take a moment.'

Kate placed a vase of flowers on Rose's table and kissed her daughter's forehead. She drew the plastic curtains and joined the rest in leaving for the café.

The physician pulled a chair beside the bed. 'So, Rose Tierney, how are you feeling this morning? I must say, you were incredibly lucky to survive such a traumatic experience, especially given your condition.'

A doctor insulting a patient? 'I beg your pardon?'

He shuffled papers. 'What I mean is that your boyfriend couldn't risk losing you and his unborn child, and he risked his own life to prove it.'

'Unborn—what do you mean?'

The doctor, evidently amused, moved closer. 'These things do show up when we carry out our observations, you know. My dear lady, you're pregnant, and have been for three or four months now.'

Rose lay still, trying to absorb the news. 'Don't be daft. I had no idea.'

'Shall I share the good news with your family?'

Dazed, Rose could only think to say, 'What? No, don't say anything yet. Please. I'd like to wait until I feel better.'

The doctor whispered, 'As you wish. Good luck to you.' He slipped away through the curtains.

Kate, popping her head back through the curtain, grinned. 'Nice man. Can't tar them all with the same brush. Heroes some, but mostly bastards.'

***

Back home the next day, Rose worked with Kate in the kitchen.

'Mum,' Rose began, 'I have something on my mind, something I found out yesterday.'

Kate looked worried.

Rose raised her hands. 'Ssh, I'm okay. It's nothing to do with the lake accident. In fact, it's good news.'

Her mother's expression shifted from concern to a soft glow of contentment. 'Oh, thank God, Rose.'

Rose wiped a tear from her mother's face and kissed the skin where the sorrow had fallen.

Knives and forks clashed against plates as they finished their dinner. Rose tapped a glass. 'I have something to tell you all. Chris is gonna be a dad. Yesterday, the doctor said I was pregnant.' She looked towards Chris. 'Two months, now.'

Thomas leaned over to hug her. 'That's fantastic news.'

Chris looked ecstatic. He stood and raised his glass. Everyone joined him for the toast.

***

Later that evening, Chris had to visit the office and hand his weekly report in. He would never have guessed that the owner of Smiths Ltd, was a certain Mr J. Tierney. He described the debts he had settled that week and how the Tierney family were fairing. However, he said nothing to Tommy Collins about the lake incident. Chris was there to protect Rose, but not to watch her nearly die.

***

Everyone but Rose had gone to bed; she still lay awake. A thought had only just occurred to her. She hadn't slept with Chris during the period necessary for her to be pregnant now, and she hadn't slept with anyone else then either. *Oh, the doctors have the timing wrong, that's all*, she decided. *It must be so.*

On the other side of the wall, Kate also lay awake. A thought had only just occurred to her. Had John known something? It made sense, considering all the time he'd spent with Rose. There must have been some logical reason?

Oh, but that was stupid. How could John predict a pregnancy? Besides, he was on the other side of the planet.

Now where will we buy all the baby clothes and supplies? she wondered. Finally, she fell asleep.

Chapter X

One night in late June, Rose was resting by the fireplace. Rose knew Christopher was at the office talking to his boss, Tommy Collins – an old man her mother knew well.

Christopher saw his boss differently; to him, Tommy was a colossus of a man who commanded vast respect. His boss poured two glasses of whisky and pushed a chair towards Chris. Chris, in return, placed his weekly report in front of Tommy's eyes.

Christopher had a problem on his mind he needed to clear. 'Boss, since Rose has been pregnant, I've been doing these new weekly reports since April. How long must this go on?'

Tommy was in a deep trance reading the report. Page after page flicked over without a reply.

'Boss,' Christopher repeated. He was getting anxious for a reply.

Tommy took an envelope out of his top drawer and placed the report inside before looking towards Christopher with his answer.

'Chris, you knew what the deal was didn't ya? You look after Rose and the Tierney family and make a weekly written report and pass it on to me. Now you've gone and gotten her pregnant, which sheds a different light over the situation regarding questions, and now you're asking more questions.'

Tommy stood, spat on the envelope sleeve, sealed it with his tongue, and walked over to the door. Tommy said, "We want you to take time off and help Rose until your baby is born. You've done a grand job. You deserve it.'

Chris sipped his whisky. 'I deeply appreciate that, Boss.'

'Nevertheless, you still have to stop by and deliver your weekly reports until the baby is born.'

Christopher nodded and straightened his tie. 'Sure, Boss.'

Tommy opened the door that led out onto the landing. 'Now be on ya way, son. I have work to do…'

Although Chris didn't know it, his boss's orders came directly from John, whose organisational skills had put him in good favour with the Irish Republican Army. They could always use a good thinker, somebody with ideas and the ability to make them happen.

As Christopher walked slowly down the stairs, a little bemused, Tommy shut the door behind him and placed the envelope on the desk next to the window. He then watched Christopher crossing the road. Then he let the venetian blinds he was holding open snap shut and looked seriously down at the envelope. John Tierney, Boston, United States of America, glazed in his eyes.

***

Weeks passed, and Rose awaited her child's birth. Now she had physical evidence to support her belief that the physician's calculations had been incorrect. She felt ill, bloated, tired, and angry. Yes, she knew it would be worth it, but only John knew it would also be the day the family had waited over four hundred years to arrive.

Holding the stairway rail, Rose struggled to make her way up to her bedroom. Then she noticed her water had broken, months to early. Childbirth had begun.

Okay, just keep calm, she told herself. *Lie down and wait.* Grabbing the sheets, she slid onto the bed, staring at the ceiling. *Sleep. Maybe I can drift away and leave this pain behind.*

No such luck. The pain ebbed and flowed like the water in which she had almost drowned. Her chest heaved, blood throbbing in her temples. Sweat gleamed on her forehead. Anxiety washed over her, her oxygen running out. Bird-like shadows swooped over her.

'Breathe, Rose, breathe. There's a good girl.'

Amid her inner turmoil, Rose had missed the midwife coming up the stairs. *Funny*, she thought, i*n the most important moments of my life, I always have to rely on others.* The midwife placed a cool flannel across Rose's forehead.

'Stay with me, Rose. You're doing fine.'

Downstairs, someone opened the front door then slammed it so hard that a tremor rumbled through the house. It was Chris running up the stairs, with Tommy Collins right behind. The news had travelled quickly.

'Rose, is everything okay?'

'It's fine, sir,' said the midwife. 'Maybe it would be better for Rose if you waited outside a while.' She expected a crude retort.

Chris sighed and wandered onto the landing, where he paced with anxiety. The clock was ticking. Time went by, and while Chris paced, Rose panted.

'We're getting closer. Try to push, Rose. Give it a go.'

Rose gulped air and pushed so hard she thought she'd ruptured a muscle.

The nurse took her hand. 'Do another one. That's it, breathe.

'Again. That's a good girl. You're getting the pattern.'

Chris studied his watch. The damn report had left him in the office longer than usual, waiting for a late boss. What perfect timing. Rose screamed. 'For Christ's sake, someone just stop it.'

The midwife yelled, 'Keep going. Not long to go now. Breathe and push.'

Thirty seconds later, at last, a body appeared. The baby was somewhat premature, but all the same, Rose had delivered a beautiful baby boy. Rose, gasping for breath, lay as if she had just run a marathon. The midwife took a fresh towel and spread it across the new mother's bed. She lifted the baby and set him on top of it.

'No sound, no sign of respiration. God.'

Rose panicked. 'What's wrong?' She lifted her head and noticed something over the child's face. 'Please, help my baby. For God's sake, don't let him die!'

The midwife removed a surgical blade from her purse. 'I'm not sure I've never seen anything like it. I'll need to remove it. But first, I must pierce holes for the baby to breathe and see.'

'It' was a layer of dark fleshy-coloured skin enshrouding the baby's face. The midwife tried to remove it as if it were a garment. How fragile it appeared; she discovered it to be resilient to force. It seemed to be attached by some kind of skin-type loops around the ears.

The silver blade, in the light of things, presented the last option. She sliced the skin at the back of the baby's neck and continued dissecting to the top of the head. No blood, everything in order. The midwife peeled the skin away. With two fingers, she tapped the baby's hand. The fingers and toes moved. A cry bellowed through the room. She dropped him on the scales before wrapping him in a small towel and handing the child over to Rose.

'Here he is Rose, a beautiful, eleven pound eleven ounce baby boy.' The midwife then looked at her watch and wrote the time and date of birth in her note pad. 'Eleven minutes past eleven,'

Rose was elated cradling her child.

The midwife drove back to surgery and reported to her boss what she had seen. 'You wouldn't believe it.'

Her boss reached for a telephone directory. 'I've a call to make.' The book slammed shut as he dialled the number.

***

Three hours later, Chris heard a knock on the door. He opened the door slowly. 'Can I help you?'

Two men in white coats stood side by side, one taller than the other. 'Well yes,' the tall one. 'We've been informed that your child was born with a profound abnormality. Do you mind if we come in? It won't take but a moment.'

Chris stepped back and gestured for them to enter. The shorter man closed the door. 'You're not going to tell me there's something wrong? Because if you are—'

'We didn't mean to offend you in any way. We need to see the skin, that's all.'

'What d'ya mean skin? What skin?'

The men looked at one another. 'The skin that was covering your baby's head when he was born. You do have it here, don't you?'

Chris knew whatever they were talking about had to be upstairs in the bedroom. 'He was born up there, so I guess that's where we'd better go.' The men looked pleased and headed for the stairs.

'Wait a minute,' Chris said. 'Before you go barging through my property, I'd like to see some kind of ID.'

The taller one removed a card from his pocket.

Satisfied, Chris proceeded behind them up the stairs. Beneath a microscope, the skin looked like, like skin. But why had it grown over the baby's head? Moreover, how had it grown? The taller man shook his head as Chris stood by Rose, observing their every move. 'We'll have to take this with us for further analysis. That should clarify its purpose and origin. There may be a history of such births.'

'No bleedin' way, you can forget that. How dare you come into my home this way? I don't care who you are; that's part of my child. Just because I had a gypsy upbringing and you two spent your youth with public school ponces doesn't make you better than me.'

Chris, standing against a backdrop of wine red curtains, shrugged. 'Don't look at me. She's right. I think you've done enough damage here. Now I'll thank you two gentlemen to show yourselves out.'

Chris and Rose hadn't noticed that the man with the microscope stood in front of the shorter man, shielding him from the sight. The shorter man held the skin behind his back, standing next to the bedside cabinet and facing Chris. His scissors finished the job with a single snip. It was done. They had what they needed.

'In that case, thank you for your hospitality.' He snapped his briefcase shut; then both men left, never to be seen again.

Chapter XI

The next day, the family gathered around Rose, who sat in an armchair cradling the baby. Thomas knelt beside her.

'Can I hold 'im?'

Rose nodded, carefully passing the little bundle. Thomas laughed. 'He's wide awake an' all. Starin' up at me, he is. Hello, little fella. You're the biggest Tierney ever.'

'Yeah,' Chris said, 'with the biggest mouth.'

Kate walked in with a tray of tea. Thomas's dog barked as the letterbox rattled.

'Shut up, Teddy.'

She placed the tray on a small table and went to the door. She opened it just as one of two boys had his fist ready to knock again. He blushed. Kate slipped on her glasses, which hung from a chain on her neck. 'What can I do for you?'

The boys wore sailors' uniforms. The light-haired one spoke first. 'Is it true your daughter drowned and was given the kiss of life while pregnant? And that yesterday, she gave birth to a baby boy with a veil of skin?'

Kate pulled her cardigan tighter. 'Why do you ask?'

The dark-haired boy said, 'Well, we talked to our

captain yesterday, and we want to buy this skin from you. He instructed us to come and ask you.'

Kate, fiddling with her rosary beads, couldn't help but laugh. 'Madness. What on earth would you want with it?'

The same boy raised his eyebrows as if to say, you don't know?

It will bring our shipmates luck.'

Kate stepped back and said, 'It's not for sale.'

The blond boy stepped forward. 'Will ten pounds be enough?'

That does sound like a good offer. She signalled them to wait and returned to the front room.

Rose looked up. 'Who is it, Mum?'

'Pair of boys. Sailors, they are. They want the skin. Ten pounds they'll pay. It's your choice whether you need the money or not.'

Everybody looked at Rose, who was studying Chris's expression. 'Don't know what the hell they want it for, but ten pounds sure sounds good to me.'

'Well then, it's settled. I think maybe we should let them have it. The money would do us well, especially with your time off, Chris.'

'Makes sense, I suppose,' he said.

Kate went to a cabinet and removed a tiny key from her top pocket. 'Well, all right, then, I'll give it to 'em.' She lifted a small package wrapped in brown paper and went to the front door.

'Give me twelve pounds.'

'Eleven.'

'Look here, sonny, I'm not about to start haggling with ya, especially on me own doorstep. Either you want it or you don't. That's the end of it.'

The blond sailor paused; his captain had told them to

get the skin at whatever cost. 'Oh okay,' he said, 'but can we see it first?'

Kate lifted the package and parted the paper, exposing the skin. 'Look.'

The young sailors gasped. 'It shines, like they told us it would. And it feels like—'

The blond boy pulled the money from his pocket and placed it in Kate's open hand.

She smiled. 'Now, on your way, boys; I've lots to do.'

She watched them walk down the street, chattering. Something about the episode was troubling her, despite having accepted the money. Who was 'they' who had told the boys about the skin in the first place?

She closed the door behind her and peeked through the curtains. Through the rear window, she saw the boys climb into a car parked at the end of the street. Its purpose, she guessed, was to throw her off the scent. Two men sat in the front of the car. *Oh, and Tommy Collins told me to put it in a safe place for the time being.*

***

'All is well, it appears,' the driver said. 'Good job, boys.' The driver wore jeans and a leather jacket.

The other man adjusted the gold chain around his neck. He zipped up the top of his tracksuit. 'It's time we should be getting back. We can't arouse suspicion.'

The driver glanced at his companion. 'The only suspicion you could arouse is that you have no sense of fashion.'

'Shut it and drive.'

The driver turned on the radio tuner, and the car reeled round in a cloud of dust. A voice came over the radio:

We're sorry to interrupt this programme, but this is a news bulletin just in. There's a traffic hold-up on the motorway, due to an accident. If you're heading towards

London or the south, we advise you to refuel at the nearest station.

'Fantastic,' the driver said. 'Another excuse to bitch at us.'

They continued to the nearest petrol station and pulled alongside a pump. The boys got out of the car, leaving the skin with the men.

'I'm sure your cooperation will be much appreciated,' the driver said. 'Tell your captain the object of study will be returned to you once we've completed the necessary research.'

The boys nodded. The car seemed to disappear at the peak of the main road.

'I hate to bring this up,' the driver said, 'but weren't you supposed to get petrol back there?' They were going the wrong direction on a one-way system!

***

Back in Sheffield, Chris worked at the office, writing the usual weekly report. He was distracted, unsure of all that had occurred in the past few weeks. *People think they have the right to invade my family life*, he contemplated. *Why?*

However, the situation had progressed too far. It had escaped his control so quickly. *How could I have been so careless?*

***

Elsewhere, John was no less concerned. The bank had been mapped. Safe locations had been arranged. Security operating codes had been cracked. *A master plan. Don't leave it on the heat too long.* But John had done just that. He'd been waiting all his life for such a perfect set-up, but despite all the planning and preparation, something seemed to go dreadfully wrong.

Chapter XII

A month later, a package arrived on the HMS *Sheffield*. A blond-haired sailor ran across the deck, clutching the square object, which was wrapped in brown paper. Shoving through a pair of swinging doors and into a wood-panelled room, he put it down on a small table in front of him.

Behind the table stood a thick, fifty-something man, his navy jacket adorned with pins and medals that sparkled in the orange light. Biting the cigar hanging from his mouth, he laid his hand on the parcel, glancing at the boy apprehensively. 'This could be it, lad.'

Leaning over the desk, he tore the string from the parcel With a penknife, he made an incision across the top of the box. Barely able to contain his excitement, the man lifted the lid with shaking hands.

'Look at 'er. Can you feel that? I have a strange kinda feeling about this. She'll take pride of place right 'ere in the heart of the ship.' He lifted the frame to the light.

The boy stepped forward and picked up a small folded note from the table. 'Captain, there's a letter here. Shall I read it, sir?'

The captain had his back to the boy. He turned a

screwdriver to remove a photo frame that was screwed to the wall. 'Aye, lad, let's 'ear what them there land rats gotta say for 'emselves!'

The boy read:

To the rightful owner,

We are happy to inform you that your cooperation in this matter has been of great assistance to us. Your involvement will be noted in our records. Should you have any objections to the inclusion of these records in your file, please do not hesitate to contact the public services office of the main headquarters, number printed overleaf. We thank you once again and wish you the best of luck in future missions.

Yours confidentially,
Vladimir Roscoff
MI5

***

On the day of the christening, Rose and Chris finally agreed on the baby's name, and to no one's surprise, they chose John.

Kate had sent a letter to the baby's namesake, informing him of the good news and, naturally, to ask when he might return.

In the church, sunrays lit the arched windows, sending rainbows of colour upon those gathered to watch the priest dab holy water on the baby's forehead. Unfortunately, John had missed this special day. He had never returned any of Kate's letters. Maybe hers had never found their way to him.

Rose lit a white candle. Kate leaned forward to watch the flame. It burned for both Johns.

Chapter XIII

Throughout young Tierney's childhood, he had rarely been separated from his devoted mother, Rose. He had fair hair and blue eyes. Rose adored him to the point of obsession. By the time he was ten, John's golden hair had faded to brown, a typical curly Tierney mop underscored by a porcelain-coloured complexion. He was known for his politeness. He would speak when spoken to but, otherwise, keep to himself.

Christopher and Rose lived with Thomas, who had just come back after moving to Ireland ten years earlier. It was healthy for young John to have a male role model, aside from his own father. Thomas was like an older brother, even if he had left the family behind.

One afternoon, after Thomas had gone out on his motorbike, what sounded like a cymbal echoed through the house. John dropped his fork onto his plate. He hid his face in his folded arms. Rose reached over, touching his shoulder. 'What's the matter, love?'

John sat up. Teardrops fell like rain.

Chris rubbed his arm. 'John, come and tell your dad what's wrong.'

John took a few deep breaths. 'It's Uncle Thomas.'

Chris rubbed his sons back. 'He'll return soon.'

Yet John became still more anxious, the volume of his voice louder as he fought his despair. 'No, he's had an accident on the motorbike. His leg is hurt. I know it.'

Chris didn't understand. He spoke so fast that his words were nearly incomprehensible. 'Now come on, son, you don't know that.'

Rose walked into the kitchen, her shoulders hunched. Nearly ten minutes of silence passed, broken only by a loud knock at the door. Chris opened the door. Two police officers faced him. One firmly held his hat as if it might fly away.

'Good evening, sir. Sorry for any disturbance. May we ask if this is the current residence of one Thomas Tierney?'

'Yes, it is. Why?'

The second officer stepped forward, hands behind his back. 'We've been sent to inform you that Thomas Tierney has been involved in a motoring accident. He's currently at the Royal Infirmary Hospital. They're working on his broken leg.'

Christopher and Rose exchanged shocked expressions.

Christopher said, 'Thank you, officers. I appreciate the information.' He closed the door and said to Rose. 'We need to talk about this, Rose. Upstairs please, now!'

Rose followed him up to the bedroom. Chris closed the door behind them and sat on the bed. 'Rose, there's something I've been meaning to ask you for a while now. I can't ignore it any longer. What just happened made me think about it again. Help me understand, Rose.'

'Understand what, Christopher?'

'Oh, come on, Rose, look what just happened.'

Rose, standing against the opposite wall said, 'That's our son you're talking about. I know what you're gonna say next.'

'Leave off, Rose; you know exactly what I mean.'

'Well, I've had enough, Chris. You don't even understand our son. Look at you. It's the same every time. Don't worry about me; I'm alright, Jack. What are you thinking, Christopher? And you're the boy's father?"

Christopher took a deep breath before standing up, pointing his finger. 'Don't think others haven't added it up. You wanna know something? I was embarrassed to revisit John's school, to show my face, the way that teacher joked about him. "Sometimes, sometimes I feel your son can read my mind. It's as if he knows what's going to happen next."'

'I tell ya, it's a good job she started laughing because I didn't know what the hell to say. How would I, when nobody's telling me the truth?'

Rose advanced towards him. What he had said made sense. She rubbed his arm encouragingly. 'He's special, that's all. We have to take good care of him.'

Later that evening, after reading the newspaper, Christopher thought back to the start of his relationship with Rose. It occurred to him that he had met her under rather strange circumstances and that, perhaps, there was a reason for that.

Chapter XIV

3 May 1983, Sheffield.

The school holidays had arrived, and England was at war with Argentina over the Falkland Islands, which had resulted in several battleships surrounding the islands, as well as paramilitary regiments, which were ready for action. The battle had heated up with the sinking of the Argentinean battleship, *General Belgrano.*

Rose was shopping with Christopher and young John. They went to a small café for lunch. Rose pushed her plate towards Christopher.

'What's wrong, love?'

'Just remembering, Mum, that's all.'

Rose's mum, Kate, had passed away five years before to the very date, and Rose wanted to pay her respects at the cemetery.

After lunch, she took John to a florist. 'I'm just goin' to get some flowers, love.'

Chris, no longer employed by Smiths Limited, had gained freedom from the need to visit the old office. Another company had purchased Smiths Limited, though whether they had any connection to the older John Tierney seemed unlikely, for his whereabouts had been unknown for some time.

When young John, now known as 'Young Tierney,' returned to school, the war had reached boiling point.

***

One of the ship's in the worst area happened to be the HMS *Sheffield*. The commander, Captain Salt, had shut off the EMS equipment to activate the satellite transceiver. Thus, the seeker alarm that was capable of detecting Exocet missiles had been silenced.

***

Unknown to Captain Salt, two Argentinean fighter jets had taken off at 9.45 a.m. from Rio Grande, Tierra del Fuego naval airbase. Captain August Bedacarratz 3-A-202 and Lieutenant Armando Mayora 3-A-203 were twenty-five miles west and closing in on the HMS *Sheffield*.

Captain Bedacarratz acknowledged the HMS *Sheffield* had come within missile range. 'Battleship within striking distance, missiles ready, reducing altitude to avoid radar detection, over.'

A buzzing noise could be heard in the cockpit. A red light flashed towards a sea of blood.

'Captain August Bedacarratz, target locked, missiles ready. Permission to fire, sir? Over,'

A short silence that seemed like a lifetime followed. No reply. Maybe he was having second thoughts.

Then, unannounced, the order was given. 'Rio Grande command to Lieutenant Mayora, fire at will.'

The first Exocet missile was launched, shortly followed by the second and the telling words of Captain Bedacarratz. 'These babies with love from the *Belgrano*.'

***

Captain Salt sent an SOS out to HMS *Coventry*. 'Sheffield hit. Repeat, Sheffield hit.'

Aboard the ship were the two sailor boys who had bought Young Tierney's caul from Kate. The caul had remained on board, in a glass case screwed to the wall behind the captain's place on the bridge. They had purchased it for luck, yet an Exocet missile had struck the heart of the ship. Fire spread rapidly. Twenty crewmembers were killed and another twenty-four severely injured.

Six days after news updates were released, the *Sheffield* sunk, taking with it everything on board, not to mention Young Tierney's caul.

***

At that very moment, Young Tierney sat in science class. His friends were throwing scrunched up pieces of paper around. Somebody whispered, 'Johnny, what's up?'

The teacher, writing on the blackboard with his back to the class, was alerted to the unsettling noise coming from the children. He paused and turned.

'Is there a problem in your corner, David?'

John's friend sat up straight. 'No, sir. I was just asking John if he was all right.'

The teacher's voice softened when he saw John's glowing red face. 'What's the matter, John?'

All heads turned as John spoke.

'I'm not feeling too well, sir. I feel dizzy.'

The teacher filled a plastic cup with water and placed it in front of John. 'My God, you're bright red. Drink up, John.'

Suddenly, John fell off his chair, eyes crossed as he passed out. His friends tried to pull him up. One girl cried. The teacher shouted for someone to run to the headmaster's office and have an ambulance called.

***

John regained consciousness and saw two indistinct faces looming over him. The men wore green and white uniforms. The one to the right aimed a flashlight at John's face, which for a moment, blinded the boy.

'John, look at me. How many fingers am I holding up?' In a shiny white sterile latex glove, three fingers were displayed.

"Three," replied John.

The man removed an oxygen mask from John's face. 'Good. Are you feeling better now?'

John attempted to sit up then fell back. 'I don't know. It felt like I was drowning, with water everywhere.' He shook. 'I want to see my mum.'

The man gripped John by the arms and helped him stand. The other man, short and bald, said, 'John, everything's all right. We just need you to come with us for a bit. Your mum can accompany us.'

John took the cup and guzzled the water. 'Okay.'

As he sat down, the men asked for the teacher's account of events.

'Well, it was strange. He complained that he felt dizzy and overheated. Then he shouted something like, "Water, water." I can't tell you more than that because, at this point, the boy blacked out.'

***

Rose and Christopher had been waiting outside the office. John walked in slowly. His dad hugged him. 'There you are, son. You'll be fine. We're comin' with ya. This won't take long.'

They all walked out to the ambulance. When they arrived at the hospital, Chris experienced a strange sense of déjà vu. Nothing but the receptionist had changed since the night Chris had rescued Rose from the lake all those years back. He sat in the waiting room while Rose and John were led into a small examination room.

The doctor, a young American woman, said, 'So, what've we got here?'

She checked a list of symptoms on her clipboard. 'If you don't mind, we'd like to take blood samples from both of you. The reason we do that is to check for things like diabetes, allergies, thyroid problems, and so on. People often have illnesses and never know it.'

Rose patted John's arm, comforting him. The doctor smiled and offered a sugar-free lollipop. 'Don't worry. This is no big deal. We had a boy come in yesterday who had to have the same test. He was only eight.'

John forced a smile. An hour later, he was released from the hospital.

***

Three weeks after the incident, John returned to school. His blood test results had been negative for everything. He was in class when the head teacher poked his head around the door. He apologised and pointed at John. 'I need to borrow you for a minute, if that's okay.'

Worried, John picked up his bag and followed the head teacher down the corridor.

'Don't worry. You're not in any kind of trouble. I'm taking you to meet two doctors at the medical office. They need to ask you a few questions about what happened a few weeks ago. If you feel uncomfortable or unhappy, just knock on the door. You're under no obligation to stay if you don't want to, okay?'

John didn't reply. He stared at the tiles on the floor as he dragged his bag behind him. It seemed so odd. He'd already undergone tests, so why were more people visiting the school? *There's something wrong with me, something certain people don't want me to know.*

He left his bag on a chair outside the door. The head teacher showed John inside the office, pulled out a chair for him, and left, closing the door behind him. The room was small and rectangular, the walls painted yellow. What a perfect colour when you're feeling sick. A small, narrow, sorry excuse for a bed had been pushed against the wall. Two men nattily dressed in pressed shirts and black tailored trousers sat across the room. The medical profession must pay well.

One of the two was tanned with dark hair. He gestured for John to sit.

'John, we're doctors from a hospital in London. We've never examined somebody who suffered an accident like yours, so we thought it worthwhile to visit Sheffield and speak to you. We've a few questions to ask, that's all. For instance, how have you felt since you fainted? Has anything changed?'

Under a bright light, John hugged himself tightly. 'I don't know. I feel okay. But when I sleep, I dream of strange things, things I never dreamt about or saw before.'

The man gave a meaningful look to his colleague, who watched from several metres away. The second man, taller and older, wore small rectangular glasses that reflected the light. His blond hair showed the first flecks of silver. He simply observed John without expression, but the questioner looked concerned. He tapped a pen on his clipboard and cleared his throat. 'What do you dream about, John?'

John rocked in his chair, trying to remember. 'It's strange. Faces I've never seen before. Fighting. Some sort of war between two countries.'

'What about the water, John? You mentioned water when you passed out. Do you remember anything specific?'

John clumsily loosened his tie. Detention would beat

this. 'All I saw was water around me. I couldn't breathe. I can't remember everything.'

The man leaned towards John. 'What kind of water? An ocean? A swamp? Can you tell us that?'

'Seawater.'

A knock sounded out. The tanned man got up and opened the door. John swung around for a peek at the intruder.

'Sorry, it's late,' said one of the dinner ladies. 'We're a bit short on supplies.'

The man thanked her and pulled the silver trolley the woman had brought into the room. On it were two white cups and a pot of steaming tea, plus biscuits and a glass of water for John.

The man in the corner removed his glasses and asked his colleague to leave the room. 'Do you mind if I have a moment with John alone?'

His colleague nodded and quickly left the room without any hesitation.

The remaining man placed the tray of biscuits in front of John. 'Please, take some.'

John reached over while the man stirred his cup. 'So, John, you mentioned something about a fight. Do you remember who was fighting in your dream?'

Chewing a biscuit, John said, 'I'm not sure. Battleships – one had "Sheffield" printed on its side. Jet planes too.'

The man sat back in his chair. He could feel his nostalgia creeping up in his mind. His heart was pounding louder. It was time to end this interview.

'Okay, John, thank you. We've enough information now. It's best you get back to class.'

John shuffled through the doorway, grabbed his bag, and threw it over his shoulder. Suddenly, he wanted to run, to get back to class, as if nothing had happened. He wanted to be left alone, like the other kids, but that, he knew, was wishful thinking.

***

After a brief chat, the head teacher showed the doctors to the car park. A car and its driver awaited the men. *If I were younger*, the teacher thought, *I'd reconsider my profession*. He handed a business card to the tanned man.

'If you need more information, I'm happy to help.'

The man smiled and tucked the card inside his jacket pocket. 'We'll be in touch, Mr Mauritz.' He slid into the car and slammed the door.

Just then, suspicion entered Mr Mauritz's mind, for he had never requested proof of identity, nor profession. Why would two strangers waste an entire day travelling from London and back just to ask a boy about fainting, unless they really were doctors?

***

But he was wrong. The silent man, Vladimir Roscoff, knew a great deal about John's 'skin,' which now rested hundreds of feet below sea level.

Later that day, back in London, Roscoff ran his fingers across his lips. He knew John's situation, unlike his colleague, who had conducted the interview. The latter knew only what he'd been told, and that wasn't an awful lot.

The interviewer turned to Roscoff. 'I'm confused. Something doesn't match up. Sir, where is all of this leading?'

Roscoff sighed. 'It's leading us to a dead end, that's for sure.'

'What's our next step?'

Roscoff crossed his legs. 'I'll call in at headquarters. Then I've another meeting to attend. I'll see you tomorrow in London.'

Roscoff departed with a plan far different than that

of his colleague. He drove to a payphone and dialled the number for the main office.

'Hello. You're through to the main office. How may I help?'

'Yes, good afternoon. This is Agent Roscoff.'

'How may I help you, sir?'

'Cancel all scheduled meetings for today. Now!'

'Yes, sir. Please confirm your security number.'

'It's three-thirteen-five-three-zero-four."

'I'm sorry, sir, your access has been denied.'

'Look, for Christ's sake, do we have to go through this every time? Everyone knows the access code is nil-one-seven-two.'

'That's correct, you're now confirmed, sir.'

Roscoff slammed down the phone. He was annoyed. He picked the phone up again, and dialled the number of his own office. He kept a close watch on the passing pedestrians.

'I'm afraid Agent Roscoff is currently unavailable.'

'That's because I'm Agent Roscoff.'

'Oh, I'm sorry, sir.'

'Maria, I need you to arrange a board meeting for the head agents of each department. Schedule it for tomorrow, as early as possible, and please confirm the time with each agent.'

***

At noon the following day, the agents gathered for the meeting held in a secret location. The five agents sat around a table, eagerly awaiting Roscoff's feedback from the previous day's interview.

When Roscoff arrived, he placed a briefcase on the table. 'Mullins, Munroe, gentlemen, it's good to see you could all make it. As you know, yesterday I visited the school of John Tierney. Quite frankly, I don't know where to start. We're all aware of his birth, but I think we need to prepare ourselves for much more. My natural scepticism is always an issue, but what I witnessed yesterday eradicated that issue.'

Mullins cupped his hands. 'What are we looking at here, Roscoff?'

Roscoff stood, hands in his pockets. 'The analyst's report on the "skin" or "veil" stated that it couldn't have been human. The skin had an extremely tough outer layer, which seemed to protect any damage to the baby's face. The skin sample remains in the exact same condition as it was eleven years ago. However, our specialists inform us that the small sample skin cut off appears to have doubled in size, expanded. It's as if the skin has been growing – which means, gentlemen, that if our sample has been growing, then so too has the original skin.

'Gentlemen, on May 10, 1982, as we all know, the HMS *Sheffield* sunk during the war against Argentina. As we also all know, the 'skin,' or 'veil,' was aboard that ship, maintained in the captain's headquarters until the *Sheffield* sunk.

'Precisely eight hours after that, John Tierney blacked out. He was unconscious for more than an hour. While passed out on the floor, he screamed, "Water, water."'

An agent laughed. 'I apologise, Agent Roscoff, but I'm sceptical on this one, too.'

'Yes, I'm sure you are, but do you think you could let me finish before jumping to conclusions? Perhaps your aptitude for registering what you consider an abundance of information is inappropriate. I believe this meeting was summoned by me, was it not? I also believe the information I was about to disclose will be of immense use to us, though perhaps I'm standing here wasting my breath.'

Several agents stifled laughter at this browbeating by

Rocketman Roscoff, his nickname due to being the only Russian in the unit.

Roscoff studied the humiliated agent. 'I shall grant you a second chance to prove me wrong. I apologise for the minor disruption, gentlemen. Allow me to continue.

'Yesterday, when Tierney was interviewed, he spoke of water, as well as the other visions he remembers from his dreams. He spoke of faces he doesn't recognise and fighting between two countries. The water was seawater. All he saw was water around him. He couldn't breathe. He saw the battleships. He saw jet planes. Coincidence? Doubtful. Of course, you can dismiss dreams, if you like, but before you do, ask yourself just how many times you've heard such relevant visions before a person passes out.'

The tainted agent tried to redeem himself by introducing a fresh problem that stood in the way of Roscoff's resilience. Maybe that would help tip the balance a bit. 'We have to be sceptical, but I agree something's definitely not right here. We have to go further with it. But the boy is only eleven, far too young for us to be experimenting with him. We'll have to put that part of the investigation on hold until he's older and mature enough to understand the situation. Indeed, if these dreams are what I think they are, then you're correct, Mr Roscoff. This boy could become useful to us.'

Everybody murmured sounds of approval. Roscoff smiled with a genuine look of accomplishment. 'Correct. I also agree. However, the boy must remain under surveillance and protection at all times. We need to keep him secure until he's ready to help us. Are we all agreed?'

Each agent raised a hand to signal consensus.

Roscoff held his hands behind his back and strolled to the window. He put his left hand between the slats of the Venetian blinds to get a look outside. The weather was as ambiguous as the boy's situation.

Turning back, Roscoff pulled down his shirtsleeves and buttoned the cuffs. Placing his hands on the table's edge, he leaned towards his colleagues. 'We'll have to plan ahead. The only other problem is his parents. We have to get them involved. There's no doubt about that. They must be informed, or we'll never make progress.'

Agent Mullins stood, gathering his belongings. 'Let's not be too hasty here. A lot can happen over time, and we can only wait. We have no option but to postpone action until the most suitable moment arises. I think we've discussed this enough for now. Sorry, gentlemen, I must leave. I have another appointment scheduled.'

The agents shook hands. They had decided they must wait for their chance to discover the truth behind the 'prophecy' myth. For now, they knew only that years of work would ensue after that moment. Since the prophecy had obviously coincided with events that had not yet come to pass, they knew they would have to take heed of Young Tierney's dreams now.

Agent Mullins was the first to leave the building in a hurry. He sat in his parked Jaguar for ten minutes thinking, pondering the boy. Eventually the wait was over. Mullins scrolled through his contact list in his mobile and found the name he was looking for – Cardinal

***

Everything in the MI5 unit was running smoothly, at least on the surface. Of course, being a Russian agent meant Roscoff had connections to the KGB.

People never dared to assume, though they tried to find out. Since his diplomatic family had immigrated to the UK, Roscoff had always kept in touch with a few old friends, just in case he needed a secret underground association to help out. He could hire several pairs of eyes to watch Young Tierney, though that would be as far as things could go.

Under no circumstances would his friends know the true reason for their services.

Yet whatever precautions were taken, even Roscoff had no idea just where the investigation would lead.

Chapter XV

During his last few years of school, John's interest and concentration began to wane. It wasn't his fault. He'd scribble maths sums one minute, and the next minute, he'd be lost in a world of daydreams.

Somewhere, John had lost his sense of self. Yorkshire life in the '80s was notoriously difficult. Boys his age tended to be blamed as a group for individual failures. Still, he got on well with other children, excluding bullies. John didn't like to see them picking on smaller kids. However, if John interfered in such situations, bullies would have enough common sense to walk away. Though John rarely fought, the few who had challenged him made sure others knew the Tierney family skill had walked the genetic line.

John was also admired for his comforting effect on those involved in accidents. If somebody fell, John was always the first to help. Whether he carried some medication, no one knew. Neither did they know John possessed a secret that couldn't be revealed. During football, John preferred to sit and watch. He received offers to join teams, but he preferred his own company.

***

Once their son had finished school, John's parents had decided to move. They resettled on the outskirts of Sheffield. Considering that John was becoming more intelligent by the day, it was a wise decision. Chris didn't want unnecessary attention drawn to the family. He started by giving John a practical job at his scrapyard. That allowed Chris to keep a watchful eye over the boy, as well as gain insight into how he was progressing.

After gypsy boys had taught him how to play cards, John's gift became evident. It was more than obvious he had a special knack for gambling, which led to his exclusion from games.

John slipped into his twenties with ease and had become an attractive young man. His long curly hair and muscular frame caught the attention of young ladies. Nevertheless, few opportunities arose, since his father had banned him from the town. Apparently, mobsters and drug dealers thrived there. They would try to recruit John the minute he showed his face. However, by then, he held a black belt in karate and thrived as a runner in local marathons, thereby gaining increasing recognition, which, unbeknown to John, was the last thing he needed.

***

On 11 August 1999, John's birthday, Christopher looked out the window. The morning sun had reached the beautiful blue clear sky, yet he saw nobody working. *Why do I pay this lot per hour?* he thought. Christopher threw the paper down and walked out of the office.

John sat with four gypsy boys playing cards.

'Oh no, not again,' cried one of the gypsies.

'You're too good for us. How do ya know what the cards are?' The other gypsy threw his cards down in disgust.

Smiling like a Cheshire cat, John reached over and removed the money he'd won from the tyre.

Then Christopher walked inside and shouted, 'John, come here, and you lot, get back to work.'

John got up and walked over with his hands in his pockets. He knew he was in a lot of trouble. Christopher placed his hand on John's shoulder and, walking him outside, said, 'How many more times do I have to tell ya, son? Stop showing off. I don't want ya bringing any problems on ma doorstep.'

John was now in a sheepish mood. 'Sorry, Dad, it won't happen again. Promise.'

Christopher smiled. 'Okay, son, think your mother's waiting to take you into town. Said something about a birthday present. Don't know what she's on about myself.'

John hugged his dad before rushing out of the scrap yard. 'I'll see ya back home, teatime.'

Christopher, smiling to himself, walked back into the office and sat down. He picked up his newspaper. The headlines on the front of the paper read, 'Total Eclipse Today, Last of the Millennium.'

***

It was just after eleven o'clock in the morning. John had gone shopping in the city centre with his mother Rose. They strolled along the peace gardens. Crowds had gathered, looking at the sky. They pointed, nodding. Rose, too, looked up at the sky. Then she stopped for a moment.

'Oh, yes,' she said, 'I read in the paper this morning, John, it's the last solar eclipse of the millennium.'

John pulled his sweater around his neck.

Rose looked to John. 'You all right, love? It's not hot at all.'

John rubbed his eyes, simultaneously blinking. He came to a standstill. 'I can't see. What's happening? Am I hallucinating? Mum?" Swaying, John grabbed Rose's arm.

'Someone help!' Rose shouted. 'Please help.'

John hit the floor hard. A man ran over, removed a mobile from his pocket, and rang Emergency 999.

Within fifteen minutes, the ambulance arrived. John was already sitting up, Rose wiping tears from her eyes. The paramedic looked at John and placed an oxygen mask over his face. The paramedic raised a hand.

'How many fingers am I holding up, please?'

John didn't answer. He was thinking of a time when he was a boy at school. He was confused and had no idea at all where he was. He just closed his eyes as though he was going to sleep.

Later, John was putting his jacket on in a hospital room as the doctor returned. The doctor focused on the notepad in his hand. 'Right then, Mr Tierney, looking at your records. You passed out once before when you were a young boy. Your blood test, and your blood pressure is normal. I think you can be discharged. That ought to please your anxious mother.'

John followed the doctor out of the room. 'I just hope that's the end of these attacks.'

The doctor stopped and said, 'You ought to try and find out if there was a solar eclipse when you were a boy as well, because if that's the case, you might turn into a werewolf tonight.'

John laughed. 'Yeah sure.'

He walked up to Rose and said, 'Come on, Mum, let's go home.'

Chapter XVI

Sheffield, England – 2 June 2000

As the years passed, the fashion, food, music, places, and people changed. Even the recreational drugs favoured by those inclined to use them differed from what they had been. Ecstasy pills with a sun imprinted on the surface were known as California Sunshine. Every single club in town had become an 'E' joint with a constant flow of buyers and suppliers. In most cases, a boss sat at the top of this drug chain. The pockets of such bosses were never empty, their guns were always loaded, and their eyes always open. Without qualm, they beckoned rookies to their world.

***

By this time, Young Tierney was nearly twenty-eight years old, and he hit the casinos. No one had ever seen a player so good. Inevitably, gossip circulated. Challenge him? Hell no. The dealers weren't exactly queuing up either.

The 'big boss,' Steve Biggins, owned the Napoleon Casino and a couple of nightclubs. All the attention paid to John aggravated Biggins. *This bloke thinks he can turn up and spin the spotlight in his direction.* Biggins had grown sick of it.

He wasn't the only one. Several days later, John stood at the casino table. As usual, he was casually dressed, wearing jeans, a white shirt, and black shoes. Beneath his belt rested twenty grand worth of chips. Gambling was becoming a regular habit.

'I think that'll be enough for one night,' he said. 'It's getting late, gentlemen.'

The crowd behind him moaned with displeasure, having watched Tierney's magic for hours. One follower shouted, 'Come on, one more game.'

But John had already placed his chips in the box. He turned to the crowd and smiled.

Then from the stairway came another voice. 'Young man, why don't you stay? Let your fans witness more of your luck. That's what makes your talent so interesting at this moment.' The voice belonged to Biggins, who wore a black tuxedo. His hair was black and slick, combed back into a Godfather haircut.

John stopped walking, box of chips still in his grasp, and turned. From the roulette table, Biggins and two minders approached John. The crowd formed a circle around the man and the roulette table.

John said to Biggins, 'Are you a betting man? I'm sorry, I don't know your name.'

The crowd sniggered. Biggins blushed, his face like Mount Katmai on the verge of eruption. Biggins's own reaction infuriated him even more. He thought but didn't say, *Do you know who you're speaking to, you disrespectful little bastard?*

John answered the question himself. 'I know who you are,' he said. Then he turned and pointed to the picture on the back wall. 'That's you on the wall there and there and there and there.'

The crowd roared with laughter once more, and Biggins decided to answer the first question. 'In that case, that does make me a betting man, doesn't it?'

John rolled a chip between his fingers, yet another skill he'd developed. 'Tell ya what I'll do, since I'm in a charitable mood; I'll spin ya for the lot. I'll even name ya a number. How's that sound?' John placed his box of chips on the table.

The astonished crowd sighed. Biggins and John fixed their gazes upon one another, locked in combat.

Biggins thought, *This man's crazy, but now's my chance to wipe that smile off his bloody face, once and for all.*

'What a wonderful idea,' Biggins said. 'Please call your number.'

John stared at the croupier, turned, and, directing his question to the crowd asked. 'The most spiritual number in the world is what?'

Those gathered about the table responded with silence, having no idea what John was talking about.

John placed a single chip gently on the table. It accounted for all his chips. 'Eleven,' he confidently pronounced. He then turned to face Biggins, who signalled the croupier to spin the wheel.

John held up his hand. 'Wait.'

Yet again Biggins's angry stare met John's, but the latter seemed to show a happy smile on his face.

John pointed at Biggins. 'I want you to spin the ball,' he declared.

The crowd cheered with delight at John's suggestion.

Biggins loosened his collar. Having never spun a ball in his life, he took a drag of his cigarette and blew the smoke out of his nostrils. He motioned the croupier to hand him the ball. With the crowd shuffling behind the wheel, the croupier duly handed it over.

The light was bright from the crystal chandeliers hanging over each table. Biggins now held the silver cannonball in hand. He had brought the spotlight upon himself. *One last glance into the eyes of a winning run, running on luck alone.* Biggins was certain of his suspicions.

Without further hesitation, Biggins rolled the ball. The cigarette smoke had formed clouds that floated above the table like a waterfall. The sound of the ball seemed deafening in the now silent room. Biggins took a last look at John. *Smile now, ya bastard.*

The crowd gasped. So did Biggins. John stood there, glaring at his opponent. The ball had dropped, and so had Biggins's expression.

'Eleven black,' shouted the croupier in excitement.

The crowd roared with delight. Biggins stubbed his cigarette out in the ashtray, turned, and took a final look at John, who saw the darkness around Biggins's eyes being swallowed up by the anger stirring in his stomach. As Biggins walked up the stairs, he heard John's last words, which would ring in his ears long after they had been spoken.

'Cash me out, please. I'm outta here.'

Biggins looked down at John walking towards the cashier's desk before calling his right-hand man, aka Tony 'the Fox' Harding, over. The Fox was a twenty-stone fast food-eating yob, with the belly to match. Tony had a reputation for sniffing out a rabbit in a skunk hole then catching it and skinning it with his own teeth. In other words, he was a crazy son of a bitch!

'Tony, I want you to find out who he is, where he lives, and what colour pants he's got on. Do you fucking hear me?

Tony knew Biggins meant it, and by the look on

Biggins's face, pizza wouldn't be on the menu tonight! 'Er, okay, boss.'

***

In the meantime, John was at the desk. He smiled at the attractive cashier, filled his briefcase with well over £100,000, and took a seat on one of the casino's leather sofas underneath a low-hanging lamp.

Two men approached from behind. On closer inspection, they noticed he had an open briefcase in front of him. It was full of money. The men stood inert several meters behind John. Both were well built and taller than John but not as well toned. Dressed in jeans and basic striped shirts, they looked out of place. Eamon and Dermot were brothers. Dermot nudged Eamon. 'Damn it, Eamon,' he said in a thick Irish accent, 'you talk to him then. I'm not.'

At that moment, John slammed his briefcase full of money shut and turned around. Eamon said, 'Seems to be your lucky day, laddie.'

John shrugged, disinterested. 'Seems that way.'

Eamon said, 'Correct me if I happen to be wrong, sir, but when you were playing cards, I reckon you knew them there cards under that dealer's hand, did ya not? Or could it just be luck?'

The brothers looked at one another, waiting for John's response.

He smoothed his shirt and buttoned his sleeves, oblivious to their presence. He finally said, 'I'd say it was luck. I was very lucky tonight.'

Dermot said, 'I don't think so. I think you knew for sure. Why else would ya chuck in a king and a jack? Tell me that.'

John stifled a yawn with his palm. He turned to collect his things, replying over his shoulder, 'Like I said, it was pure luck.'

Eamon chuckled and whispered something in his brother's ear. 'Don't you forget to tell 'im about the Tierney clan, Dermot? He'll pipe down and lend us an ear, so he will.'

Eamon said, 'The next card was an ace to the dealer. You would have lost! Get outta that one.'

The chattering that surrounded them increased to a loud noise that washed over the room. A crowd of tourists seemed to swim towards the exit.

John turned to follow them. He held his arms out apologetically. 'Sorry, gentlemen, it's time I was leaving.'

Dermot put his hand out calmly. 'Wait, we got somethin' to tell ya. We've all got something in common here.'

John, at this point merely amused, stopped beneath a chandelier. 'Oh yeah, and what might that be?'

Hatching an idea, Eamon reached down to his belt, staring at John, who watched his every move. Eamon pulled his jacket back a fraction, careful not to reveal the contents of his trousers to everybody. He turned slightly, just enough for John to see the handle of his handgun.

One shot, or even a glimpse of the gun, would create chaos. *What do they want? Money? Gambling tips? What the hell are these two after?* John noticed a tiny scar on his left hand. Strange, it had always been there, but he could never remember how or when it happened.

A word echoed within blood. He put his hand to his head. In a flash, Eamon was at his side. Eamon placed a hand on John's shoulder, his breath hot, as he whispered in John's ear, 'We're all of the same blood, my friend.'

John laughed. 'How could that be?'

Eamon signalled for Dermot to return. 'We're from the Tierney clan.'

John dropped his casual mannerisms. *Well, if you're from the Tierney clan, it's not my blood.*

John paused, brushing Eamon's hand from his shoulder. He pulled his jacket tight and continued towards the exit. Dermot attempted to follow, skipping alongside him and hysterically saying, 'In fact, your mother called you after my father, John. And he told us everything you need to know about yourself.'

John stopped.

Dermot stopped, too. 'I bet ya didn't see that comin' now, did ya, sonny boy?'

The momentary shock caused the hefty briefcase in John's hand to slip from his grasp. John knelt to pick it up and, after a pause, marched back aggressively until he stood an inch from Eamon's nose. 'Well, fellas, since it's so bloody urgent, you'd better come with me.'

They filed out of the casino in a single line, John leading.

***

Unknown to the trio an undercover MI5 agent sat watching from the bar beneath a loudspeaker blaring jazz. A small keypad lay on the bar's highly polished chrome surface, numbers illuminated in blue. The agent pressed a speed dial button and plugged in a headset.

'Yes?' Vladimir Roscoff answered.

'It's about Young Tierney, sir.'

'And?''

'Well, it's hard to believe, but he played blind and walked away with a hundred grand, sir.'

'Did you get the video evidence, agent?'

'I did, sir, and the dealer talked.'

As the Tierney boys disappeared into the darkness of the night, the agents arranged a meeting point. The dealer arrived last, except for Roscoff, of course. Biggins, the casino owner, had won the race to be first. He was too scared he might be missing anything to be late, whereas Roscoff was in the habit of showing authority and thought being late was as good a way as any.

Biggins had to know everything that occurred under his supervision. He coughed, dropping a pack of cigarettes on the counter.

Roscoff questioned the dealer, taking occasional sips of bad coffee. He leaned across the table. 'Tell me about yesterday. You played a young man named John, John Tierney. Did you notice anything about his playing methods?'

The dealer smiled 'All I know is that he's been coming here for the past three weeks, and he's cleared us out.'

Roscoff smiled. 'And do you think he's cheating?'

The dealer gestured to Biggins for a cigarette. She caught it and struck a match before replying, 'Pure luck. It'll run out. It's taking longer with this guy, that's all.

'But I'll tell you one thing that bothered me. He knew exactly when to throw in his cards. A King and a Jack, he folded. Who'd do that? Okay, I only had nineteen, but my next card was still an Ace. He would've lost. He plays blackjack like nobody I've ever seen. As for his challenge bet on the roulette table, well, I don't wanna say no more.' The dealer looked to Biggins.

Roscoff stirred sugar into his coffee. 'Does he speak to you? Even a word?'

The dealer shook her head. 'Never. He just nods. He gets this look, his eyes constantly fixed on me. Makes me fucking nervous. I never get nervous.'

Turning his chair towards the casino owner, Roscoff said, 'So, Mr Biggins, we can't arrest this gambler despite your suspicions. That is, there's nothing to confirm your suspicions.'

Biggins pulled the ashtray closer. 'Well, you have to do something. He cleans us out, and it doesn't stop there.

He's into my bookies in town, went through the complete card. I've never seen this happen. Where is he getting his info from?'

Roscoff observed the owner. 'You know what I think, Mr Biggins? I think you're a bad loser. How many people come into your casino with everything and lose it all? Tierney's a natural winner. Or do you think he's a magician?'

Biggins stood and walked over to Roscoff, bending to meet the latter at eye level. 'I don't know who the fuck he is, and I don't care. He's barred from my property. He won't be coming through my doors again.'

Roscoff offered a displeased nod. 'I've heard enough, thank you.' He gathered his papers, tucking them into a leather folder. He got up, put on his hat, walked to the exit door, and left, slamming the door, leaving the sound of Biggins's moans behind him.

'He's not normal,' the casino boss cried. 'Do you hear me? Not normal.'

Roscoff struggled to find his phone as he walked down the corridor. Something had to be done. Biggins was getting out of hand and would soon get others involved. Roscoff wanted the matter under control. He dialled his secretary.

'Buona sera.'

'I need you to arrange an emergency meeting – *now*. Call Agent Munroe first, and make sure everybody gets to headquarters.'

***

Young Tierney, Dermot, and Eamon had arrived back at the hotel. The anonymity the hotel offered, a place where nobody knew one another, earned its price. Eamon and Dermot had already inspected the minibar.

'Drink?' Eamon offered.

John felt threatened, yet he also sensed a connection with Dermot and Eamon. If they were the sons of the late

John Tierney, that would explain everything. He climbed off the bed and set his briefcase on the table then fell into a cushioned chair. 'Whisky, straight,' he said. The Georgian styling of the room struck him as being almost as odd as the pictures on the wall.

Dermot pulled up a chair beside John. 'Same for me.'

Eamon handed a glass to John, who drank it fast. Dermot placed the rest of the bottle on the table.

'Dermot,' John said, 'what happened to your father?'

Dermot started to speak, but Eamon interrupted. 'Shortly after you were born, he passed away. We had letters from your granny, explaining' how you were named in his honour. Before he died, he told me everything, about you, about the prophecy, all of it. And from what I've seen so far, well, you have a lot to learn, lad.'

What are they waiting for? And do I even want to know? John pulled off his jacket and laid it over the chair then walked across to the window. Lifting the latch, he pushed a small pane of glass outward. *The night air will help.* On the road, bright lights flashed like an outdoor casino. *Two people in the room with me, and I've never felt more alone.*

Eamon refilled glasses with whisky. John pressed his face into his palms, his distress as palpable in that action as his voice. 'Sometimes I think I'm going crazy. There's pressure in my head, instincts telling me what to do all the time. But that's not what bothers me. It's the dreams. Some help me win, but others – I can't make heads nor bloody tails of them.'

Eamon gripped a glass and handed it to him. 'Listen, John, you're not crazy. You simply experience events no one else can understand. Hear me? That's why people, including yourself, think you're crazy. They don't know you're not, and neither do you. That's not a choice, is it?

You've no problem. It's a gift. Don't ask me why; I'd tell ya if I knew, but I don't.'

He sipped the whisky and continued. 'What I know, I learned from my father. That information came from Nostradamus' prophecy.

'Nostra bloody who?' John interrupted.

'Just listen please,' Eamon said gently. 'He called you, in his own words, "the high caulbearer." He predicted your birth and said the secret must be kept within the Tierney clan. Your birth was unusual, John. Your mother saw the extra skin. It's known as a caul, or a veil, but few have the knowledge of the caul, and fewer still know you possess it. That was the source of your gift. How else could you keep up your pace?

'The prophecy was made centuries ago and predicted this very day. Don't worry about any of it yet. We have friends in high places, John. They tell us you're bein' watched.'

John's mouth had dried out with whiskey and swallowed tension. 'Watched by whom? How do you know?'

Eamon suppressed a grin. Dermot stayed quiet, content to know the plan. He walked to the second window across from John and drew the curtains. The atmosphere in the room had disappeared into the space between the secrets and John's knowledge of them, blank and empty like the sky above.

'Look,' Eamon said, 'last week, we followed you to the casino in London. The Irishman sitting next to you was a friend of ours. We sent him. That's how we know you never once lost. Then you returned to Sheffield and won another game there. Members of the London mafia watched you, too. That's how the hearsay started. They started sayin' you're the best player around. Some even called ya Psychic John. And the casino boss, Biggins, met with the police, though which branch, we don't know. We do know they saw what we saw. Your next move is obvious.'

'And what's my next move?'

'Lose. You have to lose, John.'

John frowned. 'I always knew there was something wrong with me. Who am I? Why me?' He flung his glass at the wall, but it failed to shatter.

Eamon said, 'Calm down, John. Only time will tell. But we're here with you. We're your true family, so tell me what you dream about; I have to know everything, John, or I can't help you.'

John rubbed his eyes. 'I dream of people following me. They're planning to take me away.'

Eamon shook John. 'When was this?'

John tried to settle his mind. 'It's kinda blurred, but I saw a man from a casino and some other men, in dark suits. I've no idea where I was.'

'True visions, John. Think about tonight. What you dreamt happened. Tell me everything in detail. We have to sort this out before it's too late.'

Dermot shouted, 'We've gotta get out of here, fast. We can't let them find us.'

'Where will we go from here? Is anywhere safe?'

'We're heading out of England, John. Soon, I'll tell you more.'

'If my dreams are true,' John said, 'I know exactly when I'll die.'

A sudden loud knock on the door startled Eamon. Dermot slid his hand into his jacket, retrieving a gun. He waited, gun ready. A second knock and they all froze.

'Put the gun away, Dermot,' Eamon said. 'It's probably bloody room service. We have to concentrate, not get paranoid.' Eamon turned away from John even as he continued his explanation. 'You can't avoid death. In that way, you're like everyone else. You can't change life's course. That comes from the hand of Nostradamus, as part of the prophecy. Things will be difficult for you. You'll have to trust me if ya want my help.'

John studied Eamon's expression. *He sounds genuine. He's offering a solution to all my questions. Somehow, it's funny the way he claims to know everything about some prophecy, yet he can't tell whether I'll trust him or not. On the other hand, that's why he almost convinces me.*

***

The sky over Canary Wharf, as always, was stormy and grey. The tourists gathered outside St. Paul's Cathedral and raised their umbrellas, drifting towards the museums and cafés. Some piled back into the red double-decker buses.

***

Elsewhere in the city, agents gathered for the MI5 headquarters meeting at Thames house in London, with rows of occupied chairs positioned in front of a white board. The bosses mumbled to each other as they waited for Roscoff's appearance.

Seconds later, he arrived in typical cantankerous fashion. He spun around and, with a marker pen, began writing. He underlined two words on the centre of the board:

YOUNG TIERNEY

He placed the pen on the desk in front of them. 'I called upon you, as the time of reckoning beckons Young Tierney.' He pointed at the board. 'He's developed some method of, well, reading the cards and beating the casino, and it's no trick. Things are slipping. The casino's owner – a convicted drug dealer, mind you – watches our subject as if he's one of us. It's time for decision, action.'

Agent Munroe, the youngest on the team, eager to impress but so often with his foot firmly in his mouth, stood and said, 'Let's haul him in.'

Roscoff tapped a pen on the desk. 'And how do you suppose we'd go about that, Agent Munroe?'

'Make an offer to Biggins, an offer he can't refuse.'

Agents laughed, knowing Roscoff lacked the guts to offer a solution. Monroe looked bored. 'Call it that if you like. I meant that we offer him police protection from outsiders.'

'No,' Roscoff said. 'I don't believe that's the technique we should adopt in this case.'

Munroe remained nonplussed. 'The subject must be controlled. We can't take chances. We could have an epidemic on our hands, and if the newspapers get hold of it, everything leaks. Then it's over, and not only for us.'

He's got a point. Roscoff scrutinized the options listed on the board. Grabbing his coat and folders, he rushed to the door. 'Ten days and I'll have it sorted out. For now, let's stay the course.'

He headed towards his next goal, unknown to the agents pooling at the exit.

Munroe remained seated. After he was the only one left in the meeting room, he developed a new idea. He dialled the number for his understudy.

'Agent Ross?'

'Is everything okay?'

'It will be, if we move fast. Roscoff's out of the equation. Make an offer to Biggins. Do it today. Young Tierney needs a set-up now. I know Roscoff. He'll take too long, like he always does.'

An hour later, Ross contacted Biggins. The casino boss had first received an offer of police protection, followed by

Munroe's initial proposal. Biggins went for the money, and the danger for John expanded.

***

Later that evening, John and Eamon took a walk through the park. Dermot stayed at the hotel, checking flights to Berlin via the Internet. He used a laptop supplied by the hotel. If anybody tried to hack John's system, they'd find no clues through browser histories or temporary files. John had also registered under a pseudonym. He would never use the same one twice.

In the park, wires of bulbs had been strung between the trees, and a breeze projected translucent light in every direction. It seemed to Eamon the perfect time for him to reveal the prophecy to his younger cousin. John was about to learn a secret that each of his namesakes had been told and also to be given the burden they had all shared.

John and Eamon stopped near a pond hidden by reeds. John sat on a bench while Eamon stood watching the water's black surface, where he saw his reflection. Church bells in the distance struck nine o'clock.

Eamon sat beside John. 'You're a special person. You have a talent you alone possess, so far as we know. For that reason alone, you'll make enemies. The worst enemy is the secret police.'

'Secret police?'

'MI5, MI6. I don't know who they are exactly or what they plan to do. We've a strong suspicion it's them followin' ya. Aside from the London gang, it's just as important you understand that all the other mafias will join forces to squeeze as much out of ya as they can. They'd never miss such an opportunity. As for the police, they've two sides. Flip a coin; that's as good as trying to figure them out for yourself.'

John noticed something white in the pond, a little paper boat, floating in the reeds.

'You said to go away, to move away, but where?'

A star shot across the sky. 'Berlin's good. I have some good friends o'er there. We'd be put up for a while. I know a girl called Lisa; she works in the Irish Times Pub. I know her well enough to trust her. She'll help us organise a few t'ings.'

'Berlin sounds like a beautiful place,' John said. 'I once dreamt of a city with a golden angel in the sky and a great wall that led to freedom.'

Eamon laughed. 'That's it then, or was. Hey, let's walk over to another spot. We can chat about these dreams of yours and the visions you see. In return, I'm gonna give ya the information my father meant for you to hear. I was supposed to tell it – all of it.'

They returned to the main path and found a tree, under which they sat. 'An ideal spot,' Eamon said.

John removed his jean jacket and laid it on the grass. Eamon stretched his legs. John closed his eyes as if waiting for the worst of news. Eamon touched his shoulder.

'Don't look so worried, John. Relax. We're gonna be here a while.'

John leaned against the tree trunk. For the first time in his life, he described his dreams exactly as they had appeared to him. It soon became apparent to Eamon, that the dreams John could never fully comprehend had predicted the future.

Chapter XVII

A black cloud hovered above Vatican City. Deep within the walls a secret meeting was about to take place. Cardinal Bishop Rossini and Cardinal Bishop Rizzi had summoned two high-ranking officials from the College of Cardinals.

Having no windows, the room was deprived of natural light. The two officials arrived and sat silently at the round table. Under the warm glow of the fire and candlelight, the tension built as the four waited. The creaking noise of an opening door announced the arrival of the Swiss Guard. A steel box was placed on the table. Rizzi dropped his head as though it was the end of the world. Anxiety was present in Rossini's eyes. He knew what was about to be revealed. Opening of the box would strike terror into the hearts of the two senate officials.

Across the table the bishops' eyes met, glowing with fear, as Rizzi put his hand to his mouth, clearing his throat, before speaking. 'This box is from deep within the walls of our most secret of secret archives. The documents you're about to see now have only been seen by myself and Cardinal Rossini.'

Rossini removed a chain from around his neck; attached

to the chain was a key. He placed the key on the table while Rizzi removed a small sealed envelope from his pocket. The envelope had a red Vatican wax seal on the back.

'This box can only be opened by you, the College of Cardinals. As a security feature, it's necessary to have the key and the contents of the envelope to do this. We must all remain within the complex until you've read the documents and decided what we must do. This will take time, maybe even days. Once we've reached a decision that we all agree upon, we must first decide if these documents should be destroyed.'

Rossini pushed the key across the table to Cardinal Priest Bruno, and Rizzi passed the envelope to Cardinal Priest Conti. The priests were speechless and, by now, terrified. Priest Bruno lifted the key and placed it in the lock. At the same time, Conti broke the seal and started to open the envelope. The small piece of parchment revealed a coded number needed to open the second safety feature of the box.

With shaking hands, Conti fumbled with the numbers of the lock, eventually getting it right; the click of the final number released the box lid.

Rizzi crossed himself as Rossini kissed the crucifix around his neck. Words could be heard coming from Cardinal Rizzi. In a voice that was barely audible, he mumbled, "Forgive me, Father for, I have sinned.'

Chapter XVIII

In a swank uptown restaurant across town, Biggins had conceived a trap for John, thanks to Munroe's quick thinking. Biggins tapped his wine glass with a spoon, attracting a waiter's attention.

'Yes, sir. What can I get for you?'

Biggins blew cigar smoke into the waiter's face. 'Bloody better service, that's what. I've been waiting twenty minutes. Where's my tiramisu?'

A few moments later, the waiter returned with an unusually large portion of tiramisu and a bottle of iced champagne. 'On the house, sir. Signor Mancini calls you one of our most valued clients.'

Biggins inspected the tiramisu closely. An idea had begun to form.

After his meal, Biggins swaggered down the amber-walled corridor in the direction of the restaurant's bathroom. He swept past the cubicles, checking to ensure he was alone. He locked the main door and dialled his phone.

'You there?'

'Yeah, boss.'

'Here's what we're gonna do. I know that Tierney boy's

already got a table booked with us for tomorrow night. You're gonna make sure he never books one again.

'Now listen good. Tell security who they're waiting for and to call me when Tierney arrives. Now, both you and Gary know I have a stash of Charlie in the office. Go and get it.'

'What's Charlie, boss?'

'Don't give me all that bollocks. You're not on the job due to your intelligence now, are ya, son?

'Charlie's the shit you and Gazza blow your wages on every weekend, you silly sod.'

'Gotcha, boss, but I have a question. What 'appens if the old bill are watchin' the place?'

'It's under control. You grab the bags of Charlie, bring 'em out to the boy's car, and sling 'em in the boot. I'll make sure the boy's too busy winnin' to notice ya. He won't be needing money for decades where he's headin'. Now that shouldn't be too difficult, even for you two.

'But be careful; he's an ignorant bastard that boy, and he's not afraid of a ruck. So you just do your job and everything will be cool, got it?'

***

Back at the park, Eamon said to John, "D'ya remembers what I said to ya back in the hotel?'

John threw a stone at a tree.

Eamon seemed over-elated at what had been nothing more than a release of tension. 'The tree - ; focus on that tree for a minute. Imagine each leaf as a pound note. Suppose a man had an orchard full of these trees. Well, they would burst into life in the springtime because that's their peak time. D'ya get what I'm tryin' ta say?

'And if one stayed as full throughout the winter, you'd realise fast that it was the only tree without bare branches. Well, wouldn't that seem odd?'

What Eamon said made sense in a way. 'I think so,' John said. 'You mean there's nothing wrong with winning all the time, it just seems abnormal because no one else can do it?'

'That's exactly it, John. Now you have to test your theory Saturday by seeing how the crowd reacts when you don't win.'

***

Saturday arrived. John wore his best suit and waxed his hair. *I have to look the part of a loser.* He poured a pint of ice cold water and drank. Coldness usually gave him headaches. In this case, he thought it might help, since the casino would be hot. He switched off the lights. Just before closing the door, the curtain shimmied in the breeze. *Anxiety. Maybe some kind of warning. What next?*

He left the room and the hotel. He walked towards his car. As he closed the door and started the ignition, he felt a sense of relief in remembering that Dermot and Eamon would be present.

Overdressed tourists appeared as John approached the casino. Some people stopped and stared. Others mumbled and pointed at his car. John reached down for a bottle of water. He climbed out of the car and buttoned his jacket. As he reached the top of the steps, the two huge doormen nodded at each other. John ignored them and headed straight for the bar, where Dermot and Eamon waited.

The security man responsible for the bar area lifted his wrist to his mouth and spoke into a wire. 'He's here, boss.'

Several floors up, Biggins sat in a large leather chair with his feet on his desk. He pushed a button on his armrest. A large television dropped from the ceiling. He responded to a comment through the radio transmitter, 'You know what to do. Now do it.'

The transmitter crackled a silent, 'Yes, sir.'

Biggins lifted a small mirror and studied his reflection. This is gonna be a night I'll never forget. He lit a cigar and pushed the mirror away. Time seemed to slow.

Downstairs at the bar, John and the boys finished their drinks. Eamon tapped John's back and gestured towards the table. 'Guess we'd better be headin' over.'

John sat at the table's centre seat, directly below the spotlight. Dermot and Eamon stood behind him, watching as others gathered. A blonde woman looked at John and leaned towards her friend, whispering.

"Tierney" randomly resounded through the crowd. John turned to look at Eamon, who winked.

The dealer dealt the cards. John removed his sunglasses. After a glance, John carefully slid the cards into his pocket. The dealer looked discomforted. Here was the same dealer who had been in the meeting with Roscoff and Biggins just days before. The glasses usually allowed John to play blind, hiding behind some kind of invisible force field. But that was the exact reason he'd chosen not to wear them that night.

Meanwhile, two men from Biggins's team made their way down the building's secret escape route. They carried cases towards John's car.

As the game began, everyone moved closer to the table, hoping to witness Young Tierney's 'luck.'" When Biggins appeared, not a single person noticed. Biggins pushed through the crowd and sat at the bar. He spotted one or two familiar faces.

The cards were dealt. The dealer had eighteen, and John had eighteen. He nodded for another card, a seven of clubs. Perfect. He tried to mask his joy in attaining the first part of his objective. The dealer looked content as she scanned the crowd then turned back to John. 'Twenty-five, sir. You lose.'

John found it hard to believe that it was even harder trying to lose than it was trying to win. How could he pretend to lose without looking like a complete idiot? He'd have to use his best judgement to overcome a problematic situation.

Biggins studied John's silent response and noted the absence of sunglasses. *Did I hear that right? He lost?*

Biggins called for the barman. He ordered a double espresso.

'We don't have a coffee machine here, boss.'

Biggins grabbed the barman by the neck. 'Fuckin' get one.'

John was on a losing streak, hand after hand. Not only was he losing, he was losing heavily to make events seem more plausible, which to John's dismay was awfully hard to handle. Eamon pretended to comfort John, while Dermot urged another round.

Biggins laughed. *I can't wait to see his face.* Despite the bleakness felt by everyone but the involved parties, all remained focused on the games. By the time spectators drifted away, John had lost £20,000.

'Seems like your luck ran out tonight, Mr Tierney.'

John rested his head on the table as if exhausted from the shock of losing. 'It's like you said, pure luck, and it's going to run out sooner or later. I guess it finally ran out.'

The dealer's face gave away her loss of confidence. *How the hell does he know?*

Head still resting on the table, John flashed an ironic grin. He stood and put on his sunglasses. The liberation he'd gained through accomplishing such a strange goal pleased him.

Dermot and Eamon collected their coats from the cloakroom area opposite the bar. As John walked over,

Eamon slapped him on the back and said, 'Well done, John.'

Biggins was watching them from the smoky bar area. Why did they look so pleased? The boy had never lost before. Nobody ever planned to lose. There was something strange going on.

Dermot echoed Eamon. 'You did well there, Johnny boy.'

John shook his head. All of a sudden, his expression darkened. 'Let's go. I feel like shit.'

Dermot and Eamon followed him towards the exit. 'You did it for a reason, John, remember?'

John stopped and turned, 'Okay boys, one question.' They looked mystified. John leaned forward and whispered, 'Is there gonna be a casino in Berlin?'

The two boys cracked up laughing and continued towards the exit. John wedged between them.

Eamon said, 'You know, I like your sense of humour.'

'I'm not laughing.'

At the top of the steps, John hesitated as the other two ran for the car. Dermot shouted, 'Throw me the keys, John; I'll drive, if ya want.'

John watched the people moving up and down the road and the last few cars speeding away. He was almost oblivious to Dermot as his fear intensified. Eamon waved at one of the doormen standing behind John. As the door slammed behind him, John realised he'd seen all of this before. The second doorman looked down at his watch. The rain began to fall. In a dreamlike state, John had a flashback.

Men in dark suits. A splash of water, a train, and rattling tracks. He put his hand to his head. Too much.

Dermot rolled down the window. 'Come on, John. Don't let losing bother ya. It doesn't matter. It was on purpose, remember?'

John screamed. Security reached for their radio transmitters.

Back inside, an intoxicated Biggins chatted up a girl half his age.

'Piss off, you repulsive old man,' she said, slapping his face.

He slammed his glass on the bar and grabbed her by the throat. 'You speak to me like that again, you little whore, and the next time you wake up, you'll find yourself in the middle of a field somewhere, got it. You sluts don't know how to appreciate success.'

***

Outside, Eamon shoved past the car and ran towards John, who was sitting on the bottom step. Out of breath, Eamon slowed his pace to gentle steps. 'You all right, John?'

John's sunglasses had been crushed on the steps. 'Something doesn't feel right. Something's wrong here.'

Dermot watched from the car. *It's the feeling of losing. That's what John doesn't like.* He started the car.

Biggins burst through the door and pushed the girl down the stairs. 'Get the fuck out of my casino.' He looked at John, realising what was about to happen.

John was abruptly awakened from his daze as three unmarked cars approached rapidly from different angles. They surrounded John's car, blocking it from moving. Unless they operated through telepathy, it was definitely too late to call a taxi.

Eamon waved madly. 'Run, John, run.'

John sprinted between two of the cars. He put his hand on the bonnet and leapt over it. The undercover police officer in the third car opened his door, but John swerved around it.

An officer snatched John's keys from the ignition. Rain

poured down heavier. John ran through the parkland like a Ghurkha climbing the embankment like an expert. He dropped down the other side, crashing upon the railroad shingle. The two undercover cops, not far behind, stopped at the embankment's steep drop.

John caught his breath and sped off in the opposite direction, sloshing through the ankle-deep stream. He slipped on weeds gathered in the waterbed and stumbled, mobile phone slipping out of his pocket and into the water, before finding his balance. The wind, cold and sharp, blew straight into his face as John climbed the next embankment. A train approached with sirens blaring. Its lamps casting shadows. It was closer than he thought.

Jumping the tracks, he turned to find himself face-to-face with a speeding freight train. The siren sounded again. He felt pinned to the tracks, paralyzed. He couldn't breathe, couldn't move, like a rabbit caught in a car's headlights. *Don't look at the lights.* He closed his eyes, threw himself to the side, and rolled away from the imminent danger.

The undercover cops caught up and stopped, exhausted, on the opposite side of the tracks, too late to capture their prey. The last carriage zoomed past as if to stamp 'failure' on their mission. Now they were in for it.

Back at the casino entrance, Biggins lay across the steps laughing without a care in the world regarding his soaked €3,000 suit. He'd gotten what he wanted. The cars were gone and with them Eamon and Dermot. The police had handcuffed and taken them to the station for interrogation, and an MI5 agent accompanied them, as instructed by his boss.

Chapter XIX

In the early hours of the morning, an officer sat in a small interview room. He loosened his tie. His phone rang. He looked at the display and waited several rings. *I'll have to deal with this later if I don't answer now.* Heart thumping, breathing meditatively, he held the phone to his ear.

'He got away, boss.'

He pulled the phone away from his ear as the volume increased. 'What the fuck? How the hell did he get away? I give you a pair of royal marine commandoes and he gets away?'

'It's his good luck, sir.'

'Which ran out earlier tonight, and you still couldn't catch him.'

'He ran over the tracks, sir, got the jump on us. The train was coming. He was on one side. We were on the other. Then the train ran between us. There must've been more than twenty carriages.'

'So crawl between the fucking wheels, man. Jesus fucking Christ, Roscoff's gonna piss on me for this.'

***

Sometime later, John wandered past a row of small

houses. The rain had calmed, and he felt no signs of injury from his escape. The breeze began to dry his clothes. He had no idea of his location but knew he was lucky to be alive. *Lucky once again.*

Somehow, he had to find the hotel. He came to a small alleyway that ran between the houses. It led him to the Sheffield High Street TSB cash point, where he withdrew cash, knowing the authorities would track the transaction. Stepping through the litter of drink cans and crisp packets, he came to a street lamp. He waited on the corner then spotted a blur of red in the distance. Never had he felt such joy upon seeing a bus. He reached in his pockets for loose change. There was enough for the ride.

Watching the cars and buildings, John noticed a road he recognised. He pushed the button in front of him and stood. The bus slowed and pulled over. The door folded open. John jumped off the bus, bewildered, not knowing which direction to go until he saw in the distance a hotel sign in white neon down the opposite side of the road.

As he neared the Hilton entrance, he checked his reflection in the door's glass. He combed back his hair and wiped blood from a scratch below his eye.

An attendant greeted John politely as he proceeded into the foyer. The doors slid shut, cloaking John in safety, for a while at least. The hot air blowing from a ceiling vent warmed his skin. He checked his watch – almost 3.00 a.m. He went to the elevators and pushed a button. The chrome doors opened. He travelled to the third floor. He found his keys, which might have been lost had he worn something other than a simple pair of black trousers.

John followed the corridor to Room 314. He unlocked the door, stumbled through the doorway, and collapsed on the bed. Rain had made the curtain damp where the window had been left open. After a few minutes, he got up, pulled the curtain aside, and slammed the window shut. He switched on one of the small bedside lamps. He took a hot shower and changed into clothes that had been left in the bathroom. He gathered his belongings and clothes and set them in a bag. He double-checked to ensure his wallet and passport were safely tucked in his jacket.

In the main room, he noticed a magazine that Dermot had left on the bed earlier. As he lifted the magazine for a closer look, a white card dropped to the floor: Berlin. The card provided numbers, too. *Thank you, Dermot.* He grabbed the card and fled.

***

The next morning, Dermot and Eamon were still in separate cells. Munroe, with Ross in the interrogation room, prepared questions for the brothers. Munroe's forehead was glistening with sweat.

'Boss, do you feel all right?'

'What do you think?' said Munroe. 'It's a catastrophe. Now we're deadlocked. I've absolutely no desire to hear Roscoff's bitching. We might as well get on with these two and hear what they have to say.'

News of the operation's failure had already leaked. Naturally, one of the first people to find out was Roscoff's secretary, Maria, who had received a classified internal report. It was obvious to her what Biggins had planned, but she was equally certain that Roscoff would be more interested in Munroe's contribution.

***

At the same time, Roscoff was at John's parents' house drinking tea. Rose was starting to get upset.

'You know, Mr Roscoff, I always knew this day would come.' Rose wiped a tear away with her hand while Christopher offered his arm in comfort. Rose went on. 'He seems to be coming home with more money than I could ever imagine, and he's just getting—'

Rose blew her nose, and before she could finish, Roscoff interrupted. 'Out of control?'

Rose, sobbing, replied, 'Yes, out of control.'

Christopher lent abruptly closer as he wanted to get his point over. 'Look, Mr Roscoff, he doesn't listen to anybody anymore. We'll do anything. As long as John is safe, we'll cooperate with you. I told the cardinal the same thing the other day.'

Roscoff turned to Christopher, his face enlightened. 'Cardinal?' he said in an inquisitive voice.

'Yes, he's visited us as well, concerned over John. I have his visiting card here if you need it.'

'Oh yes, please,' Roscoff replied.

Roscoff looked at the card. His eyes narrowed with suspicion as he loosened his tie. A fire crackled; the flames from the open fire were making Roscoff sweat. Or could it be the fact that now the Catholic Church was also showing interest in a boy's future that was most definitely wrapped up in mystery?

Roscoff's phone rang. 'Excuse me for a moment, Mr and Mrs Tierney.' He snapped open his phone. 'Yes, Maria?'

'Just after midnight an operation took place under the orders of Agent Munroe.'

'Go on.'

'The plan was to arrest Young Tierney. Unfortunately the plan failed, and Tierney escaped, though they arrested two men who had accompanied him to the casino – the same two caught on video leaving the casino with Tierney a few days ago.'

'And where's Munroe now?'

'Well, sir, he's interviewing the two men.'

'Where are you now, Maria?'

'Already driving up, sir. I'll be at the station in one hour.'

This was the response Roscoff wanted to hear. 'Good work. I'll meet you there.'

Roscoff had been getting on so well with John's parents, and now, just when the breakthrough was at his fingertips, this. He took a deep breath. *Compose yourself, Vladimir,* he thought. He stepped back to where Rose and Chris sat next to each other.

'Everything okay, Mr Roscoff?' Chris said.

Roscoff shook his head placing the cardinal's card in his jacket pocket. 'Please, you must excuse me. I have an urgent matter I must attend to. Everything we've discussed today will stay between us. I'll get back in touch soon.'

After handshakes were exchanged, Roscoff headed for the police station. With roads deserted, he gunned the car.

***

Meanwhile, Munroe and Ross faced Dermot and Eamon across the interrogation table. The light from the tiny window reflected the shadows of the steel bars on the opposite wall. Munroe shifted restlessly and watched Ross. The good cop, bad cop scenario was about to begin, a game the Tierney boys knew all too well.

'So, gentlemen, what can you tell me about the drugs we found in the trunk of your car? And who was the third person that escaped?'

Eamon slouched in his chair. Munroe only had to make eye contact to see that Eamon felt no compulsion to surrender silence. Munroe pushed a pack of cigarettes towards Eamon. 'Please, take one.'

Eamon reached for the cigarette as Dermot whispered, 'But you don't smoke.'

Removing two cigarettes from the packet, Eamon said,

'Doesn't look like they're gonna give us much else in here, does it, Dermot?'

Dermot took the cigarette and tucked it behind his ear.

Eamon said, 'I'm afraid a cigarette won't butter us up enough for us to start answering any questions. I'll say this much until my solicitor arrives: You know who put the drugs in our car. You know who the third person is. You've been trailing him for years. That's all you're getting from me.'

The clock approached 9.00 a.m. The brothers had endured eight hours of solitary confinement. They had refused to complete all forms they'd been given.

Munroe knew a solicitor would arrive any minute. Ross's phone buzzed. Ross followed Munroe out of the room.

'Sir,' Munroe said after the phone conversation, 'they searched the car and found the number and address for the hotel room. Our men will be at the location soon.'

They returned to the room. Nine hours had passed since the boys had been arrested, and Ross had only just learned a key fact.

They sat in silence for a moment. Munroe walked over to the window. No sign of a car. He said, 'Look, gentlemen, as we talk, your hotel room is being searched. And right now, you're looking at five to eight years.'

Dermot reclined. 'Five to eight, huh? I expected at least ten to twelve. I'll do it standing on me fuckin' head, ya muppet.'

Munroe turned his back to the window. A car pulled into the parking space.

Roscoff entered the building, accompanied by Maria, who clutched her phone. 'Munroe is still in the interview room with the two men,' she said. 'I've just received new information from the hotel search. The names of the men being interrogated are Eamon and Dermot Tierney. Two plane tickets were found in a drawer. They were heading to Berlin, due to depart at 6.45 a.m.'

Roscoff touched his chin. 'That puts a different spin on things. Does Munroe know about this?'

He walked towards the interrogation room. *Come on, show yourself, you bastard.*

Maria said, 'Not yet, sir.'

Inside the room, Ross leaned against the wall texting someone. Taking off his tie, Munroe looked as if he were the one being interrogated. Eamon and Dermot appeared stoic. Munroe finally said, 'We just want to make a deal with you.'

Munroe tensed. Ross reached for his gun.

Dermot nudged Eamon's arm. "Who da hell is dat?'

Eamon shrugged. 'How the hell do I know? Look at dat face.'

Roscoff said, 'What the hell is going on in here? Why wasn't I informed of the plans for this operation? Who gave the authorisation for it?'

'Can we at least talk about this outside?'

Roscoff nodded and gestured for Munroe to follow him and Maria. Since he knew the brothers were Tierneys, he held the advantage. He'd get them on his side. It was better that he hadn't discussed John in front of his relatives.

He faced Munroe. 'Do you know what you've done? Not only have you let the entire organization down, but you've completely lost any trust I had in you.'

'Look,' Munroe said, 'we had to bring him in for his own protection. It made sense. If I had informed you, I knew you would have called the operation off.'

Roscoff edged towards him. 'That's bullshit, and you know it. If you were smart enough to run the show, then you would have followed protocol. For one thing, you never interview pairs or groups of people. It only gives them a chance to confirm their stories. I can't believe I have to tell you this.'

Munroe knew he'd been right all along, despite what Roscoff said. *Might as well give it a shot.* 'We interviewed them together because I figured that if I split the interviews, one or both would've claimed the Fifth Amendment and leave it at that. Being together might encourage them to speak for the sake of getting out sooner.'

Roscoff rolled his eyes. 'This is the UK, Charles, Fifth Amendment? Think about it. I'm still struggling to understand how the hell you could do this to me, Charles. From now on, we do things my way, every time, every way.'

He marched to the far end of the corridor, stopping to say, 'By the way, the names of your captives are Eamon and Dermot Tierney, in case you want to continue your fucking interview.' He pushed through the doors.

Munroe pulled Ross aside. 'Shit, these two bastards have us by the balls. What a fuckin' mess. What the hell should we do?'

Ross tucked his phone into his pocket. 'We'll have to make a deal with them now; that's for sure.'

Chapter XX

Far from the interrogation room, John had arrived at Berlin's Zoologischer Garten train station as planned. Walking along the platform, he could smell the fumes. The place seemed so much more orderly than London. The tourists blended in with the locals, even on tour buses. There were no excited kids, only travellers who couldn't be bothered to drive and who took their time. Everyone appeared detached, tuned to their own thoughts. They had the same way of walking, revealing a quiet arrogance. Students, pensioners, and foreigners dragged suitcases and rucksacks in all directions. In the distance, a church bell sounded. John looked up at the clock, ran down the steps, and found an empty locker. He stashed his bag inside, took the numbered key, and rushed out to the taxi area.

'Guten tag. Sprechen sie Englisch?'

'Ja, little. Where to go?'

'The Irish Times Pub, bitte.'

'Kein problem.'

Eamon's words resounded in his mind.

A girl works in the Irish Times Pub, helps us organise a few t'ings.

John had no idea who she was or how she could help. He would have to find out for himself. The cab rolled through the streets of Berlin. John was fascinated at all the tall gothic buildings in the Berlin-Mitte area. He pointed to an aeroplane hanging in mid-air over a skyscraper.

'It's a beautiful city, just as I had dreamed.'

The taxi driver looked to John and smiled. 'You've never been Germany?'

John returned the smile. 'It feels like I have, somehow.'

The taxi reached its destination, and the meter stopped ticking.

'Twenty Deutsch marks, please.'

John took the crumpled notes from his pocket and paid the driver. 'Thank you.'

He slammed the door shut, threw his rucksack over his shoulder, and looked ahead to see the Irish Times Pub. Walking to the door, John noticed a sign:

Closed
Open at eight
Karaoke night
Cash prizes to be won!

With time on his side, John decided to walk the streets of Berlin.

Chapter XXI

Over twenty-four hours had passed. Priests Conti and Bruno had returned from their sleeping chambers. Fresh coffee had been made and placed on the table. The documents had been read without a word of discussion. Shocked, saddened, ashamed, and, surprisingly, amused expressions had registered on all of their faces throughout the unveiling.

Cardinal Rizzi was anxious to hear the thoughts of the priests. 'So, now you've seen the evidence do you wish to make a comment?'

Priests Gustav Bruno and Angelo Conti looked to one another and nodded.

Bruno was first to speak. 'Yes, we've spoken about it; we'd both like you to tell us how you see these events from the start. Would you please explain?'

Cardinal Rizzi stood and walked around the table. His hands were behind his back as though he was about to make the speech of his life. 'A high-ranking member from Propaganda Due called the Black Friar came to us at the Vatican. Oh, excuse me please, gentlemen, I'm sure you all know Propaganda Due as the secret society P2. This member was a professional banker, and to this day, we're not sure if he had the permission of the Worshipful Master to come to us. However, it's now irrelevant.

'The Black Friar's contacts throughout the banking organizations and the Illuminati were enormous and stretched as far afield as America. He brought with him two photos with digital signatures attached. The photos were of the sacred book of life. It had been said that this book was once part of the contents of the lost Ark of the Covenant hidden by King David himself and contains the caulbearer bloodline of the Brotherhood of Nazarenes. Some of you within these walls call it the Book of Death.'

Bruno interrupted the speech. 'This so-called bloodline, what makes it so special?'

Rizzi looked towards Cardinal Rossini for a response. Rossini was sitting with his hands in a prayer-like fashion.

'Well, Bishop Bruno, many years ago, we, the Catholic Church, introduced the *Malleus Maleficarum*, which was a paper written to convict heretics. It was known as *The Witches Hammer,* and it allowed us, in the past, to use the law purely to justify the burning to death of these caulbearer children and the children's mothers. In 1312, the Templars and their caulbearer Grand Master, Jacques de Molay, governed the bloodline. The Church feared the seeds of these children and searched desperately for the sacred bloodline without success. Around this time, de Molay was burned at the stake, and with his death, the bloodline vanished, never to be seen or heard of again.

'As we sit here now, my friends, we find ourselves in a very compromising position. It appears the secret bloodline is upon us once again.'

Conti was quick to respond. 'Brother Rossini,' he whispered, 'most of what you've said is common knowledge among our brother cardinals. However, reading between the lines, are you trying to tell us that P2 wanted to unite the Masonic lodges and use the CIA and MI5 to bring the child called the high caulbearer into the Vatican with the agreement of the Pope? And if so, are you saying the Holy Father signed the documents without the permission of our fellow cardinals?'

By now, Bishop Conti was chuckling to himself. He continued, 'After telling us this, can we assume these are the reasons why the Pope was m—'

'Yes,' replied Cardinal Rossini in a loud tone, not wanting to hear the mention of words that killed the Pope.

'We united and appointed the new Pope within days, according to the code. The newly elected Pope renegotiated with P2, paying them over one billion dollars, providing the banker returned the original documents to the Vatican, which he duly did.'

Conti knew another twist was coming within the next breath. 'Can we presume that the banker was expendable and was disposed of?'

Rossini stood and replied, 'We had no choice, Brother Conti. The cardinals knew bringing the bloodline into the Church would signal the end of an empire. The Worshipful Master of P2 was informed about the transfer of Vatican funds paid to the banker. A list of names was presented to the Vatican. The bankers' colleagues connected to the deal were either listed as untraceable or dead.'

Conti was, by now, in total shock, but he was eager to get to the bottom of the mystery.

'Unfortunately, the banker kept threatening the Vatican, claiming that, should he be killed, a copy of the signed documents from the Pope would be revealed to the press.

'After this, the Vatican became worried about the banker and used their Opus Dei associates to find out the whereabouts of the copy of the papers. They discovered the documents were being fronted by a close journalist friend of the banker. Once we were sure we had the final copies in our possession, we ordered our secret organisations to go after the banker, who was in hiding in London. Soon after, he was found hanging from Blackfriars Bridge in London. The banker was the last name on the list. The verdict was suicide. The future of the Church was now at its strongest point once again. Now we must decide what we're going to do about this so-called bloodline.'

Chapter XXII

Munroe was under pressure now and had to give Roscoff a description of the entire John Tierney arrest operation, including the planning, preparation, and failure.

'You know you were wrong.'

The coldness in Roscoff's voice made Munroe shiver. Fortunately, the rising steam of coffee warmed his face.

'But it's done with now. Let's put it behind us and move forward. You might like to know I had an intriguing meeting with Tierney's parents. They know his situation and condition. Then again, they don't know how to approach the issue. What matters more is that I've managed to gain their trust.'

'How'd you do that? Considering we have the brothers in custody, I shouldn't think they would be too happy about that.'

'Well, I didn't exactly tell them everything, now did I.'

'I certainly hope not, bearing in mind one of them will eventually have to take the blame for it.'

Roscoff seemed too relaxed, if he ever relaxed. 'I've an idea. The first thing we'll do is see how much the boys know. Split them up; I'll handle Eamon.'

They headed back down the corridor. Munroe turned towards the interview room but stopped at its entrance. 'What did Tierney's parents say?'

Roscoff returned to his usual cool character. 'How did Tierney get away from you? That's what I want to know.'

'He outmanoeuvred us, thanks to the train.'

'I don't suppose you were aware he's got a black belt in karate and that he runs marathons for fun? Now, I wouldn't exactly call that luck, would you?'

'Point taken.'

Roscoff shoved past him and entered the room. Moments later, he had Eamon beside him. They walked into the opposite room without speaking.

Roscoff looked back at Munroe. 'You should have done your fucking homework. It's on file.'

'Okay, okay, I won't make the same mistake again.'

Roscoff kicked the door open. 'You're damn fucking right, you won't. You've been making a lot of them lately.'

Munroe returned and started over with Dermot, while Roscoff began interviewing Eamon.

***

Eamon was more afraid of the new agent, but he was also relieved to get away from Munroe. Roscoff threw his folder on the table. He spoke loudly. At first, Eamon thought he was doing it deliberately so that Munroe could hear.

'So, Eamon Tierney, my name's Mr Roscoff. Yesterday, you were arrested with your brother. What was found in the trunk of the car, we'll discuss later.

He lowered his voice. 'I had nothing to do with what happened last night. At the time, I was with John's parents. The problem is that two bosses want control, and one thinks he knows more than I do. So, to put things right, I'm taking over. Tell me what you know about John Tierney.'

Eamon crossed his arms. 'How long have you been following John?'

Roscoff said, 'Two days after he was born.'

Eamon spun the cigarette Munroe had given him between his fingers. 'What else?'

Roscoff rubbed his eyes. 'John was born with a skin around his face, passed out in school, he never loses when playing cards, and he's a fast runner.' Roscoff seemed oddly apathetic. 'Oh, and I forgot to add that he's an expert in unarmed combat.

'Listen, Eamon, last night wasn't my idea. Munroe panicked. He was trying to protect John. Then you two turned up and got in the way. Do you really think I want John in prison? The reason I've followed him all my life is to find out who he is and what's going on with him, not to injure him. I want to know more. I want to help him. I can get you out of here tonight, but you have to meet me halfway, if you know what I mean.'

Eamon corrected his posture. 'How do I know I can trust you?'

Roscoff smiled. 'Yesterday, I taped my interview with John's parents. I'll let you hear that, as well as another interview I recorded over ten years ago. But, first, I want to find out what you know.'

Leaves drifted past the window. Eamon hesitated before saying, 'We knew before he was born that this would all happen. My father passed the secret to me just before he died. Not even my brother knows everything I do. Now, before I go further, I want to hear the tapes – if there are any, that is.'

Roscoff delayed his answer by tapping his fingers on the table. 'Fine. But I still have one problem, and that's your brother. As I said, I can get you out on bail tonight. But your brother must at least be charged, to erase suspicion.

The minimum time he'll spend in jail is three weeks. After that, I'll arrange his release.'

Eamon split the cigarette in two. 'And if I refuse?'

As Roscoff was about to respond, Maria opened the door. She went to Roscoff and whispered, 'Sir, we traced the flights to Berlin. John Tierney was aboard the 6.45 flight this morning.'

Roscoff thanked her. She left the room.

'Maybe,' Roscoff said, 'we don't need you after all. But I keep my word. So guess what? We know where John is. It seems you'd better make a decision before it's too late. I'll leave you to think it over.'

Eamon stood and said, 'Don't bother. I've never trusted an Englishman before, not with my experiences. So I'm not about to start now, am I?'

Roscoff laughed. 'You can keep your "experiences" for somebody else. I'm Russian.'

Chapter XXIII

The hours passed. John found himself wandering through the backstreets. He realised he was completely lost, and there were no people in sight to ask for directions. He looked up and saw the same tower that had been shadowing him all afternoon. A sign on the street indicated Alexanderplatz.

John walked out onto the main street and heard the loud sound of music coming from around the corner. He turned the corner to see where it was coming from. It happened to be the Irish Times Pub he'd been searching for all along. He walked up to the window. It seemed he was in for a busy night, so he went inside and found a place at the bar.

A short waitress with dark piercing eyes and long straight black hair approached. 'Can I bring ya something?'

He paused, looking at the board. 'Just a coffee, please, love, and can you tell me if somebody named Lisa works here?'

The waitress wrote down the order and gathered the menus on the table. 'Oh, yes, she does, but she's on holiday in Ireland. She'll return next week.'

Who will I turn to now? Where should I go?

The waitress said, 'Is there something else I can do for you?'

'No, that's all right, just a coffee, please.'

He looked up and saw an old Guinness advertisement. He felt a sense of nostalgia. He wished he could return to the Tierney homeland and learn more about his mysterious heritage. Too late for that now. He watched the next singing act, wishing he was just another face in the crowd. His moments of glory had lost their appeal, and nobody present would have known about them anyway.

***

Back at the station, Roscoff finalised the arrangement for Eamon's release on bail. Dermot was charged, but Munroe knew it was only a matter of time before he was also set free. Munroe was inside the interview room with Dermot, while Roscoff remained outside with Eamon.

Roscoff whispered in Eamon's ear, 'I'm going to lie to Munroe, since he can't be trusted. He'll never know of our conversation, I assure you.'

Eamon nodded as Roscoff knocked on the door of the interview room. Munroe appeared.

'Charles,' Roscoff said, 'I'm going back to the office. If you need me, don't hesitate to call, like you did last time.'

Munroe thought to himself, *sarcastic son of a bitch,* then continued questioning Dermot.

'Dermot, I need some time to get a few things together. I think you've been here long enough. You'll be going back to your cell for awhile.'

Munroe sparked with exhilaration regarding his new idea. *This time, Roscoff will never find out.*

A police officer entered the room and escorted Dermot to his cell. Munroe rushed through the cloakroom and out the back door of the building, making sure no one could hear his conversation. He called Ross, who had left the station over an hour before.

'Agent Ross.'

'Yes, sir?'

'I want you back at HQ. Make it fast. Turn on the master recorder. Make sure you lock it up. Take the spare key, so nobody can open it afterwards. I'll hold all the paperwork at my end. That will stall them. And Ross—'

'Sir?'

'Don't fuck up this time.'

Eamon had mentioned Munroe's antics to John before, using the flip of a coin as an example. Munroe had chosen heads; they had chosen tails. Munroe was on the other side.

***

Back at the pub, John had consumed a few coffees while chatting with the waitress. He stirred his coffee and took a sip. 'You know, you don't make such bad coffee for a Bulgarian.'

The waitress said, 'Bulgarians are good at many things.' She curtseyed as she smiled.

'Tell me, what's your name?'

'Rositsa Zheleva. Call me Rosi if you like. I know you Englishmen have problems pronouncing names like mine.'

'And whereabouts in Bulgaria do you come from?'

'Stamboliiski.'

'Stamp-ba-lee-shi. Is that right?'

Rosi laughed. 'Stamboliiski. Try again.'

'Stamboliiski?'

'Much better.'

'Rosi, you have beautiful eyes.'

'Thank you.'

The DJ called Rosi's name. 'Your turn to sing.'

The bar had filled to the hilt. John had his coffee replaced with a beer. He was starting to enjoy Berlin life.

Rosi was in the swing of things. John clapped. He felt better as Rosi sang the Aha song "Take on Me." The crowd seemed to flow with the song. Rosi pointed to John as she sung. John had made a good impression.

When the song ended, the crowd applauded the best vocalizing of the night. Rosi strode off the stage, and John took her hand at the bottom of the stairs.

'Well, well, well, seems we have a singing talent in the house.'

Rosi laughed. She seemed in a confident mood. 'Yeah, there surely is, John. Come on, let's drink a toast to a new face in the city. Eric, can I have two schnapps, please?'

'Tell me, Rosi, do you know any casinos in Berlin?'

'There's one I know of in Berlin – Mitte, at the centre of the city. I think it's the biggest one.'

'And what time do you finish here?'

'The DJ finishes at midnight. Why?'

'I know we've only just met. Lisa was going to accompany me – as a friend, I mean. Would you care to join me instead?'

'I've never been to a casino before.'

'You'll enjoy it, believe me.'

'I don't know if I have time.'

John looked into her eyes. 'Tell ya what. I'll sing the next song and, if I win the cash prize tonight, will you come with me to the casino?'

Rosi had a suspicious look on her face, which ended with a smile as she replied, 'John, if you win this competition tonight, with all this talent in here, not only will I go to the casino with ya, I'll kiss your arse.'

John reached over and placed his drink in Rosi's hand. She smiled, unsure what to expect. John whispered a song title in the DJ's ear. He climbed on stage and took the microphone.

The music began; the crowd was silent. John raised the microphone and began to sing.

Love me tender
Love me sweet,
Never let me go.
You have made my life complete,
And I love you so.

Rosi had been cleaning down the bar with a towel, but she stopped, flabbergasted at how good a singer John had proven himself to be. She walked from behind the bar to the front of the stage. The crowd, rocking and rolling with smiley faces, rose to the occasion of a stranger grabbing star billing.

John approached the conclusion of the Elvis song. He spotted Rosi at the stage end and made his way over. He pointed at her.

Darling this I know.
Happiness will follow you,
Everywhere you go.

The crowd was rapturous, Rosie more so than anyone. John approached her. Sweating from the heat, Rosi picked up two small glasses of schnapps.

The DJ announced over the mike. "I think we have a winner here tonight, ladies and gentlemen.'

'To the casino then, John,' Rosie said as they happily downed the schnapps.

Just like that, John had a date. But already he had forgotten everything Eamon had told him.

Chapter XXIV

Roscoff was driving to the office, accompanied by Eamon. Meanwhile, Ross had already been to the office to switch on the master recorder. It would miss nothing. It would detect the slightest sound, amplifying it.

Though Roscoff was unaware of Munroe's attempt to undermine his plans once more, he knew Munroe would never hear what Eamon and he spoke about in the car. Roscoff rolled up the window and turned down the radio.

'Tell me about your father.'

Eamon focused on a distant tree. 'My father believed in a family prophecy passed on from Nostradamus himself, which had been written in his sacred book. That book was passed on to his best friend, the first John Tierney. Then it was passed down, generation to generation, over a period of four hundred years. Only the recipient knew the whole truth behind its contents and what he had been told. My father became obsessed with the t'ing.'

Roscoff's grip on the wheel tightened. 'Do you still have this book?'

Eamon opened his window slightly, inhaling the fresh

air. 'No, the original parchments disintegrated over time, and it never survived. However, a copy does exist.'

Roscoff tried hard to keep the car straight in the lane. 'And you have a copy?"

Eamon spat his chewing gum out of window. 'Yes. But until I have your trust and my brother is safe, I'm afraid I can't show ya.'

Roscoff knew Eamon had the advantage.

***

John arrived at the casino with Rosi. It was past midnight. The casino was larger than Biggins's place. John took Rosi's coat and handed it to a clerk in the cloakroom.

'See that table over there? That's the table where the money is, but first I have to play on the smaller tables. Then we'll move up to the big table.'

Rosi linked arms and pulled him towards the bar. 'You're so confident that you'll win.'

'You have to be confident of that.'

He ordered white wine. They made their way to the smaller table. John had two hundred pounds worth of chips on the board. Rosi watched from over his shoulder, not knowing what to expect.

Chapter XXV

Roscoff parked outside the office. He and Eamon got out of the car. Roscoff checked for anyone near them, but nobody was in sight. Once inside a room in the building, Roscoff locked the door, closed the blinds, and switched on a light.

'Coffee?'

'No t'anks – not unless you got whisky to pour in it.'

Roscoff turned on a portable television. 'It's cold in here; I'll turn up the heat. So chilly outside tonight.' *Now's my chance.* He made himself comfortable on the sofa, placing his coffee on the table, along with a plate of Viennese biscuits. Eamon narrowed his eyes.

'They're mine,' Roscoff said, 'but you can have one. It's not reverse psychology. I heard about the cigarettes.'

Eamon laughed and took one. 'So let's get on wid it. How'd it all start, you findin' out about John's birth an' all?'

Roscoff, talking while eating a biscuit, said, 'I received a piece of skin – or veil, as some call it – that had been wrapped around John's face at birth. We analysed it and, bingo, as they say. It's still in the exact same condition today as it was when we received it, only larger. Years later, John passed out at school screaming, "Water, water, water."'

'I don't get it.'

Roscoff took another bite and continued explaining. 'Shortly after John was born, his mother sold the veil to a pair of sailor boys. The same two boys were on the HMS *Sheffield* when it sunk in battle. The veil was still on board. The next day young John passed out at school.

'I took a trip to the school with an understudy. He questioned John while I listened. John complained of having dreams of wars, battleships, and strange faces. After that, we held a group meeting and decided he was too young to be put under pressure.'

Eamon's mind went into overdrive 'That's why my father was so disappointed that he didn't get the veil.'

Roscoff's ears pricked up even before it had the first hurdle in sight. 'So your father knew that John was going to be born with this gift?'

Eamon replied while still in deep thought. 'Of course he did.'

He paused for a second. He had something else on his mind. 'Listen, let me get this right. The veil was on the HMS *Sheffield*, and it sunk in battle?'

Roscoff replied, 'Yes, that's correct.'

Eamon stood and walked round the room. Roscoff's eyes never left Eamon's shadow, like an eagle preying on its first morning's meal. Eamon's mind was thinking of young John screaming the words, *water, water*.

Eamon turned to face Roscoff with his hands now resting on the table opposite Roscoff. 'Would it be wrong in thinking the HMS *Sheffield* was sunk for a reason?'

What kind of question is this? Roscoff thought.

Roscoff knew it was MI5 that had sent the sailor boys over to buy the caul. It was all planned so they could analyze the skin. He shrugged and raised his voice to another level. 'Eamon, you're starting to make me nervous. Believe me, the sinking of the HMS *Sheffield* had nothing to do with the veil. And even if it had, I wouldn't be in the position to find out this information. I would have to gain access to a top security level.'

Eamon had a twinkle in his eye. He leaned forward and turned up the heat, speaking in a slow soft but direct tone. 'But wouldn't you want to find out the truth?'

Roscoff rose from his chair. It seemed Eamon had touched a nerve. Either Roscoff was hiding something, or Eamon had actually got Roscoff thinking what could actually be! Roscoff walked over to the TV, switched it on, and turned round.

'You want to know what John's mum said, right?'

'Of course,' Eamon replied.

'Here, you can listen now.' Picking up a remote control, he aimed it at a black stereo unit on a shelf.

As the speakers emitted static, Eamon knew he was about to discover a completely new side of the story.

Chapter XXVI

John was raking in more and more chips. After seven wins out of ten, Rosi was amazed. Three times she'd seen John throw his cards in, as if he knew in advance that he'd been defeated.

The game changed to poker. The limit for the table was ten thousand. John, holding a royal flush, wasn't about to use it just yet. Rosi had never seen so much money in her life.

'How much have you won, John?' She followed him to the bar.

He ordered a bottle of champagne and handed it to her. 'Around forty thousand.'

When they arrived back at the table, John revealed the royal flush, beating everybody in the game – yet another ten thousand.

Counting the chips, he saw a shadow stretch across the green baize in front of him. It was the floor manager, dressed in a red tuxedo. 'Sir, can I invite you over to the main table? It appears you need bigger stakes.' He gave John a thumbs up.

'Well, that's very nice of you, but who am I playing against?'

The manager stepped back so that John could see past him. Every single player at the big table was dressed immaculately, mostly in black. Their cigars fogged the air above the table. 'Businessmen, sir.'

'And what's the limit?'

The manager said, 'There is no limit, sir.' He gestured for John to follow.

Rosi gripped John's hand. As they advanced towards the table, Russian voices swept past them. *Businessmen, eh? I wonder what type.* Rosi thought.

***

Eamon watched the reel of tape spin around through the stereo's small window. He looked irritated but also comforted.

When the first side ended, Roscoff pulled his coffee towards him. 'Well, what do you think of that.'

Moving from his spot by the speaker, Eamon sat in the armchair next to Roscoff. 'It's nothing I didn't know myself. John already told me about his dreams. Even the set-up at the casino that happened yesterday, I already knew. What holds him back is that he doesn't know when these things will happen. Otherwise, we'd do something.'

Roscoff stood and took his mug and plate to the sink. 'And what did he tell you about planes crashing into buildings?'

Eamon tried to explain. 'From what I know, that concerns America. It's some sort of terrorist attack. He spoke of weeping passengers on a plane, terrorists with guns, and the destruction of two major buildings. He saw the Statue of Liberty through the window; it will happen in New York. He keeps mentioning chaos, devastation, complete confusion, corrupt congressmen's faces, and police and firemen everywhere.'

Roscoff dropped the cup in the sink. He apologised and said, 'When does this happen?' He bagged the cup's broken pieces and tied a knot. 'Do you want some water before we carry on?' He took a small bottle of Evian from the fridge and handed it to Eamon.

'The dream becomes clearer each time, so we think the time of the attack is nearing. John thinks the event will eventually lead to economic breakdown and a new world order. The dream ends there.

'John keeps having flashbacks, saying they're making him wake up in cold sweats. That's happening more and more. Poor boy, said it was the worst feelin' in the world when you know something terrible is gonna happen, but you can't do a t'ing to stop it. I don't know how he can live wid it. And that's all I know.'

As he reached for the bottle in front of him, he realised Roscoff was leaning close to him. Eamon pretended not to notice.

Roscoff took a cloth and started cleaning the lenses of his glasses. 'But what does he see? He must have some idea what these visions mean.' He rose and took the tape out of the stereo. He turned it around to play the second half.

'I've asked him what the visions mean,' Eamon said. 'John sees two versions of what might happen. It's difficult to understand, for the visions include everything from trains to mobile phones exploding to a first black president.'

Roscoff laughed. 'First black president? Please. What year are we talking, 2050? Come on, Eamon, that'll never happen, not in my lifetime, anyway.'

Eamon snubbed out his cigarette in the ashtray. 'He only mentioned two dates, 2012 and 2023, but the rest is unclear. And I can't forget to mention what he said about gusts of wind and torrential rain at speed, and a red army marching towards the middle East. I don't understand any of it.'

Roscoff shuffled files in his cabinet. He paused and looked up. 'That can only mean one thing, Eamon – a nuclear attack.' He returned the files to the cabinet and locked it.

Eamon stood. 'Jesus Christ, then what?'

Roscoff switched off the TV. 'We have to keep this between ourselves, at least until we uncover more. It's the only way to deal with the problem now. Do you understand?'

Eamon breathed heavily. 'I understand. I'm glad you said that. Not sure I like that Munroe fella. Was like shakin' hands with a wet fish, one that lives in the darkest depths of the ocean, snoopin' around everyone else's t'ings.'

Roscoff laughed. 'That's only too true. Don't worry. Sooner or later he'll learn all about it. But we have to keep him blind as long as possible. The first thing we must do is contact John. Did you know he was in Berlin?'

Eamon closed his eyes. 'T'ank the Lord. He must've gotten back to the hotel and taken one of the tickets.'

Roscoff pulled a folded sheet of paper from his pocket, a photocopy of Dermot's ticket. 'We found your other tickets and ran a passenger check on the flight. By that time, John was safe in Berlin. But for now, let's listen to the rest of the tape.'

***

John sized up his opponent, the last man standing. It happened to be the Russian casino owner. Rosi watched from a stool on the opposite side of the table, wary of intimidating glares. She motioned to John that she wanted a drink. She hurried to the bar.

John's final opponent was named Frankie Shultz. He was a well-built man in his forties, arms adorned with samurai tattoos. He stood watching as John counted his chips. 'It seems I've met my match. In fact, I was observing the way you play. It seems to me that I was beaten by your skill, as opposed to this luck of yours everybody mentions. Luck comes and goes. Skill? That's different. It interests me, your skill. I can see have something special. Not many people earn my respect. You have. That's why I invited you over to the bar with your friend.' He gestured for a handshake.

John obliged. 'I'll accept that offer.' John gathered his chips into a bag and followed Frankie. In the bar, John sat beside Rosi. He felt slightly wary of this opponent. *That's only natural. But what does he really want?*

***

As the second side of the tape came to a stop, Eamon swilled a mouthful of water. 'I wonder what the Catholic priest wanted. And who were the other two with 'im? It's the third time they visited Rose and Chris.'

Roscoff finished a second cup of coffee. 'I don't know, Eamon. The trouble is that too many people know too much about John. If we gather all the information, we'd find the authorities and the mafia know more about John than he does himself.

'So, go to Berlin. Find him. You must. Once you've done that, call me. We'll start from there. Do we have a deal, Eamon?'

Eamon paused before he replied, 'Yeah, you've got yourself a deal.'

Eamon walked to the door. Roscoff collected his jacket and switched off the stereo. 'Eamon, you can trust me. I don't waste time with deception. I want to help John as much as you do.'

He switched off the light and locked the door. As he turned to leave, he was startled by Eamon, who stood directly behind him.

'I believe ya. That's why I'm starting to trust ya. You're a smart man.'

Roscoff put his finger to his mouth, signalling for him to keep his voice low. He whispered back. 'Smart? Perhaps. But I'm not devious, like you.'

They laughed as they left the building. It was the start of a partnership.

Chapter XXVII

John and Frankie shared a toast to John's success. Since it was getting late, John decided to cash in his chips. He said goodbye to Frankie and went to the elevator with Rosi.

When they reached street level, the doors opened, and John ran out, clutching his winnings in one hand and Rosi in the other. They jumped around madly, as John threw handfuls of notes into the air. He grabbed Rosi by the waist, lifted her, and spun her around. 'We're rich, Rosi.'

A small group of passers-by had gathered to witness the chaos. Several teenagers had the nerve to grab the notes and run away. John was in a charitable mood and couldn't have cared less about the stolen money.

As he stopped spinning Rosi around, he held her in his arms. They shared their first kiss and laughed when people wolf-whistled. Hand in hand, they made their way back to Rosi's apartment.

***

Yet again, someone watched John, this time from behind darkly tinted glass. He stood between two minders, looking down onto the street from the third floor of the casino. 'I want you to follow him – see which way he goes and which hotel he's staying at. I want to know everything about him.

'Don't let him get hurt. I like this man. There's something unusual about him. And I know one thing. He'll be back.'

As he turned, his face was exposed in the dull shafts of the city's lights.

***

John was gaining the attentions of Frankie, and, although he didn't know it, he was letting Eamon down once again.

***

Just minutes after the departure of Roscoff and Eamon, another car drew to a standstill outside the MI5 office. One person got out and locked the car door. Behind the closed blinds, he shone a torch around awkwardly. The loose air vent in the wall was an easy signal, at least to anybody searching for something. The other end of the vent on the outside of the building had been filled. A screwdriver easily opened the metal plate. He removed the long silver key from his pocket and inserted it into a wooden box. 'There you are.'

The master recorder was visible in the white beam. Soon after, the sounds of two voices in conversation could be heard in the other room. The illuminated numbers on the digital clock told him he had plenty of time. He relaxed, switching on a small lamp by the television. Munroe saw his own face staring back at him from the screen.

Chapter XXVIII

At 5.00 a.m. in Berlin, Rosi awoke with a start. John was shaking and sweating, mumbling in troubled tones. She placed her hands gently on his shoulders. His skin was ice cold.

'John? John, wake up.' She reached over and turned on the bedside light. He sat up. 'John, are you—'

Before she finished her sentence, he fell back to sleep. Gripping the bed cover, Rosi panicked. She went into the kitchen and heated a mug of cocoa in the microwave. The daily newspaper lay by the sink. After browsing through the paper, she felt relaxed enough for sleep. Instead, she thought about mundane topics, like designer handbags. Such thoughts always set her to sleeping. But if some item in her imagination caught her fancy, she experienced an adrenaline rush.

The clock sounded at 8.00 a.m. Yawning, Rosi wrapped a dressing gown around herself and returned to the kitchen. She slipped bread into the toaster and cracked eggs in a pan. She grabbed a pint of milk from the fridge. She laughed. 'God, you nearly gave me a heart attack.'

John finally rose from bed. 'Are you okay? You still look tired.'

She poured some coffee. 'Go sit at the table. We'll eat in a minute.'

When Rosi brought the tray, John took the steaming mugs from her and placed them down. 'Looks wonderful.'

She took a slow sip.

'The reason I look so tired is because you woke me up.'

He reached out and touched her hand. 'Oh, sorry. Did I snore? One day somebody'll get that on tape.'

She pushed a plate towards him. 'John, last night you were having a nightmare. You sat up at just about five o'clock. Can you remember what you were dreaming about?'

'I don't know.'

She poured more coffee. 'I can tell you what happened. You said, "September, September." Then you twice said, "Behind the palm tree." At one point, it looked like you were awake. I tried to speak to you, but you fell back asleep, as if nothing had happened.'

He took the plates into the kitchen. He returned with two bowls of fruit and yogurt, kissing Rosi on the cheek. 'You know something? I feel as if I've known you my whole life. We look good together. And last night, that was beautiful. I think we should take the winnings and go shopping.'

***

Roscoff had given Eamon his ticket to Berlin, rescheduled for Saturday. He planned to stay in England, hoping to learn more about what remained unexplained. He had heard a Catholic priest on several recordings. It seemed peculiar that John's parents would have asked him around, especially more than once. What possible interest could John's 'veil' have to the Catholic Church?

***

Still in the office, Munroe switched off the machine

and retrieved the tape. He'd heard enough. The conclusion that Young Tierney could pose a potential danger to society weighed heavily on his mind. Something had to be done. He made a call.

'What?'

'Look, I'm sorry he got away. I think—'

'He got away because your partner Roscoff tipped him off. How the hell else would he have found out what the dealer said?'

'John knew he was going to get arrested; of that he was certain. His visions had something to do with that. After all, his apparent abilities have everything to do with why John's garnered so much interest in the first place.

'But it had nothing to do with Roscoff. Everybody knows that Rocket-man always keeps his mouth shut. Even if there was something in it for somebody else, that wouldn't tip the balance. He takes his career seriously and keeps his sights fixed on the target. If somebody got in the way, they would take a bullet.'

'You know as well I do that there's something strange about that boy. The night he came here and lost was a con. I saw it with my own eyes. Nobody brags about losing. Anyway, I know you called because you want something from me. So what is it?'

Munroe switched off the light. The tone of assurance in Biggins's voice buttressed his suspicion that he was trapped. He saw no way out.

'At the moment, we know John is in Berlin,' Munroe said. 'We're trying to arrest him for fraud. You help me with this, and I'll help you progress in your business. It's as simple as that. You know what I mean.'

'Yeah, well, I could've had this sorted out already if you had put him away the first time. Now I've gotta make deals. I'll see what I can do. What were you gonna suggest?'

'Connections,' Munroe said. 'I know you've got connections to Berlin and Hamburg. I saw your criminal file. So now you can use them to find John. I'll take it from there.'

'I'll get on to it, then. But don't make a mistake this time, Munroe.'

So I help Munroe, but why? If John were really under suspicion for fraud, why would Munroe want my help? Why try to catch a culprit using illegal methods? Something in the equation doesn't work. Wait; It's obvious.

***

The next morning, Biggins was on the phone, talking to someone in Berlin. This should be easy.

***

The tape reels rotated slowly for the second time. Munroe wanted a clearer idea of the situation. He decided that a third party needed to be involved, to stop the situation from progressing further. It had to be his American friend from Texas, Casey Miller. After twenty years in the industry, Miller was known for his ruthlessness, and that would be an advantage.

'Hello there, Casey. It's been a long time.'

'Charles, how are ya? Or should I ask, what can I do for you?'

'Still got your head stuck up your ass, I hear.'

'That's why you'll never be as arrogant as me, see? So what do you need? I don't have time for bullshit.'

'Well,' Munroe said, 'it's difficult to explain, so I'll jump to it. What do you know about terrorist activity? Any threats in Germany picked up?'

'Momentum is building. Remember the battleship they sunk in Yemen? A guy called bin Laden was behind that. We made a deal with him. Afghanistan and Russia had been the first conflict. Afterwards, he openly declared war on America, which put him on top of our most wanted list. He's still there. Why do you ask?'

'When will you next visit England?'

'Not for a while. Get to the point, Charles.'

'I have a source who revealed there's a terrorist plot. America's the target. There's a shitload of paperwork I'd have to sift through to give you the whole story. I'd rather not reveal it on the phone either. That's why I need you here. There must be something you can do.'

'I know we've always been there for each other in the past,' Miller said. 'There's a better chance we'll beat this if we join forces. I can send my personal assistant your way.'

'No, it has to be you, Casey.'

'Then I hope to hell you're being straight with me.'

'Just get here as soon as possible.'

'I'll check flights for tonight.'

Munroe knew that Miller's proficiency in dealing with such problems was always adequate. He worked for the CIA. Everything was expanding, becoming more complex, like evolution.

Chapter XXIX

A light could be seen on the back wall of the Vatican room. The reflections of the fire's burning flames were fighting yellow between the dark shadows of the four Vatican officials still contemplating the decision of the mysterious bloodline.

Priest Conti arose from the table looking relieved. 'So the decision is mutual. We'll have to act immediately if we're to save what we have left of the Catholic Church.'

Conti collected the documents from the table and walked over to the open fire. While hanging the documents over the fire, he took one last look at his colleagues individually.

Bruno nodded confidently; Rizzi looked towards Bruno with a face of uncertainty and took one last deep breath before also returning a nod to Conti. A final nod of approval was required from Cardinal Rossini before Conti would release the documents to the fire and destroy the evidence forever.

Sweat trickled down the side of Cardinal Rossini's face as he felt the burden of his final decision. The brothers waited patiently for what had to be an individual verdict. Conti raised his eyebrows towards his fellow cardinal.

Rossini raised his left hand and removed his half-mast glasses, looking deep into the eyes of a confident priest. Rossini finally gave an unconvincing nod.

Conti's grip loosened as the documents fell to their eternal fate. The parchment glowed magnificently as if something wonderful had happened, but one amongst them knew this to be untrue. The four cardinals watched the evidence going up in smoke. Rossini took a step forwards looking to the photo on top of the pile, the photo of the caul, John's caul, burning in the sacrilege of the Vatican.

Chapter XXX

On Wednesday nights, Rosi worked the night shift. John went to the casino alone. The person Biggins had contacted was one of Frankie's business partners. Naturally, the information spread. All of the Russian 'businessmen' were on the lookout for an Englishman by the name of John Tierney, who was apparently wanted for fraud and armed robbery in Biggins's casino. They knew he was in town.

Just as John entered the casino, an attendant rushed towards him. 'Excuse me, sir. I need to see some form of identification before you're permitted access to this casino.'

John retrieved and opened his wallet. 'I didn't need it before.'

The attendant seemed nervous. 'New security regulations, I'm afraid. Just a quick look, that's all.'

John held out his driving license.

'Thank you, sir. Please continue. Have a pleasant evening.'

The assistant waited until John was out of sight. He rushed over to his colleague at the reception desk. 'That was John Tierney. Inform the head of security that the target's inside the building.'

His colleague snapped out of his usual trance and picked up the radio transmitter, exiting the side door to maintain secrecy.

'This is Thomas Eberhardt from reception one. Herr Mulovski has confirmed your target's in the casino.'

In the next hall, John sat at the poker table. Frankie was not yet present, which left his business partner, Kali, in charge. After being notified of John's whereabouts, the head of security passed his message to Kali, who, in turn, gave them orders.

'I want every camera on table one. I want him removed without any trouble. We can't disturb our regular clients. Take him upstairs to one of the rooms. I don't want any blood. Understand?'

By the time the security personnel arrived at John's table, the game had been suspended. The dealer had asked John to stay at the table. The others were led to the lounge for drinks. John knew somebody had tracked him down.

'I'll take my money elsewhere,' he said. As he stood to leave, a hand grasped his shoulder.

'Sir, leave the table and come with us.'

'What's the problem, gentlemen?'

'No problem if you come with us, sir.'

John pulled his jacket tight. The security men didn't move.

'Sir, we insist you follow us.'

'If you don't mind, I was just about to leave. If there's a problem here, I think I deserve to know what it is.'

'First, you must follow us upstairs.'

John continued walking. He made it to the top of the outdoor steps. There he was jumped and grabbed. One of the security men had gotten him into a headlock, which made John struggle for breath.

'You're coming with us, sir.'

In a flash, John grabbed the guard by his neck, swung him around, and pushed him down the stairs. Facing the doors, he saw the reflection of another guard approaching. John elbowed this one in the chest. As the guard stumbled towards the railing, John pounced. The guard fell backwards through the swinging door, landing on the casino floor.

At the reception desk, Thomas winced. 'He's gonna leave an imprint in the carpet. We'll have to replace it.'

Back outside, John spotted a third guard. He took hold of the steel railing and swung over it, kicking his opponent. The guard flew backwards and fell onto the hard marble floor, critically injuring his neck. John knew the guard wouldn't be getting up anytime soon.

When backup arrived, John had disappeared.

Chapter XXXI

Around lunchtime the next day, a gold Bentley pulled up outside the casino. A uniformed driver emerged and went to open the back door. Frankie stepped out onto the tarmac. 'No need to panic. I'm coming in now.' He tucked his phone into his pocket and dashed up the steps.

Despite knowing the previous night's events, Frankie had no idea the man the security staff had been chasing was John. After all, he'd been spying on John just days before.

As Frankie reached the top of the stairs, the office door opened. Kali stood behind it. 'I don't know what else to tell ya. It was bedlam.'

Frankie pulled out a chair. 'I wanna see what's on those cameras.'

He watched John in action, battling the guards.

Kali leaned forwards and paused the tape. 'Steve Biggins told us that the English police were tracking John.' He explained the situation as Biggins had described it.

Frankie shook his head and pressed play. When he had finished watching the debacle, he switched off the tape. 'So they want him for armed robbery and fraud. I don't understand it. The way he plays cards shows there's no reason for him to commit criminal acts. There are a few pieces missing from the puzzle. I'll investigate this myself. I have an address. I'll go there alone.'

'You saw how he took care of the boys. Have somebody assist you, for Christ's sake.'

Frankie pulled a cigarette from a gold case and tapped it on the table. 'No, that'll only make him more suspicious. I'll drive alone. It's the only way I'll get through to him. Don't you worry. And don't speak to anybody about last night. I want to hear his story. I think we should at least give him a chance to share his perspective on the incident.'

***

Elsewhere, Vladimir Roscoff had made a new discovery. The priest, seemingly shrouded in mystery, actually turned out to be a high-ranking cardinal from the Roman Catholic Church. His name was Domenico Santini. Roscoff sat cross-legged in his office chair. 'Thanks Maria' Roscoff hung up the phone. Several minutes later, the details of the church appeared on a laptop screen. He entered the number into his mobile phone and saved it before dialling. A man with a strong Italian accent answered the phone.

'This is the church of the Holy—'

'Is this Cardinal Santini?'

'Yes. To whom am I speaking? And what does your call regard?'

'My name is Vladimir Roscoff, MI5. I must talk to you. It's an urgent matter of security.'

'I can grant you a few minutes. If you can be at the church by seven, I'll see if I can be of assistance.'

***

At five minutes to seven, a figure trailed through the dark graveyard, dodging between the scattered tombstones. A small point of light was visible through the blue glass window next to the archway. Roscoff raised his fist to knock on the wood-panelled door. As he did so, the door creaked open. He looked down and noticed the iron bolt was locked onto the latch, though the doors weren't hooked together. Strange. Rubbing his numb hands together in an attempt to get warm, he stepped into the chapel.

'Hello? Cardinal Santini, are you there? It's Mr Roscoff.'

The chapel was submerged in a welcoming bronze light. A noise startled him. It sounded like something metal had fallen to the floor. As the noise echoed, Roscoff shuddered. *Churches and divinity. I feel no connection between them. The silence, it's more like hell if you ask me.*

He tucked his hands in his pockets and started snooping around until he came to a small arched doorway in the right-hand corner. Three narrow steps led up to it. An almost life-sized statue of an angel was mounted beside it, partially concealed by a curve in the wall. From what Roscoff could tell, it appeared to be a Grecian figure, depicting a beautiful woman with long hair that hung past her waistline; she was almost warrior-like in stature. When he stepped closer to observe her, he was horrified to notice that the facial features were contorted. Circling the statue, he counted six wings instead of two. He ran his finger across a dark line on the back of the neck. *What is it, an engraving?* He leaned closer, holding up his mobile as a light so that he could see it better. It was an inscription of miniscule Roman numerals, numerals he knew all too well.

Looking at his phone, he saw that it was four minutes past seven. *Where's the Cardinal?* He leaned around the statue and knocked on the door. He waited then knocked again. 'Cardinal? Is anybody there?'

He grabbed the door handle and turned it. It clicked open with ease. A small wooden table and pair of chairs faced him. The nearest chair was turned slightly, as if awaiting a visitor. The candle on the windowsill had burned low, and wax ran down the wall.

Cautiously, Roscoff sat and faced the doorway. As he was about to make a call, he heard a sound growing louder. A single beam of light shined past the door, capturing his focus until the door swung back.

A looming grey shadow appeared, stretching across the stone floor. Roscoff felt the blood in his veins pulsing.

The cardinal appeared, face red and sweating. He leaned against the wall with a hand on his chest. 'Terribly sorry, something came up. It couldn't wait. Church business – you know how it is.'

'I understand. I was beginning to think you weren't going to come.'

'Oh, no, no, no, my son, we never neglect our duties.'

The cardinal sat down. He held something in his hands. Roscoff soon identified the object as a chain of rosary beads. The cardinal placed the beads on the table and put his hands together as if in prayer. 'It was brought to my attention that you've come to discuss some sort of security threat. Is that correct?'

Roscoff tensed, holding his identity card in the air. 'Not exactly, but we do have a problem.'

The cardinal opened the desk drawer and removed a candle. He walked towards the windowsill and lit the candle. 'And what is this problem?'

'John Tierney and the fact that he was born with a caul – that's our problem.'

The cardinal seemed disgruntled then amused. *This is a cunning one. The confessional was sacrosanct.*

His expression changed to one of confusion. 'You mean to say you've come to see me about this John Tierney? I thought the public was in danger?'

Roscoff closed the door. He had no idea the meeting

was going to be so convoluted. 'Cardinal, you visited the same John Tierney on several occasions. Can you tell me the reasons behind those meetings?'

'John Tierney – the name is familiar. I can't quite picture his face, though.'

'Then perhaps I can refresh your memory. You sat there, with two other men from Rome, disappointed on every occasion. John Tierney never showed up, even though he was aware you'd been waiting for him. Is that correct?'

'I don't think I'm under any obligation to discuss this matter with you. It's a matter for the Catholic Church to decide. You know this already, Signor.'

'Okay, have it your way, but just remember, things could soon get out of hand if John Tierney finds himself trapped by corruption and danger.'

'Then tell me what you know about John.'

'Everything we need to know, Cardinal. I'm the one asking the questions here.'

'We only want the best for this young man. We want to give him guidance, show him the right way of life.'

'And I take it you know what a caulbearer is, Cardinal?'

'A what? No, sorry, I don't. Should I?'

'Yes. I thought that was the reason you visited the Tierneys. Perhaps I was wrong. Maybe it's all just a coincidence. What do you think?'

'I think it's time you were leaving, Mr Roscoff.'

The Cardinal gestured for Roscoff to exit through the doorway. He looked intensely aggravated and discontented with the questions he'd been asked.

Before the Cardinal had closed the door, Roscoff turned and pointed at the statue. 'An admirable piece. You shouldn't keep it hidden. I'm sure there are others who would see meaning and beauty in it.'

With that, Roscoff left.

How on earth does he know? Surely he doesn't mean—

A revelation came to the cardinal. *I'm not the only man worried about John Tierney. And I'm not the only man to know about angels.*

Back in his car, Roscoff scrolled through the photograph gallery on his phone. He zoomed in on the picture of the roman numerals. *Let's compare, shall we?*

Eamon stepped off the plane and headed down the corridor to the passport check-in. He switched his phone back on and saw he had a text message from an unknown number:

I did what you said.
No luck.
Lisa's still in Ireland.
All okay.

It had to be from John. 'Lisa still in Ireland? Bollocks. That's ruined our plans.'

He waited to collect his luggage then sat in a cafe. He called Roscoff and left a message on the answering machine. 'Just arrived. I'll call soon and let you know what's happening.'

After collecting his luggage, Eamon climbed into a taxi.

Whilst at Munroe's office, Casey Miller stepped out of another. He looked quite dishevelled after the long flight, which had taken nearly ten hours. The taxi driver got out, and Casey waited for him to open the door.

Munroe stood watching the scene. *Typical, can't even open his own door.*

Casey pulled a note from his pocket and slapped it into the driver's hand. 'Keep the change.'

Then he turned to Munroe. 'So, Charles, ten goddamn hours on a plane. Whatever you got me here for, it better be damn good.'

Munroe wasn't surprised by Miller's lack of etiquette. It's not as straightforward as that. I think we should start at the laboratory. There's something you should see.' Munroe knew the only way to convince a Texan cowboy was to hit him hard in the face. The veil's what he needed to see first!

Chapter XXXII

The next morning, Frankie sat in his car, huddled from the crisp morning air. Through his window, he watched Rosi's place across the road. He switched on the radio. He saw something move in the car mirror. It was John. Immediately, Frankie stepped out onto the street and walked over to John.

John glanced back and smiled. Frankie met an unexpected attempt at a handshake. 'Hello, Frankie. I see you came alone?'

Frankie paused, smiling back. 'Yes, I'm alone. I wanted to find out the truth for myself. I thought you deserved a chance to explain what the police wanted from you, that's all. I don't believe everything I hear.'

'News does travel fast, doesn't it?'

Frankie nodded. He moved closer to John, checking the street as they walked. 'Just so long as you don't pull your gun out in my casino, you're free to do what you want. But you must realise they'll get you eventually, my friend. In fact, I came to tell you that dogs are already sniffing for your heels. The authorities know you're in Berlin.'

John said, 'I know nothing about a gun. I do know that a casino owner from Sheffield is a very bad loser.'

Frankie pointed to the left as they turned a corner. 'I was told you're wanted for armed robbery. Apparently, you got away with a lot of money from his casino.'

John looked delighted. 'That's right. I did get away with a lot, and many times. It was hard-earned cash I won from card games, like I did at your casino, as you remember. Biggins can't stand to see somebody else win; that's his trouble. I'm armed with two hands that don't commit robbery. They just rake in chips.'

Frankie watched John's face. Something about it made Frankie trust John. One question still remained: *Why did Biggins, whom everyone knew was a multimillionaire, want to put John away so badly if none of it was true? It wasn't as if he needed a backhander, now was it?*

As they passed a row of shops, John was about to go into a café.

Frankie stopped him. 'If it's a coffee you want, John, I think I know a better place.'

Chapter XXXIII

Munroe and Miller arrived at the laboratory. Miller sat down as Munroe pulled white surgical gloves over his hands. He unlocked a steel cabinet and removed a sealed glass jar. As he placed it on the table, Miller thought it had to be some kind of joke until Munroe opened it.

'Don't touch the glass,' Munroe said. 'That's why I'm wearing these gloves.' He closed the cabinet and dropped a photo in front of Miller.

Miller leaned forward, unsure what to make of the photo. *What is it?*

Munroe said, 'In 1971, a child was born with what you see in that photo wrapped around his face, from the back of the head to the bottom of the neck. We managed to slice this small piece off, and as you can see, it's lost no colour or texture. On the other hand it's managed, amazingly, to double in size.'

'I've never seen anything quite like it before,' Casey said. 'What were the test results?'

'It's unrelated to the membrane, that's for sure. It's a different kind of tissue altogether. Nothing will damage it; it was there to protect the baby's face. That was its purpose.'

Munroe, with computer switched on, placed a disk inside, pressed play, and said. 'Come over to the computer, please, and take a look at this lab test on the skin. You can see for yourself that what we have here is a human arm used for testing purposes. As you can see on the screen, we're pouring an acid solution over an area of the arm.'

They could clearly see the acid burning a hole through the arm. Miller was shocked.

'Now, watch again as we reproduce the same experiment using the skin from the boy.'

The acid was once again poured over the skin, only this time what appeared to be steam began to rise, but the skin remained intact.

'Now pay close attention please,' Munroe said.

Miller witnessed a shining light coming from the skin, seconds after the steam vanished.

'Fantastic or what?'

Miller turned as suddenly one of the lab windows shook from a gust of wind. 'And what about the child?'

'We had him under surveillance. Then things got complicated, too much happening at once. Later, he began attracting too much attention for our taste, so we devised a way to bring him in. Unfortunately, he already knew. He left the country. Now we think he's in Berlin.'

'But how could he know you were coming? Who tipped him off?'

'Nobody. The operation was assembled at the last minute. That's what makes everything seem all the more true. He outwitted our plan the same way that he wins every card game he plays.

'What are you getting at, Charles?'

'He sees the future. He was born with that ability.'

Miller banged his fist on the table. 'You're telling me you believe this paranormal bullshit? Show me some evidence.'

'Casey, there's the evidence, in that box right in front of your eyes. Why do you think we keep it?'

Miller loosened his tie. 'If what you say is true, tell me something else this boy has seen – something that actually happened.'

'What more do you want? Okay, he beats casinos like a mind reader and never loses.'

Miller rolled his eyes. 'All right, Charles. I'll notify the security service at the Pentagon. But I think we should keep the whole thing about this so-called skin to ourselves, if only because they'll have a good laugh at us.'

Munroe stood. 'If I thought the whole bloody situation was normal, why'd I put your ass on a ten-hour first-class flight?'

Miller had cancelled an important meeting the previous day, August 22, and the only reason he'd done so was to help his old friend Munroe. Now he knew, or halfway knew, the reason Munroe had made it sound so urgent. In a moment of privacy, Miller called the CIA office.

'Book my flight back from London to Washington. I've got to make the next meeting, understand? I don't care about the damn schedule. Just book the flight.

***

Meanwhile, John and Frankie had gone to one of the latter's gymnasiums, where Frankie knew they could talk privately. They sat at a table by the window, behind closed blinds. A man placed a tray in front of them. Frankie poured the coffee.

'So,' John said, 'there's a picture of you on the wall, I see. You know Thai boxing?'

'I have three boxing gyms of my own. That's why I brought you here. I saw how you took care of my boys at the casino. Unarmed combat, and a nice display, I might add. Where did you learn that? It seems you and I share interests. You fascinate me more and more, especially the way you play cards.'

'It's all about movement and reaction in those games,' John lied. 'Body language tells you a lot. You become a better player by playing somebody better than yourself. Learn from them, but don't just copy. Instead, repair your own mistakes. That's what I've learned.'

'Who taught you?'

John tried to think of a random name. If Frankie knew there never had been a teacher, that would obviously raise suspicion. John, hating his own lies, said, 'P-Paul. Paul was his name. I can't think of his last name.'

Frankie smiled. *Who does he think he's fooling?* 'Facial expressions tell me a lot, too. At the card table, you're hard to read. But now I see your weakness. You're in big trouble. If you tell me the score, I might be able to help.'

John leaned towards Frankie. 'You want to help me? Why?'

'Because on September 10,' Frankie continued, 'one of the biggest card games in Berlin takes place. All the mafia bosses come together. I won't be present. You'll take my place. In return, I'll get Biggins off your back. Deal?'

John had already dreamed that Frankie would offer to help him. However, John couldn't remember the dream's conclusion. Hands shaking, he placed his coffee cup on the table. 'I'll stand in for you, if you tell me how you'll get rid of Biggins.'

'First, you gotta tell me what happened between you and Biggins.'

John frowned. 'I thought I already did. He's a bad loser, and that's all there is to it.'

Frankie shook his head. 'John, you're forgetting that Biggins is a multimillionaire; he wouldn't go out of his way just to regain the amount you won.'

'If you don't believe me,' John said, rising from his chair, 'let's drop the deal.'

Frankie motioned for John to sit. 'Hey, relax, hotshot. Lying won't help. There's no reason you should get yourself into more complications. As far as I'm concerned, we've got a deal.' He shook hands with John.

'It's a deal,' John *knew he had to get ready for the biggest poker game in his life. It's only a few weeks away.*

Chapter XXXIV

The cardinal had an idea. He would call somebody in Rome, a person he'd never seen before. That person belonged to a unit formed to protect the Roman Catholic Church, and that unit was known as the Angelic Angels.

'Buon giorno, Marcello. How are my angels? In this divine moment, it seems we're not alone. Our path to holiness is under threat, as well as our protectors of the Catholic Church. I need you here. Send your messenger to me at once. Deus tecum, amico mio.'

As one of the most powerful organisations in the world, the Church, had protectors sworn to defend its legacy and defend it to the death, if necessary.

***

At the same time that the cardinal placed his phone call, Munroe sat alone in his office, wondering who to call. He scrolled down the phone book menu. He finally decided to call Biggins.

'Look, Munroe, I have nothing to tell you at the moment. When I do, I'll get in touch. I already told you that.'

'Time's running out, Biggins. You know the Irishmen we arrested outside your casino? One of them has been released. Now he's in Berlin. We bugged his bag when we first found the flight tickets. Our target is also staying in Berlin. I'll pass on any information. I think it would be best if you joined our friends on their little holiday. Then we can start making progress.'

'I'll get in touch with my Russian contact as soon as possible. He'll take care of the situation.'

***

A moment later, Frankie's phone played the ring tone he'd assigned to Kali's phone. He entered a crowded café before answering. 'Yes, Kali, what's up?'

'I've some more info on Tierney. Biggins just called us. Tierney's not out here alone. An Irish guy arrested at Biggins's casino arrived here not long ago. I think his name is Eamon.'

'You're sure about that?'

'Biggins told me. He's at the centre of our information hive. He can't keep his big nose out of anyone's business. Even money doesn't shut him up.'

'Enough about him. What happens if this guy gives an address to the police? Then the authorities find out. I've gotta get to John fast before they do. I've gotta warn him.'

'Yeah, Frankie, keep your eyes open.'

Frankie next dialled John's number. 'Biggins is on the phone again. You have friends in Berlin, and they're being followed. The girl you're staying with, does she know your Irish pals? Is she connected to anybody in England, anyone at all who knows a thing?'

'She knows a girl called Lisa. Lisa is the only connection between me and them. They knew her from before.'

'Where's she now?'

'She was on holiday in Ireland, but I think she returned last night.'

'You have to get out of there. Your friends could be in

the pub now. And this girl you're staying with, she might've told them something, or maybe everything.'

'I'll get my stuff together.'

'Do it fast. I have a driver set to pick you up. He should be parked outside in a black BMW. I told him to keep the lights on.'

John looked out of the window. The car was there.

'I see it. Thanks, Frankie.'

'Get going.'

John chucked his phone into a bag. He grabbed toiletries and everything he'd brought. He zipped his bag, slipped on his jacket, and ran out the door. He sprinted down the steps, out onto the pavement, and into the back seat.

The driver said, 'Name?'

John shut the door. 'Tierney.'

The driver smiled. "Good."

***

Not far away, Eamon was having a drink at the Irish Times Pub, where he'd been for almost an hour. He had already spoken to Lisa about John.

'Be Jesus, how's it goin', darling? My God, Eamon, would you look at the size of yourself? Looks like you're in good health, anyway.'

'Of course I am. How are ya, love?'

'Perfect, t'anks.'

'Listen, Lisa, I got me a friend come over here. He's in quite a spot. Told him to find you.

'Course, you were still away in Ireland when he got here.'

'John, isn't it? Rosi mentioned him to me.'

'That's him. You've not met him though?'

'No, I just arrived back.'

'God help us.'

'Eamon, whatever's wrong?'

'I have to find that boy before he starts more trouble.'

'Don't worry yourself, darlin'. Rosi can help ya. D'ya wanna drink anyway?'

'A Guinness please. You'd better bring two. Plus a Magners.'

The black BMW pulled up outside an apartment five stories high, with an additional basement flat. As John opened the door to step out, the driver took the luggage from him.

At the top of the steps, the driver pressed the buzzer. A man in a white suit appeared. With his gelled blonde hair and thin rectangular spectacles, he looked down at the driver. Then he stood taller to peer at John. Apparently satisfied with their appearances, the man nodded and dragged John's case in carefully. John turned to thank the driver, only to find he was already gone.

The man stood back to clear the way. 'Do come in, sir. We knew you were coming.'

Inside, John noticed a decor appropriate for any modern-day wealthy kid's downtown apartment. It was mostly white, square, and contained a bevy of high-tech gear. Small circular camera heads were hidden in the most obvious places. For example, as John had stepped through the door, he had looked directly into a camera installed on the banister handle of the stairway. All of the cameras were connected to Frankie's casino security system.

The lounge was unusually large. John looked to his left and noticed that the windows had been blacked out. In front of them lingered the ghostly outline of an old man, bent and mangled by his many years. The scent of decay caused the acid in his stomach to make its way up John's throat. John sweated. The figure moved forwards, pointing at John as if condemning him for an unknown crime.

No. You're not real. I've seen those eyes before. Resist, resist.

Before he had time to evaluate the situation, John collapsed.

***

When he regained consciousness, the man who had greeted him at the door held a damp flannel on John's forehead. 'You had a funny turn there. Your temperature was unbelievably high. Do you feel any better?'

John winced at the strange surroundings, the room small and blue. He attempted to sit up, then realised he couldn't. The top half of his body felt numb.

The man saw that John's eyes were filled with tears. 'Can I get something for you?'

John shook his head. 'I never wanted this. I can't do it. I don't understand. Sometimes I think somebody chose me. They chose to put me through all of this darkness. They call it a "gift," some people do. Right. Try getting this gift for Christmas; you'll soon change your mind. How do I know whether I'm really having visions or just imagining these things? How can I tell? Would you know?'

The man said, 'I'm afraid my opinion doesn't matter, as I can't understand your experiences. I've never had anything close to them. I will tell you, though, that you have us behind you, for what it's worth.' He turned from John and opened the door.

A platoon of people gathered inside the room, three men and three women. Someone handed John a cup of mint tea.

A young blond man said, 'We're Frankie's security team. We never leave unless commanded otherwise. We're at your disposal, Mr Tierney.' They bowed.

It had been longer than John cared to remember since he'd felt so protected.

Chapter XXXV

At the pub, Eamon sat near the bar with two drained glasses of Guinness in front of him, foam gathering at the bottom. He swigged from the Magners bottle, disappointed at the emptiness of the place.

Still, he wasn't all alone. When Rosi appeared from the kitchen, he called her over.

'Hi,' she said. 'What can I get you?'

'Hello. You're Rosi, I t'ink. My name's Eamon. I spoke to Lisa yesterday. She said you knew where John was; is that right? I'm a friend of his, ya see.'

'Oh right, nice to meet you, Eamon. Yes, John has been staying with me for the past week. He should be back at my place now.'

'If you don't mind, would you be able to give me the address so I can go talk to 'im?'

'I don't mind. Give me a second.'

She took a small notepad from behind the bar and scribbled her address. Just as she was about to hand the note to Eamon, a man at the bar asked if he could pay his bill. She walked to the till and printed a receipt for him. After handing it over, she turned to see the note with her address gone. *Did I even write it?*

Eamon was inebriated, on the verge of toppling over and taking his chair with him.

'It's no problem,' Rosi said, trying to draw his attention. 'I finish in twenty minutes. You may as well come back to my place with me.'

Eamon drained a second Magners and slammed it on the table. 'John. Gotta find John.'

She sighed. A typical man, pretending to listen. No matter where the hell they came from, they were one and the same. It was just an excuse for doing the same thing a different way.

When she got back to the bar, she saw a single note next to the till. The other customer was gone.

Twenty minutes passed slowly. The bar was dead, and business was slow. When her time to leave finally arrived, Rosi rushed up to Eamon with her coat and bag. 'It's not far,' she said, jangling her keys, 'only a five-minute walk.'

Eamon seemed more sober after having eaten several bags of crisps. His anticipation at seeing John once again showed in his eyes.

Cars skidded through small puddles. Though it had been raining, the air remained warm. They turned onto Rosi's street. She pointed. 'There's my place, see? Told ya it wasn't far.'

They stepped up to the front door. As Rosi went to put the key in the lock, the door swung idly. The latch had been ripped from the wall and the chain torn off. Rosi gasped. For the first time, she knew what 'feeling at sea' meant.

Eamon seemed to snap out of his drunkenness at the moment Rosi's knees gave way. 'I—I don't believe it,' Rosi said. 'Why would John do this?'

Eamon lifted Rosi to her feet. He passed her the bag

she'd dropped while falling. 'You can't believe John did it because he didn't. Someone else did. There are people about. They've been watching him.'

'It must've happened earlier at the bar. When I came back, the address I wrote was gone, and so was the customer. It makes perfect sense now. Eamon, what's going on?'

They stepped over the furniture and objects scattered about Rosi's room. She almost cried as she picked up a torn photograph depicting her in the park at five years of age with her mother.

Eamon's fist tightened. He tried to reassemble events. *Bastards.*

He touched Rosi's shoulder. 'I'm afraid to say I'm not sure of the whole t'ing meself. But I'm not lettin' you sleep in this place alone. What if they come back? No, I'll try and tidy the place up a bit. It's the least I can do.'

She took his hand. 'Here, sit down for a minute.' She slid a stool towards him, providing him the one thing left intact. Then she poked her head into the kitchen, afraid to look. She was pleasantly surprised to see hardly any mess. The fridge was full, the appliances fine. One drawer had been ransacked. It lay in pieces on the floor. At least she knew whoever had broken into her home hadn't come to steal objects or money. It was information they wanted.

***

In an apartment across town, John slept uneasily. Another dream. The security team watched his stirrings. A short blonde woman nodded to the man who had first spoken to John. When he left, a brunette woman took his place by the window.

The man dialled his phone in the hallway.

'Mr Schulz, it's Martin White here. Under the circumstances, I'm contacting you as instructed.'

'Dreams again?'

'Yes, sir, by the appearance it seems so.'

'Thank you. I'll return after eight.'

'I'll inform the team, sir.'

***

In Rosi's front room, Eamon took his phone out of his pocket.

'Don't call the police,' Rosie said.

He held up his phone so that she could see that he was calling Roscoff. 'Friend of mine. Gotta find out what he knows about all this.'

Somebody picked up. The dialling tone was cut off. Eamon put the phone to his ear. 'Tonight I was followed to the pub by a man. Must be English. Found the address John was staying at.'

'How do you know?'

'Because we just got back to that address, and it's been completely turned upside down. John's not here, either. Whoever did it has a contact in your department. Nobody else knows. It doesn't look like we're going to have such a great working partnership after all.'

'Slow it down, Eamon. You don't know anything about who it was yet. I'll look into it. That's all I can do for now. And before you start accusing me, try finding out where John's been on his little vacation.'

The line went dead. Roscoff was deeply dissatisfied with Eamon's accusatory tone, though he could understand such outrage, given the importance of the situation.

Meanwhile, Eamon smacked his forehead. *Of course. Why didn't I think of it earlier?*

Rosi came out of the kitchen. 'I can't close my own door, but I can still make tea.' She stopped, holding a mug in each hand. 'What? You don't like tea?'

He took the tea from her. 'T'anks. Rosi, I have to ask

206

something now. What exactly did you and John get up to?'

'Excuse me?'

'No, not that. I mean in general. Did you go to clubs, shops, or what?'

'Oh, right. We didn't do a lot, to be honest. But the night we met, we went to the casino. John won a lot of money there.'

'How much?'

'Around eighty thousand euros, I think.'

'Christ. Did you see him lose even one game?'

'I don't know about the first table. At the second table, he won everything. That's when the casino boss invited him to the main table. He was with a lot of businessmen.'

'And this owner's name?'

'He introduced himself as Frankie. I don't remember the last name. He took us over to the bar for a drink after the games.'

'And where is this casino in Berlin?'

'Mitte. Basically, that's the city centre. It's not far from here.'

I should have realised it - casinos. Roscoff knows his business. John seized the perfect opportunity to escape. Now he's fallen into another trap.

Chapter XXXVI

On a warm sunny morning, Frankie's gold Bentley pulled up outside the apartment. It was 08.15. The blonde man named Martin approached Frankie. 'Good morning, sir. Would you like a cup of coffee?'

Frankie handed his 'assistant' a leather jacket, wiping his feet on the mat. 'No, I'm not staying long. You got the tape with the footage from last night?'

Martin walked into the kitchen and returned with the recording. 'Here it is, sir.'

Frankie walked into the front room and sat opposite the large television next to the fireplace. 'Play it then.'

Martin nodded. He departed, passing John making his way inside. John looked exhausted. 'Good to see you, Frankie. He stopped as he saw the television. 'What—what are you watching?'

Frankie patted the cushion. John sat, and Frankie paused the tape.

'You. John, it's crucial that you begin grasping the danger you're in and how you're putting yourself in even more danger. Lie low for the next few days, at least until the card game's over.'

John considered everything that had happened until this moment.

Frankie said, 'Come on. I'll take you to a place I know so we can eat in peace.'

Martin appeared in the doorway.

'Martin, fetch John's shoes and jacket. We're leaving for a couple of hours.'

'Please tell me,' John said, 'that we're not going to the Irish pub.'

Frankie smiled. 'No, we're not going there. Somebody I know has a few restaurants and cafés around town. Ever heard of Alfonso's?'

'I think Eamon mentioned it once. Said he'd known the guy for a while. Alfonso Santini? Something like that. Italian.'

'An Italian, of course. Used to have a shop in Rome.'

Soon, they arrived at a small café with the usual outdoor tables and umbrellas.

'Here we are. This is one of Alfonso's joints.'

The driver parked the car beneath a small bridge with a train track arching over it. John felt tense, remembering his experience a week before. Frankie noticed John's apprehension. 'Don't worry. They stop here because the station entrance is just round the corner.' He pointed. 'See?'

'Do you mind if we sit inside anyway?'

In the café, a tall woman in a striped apron greeted them at the door. "Good morning, Mr Shultz. Signor Santini sends his regards. He's not here today.' She handed Frankie and John menus.

'Thank you, Carmela.'

They picked a table in the far corner. Despite it being too early for the lunch crowd, John nervously checked the surroundings. The only other patron was a young woman by the window, sipping a milkshake and typing on her laptop.

The waiter brought coffee and biscotti. Frankie lit a cigarette. 'Here's the plan. For the game, I'll give you a million euros to play with. If you lose, you lose. I lost the same amount last year and made it back soon enough.

'What bothers me more is that I can see you have a lot on your mind, naturally. I have a feeling there's more on it than I know. Before we go through with this, I have to know what that extra weight is. You didn't sleep well last night. You saw the evidence yourself. It seems to me you're always half dreaming, when you're not dreaming. I can help you clear your mind, John. So what's wrong?'

John downed his espresso in a single gulp. He knew he had no other choice but to trust Frankie, the prospect made him nervous, even though he had a gut feeling it was right to do so. Nevertheless, he felt strangely lost without Eamon.

'Frankie, you know the situation. About the rest, you'll have to trust me on this one, just this once. Thanks to you, that bastard Biggins hasn't gotten to me yet, but it's only a matter of time. We have to get this card game out of the way first before the situation becomes more complicated than it already is.'

Frankie blew smoke high into the air. *It was clear to him that John didn't know about the phone conservation he'd had with Biggins.*

After lunch on the way back to the car, Frankie said, 'Let's go down to my gym. I want to show you some methods of relaxation and meditation, which may help you sleep better. I learned them as part of a Chinese philosophy we use when we want to concentrate or clear our minds. It's all part of the yin yang balance. I'll demonstrate, if you like.'

John agreed, getting into the back of the car.

Upon learning about the ransacked apartment, Roscoff

211

contacted one of his old friends and former KGB colleagues, Alexei Puskin. They had stayed in touch since the day Roscoff left Moscow. Both shared secrets and told no lies. If one needed information, the other provided it. Roscoff reached for the phone.

'Ah, it's you, Vladimir. So good to hear your voice. I trust you're not having problems with business?'

'Things are getting complicated for me, Alex. You still in Moscow?'

'Actually, I've been in Berlin for the past three months. I expect to go back to Russia by end of the year. Why? Are you coming to Moscow?'

'You gotta be kiddin' me, Alexei. I'm not going to Moscow. But Berlin is the perfect place for you to be right now. I need your help badly, Alexei.'

Roscoff explained everything he knew about John. That Puskin had a holiday home in Berlin made the phone call all the more helpful, though Roscoff might have called his friend long before.

I'm not telling Eamon any of this. I'll ensure Eamon hasn't double-crossed me with Puskin's assistance. And Eamon can continue looking for John.

***

In the cold silent church, Cardinal Santini placed his hands together, thanking God for the call he'd been anticipating. On the other end of the line, a man spoke with an Italian accent.

'Good evening, Cardinal. Parlare. I'm the messenger. Please call me that.'

'Marvellous. I have all the information you need, Mr Messenger. We must act quickly. Our contact has the names and locations of all the traitors. That information will be kept secret. It was written within the spiritual walls surrounding the seven signs.

'The High Lord of the Veil is upon us. The seven conspirators must be eliminated as soon as possible. Our Lord will soon join us. For the sacrifice of evil, we shall each be shown the rewards of paradise.'

The messenger replied, 'The Vatican asked about the sacred book. They want to know how long you'll keep them waiting.'

The cardinal answered in a brisk tone, 'They've been waiting over a thousand years. They need not fret anymore, for soon it will be over. Then nothing will stop us. Nothing!'

The cardinal knew the Messenger's contact had to be MI5. Those were the only agents who knew the details about John, besides his closest friends and relatives. Five agents attended every meeting, usually. It would take some time to narrow them down, but the identities of the traitors would soon be exposed.

Chapter XXXVII

September 10 had arrived. Frankie and John were at the gym. The game was scheduled for that night. Frankie had taught John principles and practices from Chinese philosophy. Massage and acupuncture eased John's tension. Meditation focused his mind.

The blinds had been drawn. Candles dimly lit the room. John and Frankie sat next to one another. Frankie said something in a language unknown to John, but John echoed the phrase perfectly. This proved the exercise hadn't been futile.

When John opened his eyes, he knew he'd been hypnotised. He swayed. Frankie steadied him.

'How do you feel now? Did you see anything?'

'It was an incredible nothingness. How'd you do it?'

'You'll learn how to do it yourself. And you'll feel better for it.'

'I saw everything. It was so clear.' *Wait. I promised Eamon I'd never share my dreams or visions with anyone. But what does it matter now? Roscoff knows. Why shouldn't Frankie?* John stopped talking.

Frankie rose and moved towards the door. The guard

next to him held John's coat. 'Come on,' Frankie said. 'Let's get out of here. You need some rest so you can practice before the game.'

Frankie looks as weirdly confident and confused as I do.

***

In England, Roscoff looked at his old friend and new enemy, Munroe. They had agreed to meet and devise a new strategy regarding John. Both knew the other was looking for information elsewhere and the meeting was a formality or, more accurately, a waste of time. Roscoff yawned. Munroe's phone rang.

'It's Ross.'

Roscoff shrugged.

'Yes, Ross, what now?'

'Bad news, sir, real bad.'

'How so?'

'This morning, around eight o'clock, they found him.'

'Found who? Fucking spit it out, Ross.'

'It's Biggins, sir. He's dead.'

Munroe nearly dropped his phone in shock.

Roscoff sat up and leaned forwards, trying to get the gist of the conversation with an inquiring gaze. Whatever it was, it didn't make Munroe look any younger.

Regaining his focus, Munroe said into the phone, 'And where'd they find him?'

'His doorstep, sir.'

'Cause of death?'

'Some kind of dagger. They stabbed him straight in the left side of his neck. The dagger was still there when I got to him.'

***

The killer and the cardinal knew that the first of the traitors had been eliminated. The spectre John had seen at

Frankie's apartment had been a forewarning of Biggins's murder.

***

Now Munroe sat in silence, listening to Ross's description of Biggins's body.

'Okay, already,' Munroe said. 'Follow up the leads. Keep me posted.'

Munroe closed his phone. Guilt poured through his increasingly porous conscience. In a way, the murder had been his fault, for he had contacted Biggins and involved him in the whole operation.

Munroe had no choice but to explain what he knew Roscoff would soon discover. 'Looks like somebody had it in for my contact, Biggins. His body was found this morning – on the doorstep of his own home, stabbed in the neck.'

Roscoff spoke more softly than usual. 'Biggins dead. Well, he had so many enemies. Even you know that.'

Munroe had one question on his mind. 'I just can't piece it together. What connection is there? I don't suspect for one minute that Tierney had anything to do with something this sinister. He's not even a thief. Where's he now, anyway?'

Roscoff said, 'We haven't found him. A sighting was reported, but that was days ago. He vanished once again. His Berlin apartment was broken into and completely ransacked. There's nothing leading to his whereabouts or business in Berlin. He hasn't returned to the scene of the burglary, if it even was a burglary.'

Munroe knew Roscoff's goal. *He's trying to coax more information from me. But I know even less than he does. We both know it.*

***

By the time John awoke, the sky had begun to darken. The casino hall was being cleaned and polished, ready for the big game. To make the cover story less dubious, Frankie had mentioned to one of his fellow players that he felt ill but would hopefully improve in time to play.

Six years before, the first such game had taken place. After a successful turnout, the mafia bosses agreed to make it an annual event. Each time, winner took all. Out of the previous five games, John's game being the sixth, Frankie had won two. That had put him in good favour. He knew his absence would be appreciated by some who would have had to face him.

After reviewing the rules and unnecessarily swapping tips, Frankie and John noticed the time for the game was nearing. Frankie stood. 'I'll go there alone. That way, no one will suspect you're showing up to cover me. We'll let them wait around twenty minutes and make it look like you have to prepare at the last minute. Don't worry about time. My men know the plan. After Rubin drives me to the casino, he'll circle back and wait here for you. We'll travel in the black Jaguar.'

He tapped John's arm. 'I sense you're ready. Thank you in advance for doing this. Now get dressed. Your tuxedo is in the guest room. Rubin will notify you when it's time to leave. I have some business to get out of the way, but I'll see you later. Now let's do this.'

By quarter to nine, all the players had assembled in the hall. Frankie waited for a moment of silence then signalled that he wished to withdraw. The thought of the plan going wrong nauseated him. He provided his opponents several minutes to confer. They huddled together.

One of them, a tall Jamaican-born man named René Rousseau, had travelled all the way from Paris. 'Well, it's a million less we can use. It's unusual. But Mr Shultz has already won twice. Maybe without 'im, somebody else'll have a better chance.

'Besides, it wouldn't be fair to let him play if he's ill. It would affect his abilities.'

In the few audible words, Frankie detected a general agreement with Rousseau's points. Finally, Petr Levzski, a silver-haired Russian man, announced their decision. 'We've agreed that you've been excused from this event, Frankie Shultz.'

Frankie wiped his forehead, feigning fever.

Petr continued. 'Therefore, you've been granted both the permission and the authority to elect an individual of your choice as a replacement. Our game will then continue in the usual manner. We've agreed to postpone the game until you've located a suitable replacement.'

The bosses left for the lounge, where they discussed general matters of business. By this time, it was forbidden that anyone discuss or even mention the game. Levzski ordered a vodka and Coke. Rousseau preferred coffee with a dash of Cointreau. Most of the men were soon smoking cigars. A haze filled the room.

***

At five minutes past nine, John hopped out of the black Jaguar and ran up the steps to the casino, oblivious to Eamon's shouts from across the road. Eamon, waving his arms, sprinted towards John. When he reached the top step, the door closed in front of him and behind John. It was too late.

He looked at the doormen on either side of the entrance. He bent forward with his hands on his knees, catching his breath. He pointed towards the casino. 'I have to speak with my friend. He just went in.'

The men didn't move. The one to the right spoke like a talented ventriloquist. 'Sorry, sir, but without an invitation, your entry cannot be permitted.'

Think fast and talk slow. 'I'm a friend of John Tierney. I lost my invitation. Can't you check for me?'

The guard touched his headset. 'I'll get someone to double-check the list. What's your name?'

My name; that'll get their attention. 'Tierney,' he said, 'Eamon Tierney. I'm John's brother.'

The man nodded and spoke into the headset's microphone.

Frankie. Surely he'll be inside, if he's the guy Rosi's been going on about. Eamon zipped his jacket, pretending not to care too much. He assumed a casual voice. 'Frankie won't be happy when he finds out I'm stuck out here.'

The doorman glanced at Eamon then quickly sent another message to his colleague, only it wasn't just any colleague but rather Kali, who sat by a window in an office two floors above, right beside Frankie.

'Says his name's Eamon Tierney.'

'Right. Just wait there. We'll have the guys inside bring him in.'

The guard turned his back on Eamon, whispering another message into the headset. The other guard held a small key. 'Sir, if you'd like to follow us.'

Eamon looked pleased with himself, then frowned, remembering he was supposed to look angry for being kept waiting. But just as he expected them to lead him through the revolving doors that stood between him and the casino, they turned sharply to the left and descended a narrow stairway. Eamon slowed, sensing danger.

Four flights of stairs later, they moved an underground car park flooded in orange light. The only noise came from the air vents trailing through the building's steel skeleton. They stopped by the wall. Eamon relaxed, remembering he still had a gun tucked in his belt. What were they waiting for?

As if in answer to his question, the screech of tyres startled him. A silver BMW approached from the opposite end of the car park, gleaming beneath the lights. When it reached them, one of the guards walked around and handed a piece of paper along with a key to the driver, who tucked it into his jacket. The guard opened the passenger door. He said. 'If I were you, Mr Tierney, I'd get in. That's if you ever want to see your brother again.'

***

Back in the UK, the Biggins's murder investigation gathered momentum, for a second body had been found, this time that of an MI5 agent. He'd been found in a London car park, slumped over the steering wheel of his car. Ross had just arrived at the scene. He called Munroe from a corner phone.

'Sir.'

'Hi, Ross. Any news on Biggins?'

'No, sir, well not exactly, sir.'

'Ross, I do wish you'd stop talking in riddles. What's going on then?'

'A second body's been found, sir.'

'What do you mean, a second body?'

'An agent. Agent Mullins, sir.'

'Jesus fucking Christ, Ross.'

'You'd better come see for yourself, sir.'

'Yeah, sure, I'm on my way. And Ross?'

'Yes, sir.'

'Do me a favour and keep this one under your hat, please.'

'Yes, sir, will do, sir.'

Munroe put the phone down shakily. *What the fuck is going on?* He took his mobile from his pocket. Seconds later, Roscoff was on the line. Munroe explained. 'Fuck, Vladimir,' he concluded, 'this is turning into one hell of a mess. Don't worry. I'll meet you at the murder scene in ten minutes.'

When Roscoff arrived, Ross was waiting. A forensics team observed the victim's dark blue Saab and various pieces of clothing. They circled the car for a clearer view of the scene. Munroe hid his eyes. Roscoff coughed. Ross looked sickened, having until that moment managed not to look too closely.

In the case of Biggins, he'd been given a photograph for the sake of his well-known queasiness. He removed the photo from his pocket and handed it to Roscoff.

'Sir, the photo from the first murder. In front of us is the second victim, Inspector Mullins. There's a correlation between the two – both killed using the same methods and the knife left in both bodies. Even the weapons themselves are identical.

'They *are* the same knives, except the engraved lettering at the top of each blade is quite different indeed. Roman numerals. That's significant. We have to learn what it means.'

Munroe glanced at the corpse. 'If Tierney's tied to these murders, where's the connection between Biggins and Mullins?' He pulled Roscoff aside. 'Vladimir, this could be an inside job. The more I think about it, the more I'm certain of it.'

Roscoff tucked the photo into his pocket. 'I agree. Somebody close to us is leaking information. And Mullins was present at every meeting we've held regarding John Tierney. I'm sure of that.'

He turned around and shouted over to Ross. 'Get in touch with the rest. Put them on red alert and give them police protection. We must take every precaution against further deaths.'

Munroe scratched his head and said, 'And, Ross, find

out about the knives. I want to know every detail, and I want it all on my desk by tomorrow morning. Clear?'

Ross answered from behind the car. 'Yes, sir,' he said, taking off his vomit-soaked jacket.

Roscoff walked back towards his car, stopping and shouting, 'I'll see you both in the morning. I have to go back to the office before I head home.'

Chapter XXXVIII

In Berlin, the five players assembled around a large circular table and settled in for the game. The dealer filled the sixth space. He opened the crisp new cards and placed them perfectly in the dealing box before declaring the start of the game.

***

Eamon watched the shops, flats, and people whizzing past. Then it all seemed to slow as the car came to a standstill outside a magnificent penthouse. He craned his neck to look up, impressed by the sight. The white building stood apart from the entire front glass façade. There were only five separations in the pane, all at floor level. Eamon thought about the five panels, all glass. Not exactly conventional. *Bullets can obviously pierce glass, and people can see into the building. Not to mention the light.*

The driver turned round as if he'd heard Eamon's thoughts. 'That glass is bulletproof and triple-gas-glazed,' he said in a New York accent. 'It protects against harmful UV rays. An automatic screen drops when the brightness reaches a certain level. It can be altered according to personal preference.'

The driver got out of the car, strolled around, and held the door open for Eamon. The driver pointed at the building. 'You've been staring at yourself for a long time. The glass is mirrored. If somebody stands inside, they see us, but we can't see them. Cool, huh?'

Eamon was led towards the door, reflected by the mirrored glass. The driver pressed a button, and a buzz allowed them entrance. As the door closed behind them, Frank Sinatra's 'Under My Skin' rang out from circular speakers in the ceiling. Eamon and the driver followed the narrow corridor, dark with a high ceiling, which ran the length of the building. A pair of chrome doors slid open before them as if in expectation of their arrival. Eamon cautiously studied the elevator. He saw no gun barrels. The driver held onto the rail, leaning back against the mirrored wall.

'Don't worry,' the driver said. 'Most things run by sensor in this place. You don't gotta touch nothing, dude. The heating, sound, and light systems are all automatic. But again, it's down to preference.'

He pressed the button for the fifth floor and entered a security code. Eamon concentrated on the floor's mosaic patterns. When the doors opened, a cool draft greeted them.

The driver walked past Eamon towards heavy wooden doors. He inserted and removed a small key. As the driver returned to the lift, he pointed at the gap in the doors. 'Go ahead.'

Eamon timidly slid through the gap. An even chillier breeze met his skin. The door creaked. He found himself facing two security men, or what he thought were security men. They lacked the usual black suits and shades. Instead, they wore silk Chinese robes, gold with black dragons across the back. *Somebody's probably watching me on camera, pissing themselves laughing.*

Somebody was watching him, but he certainly wasn't laughing. Without so much as a blink, the guards on either side of him gripped an arm and led Eamon around the corner to yet another pair of doors, this one bright red with a large yin yang symbol embossed in the centre. Whoever sat behind this door had great importance, and the guards acknowledged it by bowing, falling to their knees and chanting a short Chinese hymn. Then they rose and finally opened the doors.

Immediately, Eamon was almost blinded by the outside city lights that glared through the glass. Eamon, eyes having adjusted to the darkness he'd encountered on the way, could barely make out a table on the opposite side of the room and the silhouette of a large chair behind it. He turned around. The door was shut and the guards gone.

A man spoke in an accent that Eamon had never heard before. 'Good evening. Please don't stand. Take a seat.'

Eamon shuffled sideways, towards a dark corner. A tall lamp came on automatically, making visible a white leather, six-seat corner sofa. He dropped onto it, rubbing his tired eyes and looked up.

The man said, 'Can I offer you a drink?' He wore a black Chinese robe but sounded, Eamon now realised, Russian.

On a small desk in the corner, a silver jug was surrounded by an array of liqueurs and tonics and God knows what else. Eamon nodded, unsure what he was about to imbibe. He watched the man mix some odd concoction. *Remember why you're here.*

'But where is John?' Eamon asked.

The man turned to the wall on the right, holding a remote control. He aimed it and pressed a button. The wall was a screen, and on it appeared John.

Eamon looked at the sparkling liquid in the glass. He tipped it back slowly. *Club soda or vodka, I hope.*

The man pointed at the screen. 'Second seat on the left. That's your brother, isn't it? You almost got him killed.'

Eamon almost choked. 'Would ya mind tellin' me how ya got to that conclusion?'

The man sat beside Eamon and mockingly said, 'Not at all. You were followed by the police from England. After John left the apartment, I had it put under surveillance. Four men were seen entering the place. Ten minutes later, you arrived with the girl. These pictures were taken by one of my men.' He was interrupted by the sound of his phone ringing. He answered the call.

'Frankie,' Kali said, 'you won't believe it; I've just received a call from Hamburg about a murder. A man's body was found on the doorstep of his own home in England.'

'So?'

'It was Steve Biggins.'

As if the words were too disgusting for his ears, Frankie put down the phone, cutting off the call. If someone had reason to kill Biggins, then there was another side of the story yet to be revealed.

He walked over to the window. Eamon had not heard anything. Nor had he tried to guess what had been said, as he was too concerned about their previous conversation, which he continued. 'How did you know they followed me?'

The man returned to the seat behind his desk. Suddenly, he sounded older. 'Biggins told us. The men responsible for the break-in were police. A week before, John had requested a meeting with me. Biggins had already told us John was wanted for armed robbery, so I made a deal with John. If he played for me tonight, as my replacement, I'd keep Biggins off his back. Simple as that.'

Eamon walked over to the desk. 'How do I know I can trust you?'

The man spun his chair around, kicking his feet up onto the table. 'You may not trust me, but John does. When this game's over, he's out. If he wins, he keeps 25 per cent of the takings, which amounts to approximately 1 million euros.

Eamon replied, 'Twenty-five per cent is 1.25 million!'

Frankie smiled. 'Not after I take my initial stake out first, my friend. He'll receive payment tomorrow if we win, when we meet for lunch. It's all been taken care of; don't worry.'

Eamon knew he had to trust this man, who so obviously wanted to help John. He seemed authentic, compared to the crooked gangsters and big shots hiding behind their so-called businesses. *Can't trust 'em, even as far as you can throw 'em – especially that Biggins bloke.*

Frankie snapped his fingers. 'Goddamn it.'

Eamon searched for the source of irritation, but Frankie looked at Eamon and offered his hand. 'My name's Shultz. You can call me Frankie. We shall become good friends, Eamon. Trust me.'

Young Tierney had been playing for two hours. Facing two other players, each down to their last chips, he easily managed to break even. He was feeling good and felt like he could play properly, without the usual spotlight blocking his vision. The entire time, he'd played in almost total silence, with the usual surrounding air of respect, no tarted-up strangers whispering about the 'amazing Tierney.'

Those knocked out of the game watched from the lounge, drowning their sorrows in alcohol. Eamon and Frankie watched from the penthouse, pouring occasional vodkas. Frankie's plan to maintain John's lack of distractions had paid off.

***

Under rainy skies, Roscoff drove up his watery gravel driveway. It had been a long journey home. He got out of his car and rushed to the door, protecting his head from the rain with a newspaper. Once inside, he fell back towards the door. Panic. *Why the hell are the hallway lights still on? The cleaning woman never leaves them on. I know I didn't.*

He slipped off his shoes and dropped them on the doormat. He went to the lounge, switched on his laptop, and opened a bottle of whisky as he waited for the computer to boot up. The bottle hit the glass. His hand faltered. *Did I just hear something?*

There it is again, a creak in the upstairs floorboards. He put the bottle down and crept towards the hallway, listening. Silence. *Maybe I imagined it.*

Lightning lit the curtains shrouding the window bay. The storm had worsened. *Maybe tree branches are brushing against the window. It's raining heavily, pelting the roof tiles.*

He turned on the stereo and played the first disc. A soothing Mozart piano sonata calmed him. He went to the kitchen and stepped back. Staring at the floor tiles, he noticed stains of three faint footprints trailing from the back door. Roscoff instantly knew the cleaning lady doesn't even wear shoes in the house, let alone leave marks on the floor.

He headed for the front door, tiptoeing towards the stairway. Another footprint. He bent down, touching the muddy patch. He felt the print, grinding the soil, which was cold and wet, between thumb and forefinger. Wet mud – *the intruder left just before my arrival, or he's upstairs, considering his next move.* He released his gun's safety catch.

With his back to the wall, he climbed the stairs. Upon reaching the landing, he noticed the bathroom door ajar. He opened the door. Nothing. He slipped inside and quietly closed the door, slid open the double shower, and turned on the hot tap to maximum. Then he closed the shower door, in order to trap the steam from the heat inside. He stepped into the bath, conveniently located behind the door. He hummed as if enjoying a shower. Then the doorknob began rotating.

Roscoff lifted the gun higher, steadying himself. The steam was so intense as to obscure the intruder's vision, providing Roscoff the edge. He saw a man's outstretched hand and a fist clutching a knife. As the figure advanced towards the shower, Roscoff kept his gun on target.

It seemed a fitting time to resume humming his favourite tune. The intruder stopped, twisted round, and came face to face with a shiny gun barrel, a big one at that. Roscoff stood steady. 'Put the knife down. Get on the floor.' The man wore a black, hooded coat, making it difficult for Roscoff to see the face.

The intruder failed to obey orders. His failure to cooperate infuriated Roscoff. He was tempted to pull the trigger. 'Put the knife down and get on the fucking floor. I ain't gonna tell you again.'

The intruder's flat glare hadn't been broken. He seemed brainwashed, living for one purpose. He lunged at Roscoff, aiming his knife for the neck.

Roscoff's finger closed around the trigger, and the bullet plunged into the target. The intruder fell backwards into the shower. What looked like a scarlet flower bloomed across his chest. He dropped to the floor. Blood met water, the man's life literally pouring down the drain. The bullet had entered the heart.

Satisfied, Roscoff lowered his gun. Fastening the safety, he slid it back into the holster and advanced towards the shower with a self-satisfied glide.

Leaning down to inspect the lifeless intruder, Roscoff remembered the dagger. Glancing back, he saw it laying a metre away on the black and white tiles. He shoved his hand into his top pocket and removed a silk handkerchief. Wrapping his fingers around the dagger's handle, he held it up to the light. Roman numerals dotted the handle in a seemingly random order, II.II; the symbols were meaningless to Roscoff.

It was, however, the same kind of dagger used in the Biggins and Mullins murders. He remembered the picture of the statue on his phone. He tore open his victim's shirt and pointed the tip of the blade just over the intruder's dead heart. 'Game over.'

Chapter XXXIX

John had won almost two million euros worth of chips. As the stakes increased, only two players faced him – Ramón and the Cuban, Señor Martinez – and as Ramón was almost out, it was up to Martinez to try and inflict some damage.

Cigars produced smoke from ashtrays, and ice cubes floated in chilled drinks. Everyone was waiting for John's decision. Picturing his ace and king, he closed his eyes and thought about what would happen.

'Raise two hundred thousand.'

Sensing something wasn't quite right, Ramón decided to fold, even though he had a pair of nines.

Martinez next to him traced his own lips deeply in thought. Two hundred thousand would take him as far as a motorized cardboard box on square wheels going nowhere. He looked at the dealer in the white suit.

'Your move, sir.'

Martinez straightened his tie. 'I'm all in.'

Well then, let us see what you've got, Mr Martinez.

'Call.' John smiled

Martinez pulled his cards towards himself, then dropped them on the table, revealing a pair of kings. Still watching from the penthouse, Frankie wondered if John had been merely lucky all along and whether that was about to change.

The flop was a queen of spades, three of hearts, and a king of hearts. Martinez, who had just turned his cards, was watching John with a smug grin of confidence. The shock of the pocket kings would normally make John think twice about his next move. No such luck for Martinez, as they were both all in. With his ace and king showing, it looked like it was all over for John, considering Martinez had three of a kind. The tenacity of the game was awesome. Bitter rivalry and extreme greed motivated Martinez. John just wanted to win.

As the dealer dealt the turn card, Martinez leapt out of his seat, pointing his finger at John, mimicking a pistol. His mannerisms reminded John of Biggins. There was something of the same attitude and cocky expression.

'I flop the nuts, and you, you score an ace on the turn card. Come on, baby, make me rich,' Martinez said, blowing the smoke from the barrel of his finger.

Across the table, John's cool demeanour broke. Elsewhere, Frankie tilted back in his chair. John felt the blood in his veins registering the tension. He looked away from the table It was time for the final card, the river card. The crowded area finally broke the silence.

The river card was an ace; John had miraculously won on the turn of the last card, barely scraping the win with a higher full house. Martinez was mortified, broken, demoralised to the point of destruction. It was over, for now anyway, and John was holding most of the chips and definitely looking like the favourite.

John's face creased in elation and relief as he realised he had won.

Standing across from him, a disfigured Columbian

known as Ramón stared at John. The Columbians weren't like Italians. They didn't have the same attitude, always giving the silent treatment, as if to say, *I've seen a lot. I'm still here. Don't fuck with me.*

Martinez huffed his way out of the room. Ramón pointed at John. 'You very much lucky tonight, Tierney.'

John whistled as if in agreement that he had won by a close margin. 'Maybe, but it's far from over.'

The dealer whispered something to one of the bosses then returned to the table. 'Gentlemen, you've been allowed a short break, since you've played for over three hours. The conclusion will commence in thirty minutes.'

Everyone left the room through opposite doors. John walked over to Petr Levzski, who repeatedly failed to light his cigar. John struck a match and held it to the cigar. 'Mr Levzski, is it possible I would be allowed to lie down somewhere? I need to rest in silence.'

Levzski nodded and pointed to Security. 'Dimitri will show you a place. But don't forget, you only have thirty minutes. Don't be late.'

On the way out, John heard Ramón ordering a whisky and Coke.

Chapter XL

Roscoff locked his bathroom door behind him and rushed down to the kitchen. He picked up the house phone and pressed speed dial. He was just about to hang up when someone finally answered.

'Hello?'

'Charles, it's me, Roscoff. Something just happened, and you may be in as much danger as I am.'

'I don't understand, Vladimir. What do you mean?'

'I had a break-in tonight. It has something to do with the murders. The same people are involved.'

'That's impossible. I made sure I gave the order that everyone on the job was offered full police backup, twenty-four hours a day. Your house should have been under surveillance.'

'So you mean to say I'm the only one who doesn't have it?'

'It looks that way.'

'So you didn't directly arrange it yourself?'

'No. Maria did.'

Maria? *The ties are truly tangled. Why would my own*

secretary betray me? She couldn't have forgotten me. We've worked together for almost two decades.

Munroe's voice made him jump. He'd forgotten he was still holding the phone.

'Vladimir? Are you still there? Are you all right?'

'I'm fine now, except that I was almost killed five minutes ago.'

'Don't tell me you found an intruder.'

'I found him, all right.'

'And what now?'

'Listen, just send somebody over.'

'Okay, done, but don't leave your house, Vladimir.'

***

After watching John leave the room, Eamon turned to Frankie, while sitting on the white leather settee. 'Mr Shultz, do you think I could see John now? I have to talk to him.'

Frankie sat up and turned off the projector. 'I don't see why not. But you'll have to do something for me in return.' He got up and walked towards Eamon. 'You tell John that you've known me a long time, that we're good friends and I'm a great guy, so great a guy that you'd trust me with your life.'

Eamon squinted at Frankie's face. *It's not like I have a choice.* 'I'll do it, but I'd like to ask what you know about Steve Biggins?'

Frankie walked back to the desk. He put on his overcoat. 'He's dead.' Frankie told the rest of the story then led Eamon out to the car.

By the time they arrived at the casino, twenty minutes of the break had passed. It was 12.50 a.m. They entered quietly through the emergency escape door, near the back of the building. Nobody from the casino hall could have seen them, unless they had circled the block and turned down the next road.

Kali had been waiting for them. 'Get inside, quick. I know 50 per cent of the bosses are almost paralytic by now, but you never know who might be watching. '

Eamon pulled the door shut. Frankie took off his hat.

'All right, all right,' Frankie said. 'Stop yammering and check the casino fast.'

Kali frowned and ran up the stairs. A minute later, Frankie's mobile rang.

'Yes?'

'I think you should come up, Frank. It's not looking good.'

'Which room is it?'

'Up two floors, first door on the right.'

Eamon knocked on the door. Kali appeared. He looked at John, who writhed on the sofa.

'He's dreaming again,' Frankie said.

Eamon ran to John's side, saying, 'What do you mean "again?"'

'He's been having the same dream for weeks.'

Eamon held John's shoulder. 'Let's wake him up.'

Frankie pulled Eamon back. 'Let him finish dreaming. You'll only make him weaker by trying to bring him out of it. It shouldn't last much longer.'

'Looks like you and John have shared quite a lot of secrets.'

'Kali,' Frankie said, 'go downstairs and let Levzski know there'll be a fifteen-minute delay. Ramón will just have to wait. Make up something. Say John's feeling sick; it's the only reason they'll accept. And for Christ's sake, don't tell them we're here.'

Kali looked as if he wanted to punch Frankie. 'I'm not an idiot.'

Watching the scene, Eamon surmised the situation. *Kali obviously knows next to nothing about John.*

Frankie pulled a chair close to Eamon. 'I think the boy has problems. I don't understand what he talks about or dreams about. All I do know is that he's a wanted man.'

The words faded as John's eyes opened. Frankie stood. 'John, are you all right?'

'I feel a bit tired.'

Frankie walked to the door. 'I'll get you a coffee. Look, you have a visitor.' He glared at Eamon, ensuring the latter remembered the deal made back at the penthouse. Then Frankie left the room.

'By God, it's good to see your face again, John. I've been trying to find ya since I got here.'

John looked depressed. 'Eamon, I can explain everything. I really can.'

Eamon patted John's shoulder. 'Don't worry about all that now. Get yourself ready and finish this friggin' game. Then we'll swap stories. This time, I want you to win, and you can, and you will.'

Frankie appeared, holding a steaming mug. He handed it to John. 'Listen, we've got to go back before someone sees us. I have the game on my screen at home. We'll see you later, John. Just win. You're ready, okay?'

John nodded.

After they left, Kali returned to the room, looking concerned. 'John, we'd better get downstairs now. They're getting impatient.' He handed John a flannel.

John rose, wiping his face. He pulled on his suit jacket. 'Let's get down to business. If it's a game they want, then by God, it's a game they'll get.'

When they arrived on the ground floor, Kali peeked through the fire exit and whispered approval. Frankie's car was gone. Kali led John down a corridor and entered a private code into the one-way security system. They continued through to the casino hall. Ramón stood with arms folded. He didn't like being kept waiting, especially by some unknown proxy.

John sat. Ramón feigned patience without much effort. John looked up, amused. 'You ready or what?' He glanced at Levzski, who hated Columbians.

Ramón paced over to the table, slamming down his glass. The chips reacted. 'I sorry for my English. Is not so good. But fuck you, man. You much lucky guy. You know why? 'Cause back in my town, you leave here in body bag. Ramón don't wait.'

John carried on as usual despite the outburst.

The dealer ran his finger around his tight shirt collar. He sipped from a glass of water. He turned to Rousseau then looked at Levzski and Martinez, who nodded. 'Are we ready to play, gentlemen?' He proceeded, sliding the new cards from the dealing box.

In the Chinese room on the fifth floor, Frankie and Eamon sat on the sofa they had positioned in front of the screen.

Eamon said, 'I'll be Jesus, it's scar face. What a bastard.'

'That's Ramón. Funny you should say that. I heard some of those scars came from dobermans that attacked him when he tried to trespass private property late at night. It was a difficult time to get hold of cocaine. He really got hold of it.'

'Stealing from the wrong guy. I suppose that's how they all get to the top, one way or another. No offence.'

Frankie passed Eamon a drink. 'None taken. I've never been interested in narcotics. Anyway, let's get back to the subject. I took John down to one of my gyms. I thought it might help him free himself from his demons. It was a good decision. I learned of these events he foresees. They become reality, directly or indirectly.'

Eamon stared at the screen, feeling sorry for John. 'I know. That's what scares me.'

Frankie leaned towards Eamon. 'Is that the whole story? Or is there something else I should know? It seems to me that there's a missing part of the picture.'

Eamon looked away. *There damn well is a missing part of the picture, and I won't solve the puzzle for you just yet. Besides, I have my own role in the prophecy.* 'He suffers from schizophrenia or something like that. His parents constantly worry about him, not to mention half the MI5. Nevertheless, he plays one hell of a card game.' He coughed and sipped his drink, trying to avoid Frankie's penetrating stare.

Frankie pursed his lips. 'Really? That's interesting. News to me anyway. It explains a lot, though.'

Eamon felt thankful for Frankie's one lingering doubt. Though Frankie believed Eamon, he still had the notion there was some other factor involved.

***

On a shipwreck at the bottom of the Atlantic somewhere off the coast of Argentina, was exactly where the other factor was. But neither Eamon nor Frankie, nor anyone else for that matter, knew about it.

***

The game had progressed. John held his temples. From what he could see, Ramón was half a million ahead. All the bosses had closed around them.

The chips scattered as Ramón banged his fist on the table. 'I raise, four hundred thousand.'

Time seemed to stand still as John hesitated.

The dealer leaned towards him and said. 'Your call, sir.'

John was unsure. Delaying, he cracked his knuckles and clenched his teeth, but when his delay met with impatient glances, he finally said, 'Call.'

Ramón grinned, displaying more gold in his mouth than he had on his fingers. 'I'm all in.'

John chuckled under his breath. *Of course you're all in.* 'Call.'

Ramón turned his cards – pocket jacks, spades and clubs. They were followed by John's cards – a queen of hearts and a matching ace. Ramón winked at John triumphantly.

The dealer dropped the flop. Five of diamonds, jack of hearts, ten of hearts.

In the penthouse, Frankie's shaky hands lit a cigarette.

Three of a kind for Ramón, and John had bugger all! The silence was overpowering. Being the extrovert he was, Ramón let everyone know his delight; he banged the table so hard, it shook.

Anyone would've been forgiven for thinking the dealer was bent after he turned the next card – ten of clubs. Ramón had a full house. John had a pair of tens, which left him only one way out.

Ramón shook his fist. 'Who's your fuckin' daddy now?' He turned to his minders, queuing to congratulate him.

Simultaneously, Frankie and Eamon stood, awaiting revelation of the river card.

Ramón folded his arms, knowing the odds of John coming back were at least twenty-five to one.

John winked at Levzski, who looked surprised. He pushed his cards to the centre of the table, stood, and said straight to Ramón, 'If I had to rely on luck, I wouldn't be here; for some players its essential, if you know what I mean.'

Ramón looked momentarily confused. It was either John's behaviour he didn't understand or the use of proper English. John nodded at the dealer. His words filled the hollow atmosphere. 'Hit the river card.'

Rene Rousseau snatched the bottle of Cointreau from the

barman and took a huge gulp, grimacing afterwards. Eamon couldn't stand still. Frankie tapped the desk and hummed a song without melody. The dealer mopped his forehead. Frankie nudged Eamon. 'Keep your fingers crossed. I think the skill in this game is on its last legs.'

Eamon crossed his fingers. 'Wait for the card, man. Show some faith.'

As the dealer turned the final card, a wave of shock washed over the room and silenced the now huge crowd. The silence was followed immediately by the crowd murmuring and finally hoots of joy as the crowd threw hats into the smoke-filled air.

The totally bewildered dealer stammered, 'K-king of hearts. Royal flush. Match to Mr Tierney.'

John had beaten staggering odds and, in doing so, had defeated Ramón. He stood. Levzski, Rousseau, and Martinez nearly suffocated John with embraces and handshakes. They had never seen anything like it. Now they knew on whom to bet. It was good for business.

Ramón sulked in silence, shocked and drained.

The barman collected empty glasses.

John said, 'Two large whiskys, with Coke and ice.'

The barman skirted around Ramón. A minute later, he placed a tumbler near enough to Ramón for everyone to realise it was his.

Ramón scowled. 'What make you think I accept drink from you?'

John picked up his glass and raised it high. 'Just wanted to apologise for being late.'

Levzski, standing behind John, laughed. 'You really showed that dirt bag who's the boss, Tierney.'

Ramón walked towards John. His minders followed. 'I don't take drinks from lucky men. You can wait for next year's game. Luck like that no repeat itself; make sure you here next year, Tierney.' He flicked his cigar ash at John's feet and turned to leave, entourage behind him.

John sipped his drink. *I don't think so.*

One of the younger Italian bosses, Gianni Zanetti, kicked the door shut behind Ramón and his minders. 'Vaffanculo bastardo, eh?'

John ordered a drink for Zanetti. He raised his own glass of wine. 'Grazie, amico mio. Congratulazione.'

***

Back at the penthouse, Frankie had opened a bottle of champagne. Eamon shook his hand and hugged him; they were jumping around like kids around the Christmas tree.

'So,' Eamon said, 'what were you saying? That the skill was gone. Or was it luck? Maybe it was.'

Frankie waved his hands. 'Oh, just shut up and drink.'

Thirty minutes later, Eamon lay sprawled across the sofa, smoking two cigars at once whilst Frankie was almost asleep across the white baby grand in the corner that Eamon hadn't even noticed.

'Oh, shit, almost drifted off there. What's the bloody time? My God, Eamon, that game was incredible. I just don't understand how it happened.'

'Ah, Jesus, how am I to know? The boy knows cards, that's all.'

Frankie struggled to stand and shuffled to his desk. He picked up the phone and ordered Kali to go get some food and pick up John at the same time.

Frankie stood for a moment, grasping the windowsill for balance. Then he turned and paced across the room. He pulled a rug from under the sofa and kicked it free.

"Hell of a rug. Wouldn't see that in IKEA now, would ya?'

'Thanks. One of a kind. Handmade. Took them two years to mix the right dyes and find the perfect silk.'

Eamon guessed the intricate patterns related to Chinese mythology.

Frankie stroked the carpet. 'A special mat, not just any old thing. It's given me many hours of peace. Eamon, I think it's best you stayed here for the night. Neither of us are fit to travel anywhere.

'John will be taken back to my apartment. We'll let him rest, for now. If you want to watch him, you can do it from here. I have a camera connected to my apartment. The security team will be there twenty-four hours a day to watch over him. Don't worry. We'll see him in the morning. Relax, man.'

Relaxing was an integral part of Frankie's life. He didn't believe in the word *stress*. Well, just maybe he'd better start getting used to it.

Chapter XLI

Eamon went to bed happy, for John was doing well, and Biggins was out of their way, not to mention that Dermot was set to be released the following week.

***

But on the next day, Monday, September 11, Roscoff awoke to a house surrounded by an armed security team. He kicked on his slippers and headed for the kitchen, where he made coffee. As the percolator reached boiling point, his mobile phone buzzed on the hallway table.

'Good morning, Charles. Yes, I'm fine. What? Who?'

'Agent Ross, my understudy, dead, murdered at 5.00 a.m. this morning.'

'Don't tell me—'

'Yes, the same method as Biggins and Mullins. Killed in his own garage. But Ross didn't go down without a fight. He got a shot off at the killer. Thanks to that, the police found the suspect's body a mile from Ross's place. Blood everywhere in his car.'

'Where's the investigation leading?'

'We need to hit the downtown morgue fast. Apparently, they have something they think we should see.'

'I'll meet you there in an hour.'

Ten minutes later, after Roscoff had finished showering, the phone rang again. He grabbed it from the bedroom windowsill. He stared at the screen. *I have to answer this one.*

'I've good news and bad news,' Eamon said. 'What do ya want first?'

'Good news.'

'I found John safe and well. But it seems your partner Munroe had some sort of a deal with Biggins. It was Munroe who sanctioned John's kidnapping, if you want to call it that.'

'So is it true somebody murdered Biggins?'

'Yes. How on earth do you know about that?'

'Biggins had contacts in Berlin. I've become rather acquainted with some of them. They took a liking to John in the casino. I have everything in writing. Munroe can't be trusted now.'

'Don't worry about him. We'll have him under interrogation soon enough. By the way, somebody tried to kill me last night, no doubt one of the gang that murdered Biggins, Mullins, and Ross, all within forty-eight hours. Somebody is supplying these people with information, and that person is just about guaranteed to be Munroe. Listen now, Eamon, keep quiet and stay low. I have to run.'

He hung up the phone, glanced at the clock, and hurried down the stairs. *Eamon is still suspicious of me. He's bound to be, since Munroe was a partner in the case. As far as Eamon knows, I'm as much a suspect as anybody in the unit.*

It was almost ten o'clock when Roscoff pulled up behind the morgue. As he walked around the corner, sunshine on the window provided irony, for it was never sunny in Peckham.

He pushed open the doors, waiting to be directed by the receptionist.

'ID? Thank you. It's just through there, sir.'

Munroe was sitting in the far corner. Roscoff cleared his throat. Munroe looked up, his eyes bloodshot. 'When is it going to stop, Vladimir?'

Roscoff sighed tolerantly then noticed the bundles of white sheets on a table in front of him. Munroe pointed. 'It seems we have a cult on our hands. Care to look?'

The sarcasm in his voice revealed his motives. *Odd how people change so completely in such extreme situations and the way particular things were altered by them. Munroe even sounds different.*

Before Roscoff had a chance to decline a look, Munroe snatched the sheets from the table, revealing two bodies lying face down, the corpses of the two dead killers. It was immediately obvious as to why Munroe had jumped to the conclusion he had; on the greying skin of the men were two identical tattoos. Roscoff swayed on the spot. *By God.*

And they weren't just any drunken Friday night tattoos. Roscoff knew because he'd seen the images before. The ink was stretched across the entire backs of the men, leaving hardly any skin unmarked. In the centre of the design was an angel. Rather, it was what he guessed to be an angel, as these angels had six wings – just like the statue in the eerie church where he'd met the cardinal. A connection was certain.

He stepped forwards to observe more closely. He noticed something. The head of the angel wasn't that of a woman, nor a man. It was the face of Baphomet. A symbol of Satanism, portrayed as some kind of anti-angel, half creature, half human. It had curving horns protruding from its head – seven of them. In front of the wings, the creature appeared to have two human arms. The left hand was held up, almost as if directing the eye. Roscoff traced the direction and realised a word was cleverly disguised between the large wings. The first letter was *A* and the next *N*.

Angelic.

Munroe's Mozart ring tone startled Roscoff.

'For God's sake, Munroe, get that thing out of here.'

Munroe knocked open the swinging doors and answered the call. Cautiously, Roscoff leaned down, looking up from beneath the table. He tried to catch a glimpse of the killers' concealed faces. No such luck. Whoever they were, they appeared nearly identical, including the tattoos. He shook his head and jumped to his feet as Munroe returned.

'What are you doing?'

Roscoff tried to look methodical and bored by procedure. He succeeded. 'Hmm? Oh, nothing. So what can we do at this stage, Munroe?'

He circled the table, pausing when he noticed something else. Another word appeared in the image. The letters appeared to be suspended in the flames of the inferno.

Angels.

This hardly surprised Roscoff, but Munroe didn't and couldn't know that. Roscoff assumed his most melodramatic voice. 'Jesus H. Christ.'

Munroe held his chin, as if afraid to speak. 'What do you mean?'

Roscoff spun around, pretending to be annoyed. 'What do you mean? What the hell is going on?' He thought about the danger surrounding John. 'Enough. I'm going out for some air. I'll be back in ten minutes.'

Roscoff was gone before Munroe could protest. Outside, he walked a quarter of a mile up the road and collapsed on a bench. He'd barely managed to survive being murdered the previous night, and now he had to face more danger. He found a crumpled packet of Marlboros in his pocket and lit a cigarette. It was the best smoke he'd ever had. Until recently, he'd never smoked at all.

When Roscoff returned, Munroe was talking on his phone outside. He appeared close to crying. 'My condolences, Mrs Ross. We'll be in touch about funeral arrangements. Please take care.'

Roscoff offered Munroe a cigarette.

Several minutes later, back in the mortuary, Munroe produced a photograph of one of the daggers. 'I've noticed a connection between the tattoos and the daggers. The writing engraved above each blade looks identical to that.' He pointed at the wings in the tattoo. Each had a series of Roman numerals inside it.

Roscoff nodded.

Munroe looked taken aback. 'What? Do you know what they mean?'

Walking towards a chair, Roscoff paused. *I know what they mean. But I'm not about to tell you.* 'We have three murders, plus an attempted murder.'

Munroe looked increasingly downcast. 'Yes, Vladimir. We've been thoroughly investigating each killing for the past seventy-two hours straight. What does that have to do with anything we see here?'

Roscoff walked past Munroe as if he were alone. Leaving the room, he looked back at Munroe. There was an uncharacteristic inertness in Roscoff's eyes, which frightened Munroe. 'Look at the angel's wings. There are six, and as you so kindly pointed out, a connection with the markings on the wings and daggers. Then that leaves two.'

Munroe's hands shook. Coldness enwrapped him. He swallowed. 'Six take away four leaves two. So what?' He thought for a moment as he leaned against the wall. Somebody had tried to kill Roscoff and failed. Munroe said, 'We need inside information on this cult.'

Outside, Roscoff sat in his car, scrolling through his phone's picture gallery. Then, something else. Munroe wasn't the only suspect. Roscoff had been so busy thinking about John and Eamon that he had almost forgotten Cardinal Domenico Santini. *Of all the serpents in this world, that bastard's disguised as a saint.*

He glanced up and saw two men in cheap suits shaking hands. One clutched a thin file. He had obviously just left a job interview. The shorter man smiled as he walked away. 'Better luck next time.'

Roscoff's foot tapped the pedal a little too hard and the car suddenly revved forward, giving himself and the man-boy a fright. He switched off the radio and removed the keys from the ignition. Just as he turned to go back in, Munroe pulled open the door. He looked as if he hadn't slept in days.

'Who? Who are the other two daggers for, Vladimir?'

Roscoff scoffed. 'How the hell should I know, Charles? If you're panicking about sleeping in your own bed, I suggest you get more protection, like I did, remember?

'Oh, wait. I didn't have any at first, did I? And look.' He mockingly opened his jacket. 'Still here.'

Munroe took out his phone and dialled.

'How's everything?' he repeated. 'How do you think? I don't have time to chat. I want security surrounding my property day and night, 24/7, understand? I have kids.'

After witnessing Munroe's unusual display of dominance, Roscoff lit another cigarette. Never in their entire career together had he heard Munroe sound so simultaneously desperate and authoritative; usually, he sounded merely desperate. *Maybe it's not him. But I'd better keep my wits about me. I'm not crossing anyone off the list, friend or foe.*

At that moment, the receptionist appeared in the

doorway. 'Sorry, gentlemen, but it's close to lunch hour. I have to close in five minutes.'

By the look of her, the receptionist had little else besides lunch to look forward to.

Munroe followed Roscoff back to the examination room. 'Won't be a minute.'

Roscoff once again checked the bodies. 'They don't exactly look like they worship God or anything angelic. Look at the long black hair. The next thing we need is to get these damn messages on the wings translated as soon as possible. Only then can we discover what these bastards have in mind.'

Munroe jotted the suggestion on a notepad. After all the anxiety about his own security, he'd been frequently forgetful of late.

A raised arm appeared behind the pane of glass. A stubby finger tapped the watch face. Munroe and Roscoff dodged around the man, thanking him gloomily as they did so. Just before he went out the entrance, Roscoff noticed an old portable television set on a little table in the corner. A poster of the famous racing horse 'Red Rum' hung behind it. Roscoff squinted, trying to decipher the words on it.

The porter jangled his keys, apologised humbly, and stepped outside. 'Used to be bookies. Only converted six months ago. Had some of my best wins in there.'

I bet he doesn't feel that lucky now.

***

It was almost two o'clock in Berlin. Frankie and Eamon had been with John since midday. Everybody had slept in late due to hangovers. When they finally recovered enough to reach Frankie's BMW, they headed to Kim Chi's Korean restaurant. In the car, everyone was silent, the radio off.

Frankie felt anxious and decided to upset the quiet. 'John, you know Biggins is dead now, don't you? You don't have anything to worry about. You're a free man. We made a pact, a genuine deal. You stuck to it damn well. Your abilities exceeded expectations. I've enjoyed doing business with you.

'Once we get to Kim Chi's, you'll receive your payment. They have a room out back I like to use – fewer eyes. I hope it's the first of many celebratory meals together.'

But John had that faraway look in his eyes. Frankie knew there was something bothering his stand-in partner and that it had nothing to do with casinos or Biggins.

Chapter XLII

By the time they parked near Alexanderplatz, Frankie and John were running ten minutes late. As they climbed out of the car, Frankie checked his watch.

'Don't worry; they allow thirty minutes for a booked table, especially if I ask politely.' He winked at John, who looked pale and depressed.

While Frankie and Eamon tried to decipher John's problem, John watched a crowd gathering outside an electrical store. The people stared at television screens. John panicked as he realised what must be occurring. *Not now. It can't be.*

As he made his way through those gathered, he noticed parents clutching their children's hands, while others seemed agitated or angered. Everyone's attention was fixed firmly on the screens. Meters behind, Frankie and Eamon saw John walking away, so they ran to catch up with him.

John barged through the crowd, for a look at the TV screen in the shop window. BBC World News. Frankie and Eamon stood behind the crowd, shocked, as John shoved people out of the way. More and more pedestrians arrived. People began crying. The camera zoomed in to a speeding white object, aimed directly at one of the World Trade Centre's twin towers.

The object collided with the tower. It instantly exploded. The deafening explosion, combined with the outburst from the crowd, could be heard blocks away.

John suddenly remembered a dream, though he couldn't fully understand the connection between that vision and the scene he'd just witnessed on television. But he did remember two American government banking officials shaking hands, even laughing and toasting one another with their glasses of wine. Though the public trusted their trademark faces, they disguised something dark within themselves. *Sell our faces, then our ideas, then our actions. The world will believe us.*

He had also dreamed of men with darker skin, speaking in Arabic accents. They discussed the value of oil, weaponry, nuclear arms, suicide bombs, gold bullion, and corruption within the government. The memory of their words haunted John like a cursed ghost that had unfinished business.

A hand grabbed John's shoulder, and he found himself facing the present moment. Eamon had shaken him. 'What's happening, John?'

John hardly acknowledged him, neither looking at nor responding to him. Eamon shook John again. John turned to face Eamon. He was lost in thought, here but also somewhere else. Eamon wished he could think John's thoughts and dream his dreams, if only to understand. Eamon felt so helpless and guilty, for nothing he could do would alter what John or anybody else was experiencing. It all seemed to have been plotted by fate.

An attractive middle-aged woman in a white suit appeared on the screen. Normally, newsreaders looked impeccable; this one didn't. Her face was creased in distress, makeup smeared, hair limp. She held the headphone to her ear, struggling to make out the live feedback.

It was no accident. A consensus formed.

'Terrorists.'

'I can't watch this.'

'God help us.'

'Those poor people.'

John said, 'The second plane will come soon.'

'John,' Eamon said, 'what the hell do you mean?'

John shook his head and began weeping, thinking about the young princess on the plane. Minutes passed in a tense draw of breath. The crowd seemed like a single organism and stood transfixed. The next thing they knew, something appeared to fall from the skyscraper on the screen. It was hard to determine what the object had been. Suddenly more and more fell. The camera zoomed towards people leaping. Those who watched would never forget.

Frankie tugged Eamon's sleeve. Eamon stumbled towards the glass. He bent forward, momentarily confused. Another plane. It zoomed towards the second tower. The newswoman read a description into her headset.

Amid the flames, the tower began spitting clouds of dust. Concrete and steel crumbled under the intense heat from the fires. The tower was coming down.

John wished he had the power to freeze the moment and subtract everyone from the equation. Let the incident happen, without victims or witnesses. He felt a pang of curiosity – an idea. *How could, minutes before the crash, the exact target already have been surrounded by the media and world news corporations? They didn't act on impulse or intuition. Might they have been tipped off? Might it have all been planned from the inside, or at least allowed to happen?*

The idea sickened him. He was ashamed to have even considered it. Still, the thought wouldn't release its grip, replaying in his mind like a scratched song on vinyl.

At the bottom of the screen, the newsreel repeated and repeated:

TERRORIST ATTACK. LIVE IN NEW YORK.

Perverted entertainment. John couldn't dismiss the notion that somebody knew exactly what effect the attacks would have. *Planned, it had all been planned. How could they?*

John's mind spun with questions, flashbacks, visions, voices. He had lost all self-control. Everybody knew it was too late for anything to be done. It was finished. History had been made.

***

At that moment, overseas, Roscoff thought about the smashed bodies, which not so long before had begun a normal day's work in an office not unlike his own. How pathetic his day seemed in comparison to theirs. He thought about the American government, the FBI and the CIA. *The most dangerous moments are those you never expected. You are left vulnerable. And even once you become aware, all the protection and secrecy in the world won't save you.*

***

Eamon leaned towards John and gripped him around his shoulders. 'This was in your dream, wasn't it? Terrorism. An attack on America. Planes.'

John's face showed pure malice. 'Nightmares, not dreams.'

From a camera at street level, just across from the tower, people could be seen scattering and running for shelter, like insects. Some hadn't been successful. Black dust and debris had already fogged the streets. Some would die from lung failure, inhalation. Others managed to dive low just in time.

The external impact and force of the explosion was too much for nearby glass to withstand.

John studied the screen. How would a plane have managed to reach such high velocity that it bypassed the safety structure of a building constructed to support each level? If one layer happened to collapse, why shouldn't the next support it?

Others would ask the same questions. It might forever remain a mystery. Possibly, it was meant to remain a mystery forever.

Frankie dragged Eamon backwards. Fortunately for Frankie, he had missed the news, as his vision had been blocked by an exceptionally tall onlooker. Frankie's voice was soft but confrontational. 'I think you missed something in our little chat before. I have to understand John, Eamon. You just saw his visions fulfil themselves.

'I can't believe I didn't figure it out. This is why Biggins wanted John so badly. It never had anything to do with card games.

'The cards – John could see them under the dealer's hand. I finally understand how.'

'Enough,' Eamon said. 'This isn't the time.'

Frankie said, 'Actually, Eamon, this is the perfect time. Schizophrenia? I can't recall hearing of a schizophrenic predicting a disaster or winning every card game he ever played. I knew he was different, but judging by what I've just seen, not only is he different, he's special.

'So tell me, what do you think will happen when that gets out? We have to make decisions now. If you want the best for John, you'd better put some trust in me because you won't get far without me, and you know it.'

Eamon winced in resignation. He moved past several people, everyone weeping, who had rushed over at the last minute. He pulled his jacket together. 'Then I need you to hypnotise John again. It seemed to work last time. You hold the key. Only you can help John now.'

Frankie nodded confidently.

***

Roscoff bit his fingernails and stared ahead, still watching, as he had from the start, 9/11 unfold on his television screen. He was one of millions of viewers. Finally, he walked to the window. The cool breeze bore the scent of rain.

Looking down, Roscoff watched cars heading towards their drivers' day-to-day business, as if nothing had happened. Concrete slabs several floors below and everything blurred, and he wished he could blame the rain for the wetness in his eyes.

An ambulance siren sounded from somewhere in the distance. He felt estranged off from his surroundings. Nothing seemed real, yet the pounding in his chest continued. *What a dilemma. I've absolutely no idea what I can do. Worse, what will I do with Young Tierney?*

***

Munroe was sitting alone in his office, behind the desk. The mobile phone in front of him began to ring and ring and ring. Then it stopped. He thought he must have gone deaf or mad. He looked down at the phone's screen. He'd missed ten calls from Casey Miller. Then it rang again, and this time he answered.

'Charles, we have to talk. I'm under a shitload of pressure. My phone's ringing itself to death. I reported our meeting to high command, but I didn't describe everything I saw. We have to get our story straight. My ass is on the line.'

'It would seem that your head was so far up your arse before, you didn't listen to what I said. Now both our heads are in the toilet.'

'Charles, don't cave in on me. We need to talk about

the boy. I need answers now. I'm gonna book another flight with my advisors. It's our last hope.'

Munroe switched off the phone. It slid out of his grip and fell to the floor. If Miller showed up, Roscoff's brain would unravel everything – the tape from the master recorder that Ross had made, from which he had found out about the terrorist attack; the dreams John had been having; all of it obvious. Roscoff had other sources of information he didn't share, one problem after the next.

Munroe opened a drawer. The bottle inside looked like gold in the light. No excuse floated at the bottom of it. He opened the bottle, anyway.

***

The sun had set rapidly. The beams of light through the church windows dimmed. Cardinal Santini prayed on his knees. He pushed against the cold stone floor, struggling to stand. He pulled the gold watch chain hanging from his robes. Not much time.

He hurried towards the confession box, his breathing strained. Any minute now, the 'messenger' would arrive. The previous task had not run as smoothly as planned. The messenger would set the next challenge.

The cardinal sat in the dark hollow, inhaling the residue of incense. A few minutes passed. Somebody turned the iron handle on the main door, which a moment later slammed shut. Footsteps, loud and fast. The messenger approached the box.

Cardinal Santini frowned. Something wasn't right. The messenger was supposed to be a man, but the footsteps sounded like they were made by someone wearing high heels. *Maybe they're a man's shoes just the same*, he reasoned. A medley of thoughts playing in his consciousness nullified his other senses.

Then sudden breathing next to the cardinal caused

him to flinch. He turned to his left silently and reached out, touching the square piece of cloth. 'Is that you, messenger?'

At first no answer, then a whisper. The cardinal couldn't make out whether the voice was male or female. His black cat purred around his feet as he leaned towards the dividing wall. He strained to hear the words from the messenger. This time the words were more clear for the cardinal to hear.

'Nel nome del Padre del Figlio e dello Spirito Santo.'

This was something the cardinal usually said to his visiting confessors, or was it the cardinal that had a secret to confess?

Chapter XLIII

Roscoff had opened his laptop. Over the Internet, he purchased two tickets to Berlin for the next morning, one for himself, the other for the soon-to-be-released Dermot.

Roscoff glanced at the blank television screen. He felt a guilty sense of relief that he had the ability to turn it all off, though he had hardly forgotten what he had witnessed. He reached for his phone.

'Eamon, are you there?'

'Vladimir. Let me find somewhere quiet okay.

'Now I can hear ya better. What's going on?'

'I'm flying to Berlin in the morning, with your brother. Remember our agreement about the books and transcripts? You told me about the images involving a satanic cult you didn't understand. I think it's time I saw the evidence for myself, before they wipe out my entire unit. And I must speak with John.'

'You know I promised my father nobody else would see the book. But you've shown your trust in me. I never contemplated showing it to you before. I can put that down to bad experiences.'

At that moment, it seemed they had arrived where they had started.

***

Eamon hung up, walked back, and joined John and Frankie in the room. They had decided they would return to Kim Chi's. Once there, John took a slow sip of the Jasmine tea. Frankie lit a cigarette. Eamon sat down, tucking away his phone.

'How are you feeling, John?' Frankie said. 'What are you thinking about?'

'That child, that poor child.'

'Which child, John?'

John stared into his mug.

'The dream was so vivid the second time around. A dark tunnel appeared, as if I was on a rollercoaster. Then the real ride started. Twisting about, upside down, going at a slow pace. Then I see the light at the end of the tunnel. Next thing I know, I'm sitting next to the child on the plane. The nose of the plane had been ripped off and my feet were just hanging, nothing below them but endless sky.

'Two terrorists had stood in the aisle. One had a gun. The other pulled out a knife. I looked down. There was a sweet child sitting next to me, just sitting and holding her teddy bear. The mother had gone mad and had forgotten her child altogether. The plane veered off towards its destination. The Twin Towers appeared in the distance. I could see the clouds of smoke from the first crash, rising. One of the terrorists kneeled and prayed. I knew we only had seconds left, and I grabbed the child's hand.

'She stared at me as if to say, *Only my daddy can do that.* I smiled at her as best I could. Then she became an adult with beautiful blue eyes and golden hair. As the plane was about to plunge into the tower, everything dissolved into a bright flash of white brilliance. Then I awoke in the casino, and I had to concentrate on playing fucking cards.'

He punched the wall. Frankie observed him tolerantly. Eamon jumped up. 'John, there was nothing you could do! You don't have to feel like this. It's not your problem.'

John laughed wryly. 'It's not my problem? Then what's this gift I've been given, eh? It's been given to me for a reason, Eamon! Look, I'll talk to you in the morning. I need some space.' He swerved around the table and jogged out of the room.

Eamon ran after him, stopping in the doorway. 'John, wait. Where are you going?'

John shouted a reply without looking back. 'To see Rosi, and I'm going alone.'

Frankie said to Eamon, 'Let him go. My security team's on it. They'll put a man in the pub before he ever gets there. He'll no doubt stay at Rosi's tonight. My men will be watching her place, too. Someone will be watching him everywhere. You must relax, Eamon.'

But Eamon was struggling to catch his breath. He called the one person of use to him.

'Lisa, it's Eamon. John is on the way to see you and Rosi.'

'Rosi's not here; she left.'

'What?'

'To Bulgaria, I think. Her mother was ill.'

'Jesus. But she's out of harm's way. Good news, I suppose.'

'That's not all. I was tidying the flat yesterday, and I found a pregnancy test.'

'And?'

'Positive. When I think about it, she had been upset for a few days, constantly asking where John had gone. I told her what you told me to tell her. That upset her even more. What do I say to John when he gets here?'

'Nothing, except that Rosi went to see her mother.'

He ended the call. Soon, John would discover the truth.

Frankie flexed his fingers, staring at Eamon.

'We have to hypnotise him,' Eamon said. 'He sees things more clearly afterwards, doesn't he?'

Frankie considered the situation and finally said, 'I'll do it, but it's best we don't warn him. He'll think he's going for a normal session, like last time. At least that way he won't get nervous. Maybe the outcome will be different this time. You wait in the background, and make sure he doesn't see you.'

***

Roscoff leaned back in his leather armchair. He was smoking again. After having informed Maria of Dermot's upcoming release, he arranged for a car that would take them to the airport the next morning. Meanwhile, he enjoyed a Chopin CD, but the office phone interrupted.

Roscoff paused the music and answered the phone.

Ten seconds later, he slammed it down. *Another murder. The cardinal? Why would they want to kill the cardinal?*

***

Munroe picked up his mobile phone. 'H-hello. Vladimir. What can I—'

'Meet me at the Church of Holy Mary in twenty minutes.'

Munroe pulled on his suit jacket, locked his office door, and made his way down to the car park. Twenty minutes later, he found himself viewing yet another murder scene.

Roscoff beckoned to him. 'Come closer. We have a problem here.'

Kneeling for a better look at the cardinal's face, Munroe said, 'Who was he?'

Roscoff stepped back, resisting the urge to vomit. The murderer had not only stabbed the cardinal but choked him with the watch chain afterwards. The chain was embedded in the neck, below the dagger, the wound crusted with blood.

'He was a highly ranked cardinal. I found out about him from Tierney's parents. He wanted to meet John, but for some reason, John never showed up despite several appointments.'

The cardinal's watch still ticked.

Munroe stared at the dagger. 'Everything's connected to Tierney. The fourth murder, and always with a knife, as if they want us to find out what they're doing. The knives are bait. They're leading us somewhere.'

Roscoff looked again at the wound. 'But why kill the cardinal? What about the other two? They were from Rome, too. They accompanied the cardinal when he met with Tierney's parents.

'I think we should bring Rose and Christopher down to the morgue. Maybe they can identify the bodies. That would clear up one thing.'

He held his forehead, partly from a headache and partly to shield his thinking from Munroe. *I've no choice but to tell Munroe I'm headed for Berlin.* He remembered the morgue. He called Maria.

'Organise a meeting. Contact Rose and Christopher Bronks. Tell them we need them at the morgue. It's crucial. A car will pick them up.'

Munroe walked towards Roscoff. 'What are you doing? You can't smoke in church.'

'I think murder beats smoking in the sin department, don't you?' He lit the cigarette.

'Munroe, I'm taking a flight to Berlin tomorrow morning. We need the results from the weapon examination

267

at the lab. Keep me informed about anything and everything that concerns Tierney. Hear me?'

Munroe seemed offended. 'I need to know what's happening with Tierney first. How else can I tell you anything?'

Roscoff shook his head. 'I think the real reason you need to know is because you're planning your own project. Gonna try to kidnap him again? I find it funny that you seem to forget you tried twice and failed already. What's the plan this time, Charles?'

Munroe tried to mask his embarrassment by redirecting Roscoff's attention. 'Tomorrow, the CIA arrives here. For the record, I taped the interview you had with Eamon that night, which, I might add, you failed to report. Luckily, I have other friends. I had them search the U.S., internal, and international airports, not to mention the private airstrips scattered across the fucking country. And what about you? Your ego took over the whole situation, as usual.'

Vladimir knew Munroe had a point. With John's dreams beginning to materialise and the increasing evidence, his breach easily overshadowed any wrong move Munroe had made.

Why must I reveal everything to Munroe, when I did the hard work and attended to every detail? I'm the one Eamon trusts. Still, I have to tell him. For Christ's sake, I even have to tell Maria, or she might start wondering about my travels and meetings.

'Follow me,' Roscoff said.

He passed the angel statue and entered the cardinal's private room where they had met only days before. Munroe closed the door behind them.

'Listen to me, Charles, since I have to spell it out. Eamon doesn't trust you. I need Eamon's trust because we won't get the information we need without his input. We're so close now that we can soon end this charade.'

Munroe folded his arms. 'Then go to Berlin, but you have to bring him in. John needs our protection and nobody else's. The agency always comes first, as you know or used to know.'

Roscoff realised that Munroe made sense. He had never felt so much self-doubt.

Munroe said, 'Casey Miller will get here in the morning. He'll want to question Young Tierney. I'll hold him off for a while but only a few days. You'll be lucky to get a week to bring John here.'

'How much does Casey already know?'

'Casey's tough to convince. He couldn't absorb what I told him about Young Tierney. But now, he can't get his arse here fast enough, if for no other reason than to cover his own arse.'

For once, Roscoff saw eye to eye with Munroe. He felt culpable for holding back information. He spun around and walked over to Munroe, an inch of space between their faces. 'You may well have listened to what Eamon told me about the book, but you didn't hear what he told me in the car as we drove back. He couldn't work it out. He spoke of an angel that had six wings and the head of a creature with seven horns. Somehow, it's connected to Young Tierney.

'The book says they'll come for him. They go by the name of the Angelic Angels. The book describes them only as the dark side of the Church. What Eamon doesn't understand is that the book also says they're protectors, protectors of the high priest, until the time of the sacrifice. This hints that the high priest could be sacrificed himself."

Munroe gasped in horror. Though the names were mostly new to him, he could tell the magnitude of the matter merely by the way Roscoff pronounced them, aside from the series of murders of course. He held his shirt collar tight, as if to shield against a sharp wind. 'We need the book! We must get back to working together, before it's too late!'

Roscoff shrugged, walking away. 'Find out about the knives. That will be a start.'

To the advantage of both parties, it seemed their working relationship was back on in a difficult time, when trust was lacking. When Roscoff got to the door, he turned around and sighed. 'I'll see you tomorrow, Charles.'

Munroe forced a shaky grin. 'Sure thing.'

***

Frankie and Eamon were back at the apartment where John had been staying. As Eamon had suggested, Lisa told John that Rosi had gone back to Bulgaria so she could visit her sick mother.

At that moment, a key turned in the lock. John appeared.

Eamon switched off the television. 'Is everything all right, John?'

'It's late. I'm going to bed now.' He turned to leave the room, then returned. 'From now on, when I say I'm going alone, I go alone.' He pointed his finger at Frankie and Eamon. 'I don't like being followed. I'm going to the bathroom now, in case you want to watch.'

In the kitchen, Frankie closed the door and put on the kettle. 'Whatever we do now, he'll know about it.'

Eamon said, 'I know. I've just found out Rosi's pregnant, and I told her John went back to England.'

'That he what?'

'It's simple. He doesn't want to see her anymore.'

'You couldn't have picked a better time. He'll find out about it; that's for sure.'

The kettle whistled and clouds of steam formed around them.

***

Drifting through an entirely different type of cloud, Casey Miller watched the sky from a CIA jet, on schedule to touch down in Newmarket an hour later.

Miller received a message on his laptop. It was from his boss, General Hanks, the only person with whom he had shared John's story. Within the ranks of the Pentagon, Hanks was second in command. Miller opened the file. The message appeared centre screen:

> After analysing the information you gave us, we have discovered that these births are extremely rare. This individual could pose a threat to society. Therefore, he has been categorized as a Section 151, with immediate effect.

Miller touched the message as if he could feel its meaning. *What the hell's a Section 151? I made a deal with the general. All operations and information will be clandestine. The Pentagon committee will stay in the dark.* Miller just wanted to clean up matters, but matters had become even more complicated.

***

Back in the United Kingdom, it was eight o'clock in the morning. Dermot had finally been released. Roscoff made sure Munroe gave the order, since Eamon hated Munroe's guts.

Dermot and Munroe left the station and headed to Gatwick airport, where they would meet Roscoff. Half an hour later, they pulled up in a busy car park. Dermot checked his ticket and passport. 'Thanks for the lift. No doubt we'll be hearing from ya soon.'

'No problem,' Munroe said. 'Not all that bad, was it?'

'Don't push it.'

He found the entrance and Roscoff fumbling with a cigarette. 'Good to see you, Dermot. Let's get rid of our bags and grab a coffee. We have a few minutes.'

***

Frankie and Eamon sat in a breakfast bar in Berlin's busy city centre.

'So,' Frankie said, 'we've agreed John will be hypnotised in the apartment and that we'll record it?'

Eamon looked around to see if anyone was listening. 'Yeah. It's the safest bet. This way might work better.' Eamon poured coffee for them both. 'Once Roscoff gets here, I'll make a deal with him. I need to get a closer look at the murder weapons, like the one used to kill Biggins.'

Frankie paused then said, 'Oh, yes, the murders. They're connected to all of this? And how?'

'I wish I knew.'

Eamon thought about his private vault at the bank, where the book had been kept for years. Frankie had accompanied Eamon to the bank the night before, after John had arrived at the apartment. Surprisingly, John asked no questions about it.

As events escalated, Eamon felt swallowed by the book itself. True, there was the honour of Nostradamus having chosen his generation for the prophecy. But the knives, unlike everything else, hadn't been described in the book. Finding the connection might require showing it to Roscoff. It was a matter of time before everything fell into place. Sacrifices had to be made.

***

Across town, the plane carrying Roscoff and Dermot had landed. They called a taxi and took it to the city.

Roscoff called Eamon from inside the taxi..

'Good morning, Eamon. In case you hadn't guessed, we're here. I need you to meet me somewhere, but I've never been here before. Where can we get some privacy?'

Eamon remembered a café John had mentioned. 'Tell the driver you wanna go to Pariserstrasse, a café called Okey. It's a good place.'

'Be there.'

Frankie returned from the bathroom. 'Are they here?'

'I've gotta go, Frankie. Roscoff wants a chat.'

Frankie nodded. *I need to get more involved.* 'I'm going to see John. I'll ask him to join me for a session this afternoon. Actually, you might as well get a lift with me.'

***

Ten minutes later, Eamon arrived at the café. Roscoff glanced up. 'I used to enjoy my coffee. Now I drink it black and wash it down with paracetamol. 'I'm confused about the murders. I want John back in England. We have an ongoing murder enquiry. It's for his own safety.' Eamon wasn't letting Roscoffs headache disappear.'

'No way.'

Roscoff felt so overworked that drinking coffee felt like weightlifting. 'I know what you're thinking. It's all about trust, Eamon.'

'Trust is your problem.'

Roscoff lit a cigarette. 'We must move on from distrust. We're so close. This is not just about murders; it runs a lot deeper. It's all leading somewhere. So, do you have the book?'

The waiter placed a glass of orange juice on the table. 'I won't take the chance.'

'But you have the book?'

'Yes.'

Roscoff revealed a sudden optimism. 'Can I see it?'

'In a week or so. When you think it's safe for John to return, then he'll return. He'll make the decision.'

'Fine. I want to see John. Where is he?'

'Nice try, but you're taking things a bit far and fast. No more risks. We'll discuss John later.'

Roscoff blew smoke to his left. *Obviously, Eamon's being deliberately obstinate. He wants things his way.* 'Look, Munroe isn't a bad guy, Eamon. He's on our side, but he operates differently. It would serve us both well to remember that.'

Eamon couldn't help but laugh. 'That's your opinion. Just keep him away from me as long as you can.' He whispered, 'And if you want to see the book, we'd best get going.'

Eamon, Dermot, and Roscoff hailed a taxi and headed back to the hotel that Eamon was staying at.

***

John's hypnosis session with Frankie had begun. John believed he was in for massage and meditation.

***

Charles Munroe heard a knock on the door of his office. Miller entered, struggling with two large cases.

'Casey, I'm so glad to see you.' Munroe poured himself a glass of whisky. Then, instead of offering to help Miller the luggage, drank his whisky and held the door open.

Casey dragged the bags into a corner. 'Rotten weather. Always the goddam same here.'

'Catch yourself a drink. I'm sure as hell not wasting my whisky on you.'

Casey laughed, but Munroe didn't share the hilarity. 'I know I underestimated what you had to say, Charles—'

Munroe interrupted him. 'You underestimate everybody, Casey, including me. That's your problem. You just can't take someone else being right for a change.'

Casey suddenly found the table fascinating. Munroe had taken charge.

He held out his arm, gesturing for Casey to take a seat. 'Things have become rather intricate. We have an ongoing murder investigation, and John Tierney is in Berlin, under surveillance. It could be at least a week before we bring him in.'

'Let's talk about it over breakfast tomorrow.'

Munroe held back a smile. *I'm keeping my promise to Roscoff, but I'm not putting my neck on the line. Miller will just have to learn the hard way.* He switched on the TV. The attack on the Twin Towers appeared and reappeared on the news. Munroe quickly switched the television off again.

Chapter XLIV

Roscoff and Eamon pulled up in a taxi outside the Adlon Hotel, after first dropping Dermot off at the Irish pub.

Roscoff looked up. 'Talk about low profile. Good job it's you staying here and not John. You could bump into anyone here.'

Eamon replied, 'Never mind that.'

A group of Chinese tourists huddled. One reached for his camera and took several snaps. Roscoff frowned at the camera's bright flashes. Cursing, he grabbed his bag and headed for the entrance, where the porter greeted him in Russian.

Здравствуйте, сэр, каким образом вы

'How did you know?'

The attendant pointed at Roscoff's case. 'I have one just like it. They're only available in Moscow.'

They chatted about the bars and other places they knew in Russia. Then Roscoff walked to the lobby, where Eamon sat reading a magazine.

'About time. Anyway, never mind this place. Keep your focus on the book, if you want to see it so badly.'

They took a lift to the fifth floor. Eamon had chosen

this room because it was farthest from the elevator. Should anyone try to steal the book, it would take longer to escape the hotel with it.

Roscoff placed his bag down by the bed and went straight to the minibar. 'I need a drink.' His hands were sweaty as he opened a miniature bottle of whisky with his teeth. He sat on the bed and drank it straight down. Eamon leaned against the doorframe, clearing his throat.

'Here, put these surgical gloves on. We have to preserve the contents of the casket.'

Eamon dimmed the light and left the curtains closed as Roscoff put on the gloves. Kneeling, Eamon reached under the bed and retrieved a large wooden box. His hands began to shake nervously, and rightly so. Other than someone belonging to the Tierney clan, Roscoff just so happened to be the first person to see inside the casket in over four centuries.

Eamon removed a set of keys from his trouser pocket. He had to push two buttons, which were actually rods that projected deep inside the casket, releasing the lock. The casket opened. He looked at Roscoff and gulped then reached inside and cautiously removed a rectangular-shaped object wrapped in a thick red cloth.

Looking over Eamon's shoulder, Roscoff moved in closer. Eamon removed the cloth and exposed the contents of the cloth. Immediately, a brilliant golden light pierced the thickness of the red cloth and projected the shape of a pentacle onto the ceiling above. At last, Roscoff's wish had been granted.

'My God, Eamon, it's incredible." Roscoff hovered his fingers over the book.

Eamon snapped, 'Careful, old man.'

The ancient leather-bound exterior was interwoven with pure strands of gold, solid as wood but flexible as parchment.

The centre was slightly curved, where many pairs of Tierney hands had gripped it over the centuries.

'Eamon, this book is a treasure. I don't know where it came from, but it's not from this earth.'

Eamon smiled.

'It's said the book came from within the mythical Ark of the Covenant and accompanied the Tablets of Stone on which the Ten Commandments were inscribed, along with Aaron's rod and manna. Being secret, there was never any mention of a book.'

Roscoff was now wide awake.

'The Ark was said to have been stolen from the Temple of Solomon and hidden by Jeremiah in the sixth century BC. After its disappearance, it was never mentioned again until the Knights Templar found the Ark at Wadi Musa, which is now southern Jordan.

'It's not certain how the Templars acquired the book, as it was said that King David removed the book before the Ark was supposedly buried under the watchful eye of Horus in a sacred tomb in Egypt.'

'You have to be kidding me, Eamon. Surely, none of this can surely be true.'

'Roscoff, this book has graced the hands of every prophet since time began,' he said as he watched Roscoff carefully turning the first page.

'Wow, that's wild, but tell me why you told me earlier that you had lost this book, Eamon?'

Eamon stood and peeped through the window. Paranoia was starting to creep in.

'Come on, Roscoff; you didn't think I actually trusted you back then, did you? We copied the original a long time ago, Vladimir, which, from now on, will be the only book we shall use. I only allowed you to see the original to prove to you my honesty.

'The copy has been translated into English to make it easier to understand. As you can see, this version is a mixture of Hebrew and Arabic. Please, be careful turning the pages.'

Roscoff turned several pages. The visual and physical fusion of the whole experience was overwhelming. Among the yellows and golds, he felt a glittery texture of the finest silks upon his fingertips, until suddenly the pages stopped turning. Roscoff froze as his eyes came across an incredibly familiar image.

'This picture, the angel – it's the same as the tattoos found on the backs of the cult members we killed - Ross and I killed, I should say.'

'Yes, it's the cult of the Angelic Angels. They're from a religious order that materialised centuries ago. Each member serves as guardian of the high priest of the church.'

'But if that's true, why would they kill a cardinal?'

Eamon walked over and switched on the main light. 'I'm as confused as you when it comes to that.'

Roscoff was so absorbed that he seemed oblivious to anything else. Eamon tapped his shoulder. Roscoff ignored him. He noticed something he'd never seen before, though it had been right in front of him the whole time.

'Here's something else. The image of the angel is suspended in some kind of compass circle. North points east. South points west. And I see roman numerals inside the circle. What do they mean?'

Eamon didn't bother looking at the image, the details embedded in his memory. 'From north to west, it reads, *35, 20, 19,* 85. From south to west, it reads, *17, 59, 30, 33*. As far as I know, the inner circle beneath the first points to a date.'

'Past or present?'

Eamon brought a beer back from the mini bar. 'I know the first one reads 2012, and the second one reads 2023.'

Roscoff swallowed for air. 'So, according to our location, our global position runs from east to west. Well, if I recall my history lessons correctly, we were told that the River Nile used to run in the same direction. Of course, it's different today, but then again, what's not? If that's true, it's telling us when the predicted events will occur, the very dates John already dreamed about.'

Eamon agreed without saying so.

'Hold on, Vladimir. You forget that a compass circle is a direction-finding device.'

Roscoff was agitated and shouted back, 'Yes, of course, but which direction? And to what? A nuclear strike? The direction of wind and rain? How the hell should we know?'

Eamon turned more pages. 'Because it's written here.' He pointed down at a paragraph and read. '"Discover the knives, and ye shall fulfil thy destiny." But here, it says, "If thy choice be amiss for the high caulbearer, thy destiny shall be forever lost."'

'Whose destiny?'

'Humankind's.'

Upon hearing these words, Roscoff knew why he never could have understood the threat, had Eamon not shown him the book.

'And why the murders, Eamon?'

Eamon paced the room. 'I'm not sure. Nostradamus wrote in the blank pages at the back of the sacred book that on the night of October 13, 1307, throughout France, King Philip's seneschals arrested the Templars. Jacques de Molay's five guardians Templar were murdered. Each was noble to his oath but alas, each was restrained and stabbed in the neck, always on the left side.

'With his guardians murdered, de Molay was arrested, but because he was Grand Master, the Church had sent three cardinals to perform the duty.

'Under the instruction of King Philip, de Molay was burned at the stake but only after years of imprisonment. As far as the Catholic Church was concerned, over a period of time, the Knights Templar had all but been eradicated, all except one called Vladimir, whom Jacques de Molay himself sent away to protect the secret bloodline.

'As the last Templar, Vladimir tracked down the cardinals, who were heading back towards Rome. With his newly recruited younger disciples, he ambushed the cardinals just inside the French border and secretly burned them at the stake. Not only did he manage to reclaim what had been stolen from Jacques de Molay, but he recovered the daggers used to murder the Knights.'

'Are you saying that these are the same daggers used to kill Biggins, Ross, and Mullins?'

Eamon closed the book. 'Exactly. It's important that you understand the engravings on them were made at a later stage, by the Templar himself.'

'I still can't piece it together. The Angelic Angels – who are they?'

'The last Templar united with a group of monks belonging to an ancient religious order. Some of them, under secret oaths, became his disciples and were known as the Angelic Angels. Over the years, there was little mention of the Templar. It seems the Templar and his disciples had all but disappeared, never to be seen or mentioned again. Only the monks and their seneschals remained.'

Roscoff thought back to the previous day, when he and Munroe had met at the church. 'So that's why the cardinal was murdered. What deep roots.'

Eamon sat next to Roscoff. 'Nostradamus had a secret

child, whose mother had died giving birth. The monks raised the child. Accompanying the child was a sacred book and from Papyrus parchments within the book, a list was recorded, written by the Brotherhood of Nazarenes dating back many hundreds of years. It was a list of Brotherhood members who had been born with a caul. The list showed that Moses and Jesus were high priest caulbearers and that Nostradamus and Jacques de Molay were also born with a caul.

'Being born with a caul was an automatic entry card into the Brotherhood at the highest level. It was said that the high priests could predict where and when the next caulbearer would be born. Those members of the Brotherhood who were not caulbearers were servants of *the way.*'

Roscoff held his hands to his ears. 'I don't know if I can take much more of this. It's as if this book goes on and on. I can't see the end.'

Eamon calmly said, 'Vladimir, I must see the knives, as soon as possible.'

Trying to remember his plan, Roscoff said, 'And I need to see John. I have a few questions that need answering. You know I'm under pressure to take John back to England. I need true answers this time.'

Eamon stood and opened the curtains. Sunlight flooded the room. 'When Frankie finishes with John, we'll go see him.'

'Who's Frankie? And what's he doing with John?'

Eamon delicately wrapped the book in the red cloth, returning the book to the casket and into the safety of the storage box. 'Frankie's like you, someone I've come to trust. Remember me saying that John had trouble remembering his dreams? Frankie knows how to get at the dreams, or to help John do so. Frankie's our key.' As soon as he said the words, Eamon regretted the revelation.

Roscoff looked unimpressed. 'Go on.'

'He's going to hypnotise John again.'

'Again?'

'He found out about John by accident. Now I believe that was meant to happen, and I trust Frankie.'

Roscoff hunched his shoulders. *A stranger understands John's mind, after everything I've done in this case.*

Eamon went to stash the box in the bathroom. When he returned, Roscoff grabbed his jacket.

'And what happened after the first attempt?'

'Nothing that we didn't know already, except he got specifics out of John, and that would be the words 'Twin Towers'.

Roscoff looked away. *How can he act so casually? But, yes, for Eamon, none of this, even the attacks, comes as a surprise, not the way it did everyone else. He has known about it all his life.*

On the way to the lobby, Roscoff spotted a sign pointing towards the café. 'Do you mind if we get something to eat before we leave?'

Chapter XLV

The clouds crept across the skyline, blocking the sun. Munroe and Miller had long since finished breakfast. Back at the office, Munroe crossed his legs and continued their intense conversation. 'And that's about the whole story.'

Miller asked, 'When did you say Roscoff arrives back in town?'

Munroe tilted his head back. 'By the end of the week, I hope.'

'End of the week? A fucking week? You've seen the news and the thousands dead. For all I know, you're withholding vital information. Americans have a good relationship with Brits, but you still owe me, Charles.'

Expecting this counteroffensive, Munroe walked straight past him. He stood by the window and took out his phone. When in doubt, he always called Roscoff.

'Hi, Vladimir. Miller is with me. We need to know more about Young Tierney. You can talk to him through my loudspeaker. Give me a second.'

'I'm doing my best. With any luck, by the end of the week, you can question John yourself.'

Miller walked over to the speaker. 'Tierney's our number

one suspect. We have to interview him. You'd better come up with something good, and do it fast. Alternatively, I'll take a flight to Berlin in the next twenty-four hours. As it stands, you're breaking departmental rules. You know how it works, Vladimir.'

Roscoff laughed, which took Miller aback. 'That's great, coming from you, Miller. Now you don't trust me or what? You Americans have short memories. As far as department rules go, why don't you try investigating the missing Russian oil files? But I know how you must be feeling, Casey. Just give me till the end of the week. I can piece this all together.'

Miller looked at Munroe and nodded. Roscoff was in the driver's seat, and there was nothing Miller could do about it.

'The best I can do is forty-eight hours, Vladimir.'

'Okay, I suppose that'll have to do.'

***

In the hotel restaurant, Roscoff placed a spoon back into his empty bowl and wiped his mouth with a napkin. Dermot paid the bill, and they all waited outside for a taxi. Roscoff sat in back. 'Where are we going, Eamon?'

'To see Frankie.'

When they arrived at the casino, Frankie was already waiting for them, with a minder in tow.

'Frankie,' Eamon said. 'Meet Vladimir Roscoff.'

'A pleasure. I've heard a lot about you, Mr Roscoff.'

Roscoff looked sideways at Eamon. 'Likewise.'

They turned and walked up the steps. Eamon held open the door. 'Is John still sleeping?'

Roscoff was eager to hear Frankie's response.

'Yes. It's been a long and interesting day. If we go upstairs, you can listen to the recording.'

***

Munroe pressed the button and rolled up the car

window. Drops of rain dotted the dashboard. He glanced over at Miller. They stopped at a red light. Munroe pressed the FM button. The radio news broadcast was still covering the attacks. Miller tuned it to serene music then turned off the stereo system altogether.

Munroe pushed the accelerator. 'I was listening to that.'

Miller shook his head. 'Let's concentrate on security threats.'

Munroe opened the opposite window. Rain blew in Miller's face. He slid a CD into the slot. 'You're CIA. You should know more than I do. I was only trying to take your mind off the subject.'

The car slowed as they turned into the car park behind MI5 headquarters. From his previous visit to the lab, Miller knew secret documents were kept there.

After Munroe buzzed in with his card, they walked a bit and greeted Roscoff's secretary, Maria, who had been waiting for them. She stood directly in front of Miller. 'Sir, no other personnel are authorised to pass beyond this point without two members of staff present.'

Munroe smiled. 'Company rules from a secretary. That's correct, Maria. That's why you're the company's favourite secretary.'

She displayed a clipboard. 'Mr Miller, you're required to sign here. It's routine for me to photocopy your security clearance.'

Miller dug into his pockets and checked his jacket. 'I don't have it with me.'

'Then I must deny access, sir.'

Munroe said, 'Maria, Maria, Mr Miller works for the CIA. We can overlook this just once.'

Maria pointed to the CCTV surveillance camera. Both

men looked up. Munroe rolled his eyes. *Lame. As if she'd take the heat.*

Maria said, 'Access still denied for obvious reasons. I cannot allow you inside.'

Munroe's blood pressure soared.

Miller didn't seem so concerned. 'I understand. I'll call my advisor and arrange for a copy to be faxed straightaway.'

***

Meanwhile, back at the casino, Frankie switched off the television. Roscoff watched dust drift through the beams of sunlight shining through gaps in the blinds. Never had he seen anything so worrying. Rather than the satisfaction he'd expected, the viewing had drained him. *What must it have been like for John to go through it all that time, knowing what he knows?*

Frankie turned to face Eamon and Roscoff, who sat side by side on the opposite sofa. 'John's mind is abnormal, too many thoughts circulating – a riddle he can almost grasp but never solves.'

Eamon stared at the dull screen. 'From what we know, the explosion in the sea must be linked to the wind and rain direction blowing at terrific speed. He said it will be nuclear?'

Roscoff took out his cigarettes and offered one to Frankie, who accepted. 'But John has already confirmed that for us, Eamon. We need to know when it will happen.'

Frankie lit Roscoff's cigarette. 'John also spoke of a newborn child with hands covered in blood.'

Eamon sharply said, 'I told you he'd find out. It was just a matter of time. Fucking bullshit.'

'What are you both talking about?'

Eamon beat Frankie to the explanation. 'John met a girl here. We think she's pregnant by him. She went home to

Bulgaria. We told her John didn't want to see her anymore. Obviously, this upset her, and that's why she left. John knows something about the situation, but not the whole story. He thinks she went to visit her sick mother. We can't let him find out the truth.'

Roscoff tried to make sense of this new thread. Another pregnancy in the Tierney bloodline was the last thing anyone needed.

'I think,' Frankie said, "it's too late for that, Eamon. He'll work out that problem pretty quickly. He works out tougher ones.'

They both looked at Roscoff, as ghostly as Eamon seemed demonic in anger – that or he was drunk again, and a little early in the day by anyone's standards.

'Frankie, you asked him about the terrorists and the Twin Towers,' Roscoff said. 'Why?'

'I remember the first time I hypnotised him. He mentioned a train bomb, somewhere in Europe. That's the next target.' He flicked his cigarette ash out of the open window.

With a mouthful of coffee, Roscoff swallowed a paracetamol tablet. 'On two different occasions, John spoke of palm trees, hiding behind some palm trees or something like that. What could that possibly mean?'

'Who can tell? That's where he lost me. But the dream scared him, that's for sure.'

'Did you question him about that?'

'No. He was exhausted. I let him sleep.'

Roscoff seized the tape from the video player. 'Then we need to take this back with us, since John is staying here.'

Frankie issued no objection. They left the room in single file. Roscoff patted the videotape in his pocket. More proof, safely in my hands.

***

Back at MI5, the copy of Miller's passport had arrived via fax. Maria reluctantly granted access. Miller followed Munroe up the stairs. 'It seems your secretary took a disliking to me.'

'I can't say I blame her, really.

Italians don't do Americans any favours, you know.'

They entered the main office. Munroe switched on the TV. Maria drifted into the room, clutching files, and passed them to Miller.

'So,' Miller said, reading from the files, 'the boy was born in 1971. His so-called skin was sold for twelve pounds, bought by two sailors from the HMS *Sheffield*, the ship that was sunk in the 1983 battle of the Falkland Islands. Hours after the ship was sunk, the boy passed out, screaming, "Water, water."

'Then, later in life, he sees visions of the destroyed Twin Towers. Naturally, the Pentagon wants to know the source of all this goddam information. I need more input here.'

Munroe waved the comment away. 'Don't worry about it. Wait until Roscoff arrives tomorrow morning. Maybe he can help.'

Miller turned to look at the television. He loved gambling; Vegas was one of his favourite holiday stops, especially when he wanted to make a killing, catching wise guys red-handed.

Munroe brought his chair closer to the TV. 'A card game, as you can see.'

'You mean another card game the boy wins because he never loses?'

Munroe winked. 'Right.'

'Then I suppose it's time I had a better look at him.'

'Play that back for me, Maria.' Miller said.

'He's playing blackjack. Just look at the cards he throws away – a king and a jack.' He pointed at the screen, as if

Miller couldn't already see it. 'Look at their faces. The other players think he's a nutter. Now watch the dealer. Four cards later, she deals herself an ace and makes twenty-one. That beats everyone.'

'You mean, he can read the cards.'

'Oh, come on. It's just not possible. The packs are new and sealed before the cards get dealt.'

'Maybe the dealer was in on it. I've seen that sort of thing before.'

'Right. So were all the other dealers throughout London, Leeds, and Newcastle. And don't forget Berlin. He always travels alone. It's the safest way for him to control his own thoughts.'

A ringing came from the corridor. Maria left the room to answer a phone then returned with it. 'Sir, it's for you.'

Munroe took the phone.

'It's Roscoff. I'm flying over with Eamon in the morning. They hypnotised John, and I have the recording. You and Miller will find it interesting.'

'Brilliant. What about the book?'

'I've seen it, but, like John, it stays in Berlin for now. Listen, I have to go. I'll see you when I get back.'

***

A couple of hours later, dusk approached. Munroe gathered his things. 'Time to leave. When we get back to my place, I want you to hear a recording I taped. It's an interview between Roscoff and Tierney's brother, Eamon. Maria doesn't even know about it. Eamon tells Roscoff about the dreams Young Tierney had. After that, you'll work the rest out for yourself. I did.'

Miller paused for a second then picked up his jacket. 'I think you're right. At least, you'd better be right.'

Chapter XLVI

Berlin was an hour difference to London. It was almost eleven. Roscoff had returned to his hotel. Compared to the Adlon, it was a dump and nowhere near the Brandenburg Gate. At that moment, he was sitting in the lounge. Suddenly, he spotted a familiar face, that of Russian, Alexei Puskin. They exchanged greetings.

Roscoff got straight to the point. 'Did you get a good look at him?'

Puskin removed an envelope from his jacket. 'Yes. I have all the information you want concerning Frankie Shultz.' He handed the envelope over. Roscoff tucked it away.

'Perfect. Remember the main objective. Don't make eye contact. Keep your distance, and report back every six hours. This boy is clever.'

The next morning, before Roscoff prepared to leave Berlin with Eamon, he had arranged for Puskin to watch over John, just as Eamon and Frankie had been doing. He took a taxi to the Adlon, where Frankie had one of his cars to take them to the airport.

***

Maria was waiting at Gatwick Airport. Munroe lounged

in his front room, drinking coffee and chatting with Miller. He switched the TV off. The room was small, the objects shades of cream or magnolia.

Miller found this typical English decor odd and in real contrast to the American alternative, where everything was big and bright – or that was the stereotype, at least.

'Now you've seen all the evidence. What's your plan?'

Miller, as always, was glad to offer an opinion, however obscure. 'I don't know. It's a position I've never experienced before. Frightening.

'I don't understand the boy. I told General Hanks about it, just before I landed here. I received a message that we need to restrain the boy and that he must remain under the surveillance of our security team.'

***

Landing at London Gatwick was never a pleasant experience; and it wasn't even in London.

During the drive to London, Roscoff received a call from Munroe. Naturally, knowing the split second their plane had touched down, Miller wanted to arrange a meeting. Roscoff knew it wasn't the right time to introduce Eamon, as he would be vulnerable to Miller's plan of attack.

He watched the hazy blocks of colour through the sheets of drizzle on the motorway. For all these years, he'd been on the same damn case. No way in hell will Roscoff sign John's life over to some con artist, even if Miller does work for the CIA. *I feel like a sheriff trying to catch a cowboy on the roof of a train. Every time I'm about to make an arrest, the cowboy ducks a brick tunnel.*

A sudden blare of dance music on the radio made him flinch. Maria tuned to the news. Roscoff and Eamon sandwiched the hand luggage between them, with one suitcase in the boot and a smaller one in the front passenger seat.

Roscoff started to question her, 'Maria, you accompanied John's parents to the morgue. What did they say?'

One of Maria's manicured hands reached up to adjust the mirror. Behind those dark sunglasses, her eyes told another story. 'I told Tierney's parents that the cardinal had been murdered and that the two other killers had been murdered too.

'Also, we've found no source of identification. We need to eliminate the two associates who visited John's house with Cardinal Santini on several occasions. Unfortunately, the results from the lab reveal next to nothing. All we have are the daggers.'

Roscoff smacked the seat. Back to square one and no leads.'

Eamon smiled to himself. Maria matched that smile.

***

John Tierney waited outside for Frankie. He grabbed Frankie by the wrist and pulled him back towards the wall. The look on his face exposed anxiety. 'Frankie, there's something I don't understand about that dream I had. It's worrying me.'

Frankie waited for the bulk of the crowd to pass. 'What's that?'

John concentrated on the series of events that plagued his conscience. 'I'm standing in a room, a white room, with people dressed in hospital whites. Lying in front of me is a newborn baby, wrapped in a white sheet. Then I look down at my own hands. Jesus Christ, there's blood all over them. People in the room start talking to me, but their voices fade as I stare at the bloody palms of my hands.'

Frankie tried to remain calm. He should've seen it coming. It wasn't that long ago that he had warned Eamon about this. He fumbled in his pocket for his cigarette case, trying to ignore John's probing expression. He signalled for them to keep moving forward. 'I'll try to help you understand your dreams. But you control your destiny. To be quite honest, after the Twin Towers, your dreams are more than scaring me.'

John halted.

Frankie reached out, placing his arm around John's shoulders. 'I mean no offence. You can always turn to me. So what are you thinking now?'

John appeared more forlorn than ever. 'Was it your idea to have me followed the other day? There were two men tailing me, right?'

Unsurprised, Frankie said, 'Eamon wanted to go with you. I thought that having my people follow you was the best option for everyone. How did you know?'

John continued as if Frankie had never replied. 'One man followed me; the other you placed inside the pub, awaiting my arrival, right, Frankie?'

'Yes, but again, John, how did you know?'

No answer. Instead, John turned away and marched up the street. The Germans passing him seemed to realise he was a foreigner. *You're not one of us. You don't belong here. Mein Gott, you're pale.*

Frankie placed one hand on his hat to stop it from blowing away then scampered along, trying to catch up. He tapped John on the arm. 'What are you doing?'

John lowered his voice, occasionally glancing sideways. Keep walking and don't look back. On the left, about two hundred metres behind us now, in a black knee-length jacket and flat cap, carrying a newspaper. He's following us. I had the same feeling yesterday at the casino.'

Frankie walked fast to keep pace. 'What do you want to do about it?'

John pulled him ahead. 'Keep walking. He's clever.

Never let your opponent know your weakness. That much, you know.'

***

Vladimir Roscoff watched a clock. *Goddam clocks, calendars – always marking time, passing time, time getting away.* 'I still can't believe how much damage the two plane crashes caused. What a tragedy.'

Miller said, 'Imagine if every finger pointed at you. I reported what Charles told me. Now they want the whole story. I don't have the whole story, Vladimir. I need your help.'

Roscoff got up, pushing his seat back. He loomed over Miller. 'We all want the whole story. It's no simple matter, Casey. If you think it's complicated now, wait until you watch this recording of Young Tierney hypnotised again.

'And look, what's this?' He reached into his jacket. 'We have it right here. Still, I'm working blind. Who can believe any of this? Let's watch the damned video.'

***

Frankie Shultz stirred the sprinkles of chocolate on the froth of his cappuccino. 'You're sure he's following us?'

John lowered a newspaper. 'He walked past five minutes ago.'

Frankie leaned closer towards the window. 'Well, I haven't seen anyone walking past who actually matches the description you gave.'

John dropped the newspaper on the table. 'Like I said, he's clever. He turned his jacket inside out, and it's white now. He put on glasses. Maybe you should invest in a pair.' John turned more serious. 'A secret agent, that's what he is. The hat he wore at first was just hanging out of his pocket. Simple mistake for an agent, wearing a jacket with small pockets. I've seen them before.'

Frankie considered John's words. He remembered faces.

He thought about the people he'd met and the people he'd heard about. Somewhere, a connection waited to be made, but for now, confusion won the day. 'Do you think the one following us is English?'

John said, 'Definitely not. He's Russian.'

***

Two hours passed. Miller, Roscoff, and Munroe remained in the office, having just watched the video. Miller and Roscoff looked ready for sedation. Munroe fed on the discontented atmosphere.

When he finally spoke, Miller sounded anxious. 'Tell me, Vladimir, what's the chance of a dream becoming reality?'

In all the seriousness, Roscoff had to enjoy some fun at Millers expense. 'Now you believe in miracles?'

Miller looked insulted. 'I certainly do not.'

Roscoff wasn't afraid of telling the truth, and he was even less afraid of Miller. "I've followed this boy from the moment he first opened his eyes. He's been my life's work. Everything that surrounds him is a mystery. He eludes us. He eludes explanation. But we're finally close to deciphering his dreams. Soon, that will be a formality.'

Miller's face registered the impact of Roscoff's statement. 'You're not answering my question, Vladimir.'

Roscoff answered with an accusatory tone. 'I wasn't aware I was under investigation, Miller. And I saw your face when you were watching the tape. It was the face of a worried man. If we work together, maybe we'll manage to prevent what otherwise will happen. And you know what's going to happen.

'We have to address the situation now. If you're still under the impression that you can sit back and wait, I'm afraid you're mistaken. It's too late for that. If you truly want to move forward, then you understand my position.'

Miller seemed sluggish in his response. 'The wind direction, a nuclear strike. Does he like Americans?'

Munroe had been perched on a stool in the corner. 'This topic must remain at level five. We can't afford fuck-ups. All we have to do is bring him in and keep him in custody. We can take it from there.'

'And what's happening with the murder enquiries?'

Roscoff moved towards him. 'That's an internal affair, Casey. You know the deal. That information is irrelevant to this discussion, and it doesn't change anything.'

Casey snatched his briefcase and barged past Roscoff. Upon opening the door, he glanced back. 'Yeah, well, I have an important meeting with my advisors in the morning. Now I have absolutely no idea what Im supposed to tell them. I'll need a couple of hours to think things over.' As he turned to leave, he noticed a wry smile on Roscoff's face.

'Oh, I wouldn't worry too much about it. You'll think of something. Bullshit's your specialty, Casey.'

***

John and Frankie were safely back at the casino. While being followed, they took the fire exit route. Inside, they ate their meals in silence.

John stood. 'I need to go out. I won't go far.'

'You know what Eamon said. We must stay together at all times, especially on the street. For Christ's sake, John, you're a wanted man.'

But it was too late, as John was already in the hallway. He felt for his wallet then shouted back, 'I'll return within one hour. I promise. I just want to call and see a friend.'

'Okay, then,' Frankie said. 'You can at least take a lift with my chauffeur.'

John rubbed his eyes. 'If you insist.'

At the bottom of the stairs, Tom, the chauffeur, waited. He nodded, holding his hat. They skipped down the steps towards Frankie's BMW. Frankie had ordered Tom to use it. They had less chance of being spotted on the road, than if they used the open roofed Jaguar. Tom held the back door open for John then slid into the front seat, checking the rear-view mirror. 'Where to, sir?'

John looked at his watch. 'The Ku'damm, quick.'

He may have shared his life story with Frankie, but he didn't tell him he had a prearranged meeting at a restaurant. Nor did the other person know.

As the car pulled up on the curb, John got out and put on a pair of dark glasses then wrapped a scarf around his neck.

Tom rolled down the window. 'I'll be here to pick you up in an hour.'

As John walked towards the restaurant, everything seemed normal. John hurried inside, heading for the booking area. A young woman came over.

'Your name, sir?'

John hesitated, scanning the scene. He had arrived just in time. He held out his credit card. The woman crossed his name off the list then headed for a table. 'Right this way, sir.'

John had reserved a table for two in the far corner. The marble column in front of it would partially conceal him from sight. He wanted to surprise the other person.

The second John sat down, unfolded the napkin on his table, and tucked it into his shirt. A pair of waiters attended to him. One placed a candle and plate on the table, smoothing the tablecloth; the other handed John a menu. 'Would you like something to drink, sir?'

'Yes, I'll have a glass of water, please – still water, please.' *Why impair myself now? I have to keep track of everything that happens – stay sharp.*

The same waiter reappeared, carrying a tray with a glass

full of ice and a large bottle of Evian balanced upon it. John handed the menu back and ordered the Russian Surprise.

The waiter hummed approvingly. 'Our pick of the day, sir.'

Something in the corner attracted John's attention. The other person had arrived, the light of a flickering candle dancing on his face.

Chapter XLVII

After Miller left the office, Roscoff had gone over to the lab to investigate the murder exhibits. He found Eamon and Maria waiting there. Apart from a single lamp hanging over them, the room was black. The shadowy figures stood around the table, studying the daggers, now in clear plastic bags.

Roscoff looked at Eamon. 'Five knives. Our contact said they could be over a thousand years old.'

'They're not exactly knives, more like daggers. You can tell by the shape of the blade. Cowardly piece of equipment, if you ask me. Gives the killer a chance to sneak up on ya.'

Roscoff recognised the one that had been used to kill Cardinal Santini. It had the most blood on it. He grimaced and stepped back. 'It seems you know more about them than I do. And the engravings above each blade mean what?'

'I only know they're Roman numerals. They mark dates, maybe. I dunno.'

Roscoff looked to Maria, blank-faced and staring at nothing in particular. 'Maria, you're Italian. Do you understand what it's all about? Why were they written that way?'

She fiddled with her necklace. 'It's old writing from many years ago. Nobody uses it now.'

Roscoff was sure that, if he looked down into his hand, this night was the last grain of sand he would hold. 'We know that the daggers are old. Are you sure you didn't learn this sort of thing at school? They always teach about the Roman Empire, don't they?'

Maria felt bombarded with questions and rather annoyed that her heritage had been brought up. Why *should I tell them more?* 'They did, and I'm sure they still do. But I left school twenty years ago. I don't remember much.'

Eamon felt the rising tension. Roscoff grabbed the table and jabbed a finger at Maria's shoulder. 'You should have found out this information already. That was your job, Maria. Much time has been wasted.'

'Excuse me, but that's incorrect, sir. I'm surprised you don't remember, since you gave the job to Ross. He obviously didn't finish the assignment. Whose job was it to reassign his part of the investigation to someone else? Not mine.'

She gestured at him. From where Roscoff sat, it looked like she was wiping something with her hand from the underside of her chin. Eamon knew it meant something else.

Roscoff straightened himself up. Complete darkness swamped his face. 'All right, but I'll say this – These assignments never stopped you before, did it? We all know you're a woman who takes advantage of any situation. You've twisted things before to better suit your own needs – like that time when there was a break-in at the church, and they found—'

'That's enough,' Eamon said.

'You bastard,' Maria screamed.

Eamon walked around the table and whispered into Roscoff's ear, 'We have five daggers in front of us, but the book said there would be six, remember? So that means there's still one more to find. Until then, I don't think we can do much.'

Roscoff apologised to Maria quietly and made his way to the door. He slung his jacket over his shoulder and looked back at Eamon. 'Yeah, you're right, but in whose neck will the last dagger be found?'

Chapter XLVIII

Though John was more concerned with discovering the identity of the unknown shadow that had followed him for the past few days, he was beginning to assemble the solution to the entire mystery of his existence and what it meant.

Early the next morning, Frankie knocked on John's door. When no one answered, Frankie opened the door. John's bed was made. Frankie rushed back to his own room and called John on his mobile.

'John, where the hell are you? I thought Tom brought you back last night?'

'He did. I just popped out again for a newspaper, that's all. I'm on the U-Bahn now. Two more train stops, and I'll be back.'

'I'm sorry for playing your father instead of your friend, but I'm worried, very worried.'

Why take the train just to get a newspaper? Why not walk up the road? All newsstands had English newspapers. None of it makes sense.

Of course, Frankie would react with concern, even though Biggins was dead, that still left the undercover police on the prowl.

What's he up to behind my back? Obviously, Eamon and Roscoff are gone from the current picture, which rules them out. There's Rosi – but she's in Bulgaria.

About an hour after the phone call, John's keys rattled in the lock. He emerged, clutching a newspaper, and a small bag of groceries.

***

Back at the lab, Roscoff unlocked the door and twisted the rod hanging from the Venetian blinds. Another ring tone played. *God, I can't be bothered with Miller.* However, it was Alexei Puskin.

Roscoff readied himself to ask questions, only to be silenced by Puskin's torrent of words.

'Ты дал мне задание следить Джон Тирни, да?'

'Woah, woah, woah, Alexei, speak English, please. This is not the Kremlin, my friend.'

'You give me job to follow John Tierney, yes? Well, I no longer follow him.'

'Why not, Alexei? What's the problem?'

'Why you no warn me? Now tables turn. He follow me now.'

'What—what happened?'

'Last night, my wife, she have birthday. We go to restaurant. We sit down, and there in corner, your man he sitting, your suspect, finishing meal. At first, I thinking it was coincidence, but after he leave, waiter bringing bottle of wine. He tell me gentleman in corner send it, your man.

Then this morning I go for newspaper, and there he is again. He buy newspaper. He turn round, he looking at me, ask if I'm following him. Then he smile and walk away, just like that.'

'Obviously, he saw you following him.'

'Definitely not. I Alexei. Nobody see.'

Roscoff needed a simple answer.

'Then how else would he know? Has somebody been feeding him information about us?'

'You want to know something else?' Alexei said, ignoring Roscoff's question. 'We not even know restaurant where we want going until we leave house. That was perhaps fifteen minute before we get there. He must be fucking my wife. She's the one who made decision. What other explanation works?'

Both men paused, overloaded with ruminations concerning what really happened. Roscoff didn't want to comment. When wives were involved, the rules changed.

Puskin said, 'Let us call it off. It not feel right anymore.'

It seemed Frankie had been right after all. Young Tierney was getting stronger, physically and mentally. Roscoff went back to the lab and closed the door behind him. His heart beat at a faster tempo. Strange how everything had progressed then had suddenly begun regressing.

A knock at the door. Eamon entered, Maria following closely behind. 'Are you all right, Roscoff? You look like shit.'

Roscoff poured a glass of water, drank from it, and then undid the top button of his shirt. 'I'm just—the stress. The stress is killing me.'

'Maria was telling me about the American from the CIA. Is that what's bothering you?'

Roscoff screwed the cap back on the bottle. 'No, no. It's the evidence I have in front of me and what's written in this book. I can't understand it.'

'Don't forget, you asked to see it. But what about John? Maybe he's the one who can work it out for us.'

Maria grabbed Roscoff's arm, her red nails digging into his skin. 'We have to give it a try.'

Roscoff shrugged her off. 'Why haven't you tried already, Eamon?'

Eamon stood. 'Because the timing wasn't right.'

'Wrong time? When's the right time?'

'I'll let you know when the time is right.' *I sound so confident, it's all a charade.*

Roscoff, however, was thinking Eamon might be withholding something else he knew about the book. His phone rang. It was Puskin again.

'Vladimir, I just read newspaper. John's photo in it. They want to know if he connected to the 9/11 terrorist cell. Another paper claim, and I quote, 'The CIA and MI5 knew of the dangers long before the 9/11 disaster. Despite this, no action was taken by any of the intelligence agencies. Sources claim their information was provided by a gambler with the supposed ability to predict future events.'

'Just what we need,' Roscoff said. 'Find out where he is. Stay on his tail.'

Puskin was adamant to find out the truth. Puskin replied, 'I have one question, I need answer. Can he see into future?'

Roscoff paused for a moment before sighing down the phone.

'Well, he's not fucking your wife; that's for sure. Does that answer your question?

'Now get back on his tail. Go.'

Puskin knows he'd better keep watch over Young Tierney. But I can't pass this information to Eamon. He can find out for himself soon enough. It won't take long before John's face appears on every TV screen.

Roscoff simply left the room. Maria turned to Eamon, shaking his shoulders. 'What will you do next?'

Eamon whispered, 'Everything was going to plan, until this American showed up. The book says five murders will take place, leaving the sixth potential victim to escape. That will determine our destiny – one knife, and whether it causes that murder.

'Who's the intended victim, Munroe or the American? It doesn't add up. Neither can be trusted. God will guide you, Maria.'

As Maria and Eamon walked down the hallway that Roscoff had just vacated. Another clue to the mysteries confounding Roscoff was within sight, but he was blind to it. All the killers so far identified had been men. Everyone involved in the investigation, presumed that would be true in all the cases. But nobody, apart from Cardinal Santini, had heard the sound of high heels approaching.

Upstairs, one floor above Maria and Eamon, Roscoff sat with Miller and Munroe. They had been looking at the exhibits before he arrived.

'So, you decided to show Miller the murder evidence.'

The pair looked up. Roscoff must have been watching them for several minutes because the door had been open, and the only movement in the room was the smoke drifting from Munroe's cigarette. Miller's face revealed no emotion.

'Got a better idea?' Munroe said. 'I think we could do with some help, Vladimir.'

'I came here simply to deliver a message. We have a more important issue to discuss now. A photograph of Young Tierney has appeared in today's paper. I know because a call came in from Germany. By tomorrow, he'll be a celebrity, and for all the wrong reasons.'

Munroe and Miller were visibly shaken.

Roscoff, pacing, spoke from behind them. 'We have to get him out of there fast – get him out of view – or it's our asses on the line.'

Munroe pushed his sleeves up and walked over to Roscoff. 'You have to agree to this now, Vladimir. It's our one chance to settle this once and for all. Give the boy a chance. Don't you think he deserves that much?"

Roscoff remembered the first meeting in the Thames house office, which had occurred almost two decades before. Now they all had the same worries and wrinkles to show for it. 'Okay. You take over, Charles. I'll make arrangements with my associate in Berlin, Alexei Puskin. He used to be a KGB spy. He goes wherever Young Tierney goes. Understood?'

Munroe knew he had finally scored a point against Roscoff. 'Understood! What about Eamon? What will you tell him?'

Roscoff dropped into the chair beside him. 'When I see John's picture in the papers for myself, then and only then. In the meantime, Charles, we still have the ongoing murder enquiry and a live press conference to sort out.

'Besides, Eamon doesn't trust you. I wouldn't bother telling him anything.' Roscoff knew he had to find John before the paparazzi did.

Miller leapt out of his seat. 'I have it. We'll take him out of Europe, move him somewhere out of sight, say, for instance, Cyprus. We have branches there. It would be a good move.'

'Yeah, that's not a bad idea. I'll make the call immediately.'

Roscoff heard his own footsteps echo down the stairway. The more times the word whizzed around Roscoff's brain, the better it sounded. *Cyprus Cyprus. It's an almost musical solution, and almost no one will ever hear it.*

Meanwhile, Miller more barked than said, 'Now the world will know. And when they learn of a nuclear explosion? I know what General Hanks will say.'

Munroe said, 'If I remember correctly, General

Hanks came under scrutiny after the John F. Kennedy assassination.'

Miller laughed. 'Yeah, that would be him. He loves his Section 151.'

'Section 151?'

Miller, knew the whole story behind John. Now he was starting to understand 'The Code' Miller said, 'for people considered a danger to society. You can't put them in prison, and you can't put them under guard. Some situations force you to make a decision. I've made mine. It's up to you whether you want to agree with me or not. But at least think about it.'

Munroe decided Miller made sense. 'You're right. I wanted him in prison, but now I understand why that would have been a disaster.'

Miller finally broke the silence of his lethargy. 'I know this tiny island. It's off the coast of Cyprus. I know it well. We'll fly in close and take a boat from there. I'll arrange for a sniper to be placed in the target location.'

The idea terrified Munroe. *Now we're going to kill a man and get away with it.* He barely whispered his next words. Whether he was talking to himself or Miller, he wasn't sure. 'You know the consequences if we fail.'

'Well, don't worry, Charles. Such a typical British attitude – always looking at the downside. I never fail.'

***

While John followed his 'enemy' to shops and restaurants, his supposed allies were planning to kill him. Puskin was only looking out for him. If it wasn't for Roscoff not wanting to disclose his extra source, John might have just as easily approached Puskin and said, 'Hi.'

Later, in the casino, Frankie and John discussed the current situation and security measures.

'Listen, John, we'll stay here for now. We have the gym.

We can relax as best possible and make use of our time. The doors will remain closed all day and night. We'll have to wait until Eamon returns before we do anything.'

***

Something extraordinary was about to happen. Ramón was in Frankfurt airport, awaiting a flight back to Bogotá, when he thought he saw a familiar face. 'Scuse me, can I look at newspaper one minute?'

The elderly woman beside him dropped the newspaper and hobbled away. He stared closely at the black and white image. There was no doubt about it; he was looking at John Tierney. Ramón still felt the bite of the public humiliation John had provided him.

Several phrases in the paragraph accompanying the picture seemed to rise from the page:

Dreams become reality…
Won millions in the casinos…
Owners call him 'unbeatable' or a 'cheat.'

Ramón was mentally strapped to his seat. Rage weighed upon him. With a claw-like hand, he beckoned his minder. 'Go get car; we drive back in Berlin now. I take care unfinished business. Tell Ramirez I want piece, 9mm with silencer. We meet him there, in city.'

Frankie's plan to trade John for gold had taken a wrong way exit. Ramón didn't negotiate.

Chapter XLIX

Roscoff laid a photograph of the Angelic Angels' tattoo from one of the dead bodies down on the table. Eamon and Maria stood behind, looking over Roscoff's shoulder.

'It shows six wings, each adorned with Roman numerals. Out of six, we still have one dagger missing. If you look to the sixth wing, it depicts the numeral III.'

Eamon said, 'Yes, numbers, but I can't decipher the code. I've no answers.'

Maria merely pretended to concentrate on the image. 'We should do what you said; let John have a look. He was born for that, right?'

She and Eamon knew John was born to decipher the code. But they didn't know they weren't the only ones who knew.

***

Frankie reached into the bathroom cabinet, grabbed something, then turned around and handed it to John. It was a pair of hairdressers' scissors. John felt a pang in his chest.

'What are these?'

Frankie slammed the cabinet shut. 'Your picture in the paper isn't so clear, but the paparazzi will want to hunt you down. They won't give up. That danger requires vital changes. First, your hair needs cutting. It's too long, and the picture shows it.'

He stared at John's palm then snatched the scissors back. 'Actually' – he placed the scissors back in the cabinet and grabbed a razor – 'we'll shave it off. We're taking every precaution. I'll even arrange for someone to pick up contact lenses that will change the colour of your eyes.'

'Will you try and call Eamon again?'

Frankie set the razor on the sink. 'Later. He said his phone will be switched off while he's in the company of MI5.'

***

On a reasonably warm Saturday night, Roscoff sat in his car outside headquarters. He was just about to make a phone call when Miller finally showed up. He fell into the passenger seat and slammed the door. Roscoff started the ignition – destination, LCY, London City Airport.

'His name is Alexei Puskin. He'll await you at the airstrip in Berlin. I have John Tierney's new ID card and passport. Give them to him. Tell him Eamon and I will arrive at the island shortly after you get there.'

Miller took the envelope and tucked it into the front pocket of his laptop carrier.

An hour later, Roscoff was on his way back from LCY. He checked his phone. A missed call flashed on the screen. Someone had left a voice message. It was Christopher Bronks, John's father, and he sounded worried.

Roscoff's nerves felt as if they had been set aflame. *How could I forget my promise, go back on my word?* He reached into the tray beneath the dashboard and pulled out a tattered map of the roads. Though it would be a good three hours from his current position, he knew it was a drive he must make.

Chapter L

Before leaving the lab back at HQ, Eamon had told Roscoff he would check into a hotel, though he had actually gone to Maria's apartment. As Roscoff endured flashbacks of the entire nightmare, Eamon wrapped his arms around Maria's waist.

'It's been so long.'

'I thought we'd agreed it would be strictly business between us now?'

His hands caressed her body. She all but yelped, laughing, as Eamon grabbed her wrists and turned her to face him. His voice was low. 'One last time won't hurt, Maria.'

Maria pulled his shirt, ripping it open. With one manicured hand firmly pressed to his chest, she forced him backwards and into the bedroom. They fell into a sea of satin. Slowly, Eamon moved his hands up her blouse then pulled down her bra. Soon, they had undressed one another, but it wasn't the nudity that bound them. It was something else, something familiar they both shared, as did several others.

***

Relief overcame Roscoff's anxiety when he saw the house

belonging to John's parents. It was close to nine o'clock. He'd been up since five in the morning. He could have used a warm cup of tea or a shot of vodka; either would do.

He parked by the kerb, shook his head to wake himself up, and climbed out of the car. He made sure to lock the doors. The car beeped.

He saw the ghostly figure of Rose Tierney in the dark doorway. The last time he'd looked, no one was there.

But when he knocked and Rose opened the door, she seemed pleased to see him, pulling her cardigan tight around her. They softly shook hands.

'Good evening, Rose. I missed the call today. As I was passing, I wanted to apologise for not getting back to you and for your obligatory visit to the morgue – not exactly the most pleasant place to visit. I hope you understand and can see our point of view.'

They stepped into the house. Roscoff closed the door, wiping his feet on the mat then followed Rose into the lounge. She had a pot of hot tea sitting on the table. She poured a cup and handed it to Roscoff, who gratefully received it. Rose sat in the lone chair near the fireplace.

'Well,' she said, 'at least it wasn't in vain. But seeing the decayed bodies of the two men who had visited our house with the Cardinal all those years back—well, they hadn't changed much. In fact—'

Roscoff choked on his tea before gaining control of himself.

Rose got up, concerned. 'Are you all right?'

Roscoff placed his cup down. 'I apologise for the interruption. You said you identified them, correct?'

Rose sat down, confused and even more concerned. 'Well, yes. I told your secretary they were the same two men. Didn't I? I'm sure I did.'

Roscoff remembered the last time he'd visited the house.

He recalled the hatred he'd felt for Munroe over the Biggins's deal. These sensations returned, and he felt a bizarre sense of reliving a time for which he had no nostalgia. *Is all this part of it, too – No Police protection outside the house. Puskin, buying a damn paper at the corner shop. Now this dam morgue identification.* He could no longer distinguish the difference between what had been written and reality.

He almost fell through the doorway as he ran to the bathroom. A few minutes later, he reappeared, dishevelled, his face still dripping the cold water he'd just splashed upon it.

Luckily, Rose had replaced the tea with a glass of water and aspirin. Roscoff sat quietly and folded his jacket in his lap.

Rose pointed at the tablet. 'Here, take that. It'll help. You might need to keep your window open on the way home, so you don't fall asleep.'

He forced a grin. He drained the glass and, while doing so, noticed a picture of twelve-year-old John on the mantelpiece. 'When was the last time you spoke with John?'

Rose sighed. 'Oh, about five weeks ago. That's why I'm always calling your office. I must have called ten times. Didn't your secretary tell you? I'm finding this a bit strange.'

Roscoff swallowed. 'Yes. So am I.' He noticed Rose waiting for him to continue. 'You mean Maria, I presume?'

'Yes, that Italian girl. She said you were busy and shouldn't be contacted. I think I remember her saying that, if I had any more questions, I should ask her, not you.'

He stared at Rose. *Maria has more to do with the situation than I ever guessed.*

***

Far below the black skies over Berlin, Casey Miller and

Alexei Puskin sat beside one another. When they met, Puskin drove to the casino car park, as Roscoff had instructed. They were there for one reason, and that was to see Frankie and John leave the building. But a surprise awaited them.

***

The Sunday morning sun had risen. Vladimir Roscoff awoke in his car. It was seven-thirty in the morning; his car was parked on the street outside Maria's flat in Primrose Hill.

He opened his laptop and ran it through to the MI5 personnel file. His throat was dry. He gasped for the need of fresh air and wound his window down. He typed in, 'Maria Bianchi.'

He knew that somebody had been leaking vital information to the cult of killers, and his suspicions told him it was time to check out a certain secretary. Roscoff didn't feel so good.

***

Back at the casino car park, Miller was wide awake and listening to morning radio. Puskin snoozed lightly. Miller woke him, shaking him roughly.

Puskin blinked, putting his hand to his forehead. 'W-w-what the? Huh?'

They watched a long black Mercedes gliding silently through the entrance, under the car park lights. The driver parked by the wall on the far side. Seconds later, an identical car appeared, parking in the space next to the first one. A door swung open. A pair of glossy black shoes touched the ground. A Columbian man appeared. Miller noted a barely visible thin moustache.

Miller was looking at a ganster, who felt around in his jacket before locking the car and walking over to the first Mercedes.

The door opened towards him. Miller's body tensed.

Puskin leaned forward to see better. The second man took off a pair of mirrored sunglasses, revealing Colombian features. It was none other than Ramón.

Finally, a mountain of a man emerged from the other side of the car, straightening his suit.

Ramirez scanned the car park. They would see nothing but the usual luxurious cars and saloons.

By this time, Miller was gripping Puskin's arm. Puskin frowned. Ramirez took something out of his pocket. He extended his arm towards Ramón. When he opened his hand, Miller thought he saw a gun.

Ramón snatched it like a magician. Miller whispered to Puskin. 'Did you see that?'

Puskin had finally fully awakened. 'They're not fucking around.'

Miller lowered the radio volume. 'What should we to do about it?'

Puskin studied the door to the stairway nearest Ramón. 'If they take the stairs, we take the elevator.'

***

It was a beautiful Sunday morning, ten to nine, Primrose Hill. Maria and Eamon were waiting for coffee in the kitchen. Maria was fiddling with the coffee maker. 'Why don't you get some fresh bread? I'm taking a shower.'

Eamon pulled on his jacket, checking for change in his pocket. 'Sure. I won't be long.'

As soon as the door closed behind him, Eamon noticed the elevator on its way down from the second floor, with no idea who had pressed the button at the bottom. Instead of waiting, he took the stairs.

***

Miller and Puskin looked on from the safety of the car as the Columbian crowd ascended the stairway. Shortly afterwards, they slipped out of the car and headed for the elevator.

***

Roscoff stepped out of the elevator on the fourth floor, missing Eamon by seconds. He ran his fingers over the name plaque outside the door and stepped back, realising the door to the apartment had been left open. He tapped on it, calling for Maria.

No response; he entered. Water sprayed from a showerhead in the bathroom. Roscoff advanced towards the kitchen. He noted the two fresh cups of coffee. Just as he reached for one, the flow of water stopped. Roscoff looked back into the hallway. Maria, wrapped in a knee-length towel, appeared. She was going through the shirt rack, oblivious to his presence.

With a single, serpent-like movement, he eased closer to her. Water trickled from her hair. For a second, he savoured her skin's sweet scent of honey. He spoke loudly and confidently. 'You left the door open.'

She dropped a shirt hanger on the floor, finding herself face-to-face with thin-lipped Roscoff, and anyone could have guessed he was angry. He sipped from a coffee cup.

'I would have locked the door if I'd known you were coming,' she said, Annoyed with Eamon for leaving it open. She next tried to defuse the situation, acting confused. 'Why are you here, breaking and entering my premises?'

She turned and headed for the bathroom.

Roscoff placed the cup down and followed. 'It was you,' he shouted, his composure finally broken. 'You bitch.'

This stopped her in her tracks. She turned and walked away from him towards the hallway.

'You organised it. You tried to have me killed. You sent the killer. Don't turn away from me when I'm talking to you, bitch. Don't even think about it.'

He grabbed her arm from behind. The towel fell, revealing the tattoo of the Angelic Angels. Roscoff was transfixed; he held both her arms behind her back. He was taking her in without pausing to praise himself. 'You'll pay for this, Maria, with interest.'

He reached into his pocket and removed a pair of handcuffs. 'I'm officially arresting you, Maria Bianchi.'

Everything happened in a flash. It took a few seconds before Maria realised she was standing naked in the hallway, while Vladimir Roscoff lay unconscious on the floor. She rubbed the red marks on her arm. Eamon, standing over Roscoff, clutched an ornament.

On his way back up to Maria's, he had heard Roscoff's hostile shouting. Eamon had gotten back just before Roscoff could make the arrest. A small stream of blood trickled from the back of Roscoff's head.

Maria picked up her towel. 'You left the fucking door open, Eamon.'

Kneeling by Roscoff's side the seriousness of his actions suddenly dawned on him. He had a flashback to Roscoff's clinical statement – *for every action, there is a reaction* – and this made him feel even worse.

Nevertheless, he got up and walked towards Maria. 'I had to do it. He would have gotten in, anyway.'

Maria was annoyed. 'What if he doesn't cooperate? What if he doesn't want to join us when he comes around? What happens then?'

Maria went to the bedroom, returning quickly fully dressed.

'How many times,' Eamon said, 'do we have to go through this? I told you, he has to join us. It's in the book.'

She inspected Roscoff's bloodied head. 'Let's sit him up and strap him to the chair before he wakes up.'

Maria found a flannel in the bathroom and held it under the cold tap, then rushed back to the front room.

'What are you helping him for?'

Maria pushed a chair against the wall. 'You gotta be joking, Eamon. I'm not.' She fell to her knees and began rubbing madly at the bloodstain on the wooden floor.

***

A golden elevator door with a diamond dragon centred upon it opened to reveal Casey Miller, gun poised. He could see the bar area straight ahead. The room was empty.

A floor above, Alexei Puskin had opened the security door. Television screens set on the casino walls. The room appeared empty, apart from an office chair and the small table in front of him. Out of curiosity, Puskin swivelled the seat, for it looked as though it had sunk. Now he knew why, as in the chair slumped Kali's corpse.

He put his hand to his heart. 'I'm so sorry, my friend. I should've gotten here sooner.' Unable to tolerate the sight, he pushed the chair so that it swivelled and faced the opposite direction.

Suddenly, footsteps approached. He turned and aimed then lowered the gun when he saw Miller.

'Thank God, it's you. I just about had a coronary.' Miller said.

Miller leaned around and saw that Puskin's expression was grim.

Puskin, listening for any suspicious sound, finally decided it was safe. He stepped back into the office. 'Miller, take the stairs on the left. I'll go straight through. Shout if you need me.'

They turned in opposite directions. Puskin proceeded through to the lounge. Tiptoeing across the vast area, he covered almost two hundred metres quickly. Edging along the wall, he double-checked each corner. No movement. A disco ball spun above a deserted dance floor.

He retraced his steps to the stairway.

Meanwhile, Miller was in the gym room. Just as he stepped out from behind one of the machines, a gun silencer startled him. The muffled blast was followed by Ramón's voice. He strained to understand the words as he noticed a hole in the back of a leather chair. Then he saw John and Frankie, flat on the floor with hands tied behind their backs. After all that time waiting for them to return, it was clear they had never even left.

He looked back through the open door just in time to see Puskin creeping up the hall to the door at the far end, behind Ramón.

Ramón stood with a foot on John's back, pointing the gun at him. 'I want you feel pain. You watch me kill your friend.'

Frankie was shaking but managed to stay quiet.

Puskin appeared in the doorway, creating what seemed like a gap in time. Miller hurried to join him. Ramirez jumped up from the chair in the corner. Ramón stood with his back to them.

As Puskin moved forward, Ramirez pulled out a knife. Miller pointed his gun at him. 'You'd better not do anything dumb, motherfucker.' Ramirez backed away. Ramón hadn't moved.

Frankie finally moaned in pain as Puskin held his gun inches from the back of Ramón's head. 'Put the gun down.'

Still aiming his own gun at Ramirez, Miller slid sideways for a better look at Frankie, who had been gagged and, it appeared, shot. Blood saturated his right knee; it had spread across the surrounding carpet. He had already blacked out from the pain and, regaining consciousness, lacked the energy to scream. Sweat covered his face.

Ramón turned and faced Puskin. He had a sick smile on his face. With adrenalin pumping, he obviously enjoyed the tension. Everyone held a gun, and no one wanted to be shot.

Puskin moved first, knocking Ramón's gun to the floor. He had won, but had a gash in his hand to show for it.

Miller looked up in time to see Ramirez advancing. Miller struck Ramirez, stopping him in his tracks then ran to Puskin's side. Ramirez issued a Columbian curse. He'd been cornered, with no way out.

'Now,' Puskin said, 'you look as though you could use a rest. Why don't you kindly lie down and put your hands above your heads.' He smiled at Ramón. 'Or would you prefer I put a bullet in your knees?'

Ramón obeyed.

Miller spotted Ramirez's blade. 'Drop it, asshole, and kick it towards me.'

Ramirez, too, obeyed.

Puskin put the first pair of handcuffs on Ramón. Then he cuffed Ramirez. Miller still had his gun poised. 'You'd better go,' Puskin said. 'I have to file report. Soon, this place will be filled with cops. Untie John. Take him to airstrip. I'll take care of Frankie and will call when I'm done.'

Miller turned to leave then suddenly stopped short. "Oh my, God."

Puskin looked up. 'What?'

'That security guard. Where is he?'

Puskin said, ' I met him on my way up.' Puskin shaking his head.

'Jesus Christ, I swear I'll drop any second.' Miller started to untie John. Puskin was confused over the situation. 'One question before you go. Why you turn away from door after the first gunshot was fired? You saw me looking at you; you turned away.'

Miller jangled his car keys. 'I wasn't sure if my gun was loaded. A passing thought, that's all.'

Puskin studied Miller's body language. He could sense something about the jerky movements. It was almost enough to convince Puskin that Miller didn't care whether John had survived or not.

Now that Puskin had the time to consider matters, it would have made perfect sense, for then Miller could have easily slipped away and taken a plane back to the Pentagon, abdicating his responsibility.

***

At Maria's flat, Roscoff finally began to squirm. He murmured something. Eamon sat in a chair facing Roscoff, observing him calmly.

Eamon's captive tried to gain back his senses, his voice faint. 'My head. What happened? What's going on? Eamon, wh-what are you doing here?'

An awareness of the peril Eamon had placed so many in swept through him like cold wind. If the blow had mentally damaged Roscoff, that would be the end of everything. Eamon decided to answer with a question, a move Roscoff knew well. If the question confused him, Eamon would know the game was up. 'More to the point, what the hell are you doing here? And what should I do about it, huh?'

Roscoff noticed a round ornament in Eamon's lap, a paperweight with a tiny model of the Roman Coliseum inside the glass. Roscoff tried to lift his arms then realised he was bound to the chair. He breathed faster. 'Where's Maria? You hit me on the head.'

Despite the situation, Eamon nearly laughed. 'That I did. Maria will be back shortly.'

Roscoff saw a picture of Eamon and Maria on the

mantelpiece. 'Now I understand. You were getting the information from Maria. You knew our every move in advance. Now it's my turn to ask a question. Why kill the cardinal? What part does Santini play?'

Roscoff's swift progression to perfect English surprised Eamon, who walked over to the mantelpiece and set down the paperweight. 'You want to know his part? He was a threat to the high caulbearer. He betrayed us. He was a threat to humanity's continued existence.'

With a sceptical tone, Roscoff said, 'But you tried to kill me. Why not finish the job? You had plenty of opportunities.'

Eamon faced Roscoff. 'Because you're the one. You'll lead us to our destiny.'

In a different context, Roscoff had heard the same insinuation. 'What are you talking about? I'm the one. The one what?'

'From the sacred book – the one who escapes death by the blade shall be thy leader.' Is that specific enough for you? That's the reason you're still alive.

'John pulls you in every time, like a magnet. You know that as well as I do. You'll risk getting yourself killed for John's sake. Now we must move, before it's too late. The book says you're the one to lead John to his destiny. And it doesn't stop there; the book names you – Vladimir – the one to hold the book. When you killed one of our messengers, we were sure it was you. Paired with your John obsession, there's no mistaking it. I almost wonder if God himself wrote the book.'

After hearing this strangely plausible explanation, Roscoff seemed content, though he hadn't put all his confusion to rest. 'But if you knew I was the chosen one, why the hell did you try to kill me?'

Eamon shrugged, looking pleased. 'We tested the book's

predictions, and you survived. The book is bulletproof. I only hope that, when I untie you, you make the right decision. You're alone. The book is yours, now.'

History had circled itself. Like John Tierney the first, Roscoff was afraid and confused. One particular line from the book echoed within him:

If thy choice be amiss for the high caulbearer, thy destiny shall be forever lost.

Roscoff's interest, his entire focus, shifted from a cult to the Tierney family history. Eamon cut the sticky tape binding him to the chair. Roscoff studied Eamon's face. Now he knew. They shared the obsession. Eamon knew the book word for word.

The ring of the elevator bell was soon followed by an out-of-breath Maria barging through the door. She clutched a newspaper. 'Have you seen this? It's John. His photo's all over the papers.'

She threw the paper so that it landed flat on the table. Eamon snatched it up. Sure enough, John's face had made front-page headlines. 'What the fuck is going on?'

Maria was clearly frantic. 'What can we do? The whole world will know about it now. Who betrayed us?'

She stared at Roscoff. Eamon, too, looked at Roscoff, waiting for an answer. Roscoff seemed smug and menacing, sitting there with such tranquillity, despite his hands still being cuffed behind his back.

He stood as gracefully as possible. 'Everything is in order. John will board a plane to Cyprus within the next hour. His face appeared in the German papers yesterday. We have to get him somewhere safe.'

Eamon lowered his voice. 'And where is Munroe in all of this?'

'Still over here. John is with a good friend of mine.'

Maria said, 'You trusted the American? What the hell is wrong with you?'

Roscoff replied nonchalantly, 'I had no choice. Miller had to be involved, no matter how many times we tried to stop that from happening.'

Maria blushed.

Roscoff's phone started ringing. He looked at Maria, then Eamon. 'Can someone get that?' he said.

Eamon quickly reached in and pulled the phone from the pocket beneath Roscoff's bound hands. 'Alexei P, it says.'

'Yes, good. It's Puskin. I told him to ring when he arrives at the airstrip with John.'

Maria took the phone. 'Mr Puskin? Vladimir is not here. I'm Maria, his secretary. He did mention something about you arriving at the airstrip with John.'

She stood holding the phone, trying to make out what Puskin was saying, his accent stronger than Roscoff's.

'We had problem,' Puskin said. 'John travel to the airstrip with Mr Miller. John made new enemies in Berlin. A Columbian gangster John defeated in poker game, shot Frankie Shultz through the knee. John nearly caught a bullet in head. If it wasn't for Roscoff ordering that Agent Miller and I go to the casino, they could've both been dead.'

'I,' Maria said, 'will tell Vladimir you called, Mr Puskin.'

' Miller is with John. I couldn't make it.'

Maria terminated the call. Roscoff wondered what had been said as Maria dropped the phone back into his pocket.

'Frankie's injured,' she said, 'shot in the knee. John's alone with the American.'

Roscoff turned around. 'Please, would you remove my handcuffs now?'

Eager to witness the assembly of Roscoff's next plan, Eamon obliged.

Roscoff pulled his phone out so hurriedly that he almost dropped it. He pressed a speed dial button. Puskin answered.

'What happened?' Roscoff asked.

'We waited for John, like you said. Some guys turned up. One handed a gun to the gangster. It had a screwed-on silencer. They looked pretty menacing. They were there to get Frankie and John.'

'And where's John now?'

'He's gone to airstrip with Miller. It was the only way to escape. Do you trust him?'

'Not when he's alone.'

'A strange thing happened in the casino today. I had feeling that, if John were killed, Miller wouldn't give a damn. He seemed afraid of John.'

Roscoff felt more apprehensive about the plan than ever, especially now that it had been brought to the attention of the global media. It wouldn't exactly earn Miller a promotion, either. Then he remembered the two murder suspects listening in on the conversation. He wrapped his hand around the phone, holding it close to his mouth.

'We must abandon the plan immediately. I'll contact you in the next hour.'

He snapped his phone shut and headed towards the door. Eamon and Maria were powerless, secretly panicking as to whether they could be arrested if they tried to leave the flat.

When he looked back, Roscoff folded his blood-spattered coat over his arm. 'Let me make one thing clear. When the situation is resolved, you're both going down. You played your cards wrong. Now you'll pay. It's my investigation, and I'm also running the show, got it?' He slammed the door and walked straight out of the building, climbing into his car, parked directly outside.

***

Inside the apartment, the discomfort eased as soon as Roscoff had left. Eamon dropped the act. He laughed to himself when he thought about all the time he'd spent trying to find a solution named 'Vladimir.'

Surely, once Roscoff had the book, he, too, would understand.

Chapter LI

John was already aboard the CIA's private jet on an airstrip outside Berlin. The same plane had flown Casey Miller from London to Berlin. John sat two seats ahead of Miller, whose laptop computer was open. Even though the sound was off, Miller knew when he received messages because a small LED would flash three times, as it now did. He keyed in his PIN code to view the message:

> Landing time, 1600 hours.
> Security on standby.
> Destination Port
> Lead target from boat to shore
> Security force preparation confirmed
> The message recipient is required to take the second boat to the shore.
> Security informed of final destination.

> Please Wait

> Confirmation:
> Immediate Affect

Section 151 Operations Active.
Confirmation Code: 0151
Sign In

The plane was three hours from its destination. John closed his eyes. Though physically tired, he couldn't sleep, as he imagined Ramón brandishing a gun at him, and not telling Frankie his initial reason for wanting to go out alone in the first place, for sometimes a street full of strangers could be the safest place in the world. And now an American agent sat two seats behind him. All these thoughts rattled John's conscience. Could he trust the American?

Miller typed a reply to the message from the Pentagon:

Recipient replies: Affirmative

John Tierney had indeed become an international celebrity, and the world wanted to know more about his role in events. How could he have known about the attacks before they occurred? Was he a terrorist? What other information had he been withholding? Of course, things looked bad for the CIA and General Hanks, too.

**

Roscoff was sitting in his car with Maria outside Eamon's hotel. Maria was reapplying her makeup in the mirror.

'Tell me about your father. What kind of a man was he?'

Maria, with lipstick in hand, stopped. She had applied the lower lip. Her mind drifted away while her heart took over her feelings.

'He was killed in Bologna, wasn't he?' Roscoff wasn't letting Maria off the hook. 'The train station explosion, correct?'

Maria now knew Roscoff had been digging deeply into her family roots, like a mole.

'That's how it happened, isn't it? He was an innocent bystander.' *Come on, let's go all the way with this interrogation*, Roscoff thought.

'An incident with a closed book – like the JF Kennedy case.' Roscoff had the fish on the hook. It was time to reel it in. 'Your father was a member of P2, the same organization that had been linked to this terrorist massacre in Bologna.'

Maria sensed the mole had entered its bunker, no longer needing to dig. She knew no more words needed to be said. Roscoff had all the information he needed to know.

Maria changed the subject. 'You know, it's strange to think how the human mind operates. People run around killing each another, yet everyone has his or her own beliefs. I just hope it all settles down.'

Roscoff rolled up the window. 'What exactly do you believe in?'

'I believe we were all born for a reason. Ours is to be the saviours of humankind.'

Roscoff laughed. 'And I suppose the murders your cult committed will save humankind?'

'The path of the high caulbearer must be kept free from hindrances. Nothing must stand in his way.'

'Yes, I can understand why Biggins and the Cardinal were murdered, but how were Ross and Mullins connected?'

'Mullins was making plans with the cardinal. Ross? He couldn't keep his mouth shut. So far, the contents of the book have come true. If the messenger had succeeded in killing you, we would all be lost, which is why we prayed for you. God chose your path.'

'I still have to take you in,' Roscoff said. 'I'm sure you know that.'

Maria eyes didn't flinch.

'It doesn't bother me. Your choice will fall in line with God's.'

***

On the CIA jet, an hour remained before Miller and John would reach their destination. Miller closed his laptop, placed it on the empty seat next to him, and walked over to John. He sat next to him.

'Trouble seems to follow you, boy. Cops are being murdered, for instance. That's why I don't like you. Americans think you're a terrorist.

And why am I really talking to you? Because I need to know whether your dreams predict the future or whether someone's feeding you information. That's what I need to know.'

John smiled sarcastically. 'Wow. Seems you Americans already got me strung up.' He leaned towards Miller, talking into the American's ear. 'One of us is going to take the fall, but the decision will be made by God. So fuck off back to your seat.'

Miller glared at John. He then turned and walked back to his seat. Surely, John couldn't know about the sniper – not yet.

Back at the Pentagon, General Hanks had spent a vast amount of time organizing alibis so that they would be covered once the assassination took place. After two bombs and open gunfire in the agency's complex, he was used to dealing with corruption from both sides.

***

Roscoff had arrived at the airstrip in Newmarket. He was waiting patiently for yet another of the agency's private jets preparing for take-off to Cyprus.

Eamon held out the sacred book. He had tears in his eyes. 'The world is in your hands now. Only you are worthy of holding such greatness. You should read it and study it in

338

depth. It's all been translated into English, as I said before. Originally, it was written in three languages – French, Arabic, and Italian. The book speaks only of the truth. Your decisions will make or break humankind.'

He handed the book to Roscoff, who had no idea what to think. *Who to trust? Nostradamus? The murderers? It's a no-win situation.*

***

Soon after, the CIA jet landed in sunny Cyprus, John followed Miller down the steps and onto the tarmac, where two American agents formally greeted them. 'We shall escort you to your destination immediately.'

Miller walked over to the white car. 'Let's go.'

They got in the back, the two agents who had greeted them taking the front seats. Miller knew there was a good chance Roscoff would try to call him, so he switched off his phone when John wasn't looking.

He reached into his laptop bag and took out the passport and ID card Puskin had given him. 'Here, take this. It's your new passport and ID card.'

John snatched the documents. 'I want you to call Roscoff – now. Eamon will be with him. I need to speak to him.'

Miller had a smug expression. 'I'm sure we'll be seeing them shortly. I'll call him once we reach our safe destination.'

***

In Newmarket, Roscoff boarded the plane. He was sitting in the back with his legs crossed, browsing the book, observing the diagrams and pictures in each section. He'd never seen anything like it. He tried to decipher their meaning.

Jacques de Molay was born bearing the caul, as was Nostradamus. Wait a minute – the bloodline. Tierney. John Tierney, of course. The third child of Jacques de Molay. Then

339

his third child, the next generation. The last of the Knights Templar joined with the monks in the fourteenth century. By the sixteenth century, Nostradamus revealed he had arranged for his secret son to be sent to the monastery.

Roscoff whispered. 'Of course, it's the same Brotherhood of monks'.

He flipped the pages with more rapidity. He stood and shouted down the aisle for Eamon to come immediately to the back of the plane. Eamon paused to whisper something to Maria.

'Told ya the book would get him in the end.'

Maria gazed up at Eamon with a loving expression.

Chapter LII

Miller and John had arrived at the destination. They pulled up opposite a moored motor boat. The agents escorted them to it. They would be taken to an offshore island where secret agents from Britain and America had already been stationed.

Miller turned to John. 'Before we get to the island, I must inform you we'll be leaving on safety rafts. The tide is too far out for the boat to reach the shoreline, so I'll have to ask you to put on the life vest.'

John ignored him. He felt apprehensive, but his confidence in fate had grown. He knew what he had to do.

***

Meanwhile, Roscoff and Eamon were examining the book together. They still had an hour before the plane would reach Cyprus. Roscoff showed Eamon the paragraph he'd been reading. 'I think I've found the family bloodline here. Nostradamus was famous for his predictions, just like John. The only difference is that we happen to be in the twenty-first century. Things are a lot different than they were four hundred years ago.'

Eamon nodded, pointing at the book. 'Turn the page to the compass circle diagram. That's the mystery we need to solve. I already know about the rest.'

'Is there anything else I need to know?'

Eamon smiled. 'Yes, you need to read about the last known Knight Templar. His name was Vladimir. Think about that. I'm going back to my seat now.'

By the look on Eamon's face, Roscoff could see there was something else Eamon was hiding. He quickly turned to the compass diagram page.

Vladimir, Vladimir, here we are, look. Roscoff ran his fingers over the entire page.

The last conquest of the Knights Templar: He will reveal the five traitors to the high caulbearer. The last of the Knights Templar shall rise again. In the last of days, let those with ears hear his words and those with eyes see his face. The dead shall walk among the living. He will go to them in a time of Great War. A war of planets. The master of planets will set his quest, before the last days. His mission will be to save humanity. Only he who has risen from the dead shall be worthy. He is the one to guide the high caulbearer along the thorny path. History must not be repeated.

'My God.' Roscoff finally accepted that he was the chosen one –that he was the one who must guide Young Tierney.

***

The jet was due to land just as the engine of the boat was turned off. It was time to go the shore. Miller spoke to John. 'When we arrive at the shore, I'll let you make that call you wanted to make earlier.'

John gazed at the landscape across the shoreline. He could see the buildings behind the beach scenery of palm trees and scattered woodland. There was a steep hill on his left. He glanced at the shore then turned to the hill. In the back of his mind, he knew somebody waited there with a gun. Now he was in control. He could switch his visions and thoughts on or off as necessary. He closed his eyes.

Miller narrowed his eyes. 'What are you thinking about, boy?'

John swivelled around, looking him straight in the eye. 'Come on – what are we waiting for? I have a call to make. And you, yes you, have to meet your maker.'

Miller blinked, unsure of exactly what those words meant. John started to climb down the ladder to the side of the boat. He leapt onto the raft, waiting to be taken to the shore.

Miller whispered instructions to the security men. 'Take the boy to shore. He looks nervous. Then come back for me.'

Miller had followed General Hanks's instructions. He watched the raft turn towards shore, only a hundred metres away.

Meanwhile, the assassin observed through his telescopic sights everything from the hillside. As the raft came to a halt on the shoreline, he saw John, soaked in sweat, jump out and onto the sand. John turned to face the woodland. Miller's men ordered him to return.

'Sir, you're going the wrong direction. We must go this way.'

Aware of the sniper's whereabouts, John deliberately tried to stay out of his line of sight. He knew the plan. He also knew how to stay alive. He had made a decision. He would trick the security team. They couldn't guess what he already knew. He turned back. 'I'll wait here until Miller gets to the shore.'

The sniper sat idle, his right eye to the telescope. Surely, the target would appear any minute now. 'Come on, you son of a bitch.'

That moment, Miller walked across to the open area. John decided to meet him, distancing himself from the woodland. He found himself in the line of fire.

The sniper saw a moving figure. 'There you are. Just a little bit farther.'

Though John was now completely visible to the sniper, he deliberately weaved between palm trees, intent on distracting the sniper.

Left shoulder, right shoulder was all the sniper could see. Then again, one shot through the head was all it would take. 'Here we go.'

Miller arrived at the top of the sand bank. The sniper had positioned himself on the north side of the mountain. He wiped the sweat away from his eyes with his thumb while his finger was paused on the trigger. A figure appeared inside the sniper's lens, walking in from the south side. It was Casey Miller.

John found himself isolated between the two perpetrators.

'Come away from the tree, you son of a bitch.' The sniper was getting agitated, nervous, in fact. Perhaps he was the wrong man for the job. Perhaps he was trigger-happy. Perhaps this could all be a big mistake.

John stood there; a sense of vigour came over his body, as though it was trying to tell him something.

God will protect you from all evil. Voices in his head gave him the spirit to walk forward.

John walked towards Casey Miller, who had come to a standstill, confused as to why the sniper had yet to fire a shot.

The sniper at last had a view.

John stopped in his tracks. 'Here we go baby' The sniper grew in confidence as he squeezed the trigger. John took a step backwards. Miller sensed John was about to run

344

off, so he reached for his gun. *I'll shoot him myself,* Miller thought.

A loud boom echoed around the hillside. The bullet was away.

The security team ducked for cover. John watched Miller sink to his knees into the sand. Blood ran down the bridge of his nose as his face hit the sand. The bullet had found a target – the wrong target.

John sprinted towards the nearby wooded area.

The assassin had shot one of his own men. He grabbed the telescope and adjusted the view, inspecting the scene intensely. He saw John running, yet he didn't fire another shot. What was the reason?

***

John dashed through the woodland. He had, yet, again been right. Miller had met his maker.

The scenery began to change. Civilization seemed to appear. A small town emerged ahead of him. He had no idea where he was going. By now, he knew he could only rely on instinct.

***

Roscoff, Eamon, and Maria had finally landed, after the jet had had what appeared to be a deliberate delay. They were on their way to the military headquarters that Miller had spoken about. Roscoff had tried to call Miller several times, to no avail. It didn't take long for them to learn about the incident.

They arrived at the scene. Miller had been left where he'd fallen. Roscoff couldn't believe it. *How on earth could this have been John's destination? Miller has been shot on a remote island miles from our main offices.*

One of the security personnel who had witnessed the event described the situation to Roscoff, pointing to different areas along the beach. 'We came to shore here. John ran off in that direction. We waited there for Miller to arrive.'

Roscoff said, 'Just tell me whose order it was to bring John here. It's the wrong side of the bloody island.'

The man's expression changed. 'Sir, this morning we came under attack. Two bombs exploded. There was open gunfire in the complex.'

'Two bombs. Any casualties to report?'

The man shook his head. 'Not to my knowledge, sir.'

Roscoff glanced at Miller. 'Nobody was injured during the gunfire?'

'No, sir.'

Roscoff spun around, taking in the surroundings. 'And the sniper – from where did he shoot?'

The man turned, looking at Miller's lifeless body. 'Judging from where Agent Miller was shot, I'd say somewhere in that area.' He pointed to the woodland just in front of the hill.

'And where was Tierney at the time?'

The guard pointed. 'There, behind that palm tree, sir. It looked as if he was taking cover.'

'So John was in the line of fire?'

'It's possible, sir.'

Maria and Eamon stood behind Roscoff, listening. Eamon tapped him on the shoulder and whispered, 'Looks like these are the same palm trees John dreamt about.'

Roscoff answered harshly. 'What bothers me more is that he was standing in the line of fire.'

The same member of security said, "Sir, after the gunshot, I quickly looked up and saw Tierney running away. That was my last sighting of him. I thought you should know.'

'But,' Roscoff said, 'there was only one shot fired. Is that correct?'

The guarded nodded. 'Correct, sir.'

Roscoff's hands trembled. He put his hand on his waist,

pointing at the guard accusatorily. 'I'm going to ask you one more time. Which officer gave you the order?'

'I'm sorry, sir, that information must remain classified.'

Roscoff turned to the rest of the security team standing close to him. 'I want you to search the entire island. Eamon, Maria, you two go with them. I'll be at headquarters if you need me. Keep me updated.'

Roscoff pulled Maria aside and lowered his voice. He removed something from his pocket and handed it to her behind his back so nobody could see. 'Here, take my gun. I know you can use it. If we don't find John by Sunday, we'll fly back to London.'

He turned towards the personnel offices, intending to learn more about the bombings mentioned by the security team member.

Something doesn't add up.

***

On the far side of the island, John managed to find a local fisherman who happened to be heading towards the mainland. He was more than willing for John to accompany him. For once, John felt thankful that he'd been given his gift. Despite all its negatives, it had its advantages.

***

In the woodland, Eamon, Maria, and the security team had started their search for John. Eamon decided to question the member of personnel who had been talking to Roscoff just minutes before.

'Did you notice anything strange about John?'

The man looked relieved at the question. 'Well, yes. There's something I remember, something he said to Agent Miller on the boat. I overheard them. "You'll meet your maker," or something like that. Shortly afterwards, Miller was dead. Weird. A bullet between the eyes. I would have sworn Tierney knew what was in store?'

Eamon said, 'Wait a minute. What do you mean, "what was in store?"'

The man stammered, 'I don't know. Nothing makes sense. I was told to come here, to this exact spot, to walk this way, et cetera. The bullet was meant for Tierney, but somehow he turned the tables, and the bullet ended up between Agent Miller's eyes. I'm confused.'

By now, Eamon was sure Miller had done all the planning. It had been an attempted assassination. Listening to the security guard, he realised that John must have dreamt about it all along. That was what the 'meet your maker' line implied. He knew that, if John didn't call him within the next two days, he was busy finding his own way home.

At the island's headquarters, Roscoff searched a filing cabinet and computer. An MI6 agent arrived. Roscoff had already notified him of John's arrival, after he had received the call from Puskin at Maria's flat. They sat at a table.

'John's destination was meant to be on this part of the island,' Roscoff said. 'What happened? Who changed the plan?'

The man clasped his hands. 'We had received a warning of terrorist activity on the island, sir. This area would have been an unsuitable location.'

Roscoff stood with as much intimidation as he could. 'Who changed the destination?'

'We got a call. Anybody approaching the island by boat should be escorted to the other side.'

'You're telling me you let this happen without seeing any official documentation verifying the order?'

'I received a verified fax directly from the American Embassy.'

Roscoff suppressed an urge to scream. 'Get me a copy. I want to see it, now.'

***

It was getting late. Eamon and Maria decided to stop their search for John. They made their way back to main headquarters. When they arrived, a man told them Roscoff had gone over to the American Embassy. He had called the ambassador for an urgent meeting.

***

'Do you know anything about this fax?' Roscoff asked. He held out the copy the agent from MI6 had printed out. 'Our agency received it at 1412 this afternoon.'

The ambassador took the sheet of paper and read it calmly. 'Yes. Everybody in this area was diverted to another location.'

'So who gave the order?'

The ambassador blinked. "It came from the American security team, of course. Why?'

Roscoff felt a new surge of anger. 'As you already know, ambassador, my friend, CIA operative Casey Miller, was shot and killed earlier today. I need the complete details to file my report.'

The ambassador threw the sheet back at him. 'I can't release that information. You know that.'

Roscoff tensed. *Think of another way to persuade him. I'll never get another chance.* 'My problem is, I think the bombings at the complex were a hoax, set up by terrorists. They knew Miller was a top operative.

'Besides, like I said, he was a friend. I need to know for my own peace of mind. How can I sleep at night if I walk away from here knowing nothing? We both work for top agencies. You understand what I mean.'

The ambassador gave Roscoff what felt like an X-ray of a stare. Satisfied with Roscoff's explanation and demeanour, he lifted his laptop onto the desk. He typed in his ID code, which gave him private access to the information Roscoff wanted. He turned the screen so that Roscoff could see. On the monitor was the name and picture of the person who had given the order.

'It was sent from Langley on the orders of a member of Congress, someone in the Pentagon.'

The ambassador merely said, 'Does that put you at ease, Vladimir?'

Roscoff pushed the screen away. 'It does. I was almost convinced it was a hoax. Now I can put that idea to rest. Thank you for your assistance.'

Roscoff rose. Smoothing his shirt, he shook the ambassador's hand, thanked him, and walked away.

His suspicions had been confirmed. It had been a set-up. The CIA was running scared from John's revelations. Besides, they had to cover their arses. That's what they normally did in these cases!

Now Roscoff would have to find out everything connected to the incident. He knew the best way for John to survive was to rely on his gift. He would share this theory with Eamon and Maria.

***

John Tierney had arrived in Cyprus. The long journey had been uneventful. He finally had time to think things through. Without Frankie's help, he feared he wouldn't begin to understand the dreams that involved blood on his hands. He wondered if he would ever hear from Frankie again.

***

A muscular but elderly man strode into the main hall at the Pentagon, General Hanks on his way to push the American summit into war with Afghanistan.

He stood at the podium, tall and proud, delivering his speech.

Coming to the end of his oration, he leaned towards his audience, firm and sure.

'We must declare war on Afghanistan. How much more evidence do you need? They may have beaten Russia, but they won't beat us. Air assault – blow them out of their mountain hideouts. Crush them.' Hanks retreated to his seat to a standing ovation.

Sitting next to him with a cheeky smile was the defence minister, James Crichton. 'George, that speech has probably just netted your company a multimillion - dollar contract.'

Hanks was still waving his corrupt hands in the air while accepting the ovation from the young American soldiers. 'Well after the pull-out of Iraq, I had to put my retirement on hold until we got rid of the stockpile of arms.'

Hanks stood alongside the rest of Congress and headed out of the assembly with the applause still ringing in his ears.

An agent named Howard motioned Hanks to join him. 'It's just been confirmed, sir, that mission 0151 has failed.'

The words hit Hanks like a drill sergeants backhand. 'The mission failed? Goddam those words. I thought I'd retire today without ever hearing them again. That's twice in my career. Get Miller's report. I want it by noon today.'

Howard awaited a torrent of verbal abuse. 'I'm afraid that's not possible, sir. We have bad news. Agent Miller was killed on duty this afternoon.'

Hanks raised his eyebrows. 'Miller?'

After twenty years of corruptly working together, his friend and understudy was gone.

'This better be some kinda sick joke, my uniformed friend. What the hell happened? There had better be a good explanation.'

Howard tried to look confident. 'Presently awaiting the full analysis of the mission, sir. We only know that he was shot through the head.'

'Who shot him?'

Howard was now sweating. 'Again, we're not yet sure, sir. We believe it may have been a mistake with the planning.'

Hanks shook his head, slapping his hand on the wall. 'Get in touch with Langley. I want to know what fucking idiot screwed this operation up.'

The day starts with a cup of coffee and a picture of John Tierney all over the media and now this crap. Miller may be finished, but the situation isn't.

Chapter LIII

John walked through the main town in Cyprus. No hope in hell they'd catch him on a plane. With thoughts of the hospital dream floating through his mind, he couldn't help but think of Rosi.

At first, he found this rather strange, but then he had an idea. Bulgaria was probably his last chance to get away. Starting from the centre of the town, he asked local tradesmen for help with directions. Their English was just good enough for him to understand their responses. Because they had less access to the media than much of the world, he was less afraid of showing his face.

***

A week had passed, and John found himself lost in the cold. Luckily, a lorry driver passing by was kind enough to give him a lift – for money, of course. He was heading straight for the city. John read the signposts they passed, until he saw one that read 'Stamboliiski – 2km.' What luck.

He went to the nearest telephone booth, flicking through the 'Z' section of the telephone directory. With his index finger, he traced down the page until he found the surname

'Zheleva,' next to the street name and the house number. He was back on track.

***

The telephone rang; Roscoff was waiting for the call, so it was no surprise. It was Agent Armstrong, the new agent who had been assigned Ross's position.

'Sir, it seems the murder suspect is back. We've just found Agent Munroe. He's dead, sir.'

Roscoff, head in hands, wasn't as shocked as he should be. 'Stab wound to the neck, right?'

'Yes, sir.'

'Okay, give me thirty minutes and I'm on it.'

Everything about the scene felt pitch black. There was a sense of impending doom in the air despite the promising light given from several scattered stars and the distorted reflections of garish orange lampposts in shallow puddles along the moist, glittering road. The sudden flare of bright white headlamps and skidding noise of car tires as they drew to a halt alarmed the men in white, who proceeded to search for clues and gather evidence. Roscoff had arrived at the murder scene.

He slammed his car door shut and took a pack of cigarettes out of his pocket. As he lit one, a tall broad-shouldered man in a dark suit strolled over. Roscoff took several hasty puffs on his cigarette before acknowledging the man's presence. 'I presume you have a summary of the events that have taken place, Armstrong?'

Agent Armstrong opened his mouth to speak, but no words came out. He pointed over to the car that used to belong to Charles Munroe. There was a sympathetic tone in his voice. 'Sir, we found Munroe here with the gun still in his hand. It appears only one shot was fired, Sir.'

Roscoff's mouth opened, an arched block of dull black, rather like a train tunnel. Wisps of grey smoke circled out lazily then rushed through his lips as he spoke. 'Any other witnesses apart from Maria?'

Armstrong frowned, flicking through a small notepad he had been holding. 'No, sir. After Munroe shot the suspect, the suspect fell into the river. We're currently awaiting the results from the team of divers, who are still searching at this very moment. It's anyone's guess where the body could turn up.'

Roscoff sighed, staring at the lifeless figure on Munroe's car seat. He took several calm paces towards the open car door, kneeling to peel back the sheet. Munroe's expressionless face stared back, the eyes devoid of any signs of pain. The Roman dagger still wedged into the right side of his neck had made him suffer.

Roscoff swallowed hard, dropping the sheet and looking back over his shoulder. He could see Maria standing with her arms folded, leaning back against the brick wall. She was wearing a luminous green police overcoat.

Roscoff threw his cigarette and smeared it into the road with his shoe as he walked towards her, closely followed by Agent Armstrong. When they were standing next to her, she barely even looked up.

Roscoff reached towards Maria's shoulder, though his fingers automatically froze inches away from her flesh. 'Are you feeling all right? Come on, let's get you home. You need to rest.' He beckoned her to follow as they walked towards his car.

When she was sitting in the seat behind him, Roscoff eyed her reflection in the wing mirror apprehensively, thinking her behaviour rather uncharacteristic. His intention was to drive back to her apartment, to clear things up with Eamon. In turn, for offering to keep Maria and Eamon out of prison, he expected Eamon to explain the whole story surrounding the mystery of the Roman daggers and their origins, at the very least.

***

As they trailed into the room, Maria suddenly decided to share her thoughts on the subject. She strode across the room, and then turned to face Roscoff, folding her arms. 'The job is finished now, Vladimir. The five murders are complete, so now the Five Knights Templar have their revenge at last.'

Roscoff looked taken aback at this sudden change of attitude. 'As intelligent as you are, I find it strange you have a difficulty with mathematics. Ross, Biggins, Mullins, Cardinal Santini, Miller, and now Munroe?'

Maria sighed impatiently. 'Yes, but only five of the victims were murdered with the daggers. In Miller's case, it seemed God himself chose the bullet. God will always protect the high caulbearer. It would serve you well not to forget that, Vladimir!'

Roscoff took a deep breath. He knew this was the start of yet another chapter, within which he was obviously destined to be involved, whether he was keen on the idea or not. However, the fact that the situation involved so much secrecy still bothered him intensely. He rubbed his chin, looking perplexed. 'So why did you make out that you didn't know where the knives came from? I still don't understand.'

He was facing Maria, who glanced over to Eamon, as if expecting him to answer the question, which he did, almost immediately.

'You remember the story I told you about the five murdered Templars and the promise to avenge them. Well, the Grand Master, Jacques de Molay, only told the Templars who were present at the final meeting about the betrayal.

356

Strangely enough, the sixth member, Vladimir, was sent away.

'If you can recall the story, you'll remember that Nostradamus had a secret son, Joseph. De Molay also had a secret son, whom nobody knew about. That's why Vladimir was sent – to look after the boy. Before he left, de Molay told Vladimir that, in another time and place, the murders must be avenged. He told all of them that he'd foreseen in a dream that the Catholic Church and King Philip had condemned them to death.

'It was written that, in time to come, your namesake, Vladimir, would return and, until the deaths had been avenged, the truth would be kept a secret. Now is the time that you should rightfully know that truth, Vladimir.'

Roscoff perched on the edge of the sofa gingerly between them. Maria stared at him with a crazed look in her eyes. Eamon focused on the floor, a downcast expression on his face. Roscoff shifted from side to side, feeling claustrophobic all of a sudden.

He ran a finger beneath his shirt collar before deciding to break the silence. 'So you know about this compass circle, the meaning of it? You do know how to work it out?'

Eamon exhaled slowly and placed his hand on Roscoff's shoulder. 'One question at a time, my friend. No, I don't know how to work it out. In fact, nobody does – not at this moment. It's something John has to work out. He's the one to show us the way.'

Maria peered around from Roscoff's shoulder to interrupt him. 'That's why the high caulbearer's path must not be obscured. We must make the way clear so that he has the opportunity to save human existence without anything standing in his way. We hope now, Vladimir, you can understand why the murders had to be. To put it plainly, it's not *the way* of *the way*, but it's the way of their way! It's

357

all part of the puzzle; the murdered Templars had to be avenged.'

Roscoff's eyes narrowed. He shoved his hands down onto the sofa and pushed himself up haughtily, swivelling to face them. 'And what are we supposed to do next? We haven't heard anything from John! How much time is there? I mean, how do we even know John's still with us?'

There was a short pause as Eamon and Maria exchanged fatigued glances. Eamon stood. 'Don't worry. Frankie seems to know where John is. Actually, he's trying to contact him as we speak.

'Think of it this way. The longer we stay away from John, the less chance he's in danger. He's the only one who'll know when the time is right for us all to join him.'

Maria's mobile distracted the conversation. She knew she should have turned it off.

Roscoff turned to face Maria with an irritated look of suspicion. *Who could that be? Do I know about this call? I hope there's a good reason for this,* Roscoff thought.

Maria looked to her cell phone; the screen read, 'unknown caller.' She half opened the glass door and, with her foot wedging the door open, she took the call. 'Bianchi, hello.'

For a moment, a cold silence of uncertainty rushed through Maria's mind. She felt a fear of melancholy running through her body. *Why don't you speak? Say something. If I hang up now, Roscoff will suspect I am hiding something from him.*

'Bianchi, hello,' Maria repeated herself before she heard a voice.

'Hello, how are you, my angel?'

Maria released her foot from the bottom of the door. She still knew Roscoff could see her reaction through the office dividing wall.

'Cardinal, please, for your own safety, this is not a clean phone,' she whispered. Maria turned to see Roscoff's suspicion still lingering in his eyes. She smiled and nodded as though this was just another call.

The cardinal replied, 'Is the boy safe?'

Roscoff moved closer to the glass, wondering who was more important than John was.

'Yes, Cardinal, he's safe. Trust me, he's safe.'

The phone line went dead.

Maria looked to Roscoff, who shrugged. She strolled back into the office as though nothing had happened.

Was this how it was going to be, more secrets kept without Roscoff's knowledge?

Chapter LIV

John realised he hadn't eaten for almost the entire day. He wandered through the narrow streets until he came to a halt outside a block of flats. Alongside the flats was a supermarket. He obeyed the urge to enter. Once inside, he drifted through the aisles. He came to a stop as if by command.

There she was. As she stretched up to reach a jar of coffee, he walked behind her.

'I hope your coffee tastes as good here as it did in Berlin.'

Rosi dropped the jar. It landed in John's outstretched hand. Her face was bright with elation.

He stared down at the bump beneath her jumper. Rosi was six months pregnant. Timidly, he reached out to stroke her stomach. He embraced her tightly. After spending most of his life concentrating on the past or fearing the future, now he could finally look forward to the next day and the one after that. He could move on, like the rest of the world. Maybe, just maybe, the rest of the world might be moving with him.

***

Everything was quiet. Roscoff had heard little on the Tierney front. It was unusual for him to be able to concentrate on one case at a time. This was great for Roscoff. It gave him the time and space he needed, not to mention the clear head he needed to devise a failsafe way to tie up the loose ends concerning the paperwork created by the Eamon and Maria saga.

Roscoff was back at the office and, at last, relaxed. He knew he had the situation all under control, providing Casey hadn't opened the envelope containing John's new identity papers, and reported it back to Langley before his fatal departure. With the CIA still hot on his agenda over the Miller case, he knew they would be chasing a ghost.

After this, he could head home and look forward to a quiet weekend. He thought that, one day, maybe people could learn to overcome their insignificant differences and live in peace with one another, instead of constantly squabbling over personal faith and belief.

Returning home, Roscoff cracked some ice, poured himself a drink, and headed straight for a hot shower. Looking in the mirror, he removed his shirt and turned his back. Through the steam of the hot water from the running tap, an image gradually came into focus.

It was the infamous Angelic Angels tattoo. It seemed Eamon's prediction had been correct after all. Who could have foreseen the sinister truth? Like the archetypical psychopath in a horror movie, Roscoff turned to face the mirror. With his fists raised in front of him, Roscoff broke out into a wry evil laugh, arguably doing more to relieve the tension than to amplify it.

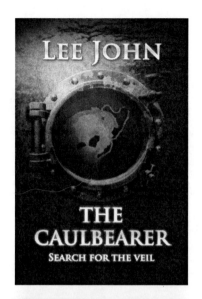

COMING SOON

Lightning Source UK Ltd.
Milton Keynes UK
UKOW031142251011

180887UK00002B/2/P